BETRAYED BY LOVE

He looked down. Desire flamed in him like wildfire. In her watermelon-pink dress with matching dyed watermelon-colored strands of coral, her lovely face was a cameo.

She was going to push it. "Did you have something in mind?"

The look on his face said he had her on his mind, but she suddenly felt bashful with him.

He sipped his wine slowly, seeking to stanch the flood of desire.

"We forgot the music." Getting up, he went to the entertainment wall in the living room, looked over one section, and chose a Teddy Pendergrass album. Just great, he criticized himself. He already wanted to make love to her. This was going to feed the flames.

Other Books By Author

Devoted
The Black Pearl
"Misty's Mothers" in the anthology
A Mother's Love
Still in Love
Lyrics of Love
"A Love Made in Heaven" in the anthology
Wedding Bells
Star Crossed

Published by BET/Arabesque Books

BETRAYED BY LOVE

Francine Craft

BET Publications, LLC
www.bet.com
www.arabesquebooks.com

To Betty and Billy and family.
May your lives continue to be blessed.

ARABESQUE BOOKS are published by

BET Publications, LLC
c/o BET BOOKS
One BET Plaza
1900 W Place NE
Washington, D.C. 20018-1211

All Kensington Titles, Imprints, and Distributed Lines are available at special quantity discounts for bulk purchases for sales promotions, premiums, fund-raising, and educational or institutional use. Special book excerpts or customized printings can also be created to fit specific needs. For details, write or phone the office of the Kensington special sales manager: Kensington Publishing Corp., 850 Third Avenue, New York, NY 10022, attn: Special Sales Department, Phone: 1-800-221-2647.

First Printing: November, 2000
10 9 8 7 6 5 4 3 2 1

Printed in the United States of America

PLANTING
THE SEED

One

Around ten o'clock that morning, Maura Blackwell stood at the rail of the White Oak Creek bridge, staring down at the sharply swirling water. Her heart still hurt from the oncologist's words earlier that morning, when he told her her grandfather, Papa Isaac, had prostate cancer. The doctor said they were catching it fairly early so Papa Isaac's prognosis was good, but the cancer would be very expensive to treat. At sixty-four, Papa Isaac was too young for Medicare, and his small insurance policy wouldn't be enough. So his life hung in the balance, and the simple fact was that the money they needed to treat him wasn't available.

A briskly warm mid-April wind swept over her, and Maura brushed back strands of chemically straightened, long, earth-brown hair from her clove-colored face. Her dark brown eyes overflowed with tears. She couldn't lose Papa Isaac, the dearest person in the world to her. For a moment, she felt dizzy with fear. Life had been mostly kind to her. Was it going to change now?

Joshua Pyne drove slowly, as he approached White Oak Creek bridge. A woman dressed in a straight navy skirt and a white eyelet tunic top stood looking down at the water. Josh was struck by her dejected stance and, as he drew nearer to her on the opposite side of the bridge, he recognized Maura. They had been friendly once, and he had taken her to her senior prom. After that he'd gone back to college and then did some traveling. He had gotten married, and he and Maura had lost touch.

Parking his car in one of the spaces near the bridge, Josh got out of his beige Saab and began to walk over to Maura. She never turned around.

He waited until he reached her side to speak, calling her name, softly.

She turned to him. "Oh, hello, Josh. I haven't seen you in a very long time. How are you?"

"I'm okay. It's nice to see you again. The question is, how are you?"

"I'm okay, too, I guess." She paused. "No, I'm not okay. I've had bad news that I can't talk about."

His eyes searched her stance.

She laughed, shakily. "You look really bothered and compassionate," she said. "I'm not going to jump, if that's what you're worried about."

"It happens once in a while," he answered.

"Yes," she said, quietly. "Just last summer, the Iverson girl jumped."

"That was awful," he commented. "Look, let me take you somewhere where we can talk. I'll bring you back to your car."

"I walked over." She relaxed then. Josh had that effect on her. On the one hand, when, as a high school student, she had worked in his father's office, he had turned her on to high heaven. On the other hand, she felt secure with him. Well, as secure as she could be with a man she liked so much and couldn't have. These days, all the city of Crystal Lake knew that he had sworn off deep relationships with women after his divorce from the beauteous Melodye Crane.

Walking to his car, Maura matched her steps to his and glanced at his profile. *He is a devilishly handsome man,* she thought, *and it doesn't seem to go to his head one bit.* With his coal-black, rough, curly hair cropped close, his bronze skin, his hazel eyes, and craggy features, he was something to write home about.

When they reached the car, he smiled at her and helped her in. "Have you got a choice of places you'd like to go?" he asked.

"No, not really."

"How about Wilson's, out in the countryside?"

"Okay."

He is an expert driver, she thought, as they rode along. With the windows down, it was quiet and comfortably warm.

"This is a long way to walk from your house," he said, *"if* you walked from your house."

"Yes, but I needed the exercise to get my mind off things."

From time to time, he glanced at her. He kept wanting to put his hand over hers, to comfort her.

She thought back to years ago, when he had briefly kissed her after taking her home on her prom night. He hadn't kept her out all night the way some of her classmates had stayed out, but she had floated just to be with him. He was a college sophomore that year, then he left to travel in Europe and Africa, came back, and met Melodye, and the rest, she thought now, was history.

"How are things with you?" she asked.

"Not bad. My father's mad as hell with me because I won't go along with a project he espouses."

"Oh."

"Yes, but I won't talk about it now. You've obviously got a full plate."

"That's kind of you."

"I have a feeling that you're an easy woman to be kind to."

"Thank you."

"I took you to your prom," he said, wondering why he was bringing that up now.

"I couldn't forget that."

"I was a mighty college sophomore that year. I took off to travel . . ."

"And you met and married Melodye."

He nodded, then sighed. "Enough of that topic."

"I was sorry to hear about your divorce."

"Don't be. I'm not. It was past due. A lot of troubled water under the bridge."

"Neither one of you has remarried."

Josh pondered that a moment. "Sometimes a person spoils it for you for a lifetime. Maybe I'm too vulnerable. I know I don't intend to let that kind of hurt happen to me again."

"You strike me as strong and enduring. Maybe the next time around . . ."

He smiled then, but it was a closed smile. "Maybe. But the next time around will be on my terms."

Maura sat thinking that she had begun to hurt less since she wasn't mulling over Papa Isaac. Now the same pain took her again. She was glad they were pulling up at Wilson's, with its outdoor tables, umbrellas, and lush gardens planted with shrubbery, impatiens, dahlias, and many other flowering plants.

Wilson Cartwright met them at the door. Bowing, he kissed Maura's hand and shook hands with Josh. A big, brown bear of a man, he was noted for his exquisite manners. His restaurant flourished under his guidance.

"I've got a special spot in mind for you two," he said. "It's near weeping willows, and it's the kind of cool that air conditioning doesn't give you. Just follow me."

He took them to a corner of the yard fenced in with gray stones. There was a large goldfish pond and several weeping willows. Watching the colorful goldfish leap, Maura reflected that it had been a while since she'd been here.

They ordered shrimp, crab, and oyster platters, crisply fried potatoes, garden salads, and iced tea.

"Try to eat something," he said. "It will help."

Their food came quickly, and Maura found she had a better appetite than she had thought she would.

She found the succulent seafood wonderful. When the waiter left, Josh reached over and squeezed her hand, gently.

A bit later, sitting under oak branches on a circular bench, he looked closely at her.

"Talk to me," he said.

"I wish I could."

"Try me."

She sighed, and her voice was husky. She wanted to talk with him.

"It's Papa Isaac," she said, "my grandfather."

"I remember the gentleman," he said. "He's one of my favorite role models."

A small smile lifted the corners of Maura's mouth. "He's a love, all right. He's just been diagnosed as having prostate cancer."

"I'm sorry to hear that."

"Oh, that's not the bad part. They think they've caught it early enough for successful treatment." She paused.

"Successful, *expensive* treatment," he said.

Maura looked at him, quickly. "Yes. We don't have the money if the treatment is long-term, and it may turn out to be."

She told him what their finances were. Her fledgling architectural firm was not yet making a profit and wouldn't for at least a couple of years. Papa Isaac owned a small truck farm that sold vegetables and berries to local and DC-based restaurants. For the past two years, there had been a severe drought, and their bank accounts were running on the rim.

When Maura had finished, Josh looked at her closely, thinking what a lovely woman she was. Her eyes were deep-brown and clear. With her high cheekbones and straight-across black eyebrows, not to mention her voluptuous body, with its wide hips and narrow shoulders, he considered her top drawer among the women with whom he'd come in contact. She was a woman with all the attributes she needed. He glanced at her long, slender feet in navy, patent-leather, thong sandals.

"I wonder if I could help you," he said.

She shook her head quickly. "No, I wasn't suggesting that."

"I know you weren't, but you need someone. And, in time,

you could pay me back. Truck farmers make good money. Successful architects make good money. I wouldn't be worried about payback . . ."

His voice trailed off, and he drew a deep breath. "Besides," he said, "I've got something important I want to talk with you about."

"Oh?"

Looking at her, he thought it was no wonder that she questioned him. Josh reflected that he had seen Maura fairly often at a distance, but he dreamed about her more and more. But he hadn't tried to get closer. She deserved more than he could offer her and she probably wanted love he couldn't give.

He patted her hand. "Listen, let's keep our minds on your grandfather and his illness. When we're a little further down the road on that, I'll tell you what I have in mind, and I want you to keep an open mind. Don't turn me down if you can help it. I'm desperate."

Maura sat thinking that she couldn't imagine this handsome man being desperate, yet his face had become strained.

"Of course I'll keep an open mind," she said, "and I'll help you in any way I can."

He smiled. "Make no promises you can't live up to, lady. What I've got in mind will startle you, to say the least."

"When you make up your mind," she said, "try me."

"I'll do that, and pray you don't turn me down. I can lend you the money, or, if you are amenable to my plan, give it to you."

Maura wondered what he had in mind.

"Does this have to do with my architectural skills?" she asked.

"No. It's personal, although I'll be utilizing your skills as an architect. I hear you're fantastic with drawing and design."

"I'm told I am. I love doing both."

"I expect to hear a lot about Blackwell Architecture, Inc.," he said.

"And I'm already hearing a lot about Joshua Pyne, home builder. I love your designs."

"Thanks. Speaking of houses, I really like your grandfather's house—a spacious log cabin, beautifully built. I hear your grandfather and some of his friends built it."

"Uh-huh. They did a fantastic job. They're all dead now, except him."

Maura and Josh fell into a deep and comfortable silence, and she wondered about him, what his life was like now.

"I keep thinking about your senior prom," he said. "Were you surprised I offered to take you?"

"Dumbfounded," she said. "You stopped by my desk and waited until I finished my drawing before you interrupted. I thought that was so sweet. You asked me why I had such a long face, and I told you it was three nights before the prom and I didn't have a date. Your eyes twinkled, and you asked if you could take me."

"Big college sophomore," he said. "That was me. I'm three years older than you but then it seemed a whole lot more. I wish now I'd kept seeing you. Then I wouldn't be so desperate now."

"I'm sorry you're having trouble. As I said, anything I can do to help . . ."

"I hope you don't come to regret those words."

"May I have a hint of what this is about?"

He looked at her, steadily. "It's about you and me," he said. "You're going to find it strange, but I hope not too strange. It's been done before."

"You've really piqued my curiosity. Look, Josh, there's no way I could tell you how grateful I am. I've exhausted all the possibilities for money to treat Papa Isaac. I can think of little I wouldn't do for you in exchange for this. Just don't ask me to kill or maim someone. I'll be taking full-time employment and running my architectural business on the side; that way I can pay you back faster."

He held his hand up.

"I'm an architect as well as a builder," he said, "and I don't want you to give up your dream. Your loan—or maybe your gift—won't be a pressure-ridden race to pay me back. You may not need to. Let's just wait until you're more secure about Papa Isaac and I bring out what I want from you. Okay?"

Maura smiled, slowly. "I guess it has to be, although I'm dying of curiosity."

Back in Josh's car, they rode in near silence, as he took her home. "When does your grandfather begin treatment?" Josh asked.

"Next Tuesday. We'll check into a hotel in Baltimore and let him rest a day or so."

"Then he'll be treated at Johns Hopkins."

"Yes."

"It's among the best, especially for prostate cancer. I'll get your account number and have the money transferred to you by Friday. Is a hundred thousand going to be enough?"

"I hope so. I don't need it all at once. The doctor mentioned that it would be at least that sum if he has to undergo extensive chemotherapy *and* radiation. There are new treatments available now, too. They won't know how much it will cost until they begin the treatment."

"You know, I'm thinking I could drive you over, book a hotel room, and stay overnight to give you moral support. Did you have any plans for that?"

"That's so sweet of you. My friend Odessa's husband was going to drive us over and come back. You know, she runs a beauty shop and he's a barber . . ."

"I know them both."

"Your taking us would relieve Odessa's husband of having to go. Someone needs to be there to manage their shops. I'd like it very much if you could drive Papa Isaac and me over. And thank you."

A hint of a smile crossed Josh's face. The more he could give her, the more likely she was to agree to the plan he had for her. For *them,* he amended, as a small thrill shot through him.

As they pulled into the driveway, Maura's grandfather stood

on the porch. After parking, Josh walked around the car and helped Maura out. *What exquisite manners he has,* she thought.

"Well, how are you, young man?" Papa Isaac greeted him, as they walked onto the porch.

"Hello, Mr. Allen," Josh said, shaking hands with him.

"Josh," Isaac Allen said, "it's good to see you again."

"That goes for me as well, sir."

The old man smiled. He had been mightily impressed when this man, as a youth, had taken his granddaughter to her prom. The old man thought Josh was earnest and levelheaded, and he had been disappointed when Josh had married someone else. Well, that was water under the bridge.

Isaac Allen had grown lost in his thoughts, and he realized Josh was talking to him, telling him how sorry he was about his illness.

"Yes, I'm sorry too, but these things happen. They're giving me a fair chance of seeing it through."

"I'm glad to hear that."

"He's going to give us the money we need," Maura said.

Papa Isaac's eyes filled with tears. "You don't say. I'm mighty grateful, but we may be a long time paying you back. I've thought of selling the farm, but it's going to take a while. I don't want my granddaughter's future ruined because of me. I want her to keep working as an independent architect and not have to go back to a dead end job. I'm so proud of her."

"I've done really well these past five years," Josh said. "What is money for if I can't use it to help someone I think so highly of?"

"I always knew you were a winner, young man," Isaac said. "Won't you come in and have some scuppernong wine?"

Josh glanced at his watch and shook his head. "I don't really have the time," he said. "I've got a meeting at two-thirty, but invite me back and I'll take you up on that."

"Of course," Maura and her grandfather said at once. Then she added, "Anytime."

* * *

Josh came out of the drugstore, frowning. He had a headache and had stopped in to get aspirin after leaving Maura's house.

He got into his car, sighing. The meeting that afternoon wasn't one he was looking forward to. Land acquisition was on the table. His firm wanted to build houses on the Turner property and an heir wanted twice what the land was worth. They had a fight on their hands.

Josh unlocked his car and got in, being careful with the paper cup of Dr. Pepper he held. Once in, he took the aspirin box from his pocket, popped two tablets in his mouth, and drank the soft drink.

Putting the cup in a paper bag, he switched on the ignition, let the motor warm a moment, then began to pull out.

Like a bat out of hell, a motorcycle pulled away from the curb several cars in front of him. Josh had been so intent on thinking about his meeting, he hadn't heard the roar of the bike.

"Look out, fella!" Josh yelled. "You're supposed to watch what you're doing!"

Incredibly, the youth on the bike gave Josh an evil grin, then gave him the finger, before yelling back, "Get the hell out of my way!"

Josh breathed deeply, angry now. It was Lonnie Fillmore, the mayor's son. He sure didn't do his dad's political prospects any good. The boy ran his hand over his soft, brown curls, worn too long, and pressed the handlebars on his bike. Tan-skinned, even featured, with his Harley-Davidson beneath him, he was a young god. He rode the wind. He *was* the wind. For a moment, the boy closed his eyes, daring anything to happen to him, then he sped away toward the countryside.

After Josh left, Maura and her grandfather sat in the deep, cool living room. She loved this old house with its exposed rafters and pine-paneled walls. She told him about Josh's offer.

"He's a nice man, that Josh Pyne," Papa Isaac finally said. "I thank God for people like him."

Maura nodded. "We'll be able to pay him back. He knows that. But he is a nice man."

"Do you remember him taking you to your prom?"

Maura smiled. "As vividly as if it were yesterday."

"He's divorced."

"And bitter about it."

"A woman like you could help a man get over a lot of bitterness."

"If he wanted to get over it."

"I'm sure he does."

"I'm not so sure."

"I've got a lot of faith in you, Maura. You're the best. You'd be good for Josh."

Maura sighed. "I think Josh is going to have to be the judge of that. Besides, you're getting ahead of yourself. Today he saw me standing on White Oak Creek bridge and stopped. Hardly a date. The only date we ever had was the prom, and that was light-years ago."

Papa Isaac rocked himself a little. "I saw the way he looked at you. He likes you."

"And I like him. Let's just not rush this. He's got a lot of women who're interested in him."

"And I'd put you up against any of them."

"You're prejudiced in my favor."

"You bet I am." He frowned. "I'm glad there's the farm, which means that when we sell we can pay Josh back. But, Lord, I hate being without it. Maybe in time I can get a smaller plot . . ."

Maura felt a sharp pang in her chest. She was going to miss this old house dreadfully; it had its own presence. But, if it meant the money to pay Josh back, then it was worth the pain of loss. Papa Isaac came first.

"You look tired," she told Papa Isaac.

"I guess I am. While you were gone, Martin came and got

the vegetables for his restaurants. Getting around is making me tired more and more. He's found a man who can manage for me while I'm out of commission."

Martin Ales was the produce buyer from a large chain of restaurants in the DC metropolitan area.

"Martin was late," she said. "He usually picks up much earlier."

"Truck trouble."

"Why don't you lie down? Josh and I had a scrumptious lunch. I'll fix you something good."

He nodded. "What I'd like more than anything is a grilled cheese sandwich and a glass of chocolate milk, and I can fix that."

"No, let me."

"Very well."

Going into the pine-cabineted, spacious kitchen, Maura hummed as she went to the refrigerator for the cheese and the chocolate milk. With strong sunlight streaming in the windows, she thought how dejected she'd been when she left the house that morning. Now, there was Josh's willingness to help them. It wasn't as if they were strangers, but they weren't friends either.

What was it he wanted to talk with her about? And when would he?

Two

Maura went into her home office. She looked out on the expanse of their backyard, enjoying the huge southern magnolia tree with its lush, pink blossoms. Her body still tingled as she thought of Josh, and she pinched herself lightly, smiling. Was it a dream that he would lend them the money to ensure that Papa Isaac had the best care available? Was it a dream that he had looked at her with care in his eyes?

Warmth took her whole body as she thought about Josh. He was so handsome, so tender.

She sat at the drawing table and stroked in lines for the planned houses of the Midland Housing Development, still a dream that she hoped to bring to reality in the near future. A small-scale model sat on another table. Crystal Lake needed those homes for moderate-income people who already lived there and for those who wanted to move there. It was a great town, and she wanted to do her part to keep it that way.

Getting up and walking over to the model of the development, she tried to focus on it, but kept thinking of Josh Pyne. To clear her mind, she thought of Malcolm, her young husband who had died suddenly of a heart attack three years before. That had been such a shock. He had seemed so healthy and had always refused to get yearly checkups.

"I'm going to live forever," he had often said. "I'll be here when the doctors are all gone."

He had been wrong, and it still saddened her to think of the heartache she'd known in the three years since she'd lost him. She had dated sporadically after her mourning period, but there had been no one who appealed to her.

Until now, she amended.

Maura looked at her long, slender fingers and glanced at herself in the mirror across from the table. Her face was a rare oval, her lips full. With her upturned nose, wide-spaced dark-brown eyes, and rounded chin, she thought she was attractive enough, but no beauty queen. Others gave her much more credit. Men often gave her a second look.

"Malcolm," she said, softly. "We had such a good life planned." There were going to be several children. Four years older than Maura, he was just getting set up as a dentist, and he had hit the ground running with his practice.

They had lived with Papa Isaac while saving money to buy their own home, and the two men had been fond of each other.

At first, her grief over Malcolm's death had been terrible, but Papa Isaac had counseled her. "You do his memory an injustice," he had said. "He would have wanted you to go on full speed. You two loved each other; let your life be a monument to that love." And she had tried; there just hadn't been anyone who interested her.

A small voice said again, *until now,* and she smiled a bit. She did seem attracted to Josh on a much higher level than she had as a high school senior, and heaven knows, she thought, there had been enough attraction then on her part. It had hurt when he got married, but Malcolm had quickly come into her life, and she had been happy to marry him.

Papa Isaac knocked and came into the room at her invitation.

"My pains are kicking up again," he said. "I couldn't rest. I think it's a wonderful thing that Josh would lend us the money." He smiled. "He looks at you in a way that says to me that he likes you."

Maura shrugged.

"How do you feel about him?"

"Papa," Maura protested, "I haven't had a long conversation

with Josh before today, and I've barely seen him since that long-ago senior prom. I don't feel one way or the other about him. He's a nice man."

A mischievous smile crossed Papa Isaac's face. "Things happen swiftly in the land of love."

Maura held up her hand. "Stop that right now. People who know Josh say he wines them and dines them, then breaks their hearts by dumping them. We're talking about women here, and I'm sure he's had his pick of some of the best."

"You'd make any man change his mind about women."

"You love me and I'm glad, but you speak for yourself. Besides, until you got sick, I'd begun to be happy again."

Papa Isaac came and stood very close to her; he placed his hand over hers on the table.

"I've had the pleasure of having you with me a long while," he said, "and I've got no complaints. If God chooses to take me, I'll cheerfully go along with His plan." Then he added wistfully, "The only thing I'd like to do is see you in a loving relationship again before I die."

Maura blushed. "You're not going to die. You're going to get well."

"God willing," he said, softly.

Driving, Josh knew exactly where he was going. Just ahead of him, Crystal Lake rippled in the early afternoon sun. He had an hour to get to his meeting, and he wanted to think. He pulled into a parking space near the Keene house at the foot of the mountain and cut the car's motor.

For a moment, he let the side of his face rest on the steering wheel, still seeing Maura's face. *She has certainly grown into a beautiful woman,* he thought. She'd been good-looking enough as a high school girl who worked in his father's office. Her sloe-eyed smile had gotten to him this morning. It was a damned shame about her grandfather.

With Maura and her grandfather, he'd been aware of feeling

too much. His father, Carter Pyne, *rich* Carter Pyne, had always warned him against leading with his heart. Before his mother passed on, fifteen years ago, she had lovingly interceded on his behalf. "You're like me, darling," she'd often said. "*Do* lead with your heart. Your father isn't as cold as he'd have you believe."

Carter Pyne would look at his wife, his eyes twinkling. "Not *cold*," he'd tell her, "*sensible.*"

Josh's father still cautioned his son against feeling too much. "If I'd loved your mama just a little more," he'd once told Josh, "my death would have come soon after hers."

It was one of the few times Carter had hugged his son—one of a few times Josh had felt close to him.

Although Josh had given up smoking, he longed for a cigarette now. Thinking about Maura again, he felt a rush of admiration for her strength and her courage, and yes, for her warm sensuality that seemed so beautifully contained.

"Whoa!" he told himself.

He'd been glad he had the money to lend her and had no fear of not having the money returned. Their place was worth the money, but it would take some time to sell. Frankly, he hoped he and Maura could come to terms on what he wanted from her. He hated the thought of their house and small farm being sold to someone else. The place had been in their family since the turn of the century.

Josh got out and walked over to the edge of the lake where the weeping willows grew. Behind him was a grove of sycamore trees, with pale bark, beautiful in the sun. He paced the water's edge. Yes, he was beginning to feel again, and he wasn't sure he wanted to feel just yet.

Melodye's name came to the tip of his tongue and he bit it back. A sensitive, loving man, he had already begun to dream a bit of Maura. He reminded himself that Melodye had turned his dreams of her and his life into a nightmare.

He'd found himself attracted to Maura when she worked in his father's office, but after that first date, he'd met Melodye and fallen head over heels in love. Melodye—with her shining, dark-auburn hair and pale skin, her sea green eyes, and dark lashes. Her sylphlike figure. Her demeanor was haughty, but he'd loved her too much to take much note of that.

He thought now that if his mother had lived, she might have been a buffer against his marrying Melodye. The old man had adored her.

"Boy, now you're getting smart, like me," he'd told Josh. "You're getting a woman like your mother."

Josh had shaken his head.

"No," he'd said. "Mom was a sweet woman, very gentle. Melodye has a fiery streak, and she's not always kind. But I love her."

"Don't let that precious cargo get away from you," his father had said. "She's a beautiful woman, and she looks good on your arm. If a man's going to get ahead, a beautiful woman always helps."

That had proven to be one of the lies of his life.

He and Melodye had traveled before and after their marriage. Europe. Africa. Central and South America. She was full of energy, always on the go. He had soon grown tired of so much activity and wanted to settle down, but he wanted her to be satisfied.

"When do we get you pregnant?" he'd asked her, early on.

She had shrugged. "There's no rush. Children tie you down. I know what my sister's life is like."

"I don't think she'd change her life."

"Men never know what it's like," she'd said. "Little crumb-crushers clinging to you every minute, their sticky little fingers all over your designer clothes."

She had laughed and come close to him. "I'll take wonderful trips over having children anytime."

She had lain on the bed and pulled him down to her. "Make love to me," she'd said, "and we can talk about making babies later."

Smitten beyond the telling, he had, as always, gone along with her wishes. They had stayed married seven years and been divorced three. He had long ago guessed that the Cartwright money had given her an unshakable sense of superiority.

She could turn on the heat and leave him gasping, but he soon found that she could be cold and hostile if she didn't get her way.

After six years of a childless marriage, his joy knew no bounds when she began to have morning sickness and thought she was pregnant. He'd gathered her to him, stroking her resisting body.

"I'll love you forever," he'd said. "Thank you."

She'd wriggled out of his arms. "Maybe I'm not pregnant," she'd said.

"You've got to be. I've—we've put too much effort into this."

Melodye had thrown her head back, laughing.

"You speak for yourself," she'd said, coolly. "Getting pregnant isn't what I want right now."

At his insistence, they'd seen their doctor and found that Melodye was pregnant.

He couldn't do enough for her, couldn't hold her enough. He bought her expensive gifts, daily flowers, and she grew more and more restive.

Three months into her pregnancy, she went to visit her sister in Michigan and returned a month later.

"I lost the baby," she said, evenly.

Josh had been sick with shock.

"And you didn't tell me, or ask me to come to you?"

After a while, she had said, "I'm not going to lie. I had an abortion. Very easy. Therapeutic. Josh, our marriage isn't working to my satisfaction. I want a divorce."

He had wanted to shake some sense into her, had wanted to beg her to stay with him. He had thought of promising to give up the idea of their having a baby, but he knew how much he wanted to father children, so he was quiet and withdrawn.

It was one of the few times in his life he'd confided in his father.

Carter Pyne had sighed. "It's not the end of the world if she doesn't want children," he'd said. "Beautiful women often come with a price. They're spoiled. You could adopt a child."

"Melodye doesn't want children, period," Josh had said. "She wants a divorce."

Carter's head had jerked up. "I love Melodye like my own daughter," he'd said. "I hope she changes her mind."

Josh's grandmother, Addie, a tender, snow-white haired octogenarian, had thought differently.

"I always knew she wasn't for you," she'd said, quietly. "Let her go and get someone who wants what you want for yourself."

He had smiled bitterly. "You remember our talks about my naming my first girl after you?"

Her soft hand had squeezed his. "I remember a lot of things, Josh. You're an only child, but my daughter-in-law wanted other children; she just couldn't have them . . ."

He'd told Grandmother Addie about the abortion and found himself bent over with burning tears stinging his eyes as she stroked his back, leaning forward in her wheelchair.

She had cried with him. "Josh. Josh, my love," she'd said. "Let her go. One day you'll find someone who's for you and who'll love you the way you love Melodye. And she'll be delighted to have your babies. You'll be happy then. I promise."

Drawing a deep breath, Josh smiled a bit grimly now. Melodye had left him in tatters, and he wasn't sure he *wanted* to find someone else to love. He'd caught onto the brass ring once and, after a thrilling ride, it had sent him crashing. He found himself liking Maura Blackwell a lot, but he saw no chance of falling in love with her. He had other plans for his life—and hers.

Three

The rest of the week passed very slowly for Maura, but at last Papa Isaac was in Johns Hopkins Hospital and she, Odessa, and Josh, who had driven them over, were back in Maura's hotel room near the hospital.

"I know we prayed in the hospital chapel," Maura said, "but let's pray again. Josh, why don't you lead?"

Josh came away from the windows, kneeled, and began, "God, be with Papa Isaac now in the time of his deepest need."

Both women kneeled and Odessa prayed, "Bless him as you have blessed him before. We are grateful for his presence on this earth."

Maura felt choked as she added, "Keep him here with us a while longer, Lord. We need him so much, and he has given help and succor to so many of us."

Each added small prayers once again and rose. Josh and Odessa sat in big, comfortable, overstuffed chairs. Maura sat in the padded rocker.

"Josh, thank you so much for bringing us over yesterday," Maura said.

"I was happy to do it," Josh said. "The test of friendship comes when you need someone."

Odessa, an attractive black-haired woman with ebony skin and brown eyes, glanced from one to the other, bemused. Were these two getting hung up on each other?

Josh seemed to have read her mind, and he looked down. He

was going to have to be careful. He didn't intend to lead Maura on, have her getting the wrong idea. He liked her a lot, but what he had in mind was a business proposition. Nothing more.

Maura had been aware of Josh's eyes on her and she, too, looked down. Her mind was full of Papa Isaac now, but she couldn't help glancing at Josh from time to time. She was not aware that she wrung her hands.

"Relax," he told her.

"I'm going out for a walk to the hotel gift shop," Odessa said. "Can I get either of you anything?"

Both shook their heads.

"When I get back, I'll call Mike and tell him what I got for him. He has a fit if I go away and don't bring him anything."

Maura smiled. Mike was an all right guy in her opinion. He and Odessa adored each other. He was fifteen years older than the thirty-five-year-old Odessa and had two grown children. He and Odessa had no children together.

She picked up her purse and left.

Maura rocked slowly, thinking, as Josh paced the room.

"Does the doctor know how long his first treatments will take?"

"About a week. The doctor said he didn't want to raise any false hopes, and they can't know until the treatments get further underway, but he's feeling positive about the whole thing."

"Papa Isaac has never had anything like this before?"

"No. He's been as healthy as the proverbial horse. Active. Forward looking. Positive all the way."

"I want you to relax," Josh said. "He's in the best of hands. You can best help him by keeping a grip on yourself."

"I know," Maura breathed. "I'm trying to relax."

She looked like a waif sitting there and, without knowing he would do it, he came to stand beside her rocker, then bent and kissed her brow.

She looked up at him and smiled. "I needed that," she said.

His kiss put Josh in a quandary. He didn't want her to read too much into it, but he had to comfort her.

She wanted to question him about what he wanted to ask her, but now certainly wasn't the time. She was too bothered about Papa Isaac.

Josh saw her tense again and smoothed her hair.

"I'm going to be here for you," he said, "all the way through this."

"For which I thank you," she said, quickly, "but I'd like to ask you why."

He squatted beside her chair. "Well, I don't want to lead you on, Maura. Call me Peter, Peter, pumpkin eater. I had a wife once and couldn't keep her. Anybody who knows me will tell you I'm not looking for trouble again. But a man needs friends, and I want to be friends with you."

His eyes were solemn as he looked at her. "Well, yes," she said, softly, her voice catching in her throat. "I'd like to be friends with you, too."

I'd like to be your lover, she thought and blushed at thinking it. *I'd like to have you come home to me. I'd like a house, babies for you. The whole nine yards.* She began to scold herself. What in the world was the matter with her? As a high-school senior, yes, she had dreamed of Josh, but their marriages had certainly stopped that. His lean, muscular body was so close to her. He smelled faintly of really good cologne, and she wanted to reach out and stroke him. His kiss on her brow had been sweet, nothing to get excited about, but his very presence excited her, turned her on to high heaven. And she wondered where this was going to lead.

"I think I'll drive over to the harbor," he said. "Would you and Odessa care to come with me?"

"I don't think so. I'm worn out from tossing and turning all night. Odessa might like to go."

"Okay. I'll go to my room and pick up a few things and wait until she gets back."

"Josh," she said, quietly.

"Yes?"

"I keep wanting to thank you again and again. Can you guess how much your coming over with me means?"

"You'd do the same for me."

"I would. You're a great guy."

His expression was grave. "Don't give me too much credit. I've got my negative points. You'll find out soon enough."

"You don't give yourself enough credit."

"I've been burned, and you know what they say about fire and the burned child."

"I insist that you're a great guy."

"Have it your way, but don't cry when you find out I'm not always what I seem."

Maura threw up her hands in exasperation.

"You just don't see yourself clearly," she said. "But, then again, you know yourself better than I do."

"Now, that's my girl."

Maura glanced at her gold Seiko watch. It was three o'clock. Papa Isaac should be out of surgery now. She dialed the hospital patient information number and asked about him.

"He's out of surgery," a pleasant voice said, "and doing well. Shall I connect you to the nursing station? They can give you more information."

"Yes, please do."

Papa Isaac's nurse came on the line and, in response to Maura's question, said he had pulled through very well indeed.

"I'm immediate family," Maura told her. "Could I visit him this afternoon?"

The nurse thought a moment. "Tomorrow morning would be best. He does seem tired, and the more uninterrupted rest he can get, the better."

Maura thanked her and said she would visit the next morning.

Josh came back into the room; she told him about the call.

"You can relax a bit now," he said.

"I can try. You know, I think I'd like to go to the harbor with you, after all. I love visiting the aquarium. Take me there?"

"With pleasure."

While Baltimore's harbor was spectacularly beautiful, it was the aquarium that held the most interest for Maura. Once there, she, Josh, and Odessa watched the many fish swim idly and sometimes purposefully by. Along with the crowd, they traversed the length of the glassed-in aquarium walls until they reached the octopi and lingered there.

"I can't believe people actually eat these creatures," Odessa said, smoothing her beige linen dress.

"Don't knock it if you haven't tried it," Josh said. "They're not so bad." A smile tugged at the corners of his mouth. "On the other hand, they're not my favorite fare."

Odessa walked a short distance away from them to watch a school of blue-and-white striped fish.

"They're like the ones I saw in Tahiti," Maura said to Josh.

"You really seem to be enjoying yourself."

"I am. Aren't you?"

"Good company. All that."

She glanced at him, liking his languid body and stance.

"Thank you. I'm just so relieved that Papa Isaac pulled through the way he did."

"I have an idea that gentleman takes care of himself. That always helps."

"You bet he takes care. He stopped smoking eons ago. Eats small portions, plenty of vegetables and fruit, and anything you mention about good health, he's in on. Papa Isaac is out there early every morning helping to get his produce gathered and loaded for shipping. He's a wonder."

"He looks like a young man."

"Well, he married very young and my mother married young. So, he's not all that old. Sixty-four isn't old anymore."

"And how about his granddaughter? Is she a health nut, too?"

Maura laughed quickly. "I wouldn't call myself a health nut, nor him. I stopped eating ice cream, but I do enjoy frozen yogurt, and I've been known to nibble on a couple of chocolate nuts or creams."

Odessa caught up with them.

"I wish Mike were here," Odessa said. "He's going to drag me back to see all this with him. We haven't been here in quite a while."

"If you twist my arm, I'll come with you," Maura told her.

"I like the whole sweep of this place," Josh commented. "It has been a developer and a builder's dream. And to think this was once a slum, or a semi-slum."

"It's beautiful, all right," Maura said.

They walked over to the food court where, at Maura's and Odessa's urging, Josh purchased double-chocolate ice cream cones.

His eyes twinkling, Josh told them; "Don't come crying to me when the hips measure a couple of inches more than you like."

"Spoilsport," Maura said. "You're getting near the age where men collect flab, too."

"Ageist," Josh said, laughing. "I've got a few years yet."

Odessa rolled her eyes. "For my money, you've got a lot of years left before *anything* negative sets in."

"My buddy," Josh said, putting his arm around Odessa.

Maura pursed her lips. "I hope you two are having fun, patting each other on the back."

They went outside and stood looking at the Chesapeake Bay, as its greenish-blue waters gently rippled before them. Maura's mind went back to Papa Isaac, then flashed over to Josh. Strange how the two men seemed so alike to her. Josh had warned her that he was not always nice. But, who was? It was as if he knew that dark forces were operating inside him, and he gave warning to anybody smart enough to listen. He certainly sounded bitter about his divorce.

Maura, Josh, and Odessa came back to Maura's room to find the telephone ringing. With her heart racing, Maura answered.

"Mrs. Blackwell, this is Dr. Lessing, your grandfather's oncologist."

"Yes?"

"I knew you'd be concerned about him, and I just didn't want you to have to wait until tomorrow for the good news. The operation was an unqualified success, and we think we've gotten it all out. Your grandfather is a remarkably healthy man. That has served him well."

"Oh, thank God."

"So far—and it's very early, I know—so good. But, we'll have to keep our fingers crossed."

"Thank you, Dr. Lessing," she said, weak with relief. "When can he leave the hospital?"

Dr. Lessing thought a moment. "In about a week," he said. "It was a large tumor. Another thing I want to mention early is that I believe in alternative medicine as well as allopathic, regular medicine. Saw palmetto has worked wonders for me with my patients, and I want to start him on it. I'll order some for him while he's here. It's available from any health-food store."

"Thank you so much, and I'll see that it's on hand for him when he leaves the hospital."

"You'll find it amazingly helpful. And with that, I'll sign off. But I'm forgetting, how are you holding up?"

"Fine. Now that I've gotten this good news, I couldn't be better."

At the hospital two mornings later, Maura, Josh, and Odessa found Papa Isaac sitting up in bed, looking at a gospel choir on TV.

Maura went to him and hugged him.

"It's hard to believe how good you look," she said.

"Can't kill an old salt like me," he said. Papa Isaac had served in the U.S. Navy and had been fond of it.

"For which I'm grateful," Maura said, fondly.

"I like your choice of music," Josh said. "And I'm really happy that you're coming out on top."

"That goes double for me," Odessa told him. "Mr. Allen, you're looking amazingly well." She hugged him.

The telephone rang and Papa Isaac answered it, talked a few lively minutes, then hung up.

"You'll never guess who that was," he said. Then he told them, "Lona."

"Mrs. Greer?" Maura asked. "The woman who's going to be taking care of you, with my help?"

"One and the same." Maura noted that his face had lit up.

"She's a charming woman," she said.

Papa Isaac smiled. "Your grandma and I once had words over this woman. I wasn't guilty, but she accused me of flirting with her."

Maura looked at him steadily. "Well, you've surely settled down, but Grandma used to say you were flirtatious to the bone."

"It's just my way," the old man said, "I mean no harm. You two ladies are looking lovely today." They thanked him and he turned his attention to Josh.

"You're a fine man, son," Papa Isaac said. "Not many people are as kind as you've been to us."

"I'm happy to help in any way I can," Josh aired him.

Two large fruit baskets, from Papa Isaac's church and Josh, sat on the dresser.

"Now," Papa Isaac said, "I'd like to sample one of those bananas. I didn't eat much breakfast."

Maura opened the basket and took out a banana, pulled some of the peel back, and handed it to him. He bit into it.

"Great fruit," he said, leaning forward and shushing them. One of the gospel singers had begun to sing the Lord's Prayer and Papa Isaac listened carefully. When the man had finished singing, Papa Isaac sighed.

"It does my heart good to hear music like that."

"Beautiful," Odessa said.

"Reminds me that my church group is coming over tomorrow morning," Papa Isaac said. "They've really stood by me."

"Well, I don't wonder," Maura said. "You've gone out of your way whenever any one of them was sick or in trouble."

"It's the way to go," Papa Isaac said. "I wouldn't give anything for what I feel about people."

"And I," Maura said, smiling, "wouldn't give anything for the way I feel about you."

Papa Isaac's glance lingered fondly on his granddaughter. "I never fail," he said, "to thank God for sending you along."

Maura selected a small bunch of grapes from the basket, went to the basin and rinsed them, then blotted them on a paper towel. The grapes were black and sharply tasty, her favorite kind.

"Try these," Maura told them. "They're delicious."

Odessa demurred, but Josh got a bunch and washed them. When he'd bitten into several of them, he commented, "These are some of the best I've tasted lately."

"That's a whole lot of fruit I've gotten," Papa Isaac said.

"Well, I'm glad you like the baskets, because Mike and I ordered one for you to be delivered tomorrow," Odessa told him.

A smiling, petite, dark-brown-skinned nurse came into the room. "Mr. Allen, I have to take your temperature."

"For you, anything," he gallantly told the nurse. Maura, Josh, and Odessa went a short distance from the bed. Papa Isaac smiled the whole time.

"Temperature's fine," the nurse said.

"I wouldn't trust just taking it one time," Papa Isaac said. "I'd take it again if I were you."

The nurse chuckled. "Once is enough. You're doing fine. Keep it up."

"Thank you very much, young lady."

The three people came back to Papa Isaac's bed when the

nurse had gone. A misting rain had begun. It was a gray day, but the spirits of the people in the room were glowing.

"My okra needs that rain," Papa Isaac said, "not to mention my tomatoes. I hope Jim Tucker's taking good care of my place."

"Papa Isaac, he's known you for ages. You know he will."

"You run a tight ship, Mr. Allen," Josh said. "Your farm is one of the best tended I've seen."

"Thank you. It's a big part of my life." Papa Isaac was silent then, remembering that the farm would be sold to repay Josh. And Josh was silent, remembering, too, that the old man would be selling the farm. Well, maybe he wouldn't have to.

Dr. Lessing swung in, his ruddy face beaming.

"How is my best patient this morning?"

"Doctor, I don't know what magic you worked, but I'm feeling really good."

Dr. Lessing grinned. "They don't call me Dr. Magic for nothing."

The assembled group asked if they should go out. Dr. Lessing shook his head and began pulling a curtain around the bed.

He checked Papa Isaac thoroughly.

"The nurse has already taken my temperature."

"Pretty little woman, isn't she?" Dr. Lessing said, then clapped a hand to his forehead. "Lord, forgive me," he said. "If she or one of the other nurses heard me say that, I'd be hounded out of the hospital on a sexual harassment charge."

Papa Isaac laughed heartily. "I'll never tell."

Dr. Lessing finished his examination and patted Papa Isaac's shoulder. "You're coming along splendidly."

"Thank you, doctor," Papa Isaac said, getting a lump in his throat. "Prayers have always worked for me."

Dr. Lessing opened the curtains around the bed and stood beaming. He bowed.

"Witness," he said, "some of my finest work."

Four

Papa Isaac was back home a day sooner than expected. In the week that followed his homecoming, Lona Greer, a middle-aged woman, bustled about, her pale face alight with helpfulness. She had moved back to their town. Widowed and retired, she offered her services to people who needed help. A newcomer in town and a fellow church member, Mrs. Kemp, also visited Papa Isaac.

Late that afternoon, installed in his bedroom, Papa Isaac lay back on stacked bed pillows, resting, when the door chimes rang. Maura answered it to find Josh standing there.

"I had to be in the neighborhood and decided to come by. I hope I'm not intruding."

Maura blushed hotly. "No, of course not," she assured him.

"These are for you," he said, handing her a bag from an exclusive shop and a big bunch of pink peonies.

"Why, thank you. How lovely they are."

"And these are for Papa Isaac." He handed her a bunch of deep purple dahlias surrounded by lush green fern.

"I'll handle the dahlias," he said. "You're getting overloaded."

Lona came into the room. "How be-yoo-tiful," she said. "Let me get vases for them."

Lona took both bunches of flowers and went into the kitchen. Maura opened the bag Josh had handed her to find a two-pound box of Godiva chocolates.

"Oh, thank you," she said. "You're something else."

She found him very quiet and asked about that. "I've got a lot on my mind," he told her. "Is there a chance of you getting away later for a ride, or a walk with me down to the lake?"

"Yes," she said, looking at him closely. The lake was about seven blocks away, visible from their house on a hill. "Just say when."

Maura and Josh walked into Papa Isaac's room. "Josh! What a thoughtful thing to do," Papa Isaac said, thanking Josh for the flowers.

Josh shrugged. "People forget about you once you leave the hospital. I wanted to make sure you don't suffer that."

"I knew he'd get well," Lona said. "Nobody's heard Theena weeping."

"Poor Theena," Papa Isaac said, softly. "She had quite a bit of sadness and despair at the end of her life."

"This Theena," Mrs. Kemp said now. "I've heard a bit about her. What's the story there?"

Papa Isaac nodded to Maura. "You tell her. Your memory for details is better than mine."

"Well," Maura began, "it seems there was this beautiful slave girl, Theena, back in the late 1850s, who caught the eye of plantation master Lionel Halaby and had a child by him. Before the Civil War, he freed her, but she wouldn't leave him. He was a widower with no children save the one Theena bore him. He moved her into the big house with him after the war was over, but I don't have to tell you his friends and neighbors didn't like it one bit.

"Nothing they said would dissuade him, though. He took the child, a lovely little girl, everywhere with him. And he was rich enough to get away with a lot where poorer people couldn't." Maura paused.

"Go on," Mrs. Kemp prompted.

"Well, Theena was poisoned and died. The legend has it that Lionel Halaby was beside himself with grief. There is a crypt on what is left of the Halaby Plantation, deep in the woods.

The inscription reads THEENA, WIFE OF LIONEL HALABY. People said he had gone to Paris and married her and that was why she wouldn't leave.

"He sent his daughter abroad to be raised and educated. She returned, married a prosperous black merchant, and bore him one child. Have you met Ellen?"

"Yes," Lona replied.

"Ellen is the great-great-great-granddaughter of Theena. People now say she is 'fast.' I believe she is heartsick for some reason. She's a gifted musician with a beautiful voice and lives in the small stone house on the former plantation. There are now only two hundred and thirty acres left. Ellen owns seventy acres. Josh owns forty. I own sixty acres next to hers, and Josh's father owns the remaining sixty."

"And that's where they want to build the moderate-income priced houses," Lona said. "I'm anxious to move into one when they get finished."

"That's right. I'm the architect for that project and Josh will be the builder."

Deep dimples appeared in Lona's cheeks. "Hurry the project," she said.

Josh laughed. "I think that's how we all feel."

Lona went into the kitchen as Josh sat at Papa Isaac's bedside.

"You certainly seem to be doing well," Josh said.

"Pretty women around. Fine fellows bringing an old codger like me flowers. How can a man resist getting well?" They heard the whirr of the big blender.

"Now, what's she whipping up in there?" Papa Isaac asked.

"That reminds me," Maura said. "Josh brought me heavenly candy." She got the box from the dining room, opened it, and put it on the nightstand beside Papa Isaac's bed. He took one piece and closed his eyes as he chewed it.

"I'd better make that my last piece for now," he said. "I think Lona's fixing me some lunch."

Lona came back in with a crystal pitcher and four chunky

glasses. "Summer punch a little early," she said. "My specialty."

"You sure know the way to a man's heart," Papa Isaac said.

"I hope you two will have some," Lona said to Maura and Josh.

"I could never pass up fruit punch." Josh took a glass and Lona poured it almost full, sprinkling cinnamon on the delectable drink.

Maura groaned. "I can see you're in a conspiracy with Papa Isaac to put a lot more meat on my bones."

Lona raised her eyebrows, "Well, you're a fetching young woman, but a few pounds wouldn't hurt. What do you think, Josh?"

Josh laughed, his eyes crinkling shut. "What I think is I'm going to avoid comments on that subject. I'll say though, she's a fine figure of a woman the way she is, but she'd be still finer with a few extra pounds."

"You certainly know what to say." Maura blew him a kiss. "Getting back to Theena," she said. "It's said that shortly after she was poisoned, Mr. Sampson could hear Theena's wails and weeping near the stone house Lionel Halaby had built for her before they married. Ellen is a gracious person and allows people to hunt on her land. She was so attached to her mother that although she was in school in the north, she returned here to nurse her when she took ill. She seemed shattered by her mother's death and stayed on. But, she rallied and began to collect wildflowers. We work together sometimes. I gather the wildflowers and she frames them. She has a wonderful voice."

Maura's hand swept out to show Josh one of the framed wildflower groups in the room.

"Lovely," Josh said. "I would like to get several of these from you. My grandmother loves wildflowers. Have you met her?"

"I've seen her out riding with you or your father, but no, I haven't met her."

"You really have to. She'll love you."

Maura felt the heat rise in her face. He seemed closer to her than ever, but he seemed distant too. That was strange.

Maura glanced at her stonewashed blue jeans and her crinkled, pale-blue cotton blouse. Pulling on a blue cashmere cardigan, she touched the big silver hoops in her ears and wondered whether she ought to change before going out with Josh.

"Are we going farther than the lake?" she asked him.

"No. I want to talk with you, and it's going to take a while, I suspect."

"Why don't we set out? We're right in time to get a stupendous sunset. We've just had rain. There'll be a fiery sky this evening."

Outside, the air was fresh with the just-over rain. At the corner, Josh put out his hand to stop her.

"I'm really caught up by your house," he said, admiring the log house with its stained spruce logs and slate roof.

"I've always loved this old house," she said. "I've been really happy here."

"You look happy now."

Being with him was making her happy, but she couldn't tell him that.

They walked slowly to the lake and sat on the steps that led down to the water.

"How do I get started?" Josh asked her.

"Started with what?"

Josh was silent for a long moment before he said, "Hear me out with what I'm going to ask you."

"Of course."

He cleared his throat, but his voice was still husky.

"I like you a lot, Maura. A hell of a lot."

She held her breath for a minute before she responded. "I'm glad, because I like you a lot."

"I'll jump in at the end and go back as far as you want me to."

"What are you talking about?"

"Something that may blow your mind."

"Try me."

"All right. I want you to have a baby for me. An heir."

Maura's breath caught sharply in her throat.

"You're kidding."

"No, I'm not. I'd want us to marry for legitimacy and stay together until we knew the child was healthy. After that, we'd both be free. Your loan would be taken care of . . ."

"I'm not worried about the loan. I can pay that back at some future time. I own sixty acres of the old Halaby plantation, and Papa Isaac and I plan to sell the house and the farm if we have to. I plan to succeed."

"And I know you will."

It was strange how levelheaded she felt. "How long have you been thinking of me as the mother of your child?"

He mulled over her question. "I think you've been in the back of my mind for a couple of years. When I saw you standing on the bridge looking so despondent, I wanted to rescue you, take care of you. That feeling made me focus on my dream. You know about my marriage. No, how could you?"

"Word gets around," she said. "Josh, this is such a shock."

"I'm sure it is. I'm thirty-five, nearly thirty-six."

"In December."

"How did you know that?"

"We talked about each other's signs at—"

"The prom," he said, laughing. "We talked about so many things. I enjoyed being with you."

"But you never called again, except to say you had enjoyed our date."

"I left for Africa a few days later. When I came back, I was head over heels in love with Melodye. We traveled together. She was like a drug to me."

"Were you happy with her?"

"At first we were very happy, then she began to play the field again, and my presence didn't matter."

He told her about the miserable time when Melodye had aborted their child. She reached out and placed her hand over his.

"I'm truly sorry about that," she said.

"Being you, you would be. I've always wanted to be a father. Melodye said she wanted children, until after the abortion; then she told me she'd never wanted children. She just said she did and became pregnant to please me. Then she found she couldn't follow through with it."

Maura saw the glimmer of tears behind his eyelids, and hurt for him.

"This is all so strange," she said.

"I know it is. I'm not going to lie to you. I've been savaged by love, and I'm bitter. I don't think I'm ever going to be able to love again and, like I said, I won't lie about it. I like you better than any woman I've ever known, and I admire you deeply.

"You know there are places on this earth where there isn't even a word for love. It can fade fast. Arranged marriages have sometimes worked best."

She was surprised to find herself saying, "You don't expect an *immediate* answer, do you?" She was discussing it as if it were a viable plan.

"No. You think about it. You're still getting over Papa Isaac's illness, and you don't know if he'll keep on healing so fast. You need time, but if it makes *any* sense to you, say yes."

"Are you still in love with Melodye?"

"I think I hate her for what she did to me."

"Hatred is the other side of love."

"So I've heard, but I think this is a special case. I don't think I'm still in love with her. My father worships her. I guess he always will."

"If you wait," she said, gently, "you may find yourself falling in love with someone you'd be happy to marry."

"I *have* waited. Three miserable years. I'd be happy to marry you, make no mistake about that. Love isn't the only thing that goes into a viable marriage. No, I've waited for more than three years, and I don't find myself falling in love. What about you? Have you found anyone to love since your husband's death?"

She shook her head. "No. I've just sort of coasted along." She added to herself, *but I've dreamed about you. I've kissed you in my dreams until I was dizzy with joy.*

"You see?" he said. "I've got a feeling we could become the best of friends."

Looking at her clove-brown, silken face, he reached out and touched her cheek. "We'd be good for each other. Sometimes friendship is better than love. I like the thought of you carrying my child, but I won't pretend to be in love with you; that would be unfair to you."

"What if we fall in love?"

He shrugged. "Then it would just happen, and we'd deal with that then. I want a kid while I'm young enough to romp with him or her."

"A good parent is a good parent at any age. Papa Isaac romped with me when he was older than you are. I don't know, Josh. What if one of us fell in love with somebody else during the time we were married?"

"We'd have to deal with that. We're both mature."

He took her hand. "Start thinking about it now. Ask me any questions you want to, and I'll answer you as truthfully as I can. I'll always be on the level with you. I can give you almost anything you'd want . . ."

"Except love," she said, gently.

"Except love."

After long moments of silence, Josh said, "What do you say we walk over to the weeping willows?"

"Okay."

They got up and started out. In the distance, they could see the old Keene house. Mr. Keene had been murdered several years before. Maura shuddered.

"I'm glad they took Mr. Keene's killer out of circulation."

"Yeah. That was quite a surprise. I thought the killer was a nice guy."

"Most people did."

Maura thought then about Lance and Fairen Carrington.

"You know, Fairen is going to do a series of articles on our Midland Heights project."

"That should help you get a head start," he said. "Have you talked with Ellen?"

"Oh, she's very much in favor. But, you know, Josh, Ellen simply hasn't been herself for the last couple of years. She's depressed and she refuses to see a doctor."

"That's not good. You can't figure out anything that might have happened?"

"No. About two years ago, she seemed terribly upset and she cried a lot, but she always said she couldn't talk about it. I gradually stopped asking. Now, she seems spacey at times, and withdrawn."

"Think she might be into drugs?"

"I hope not. Anything is possible. There's certainly enough of that around lately."

Maura still felt a mild sense of shock at Josh's proposition. *Poor guy,* she thought. His hunger to father a child made her admire him more than anybody, save Papa Isaac. He was a handsome, highly successful man, and being this close to him set her heart on fire. She could fall in love with him, but would he ever come to love her?

"Maura?"

"Yes."

"I'm sorry if I've offended you, but I had to ask. I want this more than I could ever tell you. Am I turning you off?"

"Oh, good Lord, no," she hastened to say. "I'm flattered." The words seemed to come from deep inside her before she thought about them.

They sat on a sun-warmed iron bench near the willow trees. He took her hand. "God knows you deserve all the love anybody can give you, but love isn't mine to give. Everything else I have is yours."

He kissed her forehead lightly as he had done in the hotel

in Baltimore when Papa Isaac was being treated. The first time, she had been surprised. This time, her breath came fast, and she wanted him to kiss her deeply, wanted to feel his tongue inside her mouth and hers in his. Wanted—

Stop it! she said to herself, crossly. *He's offering everything except what I want most. He says he never expects to love again. But, what about me? I haven't been remotely attracted to anyone since Malcolm died. Until now,* a small, mocking voice taunted her. She felt a lot for this man and didn't delude herself. All the more reason why she should turn him down. She would be the one to get hurt.

"Mind if I talk some more about my plans for us, and ask you what you want from me?"

"Go ahead," she said, huskily.

"If you have no objections, you'd move into my house. You'd have your own room and," he cleared his throat, "I'd bother you just enough for you to get pregnant."

A devil of mischief rose in Maura. *"Bother* me just enough?"

He chuckled. "You've got a great sense of humor."

"Sometimes."

"I'd take good care of you. Like I said before, anything you want is yours, and I'm pretty well off. My dad's the rich one, though."

"I wouldn't be marrying you for money. You know that."

"I do know that. I think the world of you, Maura."

"And I think I can let you know within the week. A marriage for a year and a half."

"With a child being born."

"What we're talking about is crazy."

"Not to me."

She wanted him to hold her, kiss her. And all he wanted from her was a baby.

He took her hand again. "You think it over carefully. Weigh the scales as much in my favor as you can."

"Yes. I'll have to think about what I want from you."

They walked back to her house then and, to Maura, it seemed they reached it too soon. She wanted to talk with Papa Isaac, but he was asleep, and she knew she would not ask his advice or anyone's on this. Not even Odessa's. This decision had to be hers alone.

Nineteen-year-old Lonnie Fillmore rode with the cool wind sweeping over him. His nearly new Harley Davidson was a powerhouse beneath him, and he never rode it without keenly feeling the thrill of all that glory. Chrome, black leather, the Harley Davidson logo, and his own black leather pants and jacket. Was he a man, he thought, or was he a god?

A good-looking youth with pale brown skin and curly brown hair, his slender body was wired with tension. Anger rode his shoulders for most of his waking hours. Whatever he wanted, his parents saw to it he got. As the only child of Ward Fillmore, mayor of Crystal Lake, and Rhea, his wife, Lonnie was spoiled, and they knew it, but saw no harm in it. They had both grown up deprived, and they swore it wouldn't happen to their son.

Lonnie raised his fairly good tenor in a ribald drinking song and laughed as he passed two older women plodding along.

It was on the tip of his tongue to say, "Get out of my way, you old bats," but, at moments like this, he was able to think of his dad's being mayor and needing votes. That fact got away from him sometimes, like when he'd pulled away from the curb and almost clipped Josh Pyne's Saab. So he raced his motor and raised his cap to them, sure that they'd heard parts of the song.

Ahead of him, a slender young girl stood waiting at the curb for the light to change. Lonnie slowed and stopped at her side.

"Care to ride with me?"

"Not on your life!" she spat. "In case you're not aware, Iris Iverson was my cousin, and she jumped off that bridge because she was pregnant with your child, and you turned your back on her. Turn your back on me and get the hell out of my face!"

His body heating to fire, Lonnie stared at her.

"Bitch!" he said, gutturally.

The girl didn't flinch. "I'm a better person than you are in your dreams." The light changed and she walked across the street.

Lonnie stared after her for a moment then roared off.

The Iverson girl crowded his brain. Like his father, the girl had adored him, but he hadn't thought much about her. She was too soft, too easy. Weak. He laughed into the wind. He liked the girls who could show a little spirit, but not too much. Too much spirit got him into trouble. Now that little hussy, Ellen—she was something. Living alone. Pretty. A little older than he was, but innocent somehow.

He wasn't sorry for what he'd done to her. She'd had it coming, leading him on. His hand tapped the handlebar. Well, Pop had gotten him out of that. Cooked her goose. She'd talked about having him arrested. He shrugged. He did what he could to keep himself happy. As much as his father loved him, his mother disapproved of his wildness. She'd said to him more than once the words that hurt him so badly.

"You're no good, Lonnie. God knows you're my child, but you're like my brother, Hal." Hal was the really wild one who had gone to the penitentiary for robbing a bank and killing a cop. Lonnie always shuddered when he thought about Uncle Hal.

When he passed a cutoff point, he looked at it longingly. He wanted to turn off there and go to see Ellen, but he was afraid she was still angry at him. There had been murder in her eyes after she had gone to his father and told him what had happened. His father hadn't let him down. His father never let him down. Only his mother did. Lonnie hunched his shoulders, thinking that Uncle Hal hunched his shoulders. Lord, he fervently wished he wasn't like Uncle Hal, but something in him wanted to be.

Five

Later that afternoon, Odessa and Mike Martin came by to visit Papa Isaac.

"You're coming along," Odessa said, hugging Papa Isaac.

They had brought him a pot of rose-colored impatiens.

"I'm going to get spoiled rotten," Papa Isaac said. "Josh brought me those," he said, pointing to the purple flowers.

"I love dahlias," Odessa said.

"But these are beautiful too," Papa Isaac reassured her. "I'm going to put in a few in the spring."

After a while, Maura left the two men to talk shop and went with Odessa to the kitchen. When they had settled, Mike came to the door. "Hey, I'm going out to the car to get my clippers to cut Papa Isaac's hair. Back in a minute."

"Trust you to think about something necessary like that," Maura said. "Thank you."

"That's what my husband is all about," Odessa said, winking at Mike.

Mike winked back. "She's so good to me, I can't help being good to others." Odessa chuckled as he went out, and Maura felt a twinge of envy. Those two had such a strong love bond between them. She probably would tell Odessa after the fact of her marriage, but not before. She caught herself; it seemed she had already made up her mind.

Odessa studied her. "Girlfriend, you look both happy and bothered. What is it?"

Maura shrugged. "Papa Isaac passed his checkup with flying colors, but there is a flareup in another spot. Josh is so precious. He offered to take Papa Isaac back before I could ask him, and he took him for his checkup."

"Seems I'm getting signs of that old love bug biting. The great sting of cupid's arrow." Odessa's look was quizzical.

Maura flushed. "Don't go reading something into nothing."

"I know the signs," Odessa said. "I've been there a few times. And heavens, when Mike and I fell in love, we really fell hard."

"You and Mike are lucky to have each other."

"We are, at that. You and Malcolm got a good start."

Grimly, Maura thought, it seemed that those halcyon days would never come again.

"You could do worse than Josh Pyne. Many a filly has set her cap for him."

"Oh?"

"Where're your eyes, girl? Fine hunk like that, and he puts himself at your disposal. It must mean something. Come by the shop and let's look at new hairstyles. Knock that rascal right off his feet with what my good-looking girlfriend has to offer. Why, if I were a free woman . . ."

"You'd be out looking for someone just like Mike."

Odessa laughed. "Guess you're right. Mike's my man. But seriously, Josh does seem keen on you. I remember he took you to your high school prom. We were just becoming fast friends. You had quite a crush on him."

"Let the dead past bury the dead."

"I like 'the past is prologue' better."

"You would."

What would Odessa say, Maura thought, *if she knew what Josh had proposed?* Mike tapped the door chimes and Lona emerged from Papa Isaac's bedroom to let him in.

Odessa and Mike were madly in love, and Odessa thought Josh was falling in love with Maura. No such luck. Josh's heart had been crushed, and he didn't believe it would ever be whole again.

"Stay for dinner," Maura said. "We're having flounder stuffed with shrimp, and artichoke salad. I'll even let you help me if you can get up the energy. I know Saturdays are rough at hairdressers."

"I took off at one o'clock and left it to my assistant. Women trying to be beautiful for men isn't going to wear my soles thin. I do what I can. I'll be happy to help, and snoop into what's going on between you and Josh Pyne."

"Give it a rest." Maura's voice was sharper than she intended. Odessa pursed her lips and studied her.

"You're a bit touchy," she said. "Why? You can hold your own with the queen. Go after him if you want him. Inveigle him into coming after you. I like the thought of the two of you together. I like rich guys. Mike and I plan to be rich one day."

Maura couldn't help but laugh. Then the laughter died. She would trade all the Pyne money for love.

"You've got a feverish imagination." Maura touched Odessa's arm, then patted it.

"I know love when I see it," Odessa said, staunchly. "And I'm staring it right in the face."

That night, the dream filtered in slowly, as Maura lay in her gauzy white gown in her bedroom. She had kicked off the blanket as she slept. Josh and she stood in front of a waterfall, and she held a precious baby in her arms. The child grasped Maura's index finger and gurgled and Maura thrilled to the joy of it. There was still so much to discuss about this wondrous, perfect child.

The waterfall cascaded merrily down the hill, obscuring conversation. She strained to hear something that Josh said to her, even as her heart beat faster from the way he looked at her. He bent to kiss her.

"I love you," he said over the roar of the waterfall.

She came awake, frustrated. "Listen, my girl," she said to herself. "You've got to get your head screwed on straight. If you're going to do this thing, go into it expecting what you *can* have, not what you can't."

She knew then that she wanted to marry Josh Pyne. She would take her chances. She knew now what she'd been thinking all along. Josh was a good man. A decent, caring man. And she *wanted* to bear his child. But she also wanted to think it through more carefully. Her mind wanted to be careful; her heart raced full speed ahead.

Six

Maura found that the next week went by with lightning speed. That Thursday morning, as Maura sat in her home office mulling over some old drawings for the recently refurbished community center, which had special facilities for teenagers, her phone rang. It was Josh.

"I don't want to make a nuisance of myself," he said, "but I think of you often."

"As if you could be a nuisance. I like your calling a lot."

"I trust Mr. Allen's okay."

"Yes, he's fine. Since you took him to the doctor, you know how the new situation is going. Josh, you've made things so easy for me with your support and help. You just took over."

Josh was silent a long moment. "I want to help you all I can. That's why I'm calling."

"Oh?"

"How about letting me monopolize your weekend. I want to do a good job of selling myself to you. So, I want to take you home with me Saturday, and I want you to meet my beloved grandmother. Are you free then?"

"I can arrange to be."

"Good. Pick you up around one?"

"That sounds fine to me."

He cleared his throat. "Are you thinking about my proposition? Thinking hard?"

"It may surprise you how hard I am thinking. Josh, you're

a wonderful man. I hope you know that. There're so many women who'd be happy to take you up on this."

"You're the one I want."

"Why?"

"Ask me when we're together."

She found it difficult to get back to work after they'd hung up. She looked down at her engagement and wedding rings from Malcolm, slid them nearly off her finger, then back down again.

Josh's white stucco, blue tile-roofed house was out near Crystal Lake, on five acres of beautifully landscaped grounds with a two-acre catfish pond. It was lovely, Maura thought.

"Like fishing?" Josh asked, as they stood watching the catfish.

"I don't know how. Papa Isaac used to fish a lot."

"He'd be in seventh heaven here. And I'll teach you now, if you'd like to learn."

"I'll think about it. What gorgeous swans."

Two black swans floated on the pond among the multicolored water lilies.

"They do add their bit of glory. And, speaking of glory, you look beautiful."

Maura blushed hotly. "Cream's your color," he told her, looking at her at her lightly draped, silk, jersey dress that exposed part of her smooth clove-colored throat and shoulders.

"Thank you," she said, following his eyes down to her strap, buff-colored, leather high-heeled sandals.

"Don't be frightened," he said. "I have to stare at the luscious legs to get to the feet I'm admiring."

Maura chuckled. "I'm not frightened of you. You're looking pretty spiffy yourself."

And he did look handsome in his beige sports shirt and dark tan Dockers.

As they walked up the flagstone back-walk to the house,

Josh stopped for a moment and held out his hand. "You wanted to know why I want you rather than someone else."

"I'd like to know."

"Because you're everything a man could want."

"Yet, I'm without a man."

"Your choice. I'm sure the field is crowded with men who'd like you for their own."

Maura expelled a short breath. "No, you're wrong there." Her face puckered with merriment. "Yours is the best offer I've had in many a moon."

"And what are you going to do about it?"

"Ask me a couple of hours from now."

"Do you need more time? Take all the time you want, but I think you know how anxious I am to get started."

They walked onto the screened-in back porch, where he took her in his arms. "We can have so much together," he declared. "Don't let the lack of love ruin it for us."

"You've been hurt. I can understand that."

"No," he said. "I'm not sure anyone can understand it. My heart is broken and may never heal. I want you to know that. But, there is so much I can give you. Since your husband's death, you say you haven't wanted anyone else. I can give you a child to love. You're a warm, vibrant woman. Just being with Papa Isaac isn't enough."

His nearness was making her sick with desire. What would it be like for him to hold her? Making a baby with him would be heaven itself, but he didn't lie to her. It would be a child conceived in deep caring, but not love.

What was love, anyway? Looking at him, she knew what it could be for her.

His house matched the grounds. Simply furnished in Spanish décor, it was light and airy with white walls, and she found herself liking it very much. The gorgeous splash of orange-red, green-and-white-flowered short drapes set off the living room and lifted her spirits.

"Love that dress," he said, touching her bare neckline.

"Love your house."

"What would you change?"

"What would I—?" She blushed again, stammering, "You mean if I were to live here?"

"If you don't like this place, I could build you another."

"I like this one. Somehow it's you."

"I'm glad you think so, but it's been another woman's house. I wouldn't mind building a new one for you. In fact, I'd enjoy it."

A deep sense of comfort came over her. "I'll think about it," she said.

His face lit up. "Does that mean you're leaning toward my proposal?"

Her throat nearly closed with anxiety. To counter it, she asked, "Will we be going to meet your grandmother after leaving here?"

"Yes." His eyes held hers. "But you're going away from something you've got to face. Maura, don't turn me down."

Maura looked at him steadily. He looked like the man he was, strong and admirable, but he also sounded like a boy who wanted something so badly he couldn't stand not getting it.

"In so short a time, I'm planning what I want to do with you. Get the rings. License. Blood tests. Get married. Everything," Josh said.

"Then the baby."

He grinned lopsidedly. "That's going to take a little while."

Maura smiled. He had her in a nearly perpetual state of warming. Her knees felt weak with desire. Yet, she had to hold back. Gently, he took her in his arms and pressed her full length against him so that she felt his arousal and his hard, muscular body. One hand cupped her chin, and his mouth came down on hers, forcing her lips open so that his tongue searched and found hers and drew the honey from it.

His other hand was low on her back, pressing her in to him. Flames of desire swept through her body, and she gasped with delight.

For Josh, this was heaven itself. The soft, tender woman he held was what he wanted for himself. He bitterly regretted that he couldn't love her, but he didn't want to lose her. He relaxed and felt her tongue in his mouth, turning him on to a high fever. He groaned inwardly. He had to have her. Love wasn't everything. There was plenty else in life, and much of it was in the presence of this woman.

How easy it would be, he thought, to lie and tell her he loved her, but he honored her too much for that.

Reluctantly releasing her, he began to tour the house with her. She found herself immensely intrigued with the large, pine-paneled library and its rich array of books.

She picked up the June issue of *Ebony,* which was devoted to June brides from different countries.

Josh saw her looking at the cover and smiled. "Even *Ebony* is on my side."

In the huge master bedroom, he paused on the doorsill, wanting to pick her up and carry her in, put her on the bed, and make wild love to her. As if she read his thoughts, she drew in a quick breath.

The house smelled clean and fresh. She closed her eyes for a minute.

"I love your house," she told him.

"I'll build you another. You deserve your own."

"We're talking as if our marriage were a *fait accompli.*"

"Is it?"

She teased him a little, teasing herself, too. "I truly am not yet sure."

Josh made brandy alexanders for them in his spacious kitchen.

"Would you like to go out on the terrace?"

"Later. I'm enjoying it in here."

"Do you enjoy being with me?"

"I do."

"Married, you'd have a chance to spend a lot of time with me."

"You're a busy man."

"I'd make time for you."

"When you could."

Maura sat on one of the pale-yellow, padded, high stools in the kitchen, her beautiful long legs pressed against the stool's cool metal. Josh gave her a wolf whistle, went to his knees, and took her hand, singling out the third finger of her left hand, kissing it. She had left Malcolm's rings at home.

"See, I'm begging you to marry me," he said.

"It's the baby you want, not the marriage."

"I'd have both. So would you."

Not fully realizing she would do so, she told him, "I must be out of my mind, but I'll marry you and bear your child."

He hugged her knees tightly and stood up, his heart racing.

"You'll never be sorry," he said, huskily.

"There's only one thing."

"Tell me."

"If it doesn't work out, we'll be faithful to our plan. We'll get an amicable divorce when the baby is under two. No bitterness."

He pulled her gently off the stool and held her slender body hard against his.

"Don't borrow trouble," he said. "Love isn't the only thing that makes the world go round. Caring matters a lot."

When Josh's door chimes rang, he said, "Damn it! I don't need more company," and went to the door.

He came back with his best friend, Rich Curry, in tow.

"I want to introduce you to my fiancée," he said.

Rich was a fiery redhead with a face full of freckles. He was of medium height and slender.

"Congratulations!" Rich said.

"Rich and I go back twenty years. He's my drywall supplier."

"And I keep him on the straight and narrow."

"Or he tries."

"I've seen you around," Rich said. "You can't live in a place like Crystal Lake without seeing almost everyone at least once."

"I've seen you too."

"Have you two set a wedding date?"

"Give us time, man," Josh said. "We just turned *this* corner."

"Well, I swear I've never seen you look happier."

Josh nodded. "I have to agree with you."

But Maura sat thinking, his happiness lay in begetting a child from her. What would Rich say if he knew the score?

"I wonder if you could excuse Josh a moment, Maura. I have a couple of things I need to take care of with him and I'm running late. I won't take long."

"Be my guest."

Rich fixed himself a gin and tonic.

"What's your choice in music?" Josh asked her.

"It's pretty catholic. I'd like to hear Rachmaninoff's 'Second Piano Concerto,' and anything by Nancy Wilson or Teddy Pendergrass."

"It's yours."

Josh went to the wall and buzzed the panels open. Racks held alphabetized and compartmentalized cassettes and compact discs, and he pulled two compact discs. In a moment, the gorgeous strains of Rachmaninoff's genius-laden "Second Piano Concerto" filled the room, as the men walked out on the terrace.

"Wow, buddy, you travel at the speed of light. She seems like one of the best. But, be careful, those gorgeous eyes alone could break your heart." He stopped a moment. "Sorry, Josh. I remember the rough time you had with Melodye."

"It's okay, Rich. I look forward to getting over that one day." He sighed. "But it sure hasn't happened yet."

"I hope you'll be happy now."

For a moment, Josh looked grim, but he told himself he was

happy. Desire for a child of his own had eaten at his spirit for a long time now. He looked forward to fatherhood from the depths of his soul.

"Well, to go from the sublime to the ridiculous, your foreman for the Huntley job wanted me to check with you on the amount of drywall you'll need. He felt he wasn't sure enough of himself to go ahead and order."

Josh sighed. "Chet's a good man, but he doesn't trust himself. You and he are just going to have to work this out. I'm training him to take over more and more. He's a bright guy. He's got to get with it. I believe in delegating responsibility You lead him along into this."

"Well said. I think the world of Chet, and, yes, he needs to trust himself more."

Josh looked closely at his friend.

"Practicing much this weekend?"

"Head on. I've knocked out a nifty song, and I've been asked to perform at the warm-up dance for the Crystal Lake teen clubhouse a couple of weeks from now."

"Yeah. It's looking great."

"Trouble is, I need at least one or two backup singers."

Josh's eyes twinkled with laughter.

"Preferably female?"

"Absolutely female."

"Got anyone in mind?"

"Yeah. Funny thing. One day when you weren't there and I went by to see you on the teen club project, I walked around and I heard a young woman, a girl really, in the woods, singing to herself. Man, it was something! It was the girl who has the stone house on the old Halaby plantation, or what's left of it."

"Theena's great-great-great-granddaughter."

"Yeah. She's a young queen. Only thing is—"

"Only thing is?"

"She's got a reputation as wild as a bucking bronco."

"Well, I'm not one to believe everything I hear."

"The entertainment field ain't laced with angels, but for a couple of years I've been hearing about her. Before then, nothing."

"Her mother died a couple of years ago."

"Yeah. That may have something to do with it."

"If you like her, invite her to sing with you. Maybe you can help her straighten out her life."

"Sure thing. I'm going to consider that. I've got to run now. I really am happy for you."

His friend sounded wistful, and Josh thought about the fact that Rich drank too much too often. He and Josh had both been divorced the same year. Rich's wife had left the country the next year with her new African diplomat husband. Rich and Josh had commiserated with each other, but unlike his friend, Rich was still looking for love in all the wrong places.

When Rich left, Maura saw him pull out of the driveway, and she came outside. Josh met her in the middle of the terrace. He kissed her forehead.

"You make me feel like a child when you do that."

"You're not a child, believe me."

"Hopefully, I'll have a child. Yours."

"I don't think we can miss, but if we do—no, I'm not going to think about that."

"I still have an unreal feeling."

"I don't. It's the realest thing in the world to me."

"I keep wondering if I'm being a fool."

"You're not being a fool. You're doing one of the most important things anyone can do—bear a child."

"I keep thinking how you're so soured on love. If you don't love me, will you love my child?"

"I like you, Maura, a hell of a lot, probably as much as I can like anybody, but love is a different kettle of fish. It's not like we're bound forever if it doesn't work. How soon can we be married?"

She looked at him levelly, and he guided her under the shade of a tree.

Her answer surprised her. "As soon as you'd like."

He smiled. "We're taking Papa Isaac back to the hospital for another bit of surgery; then, if all goes well, let's make it the next week."

"That sounds good."

"I want to make you happy."

"I am happy."

"You look so great, I want to take you to meet a couple of people. You've met my best buddy, Rich."

"I like him."

"So do I, but he's got problems."

"I'm sorry about that."

"He'll get it together one day. He was unlucky in love. Like me."

"We have to take chances," Maura said. "Look at the chance I'm taking."

"I *am* looking at it and I bless you. Right now, I want to show you off to my grandmother and my dad."

"I'm willing."

"But, I also want you all to myself."

"Make up your mind."

Josh's father, Carter Pyne, lived in the showplace of Crystal Lake, on the opposite side from Josh. Carter's house was an ultramodern one of glass, gray-beige stucco, and stone. The walls of the front section were covered with natural-colored silk, and huge Grecian urns were set about. Josh and Maura found Carter relaxing in an expensively tailored shirt and slacks. His cedarwood face was smooth and pampered. His bald head gleamed.

Josh introduced them and while the older man's handshake was firm, his gray eyes were cool.

"Actually, we're here to see Grandmother Addie. I know this is usually one of your busy days."

"No. Not really. I think you might like to know that Melodye is coming any minute."

"We won't be here very long."

"Don't run away from your troubles, lad. You can never outrun them."

Josh's mouth tightened, but he said nothing.

"It's a pleasure to meet you, Mrs. Blackwell," Carter Pyne said, as they started away. "Enjoy my house. If I didn't have guests coming, I'd give you the grand tour." He liked nothing better than showing off his opulent house.

"Thank you for thinking of it, and I, too, enjoyed meeting you."

With her elbow cupped in his hand, Josh sped Maura through the palatial house. Huge, beautiful African urns sat in several of the corners, and the Oriental rugs were a joy to behold.

"How absolutely stunning," Maura murmured, pausing to look at a Burn sunset-at-sea painting.

"Nobody ever said the old boy didn't have good taste, but it just so happens that I leaned on him to buy that."

"Your own house reflects your taste, and I love it."

Josh drew her to his side as they reached a door. He knocked. At the invitation of the sweet, older voice, they entered a room done in pastels.

A lovely, white-haired, pale-skinned old woman sat in a wheelchair.

Josh went to his grandmother and kissed her deeply wrinkled cheek.

The woman smiled, impishly. Her blue eyes were so merry.

"You didn't come by or call yesterday," the old woman said.

"I know, and I apologize, but I'm here today. Grandmother Addie, I want you to meet someone very special to me. Maura Blackwell."

Grandmother Addie proffered her buttery soft hand. Several beautiful rings adorned her fingers. Her wide, gold wedding band enhanced the other rings she wore.

"Bend down and let me kiss your cheek," the old woman

said. "I like what I'm seeing." She smiled at Maura. "I've been so afraid he'd get caught again by someone I have no love for. But I like you. You're—as the kids nowadays say—'for real.' Welcome to my little suite."

"It's a pretty spacious suite," Maura said, bending for her kiss, "and it's lovely. Mrs. Pyne, I'm so glad to meet you."

"Call me Grandmother Addie," Mrs. Pyne said. "And I hope I'll be like a grandmother to you."

"How have you been feeling?" Josh asked.

"Very well for an eighty-four-year-old. You'd better come to see me often while you can. I'll shuffle off this mortal coil one day."

Josh laughed. "I've asked for special favors, that you be allowed to stay here as long as I'm on earth. Who knows? My wish may be granted."

"How about him?" Grandmother Addie asked Maura. "Doesn't he know just what to say? His father's an only child and so is he. But I'd like him multiplied fifty times over. Cloned."

"Nope. I like having you two to myself."

Maura smiled at the easy banter between the two.

Seated, Grandmother Addie rang the bell by her chair. In a few minutes, a middle-aged gray-haired woman appeared.

"Mrs. Taylor, would you please get them what they'd like to drink?"

"Certainly," the smiling woman said.

Maura chose ginger ale, Josh, light beer.

"Have you been taking care of yourself?" Josh demanded.

Grandmother Addie pursed her lips. "I now have to leave that largely to others, but I'm having a strength trainer come out. Lord, is that man handsome. Not a day over forty. Reminds me a bit of you."

Josh laughed. "I'm happy to hear that. Did Dad give you any trouble?"

"Oh, he thinks I'm an old fool, although he dares not say it to my face. Josh, I'm determined to see my hundredth birthday and beyond. After only three sessions, I already feel better."

"Lifting weights? Light ones?"

"Oh, yes, and stretching. Breathing exercises."

"Next thing we know, you'll be doing yoga."

Grandmother Addie laughed. "Don't rule that out." She touched her smoothly coiffed white hair, then patted it.

"You're a lovely woman," she told Maura.

"Thank you. So are you."

"Oh, well, I had them dancing in the aisles when I was your age. Plenty of people thought I was a fast woman, but my husband always had faith in me. Josh's father's not a bit like my husband. And he's certainly not like me. I don't know who he takes after. Money's his god, the way love was my husband's. I think God singled me out to be blessed when he sent me my husband. Dead now some thirty years, and I'm still listening for the sound of his voice."

She sounded so wistful.

"Love is like that," Maura said.

"You look like you might know a lot about love."

"I know I believe in it."

She looked obliquely at Josh, who didn't meet her eyes.

Grandmother Addie sighed. "Nobody ever said it couldn't hurt you, though. I really grieved when my husband died. His name was Josh, too. We called him Grandpa Josh in later years to tell him from your Josh."

Maura blushed and Grandmother Addie threw back her head, laughing again. "Here I am calling him 'your' Josh. I'm giving him to you for safekeeping, when I don't even know what's going on between you two. It's not like he brings women around for me to meet, so I gather he has a serious bone or two in his body for you."

For a moment, Maura closed her eyes. *Grandmother Addie,* she thought, *you don't know how serious he is, as long as it leaves love out of the picture.*

At a knock on the door and Grandmother Addie's invitation to come in, Maura expected Mrs. Taylor with the drinks. Instead, Carter Pyne came in, his face wreathed in smiles, with Melodye Pyne, who had kept the Pyne name, in tow.

She was a knockout, no doubt about that, Maura thought, but she felt only a twinge of envy until she saw how Josh stiffened. There was still a lot going on between those two. Melodye was very subdued, her curly, dark-auburn hair cascading down her back, her creamy skin perfect. Only her sea-green eyes flashed fire as she acknowledged the introduction.

"I don't believe I've met you before," Melodye said. "Are you from Crystal Lake?"

"I've lived here all my life. We don't travel in the same circles."

"I went to Barnaby Wells Academy," Melodye said, cheerfully. "It tended to limit my friends or those I knew."

"Well, Crystal Lake's excellent public high school was good enough for me," Josh said.

His father looked at him with half-closed eyes. "It wasn't as if I didn't want you to go to a private school, but you were always so bullheaded. Wanting to mix with all classes and kinds."

"I think it added to my happiness," Josh said, stubbornly.

"That's a judgment only you can make." Carter sounded subdued. He turned to his mother. "Mother, I . . ."

Mrs. Taylor knocked and brought in the drinks on a silver tray. The cold liquid felt good in Maura's dry mouth. "Thank you," she said.

"I'd appreciate it if you'd get me a double Scotch, and," he turned to Melodye, "what would you have, my dear?"

"I think I'll take one shot of Scotch and orange juice," Melodye purred. It was plain that she and Carter Pyne had a mutual admiration society.

As Mrs. Taylor started out, Carter Pyne asked, "Where's your helper today, Mrs. Taylor? I don't want you overworked. You're too valuable for that."

Mrs. Taylor smiled. "She's just running a couple of errands for me, sir. And thank you for feeling that way."

As Mrs. Taylor went out, Carter and Melodye seated themselves.

"Don't let us interrupt you," Carter said.

Melodye raised her brows a bit. "I'm always struck by how egalitarian you are where your servants are concerned."

Josh breathed deeply. "The woman's a jewel. Why wouldn't Dad and the rest of us treat her like one?"

"Well, with what you all pay, anybody would turn into a jewel. Wish I had one like her."

"A lot depends on how you treat people." Josh seemed nettled, and Maura was fascinated—and bothered—by the heated interplay between these two.

The room fell silent and Grandmother Addie closed her eyes. She detested Melodye Pyne and wished she'd go back to using her maiden name—Crane. She suspected she didn't know the whole story behind the breakup of Josh and Melodye. She knew how badly Josh wanted children, and Melodye had confided in her that she wanted to wait. "Have a good time and enjoy settling into the marriage first," was the way she'd put it. Trouble was, as time passed, she never settled. Poor Josh; Grandmother Addie loved him fiercely. He deserved the best, and he had had to settle for a lot less.

Her voice chipper, her chin raised, Melodye began a conversation. "Did you attend Crystal Lake High?" she asked Maura.

"I did."

"Before you begin angling in order to trash her," Josh said abruptly, "Maura's an architect. Although I was in college, I took her to her senior prom. Had a wonderful time."

"You always were a great one for helping others less fortunate," Melodye complimented in a backhanded fashion.

Josh grinned a one-sided grin. "For my money, Mrs. Blackwell is one of the most fortunate people around. Frank Lloyd Wright—you don't read much out of the fashion world, but he was one of the greatest architects in the field—would be proud to have her on his staff."

"Don't lift me so high," Maura said, laughing.

"For my money," Josh answered her, "you've got everything it takes."

Melodye wriggled her shoulders. Her mouth took on a pout. "Poor me. I dropped out of college in my sophomore year and never had time to go back. You wanted us to be married so badly. I was majoring in electrical engineering. Guess I'll just have to be satisfied to be the daughter of one of the richest men on the East Coast. Money and I are very fond of each other."

Josh looked at her levelly. "Yeah. Well, some people need more than money."

"And some, like you, are never certain what it is they want."

Tapping his foot, Josh told her, "I'm well on the road to getting what I want after a long period of emotional drought."

With this, Melodye's mouth looked pinched.

Coming to life, Grandmother Addie's voice took on a conciliatory note. "Maura, I'd love it if you'd read to me from Elizabeth Barrett Browning, and a bit from Paul Lawrence Dunbar. I love them both. Think I'd like Dunbar first. Here, they're right by me."

Maura took the books. "Which of Dunbar's poems would you like to hear?"

"Oh, 'Li'l Brown Baby' would be fine."

Maura cleared her throat and began to read as Josh watched her with half-closed eyes, letting the musical timbre of her voice wash over him.

With delight, she read the poem, rife with memories of her own mother, who had been a schoolteacher, reading the poem to her. Her mother had taught her the poem and had taught her the drama of it.

Grandmother Addie watched her, and her bright eyes were sparkling. When Maura finished, Grandmother Addie clapped and complimented her. "Brava!"

Maura blushed. "A thousand kudos," Josh said. "You're wonderful."

"You read well," Carter said, dryly.

Melodye was silent.

"Now for 'Sonnets from the Portuguese.' " Grandmother Addie threw back her head and it was easy to see that she had once been a very high-spirited young woman. Easy to see that she was loving, and had been and was still loved.

Grandmother Addie smiled at Maura. "Now catch your breath and read me Browning's poem, 'How Do I love Thee?' Josh and I used to read to each other nightly."

After a moment, Maura found the poem and cleared her throat. Melodye stirred. "Carter, there're some things I need to talk with you about and I hadn't planned to stay too late. Could I get your attention now? Could we go?"

Carter seemed reluctant to leave. As fond as he was of Melodye, he had been enjoying the reading.

"Can't you wait just a bit?"

"It's okay, Dad," Josh said. "Maura does read beautifully. But you can hear her some other time. She'll be a frequent visitor."

Carter looked from one to the other of the women, then back to Josh.

Grandmother Addie clapped her hands. "Oh, wonderful," she said. "I'd like nothing better than to have you visit often."

Melodye's intake of breath was sharp. She had long begun to know what she'd lost when she divorced Josh. His kind didn't come around very often, and she'd hoped to get him back, with Carter's help.

"I'm sorry." Melodye began to get up. "I really do need to talk with you."

"Please get on with the reading," Grandmother Addie commanded Maura. "I'm impatient to hear it again."

Maura drew a deep breath and began:

> *How do I love thee?*
> *Let me count the ways . . .*

By then, Carter and Melodye were halfway across the room. Grandmother Addie was glad that Melodye didn't bend to kiss her cheek, as she often did. Shameless hussy. Probably had been cheating on Josh. Not wanting his babies. Wrapped up in self and self alone. Good riddance.

Maura finished and read more of Elizabeth Barrett Browning's poems. When she closed the book, the old woman blew her a kiss.

"I wish you and Josh," she said, "every good in this world."

When they were ready to leave, she reached and hugged Maura, and said to Josh, "Now, don't you forget you promised she would be back often. I brook no lies, you know, and I'm going to hold you to that."

A warm smile spread across Josh's face. "I promise."

"You're beginning to be happy again, and God knows, more than most people, you deserve to be happy."

Going back through the big rooms on their way out, Maura and Josh turned a corner to find Melodye and Carter locked in a passionate embrace.

Becoming aware of them, Melodye pulled away, her face flaming scarlet. Carter stared at them, coolly.

"Good-bye, Dad. Melodye," Josh said, formally.

"Good-bye, Josh," Carter returned. Melodye said nothing.

Josh took Maura's hand. "That was some kiss."

"Are you jealous?"

"I don't think so. I'm surprised. The kiss looked serious, but Dad's a ladies' man."

"I'd swear Melodye still has feelings for you. Maybe she's trying to make you jealous."

"I've got you," he said evenly, "and you're all I need."

In Josh's car, Maura turned to him. "Your grandmother's certainly a wonderful woman."

"I agree, and she likes you. I'm going to take you somewhere special."

"Oh?"

He headed downtown and, in a short while, pulled up in front of Palmer's, an upscale jewelry store.

"I wasn't sure that you'd want to shop in DC. And you still can, but Palmer's is a first-class jeweler. I like to throw all the business I can to our own merchants and see Crystal Lake grow."

"I'm in favor of that."

Inside, greeted by the owner, they looked at and tried on engagement and wedding rings.

Josh's eyes on her were tender. "Take your time. I want you to be happy."

Maura would have been happy with any set she saw, but she finally selected a marquise-shaped white diamond set in platinum, and a matching platinum wedding band.

Josh lifted her hand with the engagement ring and kissed it. His eyes were warm and gentle on her.

"To us," he said. But he had mentioned nothing about love.

Seven

Early July

For a long while, it seemed a dream to Maura that they were married. They had gone to a little town in Maryland where no waiting period was required. Telling no one in advance, they came back to have their work cut out for them.

"I think you'll be happy," he said.

Odessa had seemed a bit miffed. "I always looked forward to being your matron of honor for your second marriage. Now you go and marry 'Mr. Fine' himself and Mike and I are left out in the cold."

But Odessa had quickly rallied and hugged her. "I know you must have had your reasons, girl."

Grandmother Addie gave them a fifty-year-old silver coffee service and cried, with her blessings.

Josh's best friend, Rich Curry, had looked at them speculatively, saying quickly, sincerely, "I'm happy for you both. I think you both have the best of the lot."

Papa Isaac looked at them searchingly, kissed Maura, and shook Josh's hand.

It was the near hostility of Carter Pyne that had startled her.

"Are you pregnant?" he'd asked Maura, bluntly.

"We don't have to answer that." Josh's voice cut sharply through the denial Maura had begun.

"Well, I wonder what the rush is. You go off like thieves in the night with loot to stash away. We're a proud family, Joshua. We like for things to look right. Up to now, you've rarely disappointed me.

"I wish I could give you my blessings, but I'm too disappointed."

Quite levelly, Josh had said, "Of course, I'd like to have your blessings, Dad, but we can take it in stride if you can't give them."

Carter Pyne had turned away.

Papa Isaac was coming along splendidly, so Maura had quickly moved into Josh's house. The marriage had yet to be consummated after three weeks.

Maura had been married in an off-white raw-silk suit with an aquamarine lace blouse and high-heeled off-white leather sandals. Josh had looked at her hungrily during the ceremony. His voice had been husky when he'd said his "I do's."

They'd decided on a later honeymoon. Josh had seemed nervous as he told her, "You're going to be uncomfortable at best. I want to give you all the time you need to settle in."

Maura's heart had thumped wildly. She was Mrs. Joshua Pyne! Many words rushed to her lips. She found herself wanting him more than she had believed it was possible to want a man. The love between Malcolm and her had been slow, steady, a tame love.

What she felt for Josh was wildly passionate, filling her veins with honeyed fire. But then she told herself, with a trace of bitterness: she was the one who wanted love—giving and taking. He only wanted a child.

Now, sitting on the bed in *her* room, the master bedroom Josh had told her to take, she kicked off her shoes and tucked her feet under her.

Josh knocked and came in. He looked at her keenly, his eyes half-closed.

"I came home early, and I brought Chinese food. Won Ton has about the best. I would have called to ask what you wanted to do, but I thought I'd surprise you. You haven't begun dinner?"

She shook her head. "No, I was going to call and ask what you wanted. Chinese food would be wonderful."

"I got beef and broccoli, sweet'n'sour shrimp, moo shu chicken, and a Peking duck to freeze."

Maura stretched. "You look tired," she said.

"I didn't sleep too well."

She hadn't slept too well, either.

"Do you want to eat early?"

"Not particularly. Why?"

"I want to wait until dark, light candles—I thought that would be nice. Is that all right with you?" She finished the sentence lamely.

"Fine," he said.

She didn't want to throw herself at him. The trouble was she *did* want to throw herself at him. Whatever it took. At least he was honest. Caring. He was giving her time, and a little voice nudged her: time she didn't need.

If there is going to be a baby, let's get the show on the road, she thought.

She patted the bed beside her. "Sit down."

He reached out and smoothed her hair, loving the softly crisp feel of it.

"I'm going to go take a shower," he said. "I'll put the food on the warmer. I got fried ice cream for dessert."

"Bless you. I've wanted some for quite a while."

Why were they so awkward with each other? What he had proposed and she had followed through with was not unheard of. In some societies, marriages were arranged and sometimes happy—certainly viable. They had chosen each other, with no love in view. And, she sadly thought, she was falling in love with Josh. In some part of her, she seemed to have always loved him since her senior year of high school.

He bent and kissed the top of her head.

"Josh?" she said, slowly.

"Yes."

"If you want to go ahead and get started on the baby, I'm willing."

He dropped to the bed and took her in his arms. Turning her face to him, he kissed her as fire raced along his veins. He had wanted to get started from the day he had married her—and before.

Her slender hands stroked his back, digging into his flesh through his shirt. Her eyes were closed against the onslaught of passion sizzling inside her. Her arms locked around his neck. For long moments he crushed her body to him, feeling her soft breasts splay against him. Each could feel the thunder of the other's heart.

Would he take her now?

Gently, Josh reached up and disengaged her arms.

"I want you to be sure," he said. "I want you to be comfortable. I won't press you."

For the life of her, she couldn't answer him, couldn't tell him that she *was* sure. They had been married three weeks and he had not come to her. She felt it was because he wanted to be sure she understood that he couldn't love again, that he didn't love her. She thought she understood that. The thought flashed to mind: if the love were all on her side, she could deal with that. He was decent, honorable. He cared about her. He said so and he showed it. She groaned inwardly.

He touched her face gently. "I'm going to take a shower."

When he left, Maura sat quietly. He said he cared for her. Was it going to be enough? With him living in one house and her in another, it had been bearable. She'd never dreamed his close proximity could be so difficult.

She was in the dining room setting the table with a lace cloth, silver, and crystal. It was dusk outside and she lit the fat ivory candles in the crystal candleholders. Going to her room, she lit a small iron pot of heavenly smelling incense and took it back to the dining room.

The food looked and smelled wonderful. White wine sparkled in the crystal glasses. A low centerpiece of pink roses and fern added lustre to the setting.

Josh came and stood by the table. He had changed into a white shirt and black Dockers.

"You're a romantic," he said. "What can I do to help?"

Maura smiled. "I did it all while you were taking a shower."

"Food and incense," he said. "What smells any better?"

A smile tugged the corners of his mouth as he came toward her. "What smells any better? Except you," he said, evenly.

"Why, thank you. You and Aramis go well together."

He seated her and she picked up a Chinese fortune cookie from the batch in a crystal bowl, snapping it open. She always read and ate the cookie before a Chinese meal.

Her breath caught in her throat. The fortune read,

YOU WILL MEET THE ONE YOU WILL LOVE FOREVER.

"You look excited." Josh studied her.

She started not to let him see the paper, then changed her mind. He looked it over and his face closed. Pain narrowed his mouth. Once he had read a saying like that in a fortune cookie and Melodye had proved to be the lie of his life.

"Nice sentiment," he said. Maura deserved love, he thought. Was he wrong to have wanted a child by her when he could no longer love? Should he let her go?

"You're awfully quiet," Maura prompted him.

A smile lifted the corner of his mouth. "I'm enjoying the food and, even more, the company."

"You say the nicest things. You were certainly raised right."

"That's debatable. One thing is for certain, with Grand-mother Addie's help, I had to learn manners and consideration for other people."

"She's a wonderful woman."

"I put you both on the same level."

"That's quite a compliment."

"I mean it. Are you settling in?"

"I think I'm settled."

He looked down. Desire flamed in him like wildfire. In her watermelon-pink dress with matching dyed watermelon-colored strands of coral, her lovely face was a cameo.

She was going to push it. "Did you have something in mind?"

The look on his face said he had her on his mind, but she suddenly felt bashful with him.

He sipped his wine slowly, seeking to stanch the flood of desire.

"We forgot the music." Getting up, he went to the entertainment wall in the living room, looked over one section, and chose a Teddy Pendergrass album. Just great, he criticized himself. He already wanted to make love to her. This was going to feed the flames. He wanted her to be sure. Living together might have changed her mind.

"Beautiful," she murmured, her brown eyes sparkling like diamonds.

He reached across the table for her hand, sliding the rings back and forth.

"Are you changing your mind?" she teased. "Taking them off?"

His heart slowed. He had so much on his mind to tell her. All he could say was, "Never!"

After they'd finished eating, Maura got up and began to carry the dishes to the kitchen.

"I'll do my version of fried ice cream," he said. "Save the carton I bought for another time."

Maura found an apron for him, and he got the hard, frozen French-vanilla ice cream from the freezer, melted butter in a small iron skillet, then browned coconut, maraschino cherries, and crushed pineapple. Quickly, he put the frozen block of ice cream in the skillet, then flipped it over. The coconut and the pineapple clung to the ice cream, and he spooned the rest over it.

"Yummy!" she said.

"I'm going to go for gourmét chef one day," he said. "I think up a lot of dishes."

"If this dessert is any example, I'm rooting for you all the way."

He was suddenly quiet again. "Are you happy here?"

She took a sharp intake of breath. "Fairly. It was so sweet of you to fix up an office for me. I love it, but I have to be honest with you, I keep wondering—"

"Yes?"

Maura shrugged. She didn't know how to tell him that with every passing moment she wanted him more. She was happy about the prospect of making a baby with him, but when was he going to start the process?

She wanted to be straightforward, and for the life of her she couldn't be. What if he'd found they were a mistake?

If he could love anyone again, he thought, it would be her. But he couldn't forget, hadn't forgotten, the scalding fury that came from the bone-marrow-deep pain Melodye had left as her legacy. *Go easy, heart,* he told himself.

"I think we're coming along," Maura said. "I guess it's just going to take time. A lot of time."

"You look beautiful tonight. Desirable."

Were they getting somewhere? He often complimented her, but he hadn't used the word *desirable* before to define her.

"You're the handsome one. And you seem completely unaware of it."

"I never really thought about it much. I've always had so much else on my mind. But, if it pleases you . . ."

"You please me, Josh. Other than Papa Isaac, you're the gentlest, sweetest man I've ever known."

"You're not old enough to have come in contact with many men."

"Enough to know you're way ahead of the pack."

"You flatter me."

"No. I only tell you the truth."

She scooped up the last of her ice cream and ran her tongue over her lips. There was something going on between them that hadn't existed before. They seemed to be caught up on invisible wavelengths that undulated between them like fairy dust, silken and precious.

He broke the spell and she could have wept.

"I'll put the dishes in the dishwasher."

She nodded, wanting to cry. "I think I'll wait a little while longer, give my food a chance to settle, then take a shower. I'm a little tense."

"So I've noticed. Maura, we're going to have to talk more . . ." His voice drifted.

"About what we're doing here? A baby?"

"Yes." His throat was closing up. Lord, but she was lovely! And, yes, he wanted to talk about the baby. Had enough time elapsed? Was she ready now to begin?

"You say you're tense," he said. "Let's begin talking more tomorrow."

Maura drew a quick breath. *Why not tonight?* she thought miserably. His nearness was making her dizzy. Something in her fled, fearful that he might suggest that it had all been a mistake—the burned-child syndrome.

Josh, she thought, *I'm coming to love you, and I didn't think it would happen so soon.*

He turned toward her for a moment. "I think I'll go look over some building codes that I'll need soon."

She nodded, disappointed. She had been enjoying being with him.

She got up and, stacking the dishes in the dishwasher, turned it on and left the room.

In the living room, she read Khalil Gibran's *The Prophet* and wished that Josh would come in. She couldn't go to him because she never had, and he wouldn't want his building code reading to be interrupted. She got up and found an old CD of

Luther Vandross's, put it in the stereo and turned it on. That special smoothness of Vandross's voice washed over her. She listened for the sound of movement from Josh. Nothing.

She studied the beautiful lines of the poem and read them aloud. Khalil Gibran was the prophet. She glanced at the special cover of black leather and goldleaf. How fitting.

Opening the book again, she began to memorize some of the lines. But thoughts of Josh and her kept interrupting. Pushed by desire, she thought she'd go to him later, but alarm bells sounded in her head. Perhaps he was being quiet because he was having second thoughts.

They ate a late dinner together most days. She got up around five-thirty in the morning and had orange juice, fruit, and a muffin of some type for breakfast. He got up later. They talked about what went on in Crystal Lake, how her work and his work were going. World affairs. But never of their marriage and the baby that hadn't begun to be. He kissed her forehead from time to time, and she was going mad with passion for him.

After a couple of hours, she glanced at her watch. Ten-thirty. She got up, selected another Luther Vandross album, and put it on.

She went to her bedroom and tried to relax. Going into the bathroom, she drew a bath and put a few drops of monoi oil from Tahiti in it. Oh, that heavenly smell!

Undressing slowly, she went back into the bedroom and flipped on the radio. Through the closed bedroom door, classical music vied with the romance of Luther Vandross in the living room. Rachmaninoff's "Second Piano Concert" came on, and she listened attentively.

She had planned to take a shower, but she found she wanted the relaxation of the soda-softened water around her. Turning out the light, she got in and quickly felt more at ease.

She made her mind a blank wall, thinking of nothing at all, and it helped to soothe her. Rubbing with the loofah sponge felt good, and time passed effortlessly.

"I'll be a prune if I keep this up," she said to herself, rising and stepping on the thick cream bath mat, patting herself in a moist state. She had turned the bedroom light off. Now she plugged in a night-light that sat on a shelf and went out into the bedroom.

In his study, Josh sighed. For the life of him he couldn't concentrate. Thoughts of Maura kept flooding his mind. She didn't seem unhappy, but that wasn't the same as being happy. Building codes. What he wanted to build was a new life for himself and his new bride. He was going to be, as he once had been, a decent, kind, and concerned husband. For the past month, he had been fast proving to himself that you didn't need love to be happy. He was happier than he'd been in a very long time.

Maura had spoken of being tense. He was tense. He wanted to give her enough time before he came to her, to let her get used to him, and make her know that she was more than a carrier for his child. He wanted—hell, what *did* he want? He had Maura and he surely wanted her.

Getting up, he undressed, got into blue striped pajamas and a blue robe. It wasn't something he'd been doing, but he was going to kiss his wife good night. Maybe she would talk with him more if he touched her more. He groaned. How could he keep touching her without making love to her? But he felt she needed time.

Standing at Maura's door, he heard the radio and her singing in the bathroom. He hesitated a moment, then opened the door and stepped inside. A tall mahogany screen stretched along the space between much of the room to the bathroom. Only the nightlight shone from the open bathroom door. A sensual passage from a Teddy Pendergrass song swirled in his head.

Maura came out of the bathroom with a big, white towel around her, the rose glow of the nightlight shadowing her. Letting the towel drop to the floor, she lifted her arms over her head. The smell of the monoi oil filled the room with its gardenia-like fragrance.

Her body had the grace of a goddess, he thought. The smooth, silken, brown flesh seen in the dim rose light, the swell of the heavy hips and the smaller top, all scorched him. Those perfect breasts that he wanted to suckle forever. He closed his eyes for a moment.

"Maura," he said, his throat closing with passion.

Maura turned as if in a dream. "Josh," she said, in wonderment. He went to her swiftly.

He held her to him tightly for long moments, his face in her hair. Then his big hand held the hair back from her face as he pulled her mouth to his, his tongue probing her sweetness.

"Oh, my darling," she whispered, and he was not sure he heard her.

"Are you ready to begin our baby now?" he paused to ask, holding her with one hand, stroking her back with the other.

"Don't talk," she told him. "Please don't talk. Just come to me."

Her words sent streams of pure fire through his veins, as she undid the belt of his robe and unbuttoned his pajama top. Then, unfastening the cord of his pajama bottoms, she moaned in the back of her throat.

He held her there for very long moments, thrilling to the feel of her lush body and silken skin. She thought of nothing other than the man who held her—his leathery skin, the rippling muscles that pressed hard against her, letting her know that he wanted her—and now.

He lifted her with one hand and put her on the bed, turning down the covers as he did so. Arched over her, he cupped her breasts and suckled first one, then the other. Moving upward, he massaged the buttery flesh of her scalp. Her tongue outlined his ears, nibbling gently at them.

"Josh," she whispered. "Please. *Now!*"

He felt a wondrous rush as the blazing firebrand of his shaft entered her and clung in the honey-nectared, hotly gripping sheath he found. He moved slowly and with voluptuous wonder; she moved in rhythm with him. He brought her close and each could feel the drumming of the other's heartbeat.

This was the time of the month that she was most likely to conceive, and that knowledge swept her on. This was what she had wanted to talk to him about, but he had divined it anyway. Nature had a way of spurring on lovers. Procreation took a backseat to nothing.

"This is so good," she whispered.

His breath came raggedly as her fingers raked his back, then with the pads of her fingers she gently massaged him. Both were too full to speak.

As she gyrated smoothly beneath him, he moved into a deeper place and gasped with delight, finding voice to cry her name: "Maura!"

For long moments, they clung together as psychic starbursts flashed around them like the outside starry night. Then they were still as they held each other.

Lying side by side, they were silent before Josh whispered, "If I live to be a hundred, I'll still treasure this one time I made love to you."

"Our first time," she whispered back.

He brought her hands to his mouth and kissed them.

Maura sat up. "I want to look at the stars."

She got her robe from the foot of the bed and handed him his. Going to the window, they opened the drapes and blinds and saw the panorama of heaven. Moon. Planets. Stars spangled across the midnight-blue sky. Golden twinkling stars.

There were things he wanted to say to her and couldn't. He was caught up in the moment, her nearness, in the wonder of being a part of her, of having just been inside her body. Of the baby they hoped would come.

With his arms around her, she told him, "This is my fertile time. I was going to come to you tonight."

"Would you have?"

"I think so."

He caught her to him and hugged her tightly.

"I have an idea." He shifted her body to his side. "Come with me to the kitchen."

He got a bottle of Moët champagne from the refrigerator and held it up. She went to the dining room hutch and got champagne flutes. He popped the cork and poured the champagne.

"Oh, wait," she said. Going quickly to the refrigerator, she took out a pint of huge strawberries, plucked the stems, and put four of them under water. Placing two in each flute, she sprinkled powdered sugar over them and raised her glass.

"To us and our happiness," he said, but it wasn't what he wanted to say. He wanted to toast the baby he hoped they'd made or would soon make. He wanted to tell her that she mattered more than the baby, but he didn't want to lie to her and say that he loved her.

Baring her heart, she read him and said, "To the child we both want so much."

He crushed her to him. "You want this as much as I do, don't you?"

And he held his breath for her answer.

"Yes."

She fed him a strawberry from her flute, and he nibbled it and her slender fingers, then kissed the palm of her hand.

They sat at the kitchen table looking at each other, their eyes playing loving games. Both felt like the magnet being drawn toward the filings. Their lovemaking had been glorious, but they were still hungry for each other.

Taking a last sip, standing up, he said, "I never carried you over the threshold after we were married. What a non-romantic I am."

Maura laughed. "You can say that after what you just gave me?"

He touched her face. "There's more for the asking where that came from."

"I'm asking," she said softly. "If you don't mind, I'll walk to the bedroom threshold, *then* you can carry me across. I don't want a husband with a broken back."

Josh threw back his head, laughing. "I don't work out for nothing, Toots. I can handle you." She had called him "husband" and the word ricocheted like a brilliant diamond through his mind.

"Wife," he told her. "My wife."

He was bothered to find that there was continually something he wanted to tell her. There were things on his mind for which he had no words. He lusted mightily after her body, and he accepted that. It made him sad that he could never trust himself to love again.

Lifting her, he took her to the bedroom and put her on the bed. She slipped out of her robe, and he undid his and got on the bed with her. His tumescent shaft grew swiftly as she softly stroked it. The nightlight was on, spreading shadows across them.

Nuzzling her breasts, he kissed her belly, lingered there, then traversed her midsection and her valley of desire until she was bucking with pleasure. Fires were blazing out of control. Magnificent conflagration!

He traced kisses all the way to her feet and kissed her toes, leaving her nearly mindless with pleasure.

As he came back up her body, she wanted to cry out that she loved him, but he didn't believe in love. *Say it anyway,* she prompted herself. What she felt didn't depend on him.

"I love you," she whispered, but if he heard her, he gave no sign. He pulled her on top of him and entered her slowly and tantalizingly, seeming to hold back. Holding his hips, she pulled him in deeper.

"Baby, don't!" he said. "You'll drive me crazy and I can't last like that."

"Then, don't last," she said. "Reach the climax with me. I'm on the edge. Oh, Lord, this is heaven itself."

For moments, she felt she was falling—free-falling—into cloud beds of space. It was a wonderland up there in star country, and again they were going through the brightness of a star-filled night that they had just traversed.

Giant, glittering star-hands were shaking and shaking and

shaking her until she was limp, crying out, and satisfied in her very soul.

Josh heard her cry and drew in a sharp breath. In all his life he hadn't known what this woman had brought him. Powerful surges of passion took him and he was again doing his share to bring a new life into the world. For the moment, his fear was gone, translated into ecstasy. Had he heard her say she loved him?

Eight

Lonnie Fillmore sat in his father's big corner office, looking down at the deep teal carpet.

"Well, I want to hear what plans you've got for yourself," his father said. "I'm late in asking, but I've been busy, as you know."

"Being mayor isn't easy, Dad, and I know it." He smiled ingratiatingly.

Ward looked at his son, his eyes half closed. The boy always knew how to get on his good side.

"Enough about me," Ward Fillmore said. "I was born to be mayor of some town or other. Speak up."

Lonnie sighed and brushed his hand across his curly brown hair. "I want to stay out this year, travel through the country and maybe go to Europe or Mexico. Come back home from time to time."

The mayor frowned. "You turned nineteen this spring. You ought to be going back to college. You don't want to waste time. You said you'd go the second semester." It bothered him that the boy was so purposeless. When he was his son's age, he'd wanted to set the world on fire.

"Dad, I've got several paths I want to pursue. I'm undecided, and I want to take time to make the right choice. I'll make you proud of me one day."

Ward Fillmore grunted. "Make sure you do. I don't want any repeats of that mess you almost got into two years ago. I saved your skin then and I'll do it again, but I don't want it to become necessary. You understand? Then, there's the trouble you got into last year. . . ."

"Yes, sir. I'm sorry about that, but there was a lot more to it than came out."

"Always is. Women are so damned forward these days. Back in my day, a woman knew her place. Like your mama."

"Yeah."

"Women's dresses cut up to here at the bottom and down to there at the top. Yessir, I'd like to take a club to some of them."

"I'm glad you understand. It isn't easy being young these days."

"But, you've got it made, boy. I wish I'd had more time to spend with you, but it wasn't possible."

To his chagrin, hot tears welled in Lonnie's eyes. "That's okay, Dad. I guess you did what you could."

"Your mama worships the ground you walk on, even if she does criticize you. If you weren't my son, I'd be jealous of you."

"But I *am* your son."

"That you are. Now, is there anything else you need to say?"

"My staying out of school a year is okay, then?"

"Yeah. You tell your mother I said it's okay. She's not going to be too pleased about it, but what the hell? You're only young once, and I've got great hopes for you. Just stay out of trouble. I've got an election coming up next year, remember. I'd appreciate it if you could come back for a little while and work with me. Present a solid family front. All that gossip a couple of years back and last year didn't help my case."

Lonnie hung his head again. "I'm sorry."

"It's all right," Mayor Fillmore said, gruffly. "I've got to ask you to scoot, because I'm meeting with a bunch of old biddies who want to talk about that damned moderate housing development Ms. Blackwell—no, *Mrs.* Pyne—is behind." His voice had gone up on a high, mocking falsetto. Now he laughed.

"She and Josh Pyne sure got married in a hurry. Guess we'll be hearing the patter of little feet pretty soon."

Lonnie threw back his head, smirking. "You're a card, Dad." He got up unwillingly. He had enjoyed talking with his father. It happened so seldom. Ward Fillmore was always preoccupied, a father who was present in physical being only.

"You got friends, boy? Seldom see you around any other boys."

Lonnie's heart beat faster. He didn't need friends. He was happy as a loner.

"Yeah. Got a couple. Being alone helps me to stay out of trouble."

"Didn't help you two years ago, or last year."

Lonnie hung his head. "I'm sorry, Dad. It won't happen again." And, he thought grimly, damned right it wouldn't happen again, not even if someone had to get hurt this time to stop it.

Out on the street, Lonnie walked slowly toward his motorcycle, which was parked in front of city hall, touching his tongue to the dry corners of his mouth. She was a beauty, that motorcycle. This was his best friend. No question about control here. The motorcycle did what he told it to do and didn't talk back.

For a few minutes, Lonnie thought his heart would burst. It shamed him to think he had wanted so badly to stay in the office talking with his father. Hanging on to other people wasn't like him. That was womanish—something he hated.

Unlocking the motorcycle chains, getting on, and revving up, blessed air filled his lungs. As he roared off and around the corner, cutting it sharply, he let out a small whoop.

On the road with his motorcycle under him, he was happy, the way he was happy when he could control someone, hurt them even.

He headed toward the outskirts of Crystal Lake and reached the many-acred tract of land that was still known as Theena's Place, although others owned smaller tracts of it. Snickering, he wondered if he'd run into Ellen, and what she would do—or say—if he did. She was too damned independent, or had been before he'd gotten a hold of her. She was different now. Subdued. Sad. It made him feel good that he'd helped to change her.

Lonnie's mama always said women were too fast these days. They deserved the ill treatment they got from men. Just thinking about his mama made him uptight. The world according to Mrs. Fillmore. Mama. Rhea Fillmore had been a virgin when she married, and she still bragged about it. Two years ago, when the trouble had happened, she'd been one hundred fifty percent on his side.

"Well, it isn't like she didn't invite you in," she had said. "You just followed her lead."

Sometimes Lonnie didn't understand the ache in his chest that came so often, or the profound rage that filled him. He had it all. What was the matter with him?

Hot diggity! Ellen was crossing the road, and he swerved toward her, narrowly missing her, and roared on.

"You crazy fool!" she shrieked after him.

He shrugged. She was the crazy fool. She sure ought to know how dangerous he could be when he was crossed. Guess she would just never learn.

Nine

Two months to the day after she was married, Maura got a ride with Odessa out to Ellen's.

Maura had come along to hear them sing. Ellen and Odessa served as backup singers for Rich Curry, and they were practicing at Ellen's tonight. They found Ellen at home, looking more depressed than usual.

Odessa patted Ellen's back and briefly rubbed her shoulders.

"You need to come by for a massage," Odessa said.

"I need a lot of things," Ellen responded. "Thanks for the suggestion."

Maura studied the twenty-two-year-old Ellen. Her heavy black hair seemed less lustrous than usual, and her lovely, pale-tan, elfin face looked bereft. What was going on here?

"How are you?" Maura asked.

"I've been better," Ellen answered, quietly. "Won't you two have a seat? And can I get you anything? Lemonade? I just made some fresh and it's good. I've got soft drinks, too. Cookies."

"I'd like lemonade." Maura smiled at Ellen and got only a bleak response.

"I'm going to drive a bit further on to visit one of my customers, who's been ill. Back within the hour." Odessa swung her tote bag onto her other arm and left.

Ellen came back with the lemonade, which Maura found excellent. Two sprigs of mint graced the tall, clear glass.

"Delicious," Maura complimented her.

Ellen only nodded, her eyes still bleak.

Maura took a few more sips and put her glass on a coaster. "What's bothering you, chickadee?"

Ellen licked her dry lips. "I don't want to talk about it, but I think I'd better. I feel like I'm going crazy."

Maura moved over to sit a little closer to Ellen, and took her in her arms.

"What is it? Maybe I can help."

Two tears fell on Ellen's hands, clasped in her lap.

"I'm having trouble from Lonnie Fillmore again."

"Again? You've had trouble before?"

"Yes. You know the things they say about me—that I'm wild, that I'm pro"—she stumbled over the word—"promiscuous. You've heard the gossipy tales."

Maura nodded. She'd heard all right, for the past two years, and wondered.

"Go on," she said, soothingly.

"My mother died two years ago. We'd been so close, and I was very lonely. . . ."

After a few moments, Maura prompted, "And?"

"Lonnie Fillmore began to visit me, ask me out. I didn't like him all that much, but I was grateful for his visits. Mom and I were recluses and hardly anybody else visited.

"One night he came by. He always came by at night. If I hadn't been such a fool, that would have told me something. I could always smell liquor on his breath, but one night he'd been drinking more than usual.

"He told me how pretty I was and kissed me. Oh, God, I missed my mother so much. I wanted someone to touch me, but out of love, not sex . . ."

Ellen seemed at a loss for words.

Maura said slowly, "And he wanted to take it further."

"Yes." Tears flowed freely down Ellen's face. Her voice sounded strangled.

"Stop for a few minutes if you need to."

Ellen shook her head. "No. I want to get it all out. I've been haunted since it happened. He kept kissing me and finally he held both my hands. Lonnie's strong. He hit me and told me to stop fighting him, that I wanted it as much as he did.

"He was partly right, I thought, I did want him to touch me, but not beat me, not ra—not rape me."

Maura stroked Ellen's back, then smoothed her hair.

"I'm so sorry," she whispered.

"I feel better just talking about it. He raped me several times, and when it was finally over, he took my pants with the blood on them and threw them in my face."

"You were having your period?"

Ellen looked down at the brown-carpeted floor and took a deep breath. "I was a virgin. Mom always said to give myself to somebody who loved and cherished me. She must be turning in her grave."

"It wasn't something you could help."

"He said I was three years older and more responsible than he was. He said I led him on, that the blood was my period just starting.

" 'You won't get away with this!' I screamed at him. 'I'm going to the police.'

"He grabbed the hair on the back of my head and struck my head against the wall. 'Do that and you die, bitch,' he said. I was so frightened of him."

"Good Lord, and you've borne this in silence all this time?"

A deep sigh of despair came from Ellen.

"No, I was afraid to go to the police, but I *did* go to Lonnie's father. I'd met his mother and she really intimidates me. I thought his father would be a better person to tell. I thought he'd help me."

Ellen fell silent again and this time Maura didn't prompt her. After a few minutes, she went on. "Mr. Fillmore, *Mayor* Fillmore, said I was lying, that Lonnie didn't need to rape the likes of me; he got calls from girls all day long, every day.

"I said I'd go to the police, and he said I'd be sorrier than I'd ever been. He said it was obvious to him that I was a little tart, living alone and tempting boys. He told me to get out of his office, that there was nothing he wouldn't do to protect his son from a loose woman like me."

Ellen's shoulders sagged dejectedly. "The stories started then. Oh, yes, Mayor Fillmore told me he would ruin my reputation if I didn't keep my mouth shut. I did what they asked," she said, "but they ruined it anyway.

"Friends of Lonnie's began to whistle me down, flirt with me, and yell across the street that they'd be out to visit me that night. It was hell. I stopped going out except when I had to. Mr. Sampson shops for me."

"He's the man who lives in the woods."

"Yes."

Maura hugged her gently. "I'm going to talk with the police chief about this, and see what we can do."

Ellen reared back in alarm. "No, don't, please! The meddling's getting better. I don't mind being a recluse. Mom and I both were. I'm still scared of Lonnie. He has a killer's eyes, and he swore he'd get me if I told anyone else."

"And yet you were brave enough to tell his father."

"And what did it get me? They both hate me now. It was after I told his father that Lonnie began to stalk me. He still does sometimes. His mother looks daggers at me."

Tears of sympathy welled in Maura's eyes. "I'm so glad you finally told me. I know we've never been close, but I noticed you'd changed. I thought it was just your mother's death. I never dreamed . . . I wish with all my heart you could have come to me."

"I wish I could have too. I already wanted to die when my mother died, but after—Lonnie, I counted all the medications she'd taken through her stroke and I tried to just let go. But I'm too big a coward. I couldn't stop living. . . ."

The young woman's voice drifted, remembering, grieving her double grief.

Maura had a sudden thought. "Ellen," she said, "what if I

adopted you psychologically for now. Later, who knows? I want to take your part, be there for you."

"You'd want me, after all that's happened? I think I may have led Lonnie on, at least a little. I was so lonely. Although it wasn't like he and his dad said, that I was promiscuous, a loose woman. So some of the fault is mine."

"The fault is all his," Maura said, indignantly. "You didn't beat yourself. You didn't choose to give up your virginity to someone who cared nothing for you. Ellen, I want you to stop being so hard on yourself. See yourself as the lovely, loving person you are. And, yes, I want your friendship. I think my husband and I are going to love you, as you will come to love us. We have a lot to offer each other."

And, for a moment, Maura bowed her head. Josh had declared himself lacking in the love department, but he could and did care. That meant a lot to her. But, Ellen's tears about a sin of commission felt no less scalding than Maura's tears about Josh's sin of omission. At least he'd been honest. Maura placed the palm of her hand over her belly. Was there a child growing there yet? If so, she wanted to make it a far lovelier world for her infant.

"I feel so much better talking with you."

"I'm glad."

"I'm going to do what you said, and try to feel more confident about myself."

"You do that and I'll be glad to help you."

When Ellen went to the kitchen to get homemade oatmeal cookies for her, Maura looked around. The small living room was spotless, the furniture simple, the décor done in shades of cream, beige, and brown, with touches of turquoise and scarlet. It was a somber room for a twenty-two-year-old.

When Ellen came back, Maura bit into a delicious cookie full of oatmeal, raisins, and coconut. Ellen looked more relaxed; you'd never know from her face the horrendous tale she'd just told.

"That will probably be Odessa coming back," Maura said, as the doorbell rang.

"No," Ellen said, "it's probably Rich. He said he'd be early."

As Rich came through the door carrying his guitar, he broke into a big smile.

"Have I got another voice here?" he asked Maura.

"No, I'm afraid you get no more help. I have a tin ear and a tin voice."

"You've got a lovely speaking voice."

"Thank you."

"Your husband has a good voice. Did you know?"

Maura chuckled with surprise. "No, I didn't. But he's full of wonderful surprises."

"How're you doing? You look bothered," he said to Ellen, looking deep into her troubled eyes.

Ellen drew a deep breath, sighing. "I guess I . . . I, oh, I've just been thinking about some troublesome things. It'll pass."

"It had better. I won't have you upset."

The fondness between the two of them was palpable, Maura thought, but they seemed shy with each other.

"Listen," Rich said, "we don't have to practice tonight. Let's set up another time. You're not feeling up to this. I'm sure Odessa won't mind."

Ellen's voice held panic. "No, please! Doing the songs will help my mood. I'm sure of it."

Ellen got her guitar from a small storeroom and struck a few chords before twanging out a tune.

"That's Ellen and my latest," Rich said. " 'Losing at the Loving Game.' "

"That's very good," Maura complimented them.

As they waited for Odessa to come back, Ellen kept looking at Rich as if she wanted nothing more than to be in his arms with his hands brushing away her pain.

"I'm going to fix some snacks," Ellen announced, and went

into the kitchen. Maura followed her. They worked together, making small ham and cheese sandwiches and warming up crisply fried chicken and flaky rolls.

"I think you'll be upset for a few days," Maura said. "When you've held something like this in for so long . . ."

"I want to tell Rich, but I'm afraid to."

"Why are you afraid?"

"Perhaps he'll blame me. Maybe he's not the man I think he is."

"I'd say tell him, then you'll know if he's the man you think he is."

Odessa was back. She stuck her head in the door. "I'll let you two have kitchen duty. Rich and I are going to practice a few riffs. Fix plenty. I warn you I'm hungry."

Maura shook her head. "Sometimes I hate you. How can you eat all the things you do and never gain a pound?"

"Envy is bad for the heart. Besides, you never hear me complain that you draw like an angel," Odessa said, grinning.

Odessa went back to the living room and as Maura and Ellen worked, the sounds of Rich and Odessa riffing enlivened the air.

"Getting back to what we were talking about, I think I'll tell Rich, and soon," Ellen said.

Maura nodded. "Two years is a long time, but I'd like to run this by John Williams."

"The chief of police?"

"Yes. At the same time, I'd speak to Ward Fillmore and warn him that his son is not to come near you."

Ellen looked thoughtful. "The evidence is gone, and it was two years ago. I burned the clothes, drenched them in gasoline and almost caught fire myself."

"Oh, good Lord. Ellen, I said I was sorry, but no words can tell you the way I feel."

"I know. You're a caring person. That's why I like you so much."

"And why I'm so fond of you." The two women hugged.

The doorbell sounded again and, in a few moments, there

was no mistaking Rafe Sampson's voice. He was Ellen's nearest neighbor and rented a house from her.

Maura poured potato chips into a big plastic bowl and lined up glasses on a tray.

"Howdy, Ma'am," Mr. Sampson said, as Maura put down the tray. "How are you?"

"I'm fine, thank you. How are you?"

He bowed from the waist. "To tell the truth, I feel better since I'm seeing you."

Taking a harmonica out of his pocket, he began an absolutely wild riff on the tune Ellen and Rich were finishing. It was stunning!

Maura looked at the sixty-five-year-old man, her mouth open in astonishment.

The betel-nut-brown man threw back his head, laughing. "Young folks never know an old codger like me has it in him."

"You're really good," Maura complimented him.

A mischievous smile lit his face, and he half closed his eyes. "It were my grandpa who taught me," he said. "I never knew my pa. He walked out when I was a li'l saplin'. Never looked or come back."

A hint of sadness crossed his face, but was quickly replaced with joy.

"Ain't no use complaining," he said. "I was real little when my grandpa gave me this harmonica and taught me how to play it. I been more or less happy ever since."

The group launched into "Amazing Grace," and Maura thought their rendition was amazing. Rich's baritone, Odessa's contralto, and Ellen's soprano voices blended smoothly, and the guitars of all three meshed in sweet harmony.

Listening to them, Maura felt a sense of joy, and she also reflected on Mr. Sampson. Some called him the night watchman because of his habit of sleeping much of the day and being up and around all night throughout the town. He had been known to hike twenty miles many nights, but mostly he stayed in his own range, renting his tiny house from Ellen for a pittance. Never married, he was the grandfather Ellen had never known, and she was the granddaughter he would never have.

Winded, the group broke off and began sampling the food.

Mr. Sampson sat on the couch, his rough gray hair exploding about his face. He'd worn an afro much of his life. His coal-black deep-set eyes seemed to see everything at once.

For a moment, Mr. Sampson seemed sad.

"What's on your mind?" Odessa asked.

He stroked his chin as Ellen and Rich looked at each other.

"Well," he said, "I can't stop thinking about the fact that I ain't heard Theena crying this year. Fact is, last time I heard her was a week or so before the Iverson girl jumped."

Ellen shuddered and ran her hands over her bare arms, which were getting goose bumps.

"Poor Iris Iverson," Ellen said, softly.

"Yeah," Mr. Sampson said. "I don't want to pour cold water on our party here, but we got to take the bitter with the sweet. I used to see her and that no-good Fillmore boy in the woods across the way all the time. Knew somethin' bad was goin' t' happen. Nothin' good eva' came from that one. Then folks said she come up in the family way."

Ellen licked her dry lips. Had Mr. Sampson been twenty miles away when her own ordeal happened? She'd never said anything to him about it. She couldn't talk about it, until today. Now she felt better. Bless Mrs. Pyne—Maura.

"Well, let's get on somet'n more merry," Mr. Sampson said. "We be in this vale o' tears long enough 'thout weighin' it down some more."

They took their stations. "Let's play our signature song, 'Oddball Boogie,'" Odessa offered. And the wacky and wonderful song poured forth.

Maura was having so much fun, she forgot the time. Glancing at her watch, she gasped to find it was nearly eleven. Josh didn't know where she was, and she didn't have her cell phone on her; a perverse streak took her. Let him worry. She hadn't expected to be this late.

Odessa saw her anxious look, read it correctly, finished the set, and put her guitar down.

"Whew! We're really hot tonight," Odessa said. "But, if I'm going to be on my feet tomorrow, I'm going to have to cut it short."

"I guess I'll be on my rounds," Mr. Sampson said, intent on seeing Maura and Odessa to Odessa's car. "I had a really good time."

He looked carefully at Ellen. "You gettin' t' be such a lady, I betta start callin' you Miss Ellen, you reck'n?"

Ellen hugged him gently. "Now, you know better. I want to always be Ellen to you."

"Sure thing," the old man said.

Rich stayed with Ellen and, riding with Odessa in the smooth purr of her Mercury Cougar, Maura wondered how much persuasion it had taken to get Ellen to play with the group.

"How d' you think we sounded?" Odessa asked, as they rode along.

"Really good. I think you four are going places."

"Thanks. Isn't Mr. Sampson a card?"

"To say the least. He's got rhythm to jump by."

"Funny how he hears Theena weeping before bad things happen. Were they related?"

"I don't think so. He's very fond of Ellen."

"And she's fond of him. They add a lot to each other's lives."

Odessa changed the subject. "Josh is going to kill me for keeping you out so late."

"Oh, he'll be all right. Josh is out late himself a lot."

"You're positively blooming under those marriage vows."

"I feel good about it." That was the best she could offer. What would Odessa, Papa Isaac, all her friends, Grandmother Addie, and Carter Pyne say if they knew what was going on?

Yet, mulling it over now, Maura felt that she knew a sense of mission, of subtle peace, she had not known before. People got hurt, badly hurt, and somehow managed to love again. She would help Josh get over his hurt. She would have his baby. She drew herself up a little, her shoulders hunched. She had almost forgotten that in less than a year and a half, if all went well with the child they both thought they could have, it would be over with them.

She would keep her part of the bargain. Next week, she would get a number of home pregnancy tests and keep them on hand. If she was not pregnant now, they would serve for later. She said a silent prayer that she was pregnant.

Kissing Odessa's cheek lightly, Maura got out of the car in front of her house. Odessa waited for her to get in. As Maura put her key in the lock, the door was pulled open and Josh stood there pulling her in, his face like a thundercloud.

"Where the hell have you been?" he demanded.

"I beg your pardon."

He repeated the question.

"Well, not that it's any of your business, but I've been listening to your friend Rich Curry and his group rehearse. They're really good."

"I'm your husband and that gives me rights."

Maura's laugh was a little bitter. "Remember the terms of our marriage," she said. "It leaves us both free to do pretty much as we please."

Josh groaned inside. Damn their marriage contract. He had rushed into the wording; now he would just have to live with it. When would she be safely pregnant? What if she couldn't conceive?

Rethinking, Maura said contritely, "I'm sorry, Josh. I should have left you a note, or called. I just got caught up. . . ."

"No. I'm sorry. I had no right to come at you like that. Our vows do leave us both pretty much free, but I—"

He stopped and drew her close. "Just because we're not in love doesn't mean I can't *care* about you and want you safe. I called everyone I knew. Odessa's husband didn't know she was with you. I even asked my dad, which I hated doing.

"He told Grandmother Addie, and now she's worried. You'd better call her. She's crazy about you."

Maura laughed and went to the phone. Grandmother Addie answered on the second ring.

"Where did you slip off to?" the old lady asked. "Sounds like some of the pranks I used to pull. Keep 'em guessing."

Maura explained where she had been, imagining Grandmother Addie's eyes twinkling.

"Sounds like a lot of fun," Grandmother Addie said. "Maybe you could take me to visit sometimes. I don't get out enough lately."

"I'll be happy to. Just say when."

After she hung up, Josh put his hands on the sides of her shoulders.

"Forgive me for acting like a hothead."

"It's all right, Josh. You're out late, but you always say where you are, and I do worry about you, too. It's just that I'm always here at night. I've got to call Papa Isaac now. I'll just be a minute."

Lona answered the phone. "Well, I'm glad you're no longer among the missing. Your gramps has been worried, I'll tell you."

"Glad you're accounted for," Papa Isaac said, picking up the extension. "That husband of yours was a basket case. Never doubt he loves you."

Maura mumbled something. *He cares,* she told herself silently. *That has to be enough for now.* And the acid question came: Would he ever care enough to get over his fear and love her?

When Maura hung up this time, Josh pulled her to him, the length of his muscular body hard against her softer one. He stroked her back and ran his tongue in the corner of her mouth as fire swept through her. Turned on by the wild music she had just heard and the fierceness of his concern, she burned with wanting him.

She closed her eyes against the onslaught of the magic he

brewed. But Josh suddenly took her arms from around his neck and pulled away.

"It's been a long day," he said. "Get some rest. I've got to get an early start tomorrow."

Chagrined and stricken, Maura watched his retreating back as he went to his room. *Damn him!* she choked. She couldn't wait for this year and a half to be up. Wondrously, he'd come to her those days when she was likely to be fertile, and they'd made *love,* nothing else to call it. But it was patently not love to him, but necessary lust to create the child he wanted so badly.

Ten

In her room, Maura undressed slowly. Tears of frustration gathered in the corners of her eyes. Looking at the king-sized bed, she hated the thought of lying in it alone. Pulling on an off-white trapunto-quilted robe, she paced the room, unable to be still. Had it been long enough since Josh had come to her to tell if she was pregnant? She went to her triple dresser and got the pregnancy tests from the top drawer. Three of them.

Twenty minutes later, she sat on the edge of the bed, elated. All three tests were positive! But she would need to see Dr. Smith to make absolutely certain. She rose and pulled her robe tightly around her. She left her room and headed for Josh.

No, don't tell him yet, a cautious inner voice said. *Wait until you see the doctor.* But her heart said *tell him now; he will be so happy.*

Josh was coming up the short corridor as she left her room. They bumped into each other.

"I thought you might be fast asleep, but I wanted to check. Maura, I'm sorry I yelled at you."

"I know you were just worried about me. Josh, I've got great news. The pregnancy tests all say I'm pregnant."

Josh gave a whoop of joy and hugged her tightly. His voice sounded choked as he whispered, "How can I tell you what's on my mind? Honey, I'm so happy. How do you feel?"

"Wonderful. I've worried about whether I really wanted to go through with this, but like you, I'm happy, truly happy."

She wanted to ask him to stay with her, but she didn't dare. And he wanted to stay, but wanted to make no new demands on her. His heart felt divided. One side said to gather her into his arms and never let her go. The other side said he couldn't bear being hurt again the way he'd been hurt by Melodye. He chafed under the unrelenting inner battle.

They went into Maura's bedroom and sat on the edge of the bed. She wanted to lie close to him.

"Tomorrow I'll go with you to Dr. Smith's. What made you decide to take the pregnancy tests? You haven't been ill in the morning. Or otherwise."

"Not at all. I've been feeling great. I was just restless. I didn't think anything would come of it. I was prepared to wait."

A smile tugged at the corner of Josh's mouth. "Well, am I potent or not?"

"Now, don't go bragging. Half of the creation is mine."

"You bet it is. Talk to me."

"About the baby? If the pregnancy tests are right."

"About anything. I just want to hear your lovely voice. Tell me what you did tonight. What do you think of Rich's musical outfit?"

"I think they're good, and Josh, you wouldn't believe the places Mr. Sampson takes his harmonica to. I've heard about him but I never dreamed—"

"Oh, I've heard him and he is good. More like forty-five than sixty-five."

"Or *thirty*-five. He certainly had me tapping my toes."

"How's Ellen?"

Maura hesitated a moment. "She and Odessa sing like angels. And Rich is really good. I think you're going to be looking for another drywall supplier."

"He is good. I've been pushing him to give his music more leeway in his life."

"I hope he listens." Again, she hesitated. She wanted to talk with him about what Ellen had told her about Lonnie Fillmore.

Finally, she decided to tell him. After she was finished, he looked at her, frowning.

"That's a hell of a note. And to think the poor kid has kept that bottled up inside her all this time. Now we know where the gossip stems from. Anything I can do to help, just tell me."

"I think knowing we both are interested will help her. I hate to see her there alone."

"A good thing would be for her to take in one of the college professors to stay with her."

Maura looked at him. "You know, I hadn't thought of that. I'll run it by her. She needs someone else there, but she spoke of being a recluse and said her mother was, too. The thought of Lonnie beating her makes me beside myself."

"Likewise."

They sat in close silence.

"You know," he finally said, "I've heard or read somewhere that comfort is gauged not by our conversations, but by our silence with each other. I'd say we've got something going."

"Maybe," she said softly, thinking, *"something" isn't good enough, Joshua. I want you as my own, committed. With me. In love.*

"Guess I'd better go to bed if I want to get anything done tomorrow," Maura finally said.

"I feel I could do without sleep for the next month."

"Don't try it."

He took her hand. "You're sure you're all right about this? The more I think about it, the more I feel I had one hell of a nerve."

"Agreed. But we did it, and Dr. Smith will tell us if a baby will come to pass for us."

"A son. A daughter. God, Maura, you don't know how much I've wanted this, how *long* I've wanted it."

But Maura didn't answer. They had less than a year and a half together, baby or no baby. What did the future hold for them?

"Josh?"

"Yeah."

"Would you have asked someone else to bear your child?"

He thought about her question. "I've mulled it over a great many times, but until you, the woman I asked had no face, no body, just a lov—a presence."

She wondered if he had been going to say "a *loving* presence."

"But you asked *me,* and rather quickly."

"I shocked myself, but you've been threaded through my mind in some crazy fashion since I took you to your prom. You and I developed some kind of bond, so I thought about you from time to time. I'd run into you and remember your perfume and what you were wearing, even when I was married. I kept up with you, with your career. I asked the people at the architectural firm where you worked how you were doing. It doesn't make sense, I know."

Maura looked up, surprised. She placed her hand over his.

"I'm glad," she said. "Heaven knows I thought about you often enough."

His mind was running in circles. He felt he ought to stay the night with her, but his work was done. Tomorrow would tell the final tale.

Maura was a bundle of nerves in Dr. Smith's office the next day. Josh forced himself to be calm.

With her exam gown on, Maura fretted as the doctor examined her.

"You want this baby very much," the doctor stated.

"I can't tell you how much."

His hands probed deftly and worked with his instruments.

"I want it to come into this world on top of things," he said. "We're both going to give it the best we have. Relax, now. Just relax."

Under his ministrations, she grew calmer and time moved

swiftly. Finally, he was finished, and he put his hand on the side of her shoulder.

"Mrs Pyne—Maura—you're pregnant, all right. When you're a little more than three months along, we can test for gender."

"I don't care about gender," she said quickly. "And Josh doesn't care."

The doctor nodded. "Parents after my own heart. As you know, I've got four, and it never mattered to us what God sent us."

"Thank you so much for your help." Maura's voice was husky with caring and with joy.

Dr. Smith grinned. "Get dressed and we'll go back out and give the good news to Josh. My guess is he'll jump right up to the ceiling with happiness."

THE
BLOSSOMING

Eleven

In mid-October, Dr. Smith's eyes twinkled as he questioned Maura and Josh in his office.

"No problems? You've had clear sailing?"

"Yes," Maura replied. "Not one day of morning sickness or any kind of pain. I hope it can be this easy all the way through."

Dr. Smith nodded, his salt-and-pepper, close-cropped hair a pleasant foil to his blunt dark-brown features.

"I've been an obgyn a long time," he said, "and I've seen it all. Some babies are angels to carry and rarely give a moment's trouble getting born. Others . . ."

He broke off, smiling. "You two seem to belong on the love boat. That always helps."

Maura blushed and looked down quickly. Josh looked at her. "We do our share," he said.

Maura wondered what the good doctor would think if he knew she and Josh were business partners in a baby-making trade. At that moment, it seemed bizarre, but her happiness was real.

Seated side by side, Josh took her hand and squeezed it.

"You're glowing again," he said. "Keep it up."

"She certainly is." Dr. Smith looked pleased. "I think we'll get along fine. Now for the sonogram."

A few minutes later, lying on the long, white bed, the nurse spread the cool gel on her stomach and prepped her.

The doctor held the sonogram equipment onto her belly and

gently talked with her. She and Josh watched the computer monitor with him. Maura held her breath for a moment. The tiny infant was little more than the size of a small chicken drumstick.

"Well, here we are. Strong heartbeat," Dr. Smith offered.

"The miracle of a growing baby," Josh said, his voice thick with emotion.

Maura's heart went out to this tiny embryo. *Already,* she said to herself, *you're bringing out the best in me, as I will bring out the best in you.*

She and Josh had to talk about this baby's future, and about their own.

Josh tenderly looked at Maura. She felt a little sorry for him. If he could still love, would he love her? she wondered. She knew she bore at least some love for him. And for this moment, it made carrying his baby precious.

"So far, so good," Dr. Smith said, as he finished his examination. "Because this is a first baby, I'll want to continue to see you every two weeks for a couple of months."

He handed Maura more diet recommendations, special exercises, and brochures on childbirth. "Congratulations!" he said, as they left his office.

Outside, in the crisp, fall air, Josh took Maura's hand. Red and gold leaves drifted down.

"We've done it," he said. "Thank you."

He glanced down at her figure, thrills coursing through his body. A dream of many moons was finally coming true for him.

Out on the street, Josh asked where she'd like to go.

"I've got a craving for some of Wilson's shrimp and crabmeat. Do you have time to go out there? I guess I'm getting my cravings early."

Once in the car, Josh pulled her closer. "I'm going to take really good care of you. I'll satisfy your every craving."

"You always have. Josh, you've been really great."

"That's because you're you, but it's also because I know I

asked so much of you. You're always going to be a very special lady to me."

Helping her into his car, he handled her as if she were fine china.

"I won't break," she said.

"You'd better not. You're carrying precious cargo, and you're precious cargo yourself."

Maura smiled. "You certainly know what to say. You're gifted at the feel-good compliment."

"It helps when you've got someone worthy of it."

Wilson's was crowded. On Wednesdays he served special seafood platters to a clientele that could never get enough of his food.

"That looks like Carter's jaguar," Maura said, looking at the sleek black car.

"It sure does, but there are others who own one." He slowed as he passed the parked car. "No, that's his license plate. I remember it from when I drove it for a couple of weeks when he had a sprained ankle this spring."

"Where was his chauffeur?"

"In Tennessee visiting relatives. Actually, Carter can be as needy as any of us. He was feeling sorry for himself and wanted me around."

"So, Carter has a heart, after all."

"Don't let him know I told you. I guess I'll take what I can get. When my mother died, I was a teenager, and I was shattered. Dad had no time for a snotty-nosed kid. He had work to do and he did it."

He pulled into a parking space near the end of the lot. "Grandmother Addie saved my hide in the lo—" He stopped a moment and said "department."

"In the *love* department, you were going to say. There! I've said it for you."

Josh pulled both her hands to his mouth. "God, Maura, I'm sorry. This ought to be the happiest time in the world for you, but you can't help but feel a little anger at doing this for a jerk like me."

Maura touched his face. "You care about me. That's the best you can do right now. I understand that, and I've settled for it for the time being. You're a great guy, Josh."

His smile was lopsided. "We can be best friends."

"Friends and lovers," she said, softly. Then, "A baby. I'm going to have a baby."

"*My* baby," he whispered, and kissed the palms of her hands.

Carter Pyne had a seat up front, in life as in Wilson's, and he wasn't alone; he seldom was. Melodye sat across from him, resplendent in emerald-green silk, the top of her dress cut low to display her perfect breasts.

Carter stood as Josh and Maura approached his table. "Well, how are you two? I'll get a waiter to pull up another table."

His two male guests stood up and bowed to Maura as Carter introduced them.

Maura knew she looked good in her navy silk crepe dress with its pintucked bodice and her long strand of knotted real pearls. For once, she felt on a higher level than Melodye, pulled up there by her baby.

Melodye got up and came to Josh. "How are you, Joshua?" she said throatily, throwing back her head with its mane of dark-auburn, silken hair. She kissed him lightly beside the mouth.

Maura nearly gasped with surprise, thinking Melodye certainly liked to show off. She plainly didn't share Josh's anger. Carter Pyne looked mightily pleased.

"Melodye is doing her usual excellent job of being my hostess," Carter said. "Señors Lopez and Castillo can vouch for the wonderful way she entertains."

Both men vied with each other in singing Melodye's praises.

"And for such a beautiful woman to be so highly effective is incredible," Señor Castillo complimented.

"Another table attached to ours," Carter told the head waiter.

Josh shook his head. "Not today, Dad. We need to be alone."

"Nonsense!" Carter ordered.

"No. I insist. We need to be alone."

Carter looked at his son and heard a steeliness he had never heard before in him. "Well, if you say so, but you're welcome. You know that. You're looking well, Maura."

"Thank you. So are you."

"Nice little dress," Melodye said, cattily. "Navy's one of *my* best colors. Now, this color would be wonderful for you." Her hand indicated the color she wore.

"Thank you. I'll remember that."

Do your damnedest, Melodye, Maura thought, *today you cannot steal one clap of my thunder.*

Maura and Josh chose a table by a window where Crystal Lake could be seen in the distance.

No sooner were they seated than the owner, Mark Wilson, came over to their table.

"You are looking well and fabulously happy," he said to Maura.

Maura thanked him, blushing.

"You know, I take credit for the two of you getting together. It seems to me you became closer as you began to come in here. I told my chef the next time you came in I would have a new dessert: Chocolate Romance. He tested it today and it is wonderful, a mixture of chocolate and raspberries and the world's best chocolate cake."

"Thank you," they both said, and Maura added, "I'll certainly look forward to it. It sounds superb."

Mark lifted Maura's hand and kissed it.

"A little continental flair never hurts," Mark said. "You look especially happy, and I am responding."

Mark began his round of the tables, making his diners feel treasured. He was one of Carter Pyne's and Josh's favorite people.

Getting up, Carter strolled over to their window table. "Too bad I'm known for wanting a star attraction table," he said.

"Today, without my companions, I would have preferred a window table."

"Special reason why?" Josh asked

Carter nodded. "Melodye, Grandmother Addie, and I are planning the Crystal Lake ball for the winter. Melodye is a marvel. I don't know what I'd do without her."

Carter looked at them steadily. "You saw us kissing one day, so you know something's developing between us. Do you disapprove? I've never mentioned it before."

Josh looked keenly at his father. "It isn't my business. Melodye and I were over a long time ago."

"I thought you'd feel that way, but I'm not sure she's over you," Carter said.

"She's over me, all right. Melodye likes to play games."

"Well, I must say you both seem in high spirits." Carter was bothered that his son seemed very much his own man now, and he wondered about it.

Josh looked at his father and correctly assessed his mood of slight bewilderment. He had always deferred to the older man and today that had begun to change.

Carter got up. "Well, I guess I'd better get back to my guests. These men are thinking of building a plant here in Crystal Lake. Would you like to talk with them, son?"

"What kind of plant?"

"They would package food produced in Mexico. They're going to need a large plant. I'm thinking of letting them have my land on the Halaby tract. What do you think, Maura?"

Maura shook her head. "You know I'm committed to the Midland Heights development for that land."

"People do change their minds."

"Not this time."

At home, Maura stepped into her oyster-white cozy office to work on the Midland Heights drawings. She quickly noted that a new photograph had been hung opposite her drawing board. It was an exquisite print of famous architect Frank Lloyd Wright's residence, Fallingwater.

She found Josh in his room, sitting on his bed. She went over to him and hugged him.

"Thank you," she said.

"I gather you're talking about the photograph."

"Yes. It's perfect."

"Sit down and keep me company. Or are you too busy?"

"Well, I am busy, but you deserve whatever I can do to thank you for this wonderful photo."

"Mother of my child."

"It's just become a fetus. Don't push it."

"Still, it's thrilling."

He looked so happy that Maura was caught up in his happiness as well as her own.

"Thanks to you. I really do have to get back. I owe someone a set of drawings, and I've only got until tomorrow afternoon to finish them."

"I don't want you rushing and getting too tired."

"I won't."

He looked at her fondly, and she dropped a kiss on the top of his head.

Back in her office, she couldn't for the life of her settle in. She kept touching her stomach.

She had everything but love.

Around three o'clock, Maura answered the door chimes to find Carter standing there.

"May I come in?"

"Yes, of course."

"I see my son's car parked outside. I gather he's in."

"Yes, he's in his office. Please, go right back."

Carter began walking as he talked. "This concerns you, too," he said. "Come along."

He was so imperious, she thought. "Very well."

"What's up, Dad?"

Carter couldn't get over the sudden change in Josh. He intended to find out what was going on.

"Won't you have a seat?" Maura asked.

"I'd rather stand a few more minutes. I've been sitting most of the day."

"Well, Dad?"

"It's about Señors Castillo and Lopez. They're very interested in the Halaby land. As I told you at Wilson's, they want to construct a food processing and packaging plant. They want all the land that belongs to the four of us: Maura's, yours, Ellen's, and mine."

"And, of course they've got yours, hands down." Josh chuckled.

"It's no joke, son. They're willing to pay a couple million for the entire package."

"I'm sorry, Carter," Maura spoke up, "truly I am, but my heart is wrapped up in the Midland Heights development. I had planned to talk with you soon about raising the money to buy your land."

"You're kidding me."

"No. I'm on the level. We'll need the whole package to build one hundred and twenty-five homes, a clubhouse, tennis courts, playgrounds, and a large apartment-building, eventually. It's going to be quite a project."

Carter shook his head. "Not if I have anything to say about it. I'm going to see Ellen this afternoon."

"Carter, I wish you wouldn't just now," Maura said. "Wait a few days."

She didn't think Ellen should be pressured in any fashion just now.

"Any reason, any *good* reason, why not?"

"She's got unpleasant things going on just now, and she doesn't need more. She's been committed to the Midland Heights development. . . ."

"If I know women, she'll get committed in a hurry to the millions they're offering."

"Money isn't everything, Dad."

Josh stood and began to pace, as his father did. Were they circling each other? Maura wondered.

"No, money isn't everything," Maura said. "Please give Ellen a few more days before you approach her with this."

Carter shook his head. "Lopez and Castillo want answers, and they want them fast."

"They can wait." Maura was adamant.

"No. Ellen isn't that fragile. I want this for the development of Crystal Lake. We don't have enough of the wealthy people I'd like to see us have here. We're a beautiful town, and I'd like to see us get the kind of people we deserve."

"The *rich* kind." Josh grunted.

"Nothing wrong with being rich. I am, and you're well on the way. Coming back here, I noticed a photo of Frank Lloyd Wright's Fallingwater on Maura's office wall. He wouldn't have been caught dead poor. Wake up, you two, and help me make Crystal Lake into what it *can* be. A few more hundred 'moderate' income people and we lose the war."

"Let's stick to what's going on right now," Josh said. "Promise me you'll hold off at least a couple of days seeing Ellen."

Carter put his hands behind his back and paced harder. "Okay, but I won't wait more than a couple of days and I won't be by here first."

"Fair enough," Maura said, "but I would prefer being there when you talk with her."

"You're damned right you'd prefer being there, so you can gently guide her away from what I want. She's lived like an alley waif all her life. I'm giving her a chance to live in some splendor."

"She's no alley waif, and what we're offering isn't peanuts," Maura said.

"It isn't in the class with Lopez and Castillo, either."

"You're right, of course. It's just that there are so many people in the county who need truly decent housing and they're only moderately able to pay for it."

"I'm not playing God. I want what's best for me. If that makes me a selfish rat, so be it."

"Dad, what are you going to do with so much money? I'm your heir, and I believe in sharing the wealth."

"Who says I'm not going to outlive you?" Carter's eyes sparkled with malicious mischief. "At least I've *got* an heir. That's more than I can say for you."

Josh's smile was beatific and it startled his father. In the past, all he had had to do was mention the word "heir" and Josh withdrew. Carter's eyes drew a bead on Maura's stomach. Nothing there. Or nothing *showing,* anyway. He thought about asking, but he didn't think they'd tell him. He missed the times when Josh had been married to Melodye.

After Carter left, Maura came and stood behind Josh.

"What was that all about?" she murmured.

"Dad's losing his control over his only son," Josh said. "Thanks to you."

"Thanks to the baby. You're feeling like a father and sowing your oats."

"And, Lord, do I love those oats!"

Back in her office, Maura looked out the window at the autumn leaves, splendid in their brilliance. Midland Heights was no less her child than the baby she carried in her womb. Then again, she amended, it *was* less. Nothing on earth was like the infant she would bear.

For a moment, she felt the chill of fear. Could she carry the child safely to term? Would it be healthy? She had chosen names from the beginning, contingent, of course, on Josh's approval. Joshua Pyne, Jr., or Francesca, if it were a girl. Francesca had been her mother's name.

Carter Pyne was something else. He meant to have what he wanted. No wonder he and Melodye got along so wonderfully.

Thinking about the kiss Melodye had given Josh in the crowded restaurant, Maura felt a pang of jealousy. It was quickly subdued by the memory of Carter and Melodye together.

Hands off, Melodye, she thought. *You can't have everything. Not if part of that everything is Josh.*

For the rest of the afternoon, Maura worked on her drawings more swiftly than she would have believed possible. Josh went to his downtown office for a meeting, and she went to visit Papa Isaac.

"I'd about given up on you for today," the old man said, offering his cheek for her kiss.

Lona waved at her from the kitchen door.

"Not a day goes by that I don't come to check on you," Maura said. "Are you okay?"

Papa Isaac sighed. "I miss getting out and seeing after my vegetables," he said. "Jake's doing a good job, but my touch is even better. Sit down and stay a while."

"I'll stay longer tomorrow. I promised I'd go by and visit with Grandmother Addie."

Papa Isaac chuckled. "She's a grand old soul. I hope I can live that long with my mind in order."

"You will. I'll pray for that."

They smiled at each other and fell companionably silent.

Lona came in. "Guess what I'm practicing. I'm going through cookbooks from other countries and serving Papa Isaac unusual meals."

"She surely is, and I'm enjoying it."

"I can't guess what you're making. Give me a strong hint."

"Scones."

"English scones?"

"Yes. I've got some in the oven now, and they come buttered and with a hefty serving of strawberry jam. You've got to taste them."

"You'll get no argument from me. Need help?"

"No. You sit right there and talk with Papa Isaac. It'll take a little while to get this together. Oh, yes, and the doctor tells us he'd prefer for him to drink herb teas than coffee. So name your choice of teas."

"Have you got red clover?"

"Plenty of it. That's my favorite. I've got some all made up in a big, glass jar."

"Then, that's my choice."

Lona went back to the kitchen and Papa Isaac got up.

"I'm glad your chemotherapy is going well," Maura said.

Papa Isaac shrugged. "The doctor thinks it's going very well. As you know, he's got me on a laundry list of vitamins and minerals and food supplements. Says this way my hair won't fall out, and so far it hasn't."

"That's wonderful. So, how are you feeling today?"

"Better than I'd have ever thought. I'll tell you something, Maura, when this thing first showed up, I thought I was a goner. I guess I'm living in the past. Doc says the operation and the chemotherapy got it all."

"I'm glad."

"I'm keeping my fingers crossed. I've seen too many of my friends go down with this thing, but maybe I'll make it. Well, now, let's talk about you. How're you doing?"

Maura's face lit up. "You know, I'm pregnant," she said.

Papa Isaac's mouth fell open. "Now, you don't say. Come here and give me a big hug. I'd come to you, but I'm a mite tired. Overdid it today."

"You've got to stop that," Maura said, getting up and going to sit by him on the sofa. She hugged him and patted his shoulder.

"You and Josh don't waste time. When did you find out?"

"Some time ago, but I had another sonogram today."

"Wonderful things, those sonograms. Course I don't expect you and Josh care whether it's a boy or a girl."

"We're just happy that it's a baby. Josh wants to name it for you and Carter. I want to name it for him too. The next one's name is up for grabs."

"You plan to have a passel?"

"My husband informs me that he'd like an even dozen. He gets no more than four. I have something to say about this."

Lona came in with the scones and jam, and Maura watched how her grandfather's eyes followed the comely middle-aged woman around the room. She'd never known her grandmother, and Papa Isaac had done his share of courting, but never remarried. There was something about the closeness between these two that struck her.

Lona set the tea tray down and plumped pillows behind Papa Isaac's head in a way that Maura found could only be called loving.

Maura bit into the buttered, flaky scone and spread strawberry jam made from natural juices on it.

Then, with a start, she glanced at her watch. She had told Grandmother Addie that she was coming by today and she meant to go. She was going to have to pace herself and stop rushing. There was a little angel inside her now that had to be taken care of.

Ellen sat on her bed, toying with a yellow pad of lined paper and a pen. Her doodles were thin-lined and scrawled. Rich Curry had stopped by and she had helped him work on his latest song—on *their* latest song. She drew her knees up to her chin and breathed in long and deep. The late afternoon air that came in from the open window was invigorating, but it was getting colder. Rich had kissed her when she had thought of a word that fit his song scheme better than his own. His kiss had been gentle, and she had rested against him, then drawn away—afraid.

"What is it?" he'd asked.

She had thought of Lonnie's cruel mouth grinding into hers, of his harsh tongue halfway down her throat, and the brutal, grinding pressure of his loins.

She had pulled away from Rich, from all that lovely warmth, and a few tears had come to her eyes.

"I want to tell you something," she said, softly. "Promise you won't turn away from me."

"I'd never turn away from you."

And she'd tried to tell him, but she couldn't. The pain, the anguish, was still too raw. After two years. Well, at least she hadn't gone off the bridge like Iris Iverson.

Maura had thought she should tell Rich and she had agreed, but the words just wouldn't come. Two years of being alone since her mother died, and two years of living with the nightmare of what Lonnie had done to her, then Rich had come into her life, had lit it with Fourth of July fireworks, and she couldn't bear the thought of losing him.

"Then very soon I'll tell you," she had said.

He had looked puzzled, but hadn't pressed her. "I'm growing very fond of you."

"I like you so much," she'd answered, thinking, substitute the word "love" for "like" and you'll have the truth.

Theena, her great-great-great-grandmother had had an unhappy love life with a man who loved her enough to marry her against all social considerations. But she and Rich fit; there was no racial pain to be considered.

No. There was just Lonnie and his unfeeling lust.

As soon as it was dark, Lonnie Fillmore struck out from his house and got on his motorcycle. Tonight he was wandering, figuring out some place to go. Lonnie was a loner, but he could find a buddy or two or three if he needed one for skullduggery.

He rode without his helmet and the wind whipped past him, colder now than in the last few days.

Fifteen minutes later, he roared by Ellen Jones's stone house nestled far back off the road. He scoffed; he just wasn't thinking. He hadn't meant to come this way. He thought about riding up to her front door and honking his horn. No, maybe the back door would be better. It would scare her more.

Lonnie always felt like this after one of his talks with his mother—talks she initiated.

"You're growing up, son," she always began. Today she had said for the zillionth time, "When you get married, you want to get the best for yourself. No used goods. Get yourself a girl who's saved herself for you. Be choosy. You hear me?"

Yeah, Ma, he thought now. The only thing was he didn't have a good opinion of any of the girls around him. The way he saw it, they all had something wrong. That wasn't to say there weren't quite a few who hadn't gotten laid, but even they were pushy, aggressive, blatantly outspoken. Not like his mama, who was meek and coldly withdrawn. He never had to get married, did he?

His father, now, was a different kettle of fish.

"Boy, you get what's out there for you," he always said. "You deserve the best when you get ready to settle down, but in the meantime, play the field. Romp about a bit. You're my son and God knows, I played my hand again and again."

"How did you and my mother ever hitch up?" Lonnie had asked him once.

His father had looked startled. "Hell," he'd said, "her pa had the seed money I needed to get started."

"Did you two love each other?"

Ward Fillmore had scratched his face. "Boy, when it comes to love, sometimes I think it's the craziest word in the English language. It can drive you nuts if you let it. Listen, marriage is a business; now, it can thrive or it can die, and love doesn't come into it."

Was that, Lonnie wondered, why his mother looked so drawn and pale? Starved?

Setting his feet firmly on the pedals, Lonnie pulled his motorcycle and it reared like a fine horse. Glory! Was Ellen watching him? Was she still afraid of him? He braked and looked over at the darkened house. Last time he'd talked with her, there'd been murder in her eyes. That was not too long after he'd raped and assaulted her. He wasn't afraid of her, but he liked his women a little more willing than that.

And she *had* been willing. All soft and swoony and smelling like summer flowers. She had wanted him far more than he had ever wanted any girl.

Yeah, his father had covered that, too.

"Listen, boy," he'd said. "You're the mayor's son and there'll be girls who'll want you for that and no other reason. Don't be a sucker for a pretty face: Looks don't last. Find yourself somebody who's got plenty of the world's goods. That lasts."

A sharp wind blew up behind him. There. He had passed Ellen's house and, looking back, a light had gone on. What was she doing? What did she have on? He had half a mind to go there again, where he hadn't been since it happened. But he rode on.

Twelve

Maura decided to go home first and to Grandmother Addie's later. She felt tired and thought she really ought to rest. As she pulled into the driveway, she noted that the living room lights were on.

Going in the side entrance, she heard Grandmother Addie's merry voice from the living room. When she saw Maura standing in the doorway, she held out her arms.

"Come and give me a kiss."

Maura walked over and bent down to kiss the proffered soft cheek, and her own cheek was kissed in return. The old woman smelled of lovely lavender oil. With a surprisingly firm grip, Grandmother Addie caught her shoulder.

"My dear," she said, "I'm meddling in your business, of course, but aren't you in the family way?"

Josh and Maura looked at each other.

"I am, at that," Maura answered.

"If I could get out of this dratted wheelchair, I'd dance me a lovely dance of congratulations." Grandmother Addie's face lit up. "I'm so happy for you. Does Carter know?"

"I don't think so," Josh answered, "unless he guessed, as you did."

"No. Carter's brilliant when it comes to business. With the human equation, he can't see past a broomstraw. He's nothing like his father was."

"It takes all kinds to make a world," Maura offered.

"Don't defend him. He's my son, but he can be cold. I left him and Melodye at the house talking about the winter ball. Maybe they'll get married. They're two of a kind."

Maura smiled at the thought of those two being married, but she was glad she hadn't run into Melodye. Why was she feeling so tired?

"Have you tried the chocolate chip lace cookies I gave you the recipe for?" Grandmother Addie asked.

"Once. They came out splendidly. What do you say I make some for us now? I think I've got all the ingredients."

"I'd like that," Grandmother Addie said. "Go heavy on the brandy for my special portion."

"And if you're out of anything, I'll get it for you," Josh offered.

"Where's Joseph?" Josh asked his grandmother. Joseph was the general driver and helper for the family.

"He'll pick me up later. Save him some cookies. I swear I get fonder of that man by the day. If he were thirty years older, I'd have myself a husband."

"You'd still be pressing your luck," Josh said. "As I remember it, you always liked men older than you."

"The world's changed. *I've* changed." She threw back her head with peals of laughter. Her diamond brooch sparkled in the light.

"Why don't you two come into the kitchen with me?"

Maura quickly laid out everything she needed for the cookies. And she had the sinfully rich vanilla ice cream in stock that went with the cookies.

She separated and creamed the sugars and butter. Grandmother Addie measured the dry ingredients with a steady hand.

"I'm always anxious to get the holidays underway so I can let myself get my fill of ultra-rich cookies," Grandmother Addie said.

"You're a little ways away from the holidays." Maura touched the old woman's cheek. She patted Maura's hand.

"Go heavy on the chips for me. I love the stuff. Also, I like the way you sprinkle brandy over them when they're done. I'd like a tiny bit of brandy now."

Josh got a small snifter and poured a little brandy into it.

"You can do better than that, boy," Grandmother Addie said.

"I don't want you becoming a candidate for AA." Josh smoothed his grandmother's white, beautifully coiffed hair.

"I've been thinking," Grandmother Addie said, putting the bag of chips on the table by her wheelchair. "I've got so much stuff to give you two. Carter's been really good to me where material things are concerned. I've shopped as a substitute for loving when your grandfather died.

"I've got silver and china and crystal and jewelry without number. It's in my will and I'm telling you now. I want you two to have it all. Carter's got his share of everything, and Josh, you've got plenty. But, maybe if I leave you my things, I'll also be leaving you the happiness your grandfather and I had."

"What a wonderful gift," Maura said, quietly.

"You're a super woman, Grandmother," Josh said. "I just hope we don't inherit anything from you for a very long time."

Grandmother Addie looked wistful. "I'm eighty-four and even though my compatriots are living longer and longer, I can't last forever. A shadow comes and stands near my bed when all the lights are out. It's a friendly presence and it's been with me since your grandfather died. It gets lonesome and would like me to come with it. So, anytime now . . ."

Maura felt the start of loving tears. "I can only say stay as long as you can with us. We, too, love having you here."

"How sweet and how thoughtful of you to say that."

"You could live with us if you'd like that," Maura told her.

Grandmother Addie smiled. "Bless your heart. I've got everything the way I want it at Carter's. All your grandfather's things we shared. You've both been really good about keeping me company and I don't want to make many demands on Maura now that she's in the family way."

"Don't you worry about that," Maura said. "It's never a bother to do things for you."

Maura spooned in extra amounts of warm, melted butter over the cookie dough and finished preparing them. She placed small soup spoons of dough morsels on a heavy metal sheet and slid it in the oven.

A little while later, they sat in the living room slowly savoring the warm, delicious cookies.

"Scrumptious," Grandmother Addie said. To Josh she said, "I'm so happy you finally found someone right for you." Then to Maura, "I'm coming to love you the same as Josh."

Small chills of happiness ran the length of Maura's body. Her own mother had died when she was young. She had not known a woman's prolonged love and she had missed it all her life. Would Josh ever come to love her? And what could she do to foster that love? With the pain he plainly showed he still felt, she didn't think it would happen, but she could hope.

Door chimes announced Joseph's return. Grandmother Addie glanced at her watch and adjusted her bifocals. "He's early now. He just wants to visit a while with you two." She nodded at Maura as Josh got up to answer the door. "He's crazy about you both."

"I'm glad," Maura said. "He's a very nice man."

"He certainly spoils me rotten. There's nothing he wouldn't do for me. He almost left us when Melodye was there. He's like a family member, and she thought Carter and I were wrong not to treat him like a servant."

Joseph rubbed his hands as he came into the room. His reddened caramel-colored face beamed as he looked at them.

"Trust me to look out for your welfare," Grandmother Addie said. "I saved you some cookies. *We* saved you some cookies."

"And I certainly thank you," Joseph said, as Maura served him cookies with a scoop of ice cream on a crystal plate.

"Give him a mite more of brandy," Grandmother Addie suggested. "He likes the good stuff, same as I do."

Smiling, Maura complied with her wishes.

Maura had reserved cookies for herself that were sprinkled with a little brandy. She slowly ate the marvelously creamy ice cream that went with the cookies.

Joseph sat down at Josh's bidding in a chair near Grandmother Addie's wheelchair.

"Now, let's talk some more about Midland Heights development plans." Grandmother Addie stopped and tapped her head. "I've gotten old and forgetful. First things first. We've got to talk about the Crystal Lake Winter Ball and get it together before Carter and Melodye ruin the whole darned thing. Will you work with me, Maura? I'm the one who started it light-years ago."

"I'd be happy to."

"Then we discuss the Midland Heights development plan. Joseph, you tell her you want a house when they build."

"I sure do."

"Wonderful," Maura said. "I'll design one floor plan with you in mind."

Joseph's round face beamed. He liked Josh's second wife so much better than the first.

"Well, now, concerning the winter ball," Grandmother Addie began.

As Maura stood to replenish Joseph's glass, the room spun around her, and she slipped quietly to the floor.

Darkness flooded her being, then white light was all around her. In a few minutes, she heard someone call her name, and she opened her eyes to find Josh cradling her head in his lap. Grandmother Addie and Joseph peered down at her.

"Sweetheart, can you hear me?" Josh asked, plaintively.

"Yes," Maura whispered. "I hear you."

"Good. Now Joseph is going to hold you while I go and call Dr. Smith."

Maura wanted to answer him, but she was too tired. She wished everyone would go away so she could sleep.

Josh placed a call to Dr. Smith and left an urgent message, then he went back and relieved Joseph.

"I fainted a couple of times when I was carrying your father," Grandmother Addie said. "They put smelling salts under my nose and I got better. Medical science wasn't then what it is now."

"Should I move her before I talk to the doctor?" Josh asked.

"Well, I'm no doctor, but I got through the fainting spells. I'd guess you'd better be prepared to wait for the doctor to return your call."

Josh and Joseph got Maura to a sitting position on the living room floor, then to her bedroom and her bed. "I'll be all right," she said, faintly.

Josh stroked her hand. "Sure you will, but we've got to take care of you."

Josh pulled the covers back and removed Maura's shoes. She wore loose clothing. He rubbed her feet and hands and tucked her in, still in her clothes. Joseph went out to keep Grandmother Addie posted. It seemed hours had gone by but Josh's wristwatch said only ten minutes had passed before Dr. Smith returned his call. Picking up the phone on Maura's night table, he answered and told the doctor what had happened.

"I'm not surprised. Your wife has an iron count that's normal, but it is on the low side. Now, I live in your neighborhood, so I'll be around. I know housecalls are unheard of these days, but it will be very little trouble for me to come by."

"And for that I thank you."

"You're more than welcome. I always put myself out for my first-timers. It's such a joy to see how well they do under my care. I'll see you within the hour."

Josh breathed a deep sigh of relief.

"How're you feeling now?" he asked Maura.

"Better. Much better."

But Josh thought her face still looked pinched. He went to the door and called Joseph.

"The doctor's coming by a bit later. I think you'd better take Grandmother Addie home."

Joseph left, then quickly came back with Grandmother Addie wheeling her chair. "I've got to know that she's all right. Will you be taking her to the hospital? It's a pity you can't count on doctors to take care of you anymore. They certainly charge you enough."

But Grandmother Addie's face lost its tension when Josh told her the doctor would be coming by.

"Thank God," Grandmother Addie said.

Maura moved to sit up. "Josh?"

Josh sat down on the side of the bed.

"Let Joseph take you home," he said to Grandmother Addie.

"No. I want to hear what the doctor will say."

"I'll call you."

Maura smiled a little. "Let her stay," Maura requested. "It makes me feel good to have her around."

"That's my girl," Grandmother Addie told her. "I'll gladly spend the night if you want me to."

"Thank you. Josh?" Maura said again.

"What is it, honey?"

"There's some camphor in the medicine cabinet, near the back. That will help me."

Josh quickly got up and found the camphor and a wad of cotton and brought it back to Maura's bed. He held her head as she sniffed the camphor-tinged cotton.

Leaning back, she expelled a long breath. "Much better," she said.

Joseph answered the door when Dr. Smith got there. A hearty, portly man, he looked down at his patient with tender concern mirrored on his face.

Josh told him what had happened. He nodded. "As I told you, it's probably a bit of anemia. I'll also need to take her blood sugar. It was normal, but like the iron was normal on the low side, the blood sugar is normal on the high side. That can give trouble either way."

He took Maura's temperature and pulse and asked her what she'd eaten that day.

When she told him about eating chocolate-raspberry cake for lunch and, tonight, the cookies, his brow creased into a frown.

Josh held his breath as the doctor gently pressed Maura's abdomen in a number of places. *Dear God,* Josh prayed, *let the baby, as well my wife, be okay.* Thinking of her as his wife brought him up short. He usually forced himself to simply think of her as the mother of his coming child.

Lying there, her head becoming clearer and clearer, Maura felt sad. Tonight, Josh had called her "sweetheart" and "honey," but that added little to their tenuous relationship. A fierce longing was born then to deliver this baby safely. Her heart went out to Josh. He was so desperate for this child.

"I'll want to see you in my office tomorrow morning," the doctor was saying, as he packed his bag.

"I'll see that she's there."

Grandmother Addie had sat silently in the living room. Now, she offered her hand to Dr. Smith, who took it as Grandmother Addie introduced herself.

"I can't thank you enough for coming," she said. "I was so afraid that something had happened to the baby—or to Maura."

The doctor smiled. "I think she'll be all right. Her iron count needs to be brought up, and she might have a tad of diabetes. At least we'll find out in a couple of days. Don't you worry, Mrs. Pyne."

Dr. Smith went up the hallway, chuckling with Joseph, leaving Grandmother Addie smiling from ear to ear. The doctor, she thought, had the gift of kindness. The doctor, she further thought, had more than his share of class.

During the next few days, Josh hovered over Maura. She kept protesting that she felt okay, but she actually felt more tired than usual. In his office the next day, the doctor looked at her gravely.

"My office test shows that you have slightly elevated blood sugar, and I want you to have thorough testing done by going first thing in the morning to this lab."

He quickly scribbled a name and address and gave it to her.

"I don't find anything very wrong," he said, slowly. "This is your first child. You're in mostly good health. I wanted to take a complete battery of tests before, but you didn't come back."

"I meant to," she said, "but my grandfather has been ill and I'm helping him take care of his paperwork. I just got caught up in other things. It has only been a couple of weeks."

"You're right, but I demand that my mothers take the very best care of themselves. How can *I* if *they* don't?"

Maura smiled.

"I'll see to it that she does the things she's supposed to do," Josh broke in. "I won't let her overdo it."

"I think you're going to do wonderfully well," the doctor said to Maura. "And don't worry too much. Call me regarding the test results in a couple of days."

Maura nodded. She liked this caring doctor.

The next two days passed slowly for Maura and Josh. The first day he had a meeting, which he cancelled to be with her.

"I hope the tests come out okay," she told him, as they drove to Papa Isaac's house.

"I fervently hope so," he responded.

Grandmother Addie had called daily to check on Maura's health and had told her that she, too, anxiously awaited the test results.

"Could we stop by and see Odessa and Mike?" Maura asked.

"We could."

Odessa's beauty shop was a homey place with a pleasant black, silver, and rose décor and plenty of light. It was early, and only a few of the sinks and hair dryers were occupied. The operators looked attractive in their pink smocks and black skirts.

Odessa hugged her. "Sent for you yesterday," Odessa chirped. "Here you come today." She blithely sang a few more bars of the old, still-popular song, then hummed the rest.

"Knock it off," Maura said, laughing. "I'm here anytime you need me."

Maura had called and told her about fainting and she had come over the next afternoon.

"So, how are you?" Odessa asked.

"I'm fine. Josh is waiting for me. He has a horror of being around a passel of women. He claims we turn into monsters, en masse."

"What's he doing being around a passel of women all by himself?"

"Come out and ask him," Maura said, and took her arm.

Outside, Josh had gotten out of his car. He and Mike stood talking. Maura walked over and kissed Mike on the cheek.

"Mike's giving me some pointers on the Midland Heights plan," Josh said.

"Sure," Mike said. "We're getting a piece of the action as soon as you get started. We'll save a bundle getting in on the ground floor."

Maura looked at Odessa. "Talk to me about what you want included in your plans."

"Well, first of all," Odessa said, "I want a few touches of luxury. Marble foyer. Is that possible on a beer budget?"

"Maybe. I'll certainly look into it." Josh rubbed his chin. "You know, this is going to be a boon for Crystal Lake. Your development should get us some good, solid people." Mike pursed his lips. The more he heard about this development, the more he liked it.

"We're going to be getting a new house, too," Josh said. "As the lady desires: fieldstone."

Maura drew in her breath sharply. So, he was really going to do it. Josh came up behind her and put his arms around her.

"Nothing's too good for my bride."

"Which reminds me, I haven't had a chance to congratulate you on being, as they say in Mississippi, in the family way."

Maura and Josh thanked him.

"We'll get there one day, honey," Odessa said to her husband.

"Sooner than later," Mike said. "I'm getting restless for the patter of little feet."

Odessa groaned. "I've got a business to run and so have you."

"So have these two. That didn't stop them."

Josh glanced at his watch. "We've got an eleven-thirty appointment with Dr. Smith, so we'd better get moving."

Odessa and Maura hugged again, and Odessa patted Maura's slightly rounded belly.

"I've needed another godchild for some time," she said.

"Baby, they haven't asked you." Mike laughed.

"Ah, well," Odessa said. "Some things we take for granted."

"That's right. And I'm going to demand that you be a thoroughly hands-on godmother," Maura told her.

"Only if I get to name her."

"Odessa!" Mike laughed at his wife. "Do you want to also bear this child for her?"

"Okay," Odessa answered, "so I'm pushy. What are friends for?"

"If it's a girl," Maura said, "I'll give her two or three names and you can choose one. If it's a boy, we'll be choosing Josh and Papa Isaac's name, and for the sake of smooth family waters, Carter's."

Josh's eyes twinkled. He liked the idea of his son having all those names. He'd never felt that his father loved him half as much as he could have. He'd never do that to his son.

"Another thing," Maura said to Odessa, "Grandmother Addie wants you to be active on the entertainment committee for the winter ball. Are you willing? Both of you will just be getting over the Christmas rush."

Both said they'd be honored to serve.

"We'll start meeting in November."

"And we'll be ready, willing, and able," Odessa promised.

Dr. Smith saw Josh and Maura almost as soon as they arrived. He settled them in his office and drew more blood from Maura.

"I also want you to fast after midnight, and tomorrow morning go to a special lab I use. They freeze the blood immediately and send it out. We get the best results for some things that way."

Dr. Smith took a small sample of blood from Maura's arm and took it out to his nurse.

In a few minutes, he went out to the nurse's desk and got the results: a glucose reading of 160.

Dr. Smith looked at the paper, pursing his lips. "Not too bad, but normal is 115 at the top. While you're carrying a child, I don't want it to go over that."

"So, she's got a little bit of diabetes?" Josh asked.

Dr. Smith smiled. "Josh, saying that is like saying someone is a little bit pregnant. Her mean blood sugar will be higher. No, we'll just nip this in the bud. No more alcohol.

"There are many, many things we can do for diabetes today: diet, exercise, and food supplements. I'm going to prescribe what has proven to be a wonder drug for me, and, in addition, a wonder mineral. I'm hoping the natural things I'm asking you to do will eventually make the prescription drug unnecessary. We'll see."

"I'm glad you like vitamins and minerals and all the good stuff," Maura told him. "I was afraid you'd only believe in strictly medicating me."

"No way," the doctor said. "I've had wonderful results with vanddyl sulfate and other minerals and food supplements. It's all out there for our use. Why fret and stew over whether we'll choose ayurvedic or allopathic medicine? We badly need them both."

"*Ayurvedic* meaning the natural medicines, and allopathic being a more manufactured medicine?" Maura asked.

"That's close enough. I've had really good results using blue and black cohosh, a couple of cups a day—a decoction, which means covering the cup to let the tea steep longer. All health food stores carry it. I have a special way I like it made."

He handed her a sheet of paper. "Make it this way for best results. And when you come back, I'll have more printouts and more to tell you about herbs. Plenty of freshly squeezed orange juice, at least six ounces of V-8 juice daily."

They all stood and Dr. Smith shook each one's hand. "I'll want another sonogram about two months from now. And come back in two weeks so we can check your blood sugar. I don't want anything to go wrong."

With a start of alarm, Maura asked him, "Is anything likely to go wrong?"

"I'm not expecting it to, but I try to cover all bases."

"I'll see that she does what you've asked, Doctor," Josh said.

Smiling, Maura also frowned. "Josh! I have every intention of carrying out the doctor's advice."

Josh pulled her to him and hugged her. "I know you will, honey, but I'm here to serve as backup."

Josh and Dr. Smith exchanged a we're-men-in-this-together look and smiled.

Walking out into the warm fall day, Maura reflected on how well she and Josh fit. Probably no one would ever dream that theirs was a marriage of convenience, not love. As Josh took her arm and they crossed the street to his car, she felt a pang of longing for him to love her as much as he already loved the coming baby.

Thirteen

Ellen had gotten up at sunrise. She wanted to bake some of her extra special cloverleaf rolls. Rich and Odessa would be by this afternoon to rehearse for their group, Love'n Us. Her heart lifted just thinking of Rich.

Brushing back her super-curly, abundant black hair with her hands, she walked to the dresser and found a barrette, fastening her hair into a ponytail.

A couple of months had passed since she had talked with Maura about Lonnie Fillmore. She still hadn't told Rich, but she thought she might tell him tonight. Had Maura told Josh? The two men were friends. She thought if he had told him, Rich would have said something. He was the one she wished she could have saved her virginity for.

She picked up a framed photo of her dead mother from her night table and pressed it to her breast.

"You would love him, Ma," she said. "It hurts that you can't meet him. And you would despise Lonnie for what he did."

For long moments, it seemed she could feel the actual presence of her mother with her. They had been so close. Ellen's great-great-great-grandmother, Theena, had been a psychic and a herbalist. Now Ellen wished for that gift.

Theena only cried when someone was going to die a horrible death—like the Iverson girl Lonnie had plundered. The way he had plundered Ellen.

Theena had wept before a little Crystal Lake girl had been killed in a tornado and before a man had been found murdered.

Only Mr. Sampson definitely said he heard her weeping, but others said they thought they'd heard her.

Lonnie sat on a short hill in the deep woods behind Ellen's house. His mother would have conniption fits if she knew he was there. He thought his father would understand that he was only sowing his wild oats. And if he denied being there, his father would believe his story.

His motorcycle was hidden by bushes on the opposite side of the road. That, too, was a forest on land belonging to an absentee friend of his father. Lonnie spent a lot of time there. Taking his black binoculars from the case, he trained the lenses on Ellen's house, only to find that a big tree obscured his view.

Moving in closer, he finally found a clear line of vision to the house. Her shades were up. He snickered. What would the little hussy think if she knew he was watching her?

He wasn't going back to school, not this year anyway. Maybe never. He had more important things to do. Since he's a whiz with computers, he thought he would get through just fine. He needed to find a mentor. Maybe one day he could be as rich as Bill Gates.

He segued his lenses back to Ellen and saw her in her bedroom, binding her hair. She had on just a bra and panties and his breath caught in his throat. *Bitch,* he thought, *parading around half naked for anybody to see.*

It never occurred to Lonnie that Ellen was in the privacy of her own home, that he was the interloper.

Anger filled him when she pulled on a green shift. She was cutting him off! Damn! He'd come back around at the first sign of dark. Maybe she'd leave one of her shades open for him. Too bad she wasn't a good girl that he could admire.

He saw a car begin to pull into the long driveway that led to Ellen's house, and he stiffened. No, it was merely turning around. He relaxed. That architect broad had been coming out to Ellen's a lot, especially when that group that Rich Curry headed came to practice. He grudgingly admitted that they sounded good.

Had Ellen told the woman what had happened? He thought he'd scared her up pretty bad so she wouldn't be running around shooting her mouth off again. His daddy had probably scared her worse. He hoped he wouldn't have to run a number on the architect woman. Two years was long enough for anything to be done.

So, he'd lost his head and forced Ellen. It happened. He thought again as he'd thought so many times —she shouldn't have led him on.

Sighing, he flicked a bug from the side of his face onto his pants leg and squashed it, an act that somehow gave him pleasure.

When the phone rang, Ellen quickly dusted flour from her hands and answered it.

"I hesitated to call this early," Rich said.

"Call anytime. I told you that."

"I wanted to know if there's anything I could bring. When I get busy, I may forget to call and ask."

"I can't think of anything."

"Tell you what, I'll stop at the store and get a ham and buy some fried chicken from Popeye's. That should save you a little trouble."

"That sounds wonderful. You're so thoughtful."

"It's the least I can do. We're getting ahead with Love'n Us."

"I'll say we are."

"You seem sort of quiet."

"I'm thinking, I guess."

"Anything special?"

"Yes."

"Can I help? I give pretty good advice."

"I have something to tell you when we're through practicing tonight." She hesitated. "You may not like it."

"Well, I want to hear it."

"Can you think of any reason you'd turn away from me?"

"Turn away from you? No."

"Rich, I like you so much."

"And I'm beyond the *like* stage. Ellen, we ought to get together for real. I know you're only twenty-two, but you're mature. I can't get you out of my mind."

"And there's never a time when I'm not thinking of you. But wait until you hear what I've got to say, then make up your mind."

"Too late for that. My mind's made up, but I'll gladly hear you out. I've got to go now. See you late this afternoon."

Ellen went to the kitchen window and stood looking out at the forest in back of the house. It was so beautiful there. It was very still, and she thought she saw movement behind one of the bushes. Maybe Mr. Sampson was on one of his walks through the forest. She hunched her shoulders and hugged herself. "Rich," she said softly, and went back to making her rolls.

"What're you up to, young fella?" Mr. Sampson's voice sounded a few feet behind Lonnie, who jumped up, dropping his binoculars. Mr. Sampson looked at him in surprise.

"What the hell business is it of yours?" Lonnie asked.

"It be my business, all right. It looks like you got a fancy pair a' spyglasses lookin' at somethin' you oughtn'a be lookin' at."

"When did you get out of the lunatic asylum?" Lonnie asked, testily.

"Nev'a been in. That was all a pack a' lies like the lies they tell on that sweet li'l young woman you prob'ly tryin' t' spy on."

Lonnie swallowed hard. The old fool had his number.

"Well, that's where you ought to be anyway," Lonnie said.

In spite of being interrupted, his mind was still dreamily on getting to Ellen. He hadn't given her any more grief in the two years since he'd raped her. He wondered why he was so obsessed now, and it came to him that he'd gotten that way when that clown, Rich Curry, had begun to come around, when they'd gotten that gang together and made music.

Lonnie thought wistfully, he liked music. He'd have liked to join that group. Thinking about the group, his mind slid away from Mr. Sampson.

"Well, boy, maybe you should be leavin'. I ain't goin' anytime soon."

Lonnie thought about hitting the old man across the head with his binoculars, but that wouldn't do. He was a voter, and Dad wouldn't like that. Funny. Sometimes the thought of his father losing votes because of what he, Lonnie, did, stopped him in his tracks, and other times it didn't.

"It's a free country," Lonnie said. "I'm staying."

"This here's private land, like you know. You trespassin'. It's Miss Ellen's land yore on."

"*Miss* Ellen? Not to me she's no damned miss."

"Well, all I c'n say is somebuddy like you cain' take nothin' away from somebuddy like her. She's worth ten a' yore kind."

Lonnie's blood boiled then. Mr. Sampson looked at him steadily.

"You be goin'. Got no business here. And I'd advise you not to let me ketch you snoopin' aroun' here ag'in."

Well, Lonnie sure as hell wasn't going to be pushed around by the likes of this cretin. Nobody told him what to do, not even his parents. He was a free nineteen-year-old. And strong.

Lonnie sucked in his jaws. He gauged the strength of the old man, picked up and gripped the binoculars and started to swing; then he thought better of it again. He would never know just how he controlled himself, but he did.

"You got a pa," Mr. Sampson said, "who thinks you one a' the angels. How'd you like it if I went t' him?"

"He wouldn't believe you."

Mr. Sampson licked his lips. "I expec' you right, but I could write him a letter or call him and he might think about it. You reck'n?"

"There's nothing an old fool like you could tell a man like my dad about me."

"He loves you, you say?"

Lonnie expelled a harsh breath. "Yes."

"Pity you don' love y'self more."

"You shut the hell up," Lonnie exploded. Self-esteem was a poor subject for him. He always felt he was given so much and had so little to give in return.

Lonnie's temper was beginning to get the best of him. He had been having fun with his 7x50 binoculars and he was a poor sport. He could take this crazy down in a few minutes, he felt, but he didn't want it getting back to his parents.

Lonnie walked back into the woods opposite him and got on his motorcycle. There were wide paths in this woodland. He'd be back tonight, and he wouldn't bring his motorcycle. Mr. Sampson watched him. Lonnie thought, Sampson wasn't going to stop him. He was the mayor's son. He hadn't stopped him before. *Miss* Ellen. Maybe the old coot had the hots for her.

By four o'clock that afternoon, Ellen had set her house to order, dusting and polishing and putting spots of wax on the duller parts of her living-room floor.

The house smelled of soft jasmine and fresh-baked rolls. She had put on an indigo-blue jumpsuit and fastened big silver hoop earrings in her ears.

Rich came early, loaded down with fried chicken and a honeybaked ham.

"You're so wasteful," she said.

"And you're worth more than I'll ever have."

"Don't say that. You don't know me."

Rich put the packages on the table. "Let's put these away,

and then we're going to talk," he said. "Odessa is coming over a little later. Mr. Sampson is usually late. We have time."

What he wanted was time to hold her, kiss her.

Eluding his touch, she quickly put the food on the stove to stay warm and brought a buttered roll to Rich, who bit into it from her hand.

He took the roll from her and finished it.

"Divine," he said. "For just your rolls alone, I'd . . ."

Ellen placed her fingers over his mouth.

"You're right. We do have to talk. Let's go into the living room."

Seated on the sofa, Ellen began. "You hear the gossip about me. Have you any idea how it got started?"

"You're a good-looking woman, Ellen, and you live alone. You're gifted with a great voice, and I'm going to try to get you to take it further."

"I don't want to rush you, Rich, but I want to get this said. . . ."

She was silent so long that Rich said, "Now, who's stalling?"

Ellen cringed inside. How to tell him? What would she do if he were through with her? Had it been her fault as Lonnie said?

She drew away from him, forcing herself to speak. Her throat had gone bone dry. She drew a deep breath.

"Someone raped me two years ago. . . ."

Rich's mouth tightened. "Who? I'll get the bastard."

"You don't understand, Rich. He's not gettable."

"Who was it? Was it here in Crystal Lake?"

"Yes." Her voice was a near whisper. "I'll tell you who later. Not now. I knew you'd take it hard. You're that kind of man."

Rich reeled with shock and he took her hand. "You poor kid." He reached out and tilted her chin. "I had a sister who was raped. In Chicago. It was hell. But the man was sent up. He beat her nearly senseless."

She nodded. "I was beaten too."

"I'm so sorry."

His words were bringing blessed relief to her, but that was his sister, and different.

She had to say it and the words burst forth. "Was it my fault? God, my mother had just died and I was lonely. Did I lead him on?"

Rich moved closer and pressed her face against his own.

"I doubt you led him on, and even if you did, there was no reason to rape you. Women do change their minds at the last minute."

She had to be brave, prepare for defeat and loss.

"Thank you for saying that. Can you can you still care about me?"

There, she had said it.

"I can and I do. I'm coming to love you, Ellen. You weren't responsible for what happened. You're a passionate, high-spirited woman, and I love that about you.

"I want to kiss you so badly, but I've noticed you're drawing away from me. Is that why? Do you care about me?"

Tears filled her eyes. "I can't tell you how much I care, and, yes, I've drawn away from men all the way since it happened. I felt I was to blame."

"Well, you're not. And I'm going to help you get over this. I'll be patient, tender, kind."

"You've always been."

"And you won't tell me who?"

"I will later on. I just can't face that part of it now. You would hate him. Most people do."

He took her into his arms and held her against him, listening to her pounding heartbeat. "I'm ready when you want to tell me."

"Promise you won't do anything foolish?"

"I promise, although that will be hard."

"The two of us are beginning to have what he will never have—a life. Oh, Rich, thank God for you."

"No, you're the one."

The doorbell sounded with a musical coda rhythm and Ellen

got up, feeling weightless with joy. Mr. Sampson was there and ready to roll.

Driving along on her way to visit Police Chief John Williams, Maura touched her belly. Josh had gone with her the day before to have a sonogram. The baby was a boy. Not that either of them cared about the gender of the child. She and Josh talked often of names and had largely settled on Joshua Isaac Carter.

As she pulled into the police department parking lot, Maura couldn't help thinking about Crystal Lake two years before, when Pete Nelson had gone on trial for killing Lance Carrington's wife, Erika.

Pleading that he hadn't meant to kill her, but rather to frighten her back into his arms, he'd drawn thirty years in prison with time off for good behavior.

Police Chief John Williams was getting out of his car a short distance away. He waved and waited.

Catching up with him, she smiled as he asked, "What brings you this way?"

"I have a few questions I want to ask you about a matter."

"I'll be glad to answer if I can."

They walked in silence through the busy front section and back to his office.

"Coffee?" he asked. "A Danish?"

Obliquely, he eyed her swelling figure. He and his wife had gotten Maura to design their house, and they had remained friends.

"I'll take both," she said. "Please cut the Danish in half."

"I remember you like cream and sugar."

Without meaning to, she touched her belly again. "On second thought, I'd rather have herb tea, if you have it."

"We've got it. Red clover's about what half our staff has come to prefer."

He went out and returned in a few minutes with the tea and Danish and coffee for himself on a small metal tray.

He dropped down in a chair by her side. Both sipped their beverages in silence.

"What are the laws like in this town where rape is concerned, if it isn't reported right away?" Maura asked.

He hesitated a moment.

"It doesn't go too well anywhere if it's not reported immediately. Our town's about like all the rest."

"Two years later?"

He whistled. "That's a long time. Can you tell me who we're talking about here?"

"Could the name stay in this room for the moment?"

"Sure thing."

Maura thought about how to phrase her story and decided to be straightforward.

"Lonnie Fillmore raped Ellen Jones two years ago, just after her mother died."

The police chief raised his eyebrows. "I don't mind telling you we've had a lot of trouble out of that boy. If his father weren't the mayor, he'd have spent time in a juvenile facility.

"The girl, now, Ellen Jones certainly hasn't got the best in the way of a reputation. Not that I've ever believed all I hear. She's like a walking ghost sometimes. I feel sorry for her more than anything. She's too young to be living alone out there."

Maura nodded. "I've found out that Lonnie's friends—or his acquaintances—spread the lies about her when she went to his father and told him what had happened. He and his father threatened to ruin her reputation, and even though she didn't turn him in to you and file charges, they went ahead with it anyway."

"It happens. You see, in two years, most of the evidence will have disappeared."

"You're right. In a rage, she burned the clothes after talking with Ward Fillmore. She felt helpless."

"I'm sure. There's no statute of limitations, or anything like that. The thing is, most jurors would consider it water under the bridge and wonder why she was bringing it up now. Remember the Iverson girl?"

"I'll never forget her. As gossip has it, she was pregnant by Lonnie Fillmore, with him daring her to bear the child."

"The girl's mother came to me. Lonnie had threatened to kill her if she didn't have an abortion. *Maybe* kill her, the mother said. Ruin her reputation for certain."

"I didn't know that, of course. Her mother used to help me around the house sometimes. A lovely woman, and so was the daughter. You're saying, then, that nothing can be done?"

"No, that's not what I'm saying. If the girl—the young woman—is willing to press charges, we can go ahead. What I'm saying is, don't expect the results you'd want. It ought to have changed by now, but rape is often suspect, and when a woman's reputation has been trashed like Ellen Jones's has, not much will come of a trial. I'm sorry."

Maura nodded. "I thought it may be like that." She felt chilled thinking how Ellen blamed herself.

"Does the young woman want to press charges?"

"Not really. I thought it might be good for her self-esteem if she did. She's afraid of him."

"That won't do. She's got to have courage."

"What would you suggest?"

"You say she went to Ward Fillmore. He and the mother are fiercely protective of that boy, if he's right or if he's wrong. That's part of his trouble. He doesn't feel responsible for what he does. Thing is, Ward Fillmore is a popular mayor. He goes out of his way to do things for his constituents. His only failing seems to be his son. And that's one hell of a failing."

"He was born late in their lives. Maybe that explains it."

"I don't believe in the bad-seed theory, or I didn't until I began to hear about him—and to have a few run-ins with him."

"Could you tell me why you have run-ins with him?"

"Speeding on that damned souped-up motorcycle. Warnings about driving without a helmet. Threatening others. Stealing hubcaps—only we were never able to prove that. Breaking and entering. We got him on that, and he got a suspended sentence. His friends ratted on him.

"Lonnie Fillmore is an all-around heller. It's my feeling that he's going to do himself in one day. I wonder if he doesn't have mental problems."

"That's an idea. The only thing is he's brutalizing young women and getting away with it. Two down. How many to go? Maybe if we had stopped him when Ellen was raped, he wouldn't have been free to savage the Iverson girl."

"There's nothing we could have done about the Iverson girl. It was her word against his. Her mother didn't hear him threaten to kill her if she went through with the pregnancy. Her mother didn't hear him curse her and call her dirty names. No, we just have her word on that. Pity."

"I didn't think much, if anything, could be done about it, but I thought I'd ask."

"I'm glad you did. What I can and will do is keep my eyes on young Fillmore. It's been my experience that with people like him, the more he gets away with the more he does until he makes a wrong turn somewhere and it's curtains one way or the other."

She began to get up. "Thank you so much for your time. I'll talk to Ellen and find out what she wants to do."

"If she's going to go through with it, get a damned good lawyer. She's going to need him or her."

Maura smiled grimly. "Frankly, I don't think she is going to want to go through with it, especially when she finds out her chances of getting a conviction are almost nil. I just thought bringing all this out in the open would help her with her self-esteem. . . ."

Maura stopped and smiled, her eyes half closed. "But she's falling in love, and if all goes well, *that* will do wonders for her self-esteem. Wonders."

John Williams chuckled. "Doesn't it always?"

"Give my regards to Linda."

"I certainly will. Are you and Josh free to come over for dinner one weeknight or one Sunday?"

"Either. We'll talk and settle on a time."

She extended her hand to him. He took it and pressed his other hand onto it.

"Don't be a stranger," he said. "We've all got work to do on the Midland Heights project. Linda's very excited about working with you in the spring for the series of dances you all are giving at the Town Teen Center."

"I'm excited, too," Maura said. "But I'm going to have to take some time out for an act of nature."

John Williams laughed. "I've been wondering about that."

Fourteen

At Papa Isaac's house an hour later, Maura found him in good spirits.

"I'm a mite tired," he told her, "but Doc Lessing's been giving me something for that. I've surely learned the power of herbs and vitamins, minerals and food supplements. You see I've still got all my hair."

Lona touched his grizzled head. "That you have."

A fond look passed between them that gladdened Maura's heart. They both needed someone.

"How's your life going with the baby coming?" Papa Isaac asked.

"Fine. I don't seem to be having any trouble at all, not even morning sickness."

Lona nodded. "Some babies are like that. My firstborn was a love to carry, but the last boy made up for that; he never seemed to stop kicking."

"Does he have an active personality now?" Maura asked.

"Gentle as a lamb," Lona said. "It's the firstborn, who never gave any trouble, who's the heller. He's been in about every accident you can name. Restless. He's a card, that one, but I love them both to pieces."

Papa Isaac watched her as she spoke. "We had a visitor this morning," he said.

"Oh?"

"Man by the name of Stubbs said he was just passing by

and stopped in. Wanted to know if I was interested in selling the place. Said he'd heard I had been sick. He's only been living here a year or so."

"What did you tell him?"

"I said I'd think about it."

Lona got up. "You two're going to want to talk," she said. "I'll fix lunch for us. I'm sautéing oysters and shrimp, Maura. Does that strike your fancy?"

"You bet it does," Maura answered. "This kid I'm carrying is setting up a lot of cravings, and seafood is one of them. Would you believe I wanted strawberries in the middle of the night a couple of nights back?"

Papa Isaac and Lona laughed. "Well, if you wanted them, you got them," he said. "That husband of yours is the most doting husband . . ."

The smile stopped on Maura's face. Yes, Josh was kind to a fault. He was everything she wanted in a husband, but . . . She forced the thought back. Time was passing, slowly, inexorably.

Papa Isaac saw the shadow that passed over her face and wondered if everything was all right with her. He wasn't a man to pry.

"About the farm," Maura said. "I'll sell my land first to help you pay Josh back."

"That wouldn't be fair. I'm the one the money's going to cure. You'll need all you can get for your child. Not that Josh can't take the best of care of him, but you'll want to do your share."

Maura went to him and kissed the top of his head. "You're such a sweetie," she told him. "But we'll sell my land first. No argument."

"Funny thing," Papa Isaac said. "Josh talked about that this morning, coming back from my checkup. He said he didn't need to be paid back, that the debt was null and void since your marriage, that he was doing well. But I insisted. I wanted to be a good in-law, not a trifling one."

"You couldn't be trifling if you tried. I'll talk with Josh about it. I'm going to be selling the land anyway to the Midland Heights development program. Ellen, Josh, and I are all going to sell at under price because we so badly want that project to be successful."

"I think it's a wonderful thing you all are doing. It'll add to Crystal Lake, all right. We've got nearly no slums here, and I hope we can keep it that way."

"We'll do everything we can."

Papa Isaac shifted in his chair. "Josh stopped by the drugstore to get my prescription refilled, and Mayor Fillmore came to the car to talk to me. He asked for my vote."

"I guess he would with election coming up next year. It seems a long time away, though."

"Yes, he said the same thing. Said he's running early and he's got to get to people like me early. You like him?"

She toyed with the idea of telling him about Lonnie, but decided against it.

"I hear his boy is a handful," Papa Isaac said. "I used to see and hear him roar past my farm on that motorcycle of his. Seems kind of wild."

"We probably don't know the half of it. Are you voting for Mayor Fillmore?"

"Like you said, it's a long ways away. What about you?"

"Only if Genghis Kahn runs against him."

Papa Isaac laughed, his eyes wrinkling at the corners. "I take it he's not your cup of tea."

"You could say that."

"Why not?"

Maura laughed. "Why do I need a reason? We're not put on this earth to be liked by everybody."

"He's a good friend of your father-in-law."

"I know."

"How're you and Carter getting along?"

"We co-exist. He's very fond of Melodye. But, it doesn't matter. Josh's grandmother is great, and she tells me she's quite taken with me."

"She's a love of a woman. Every dance we used to turn up at together, she asked me to dance. She's a wonderful dancer and I miss her since she's not able to get around."

Maura chuckled. "I remember she used to come to Crystal Lake ball dances, then had her second stroke and couldn't get around well. She's well enough now to attend this year. She's a remarkable woman, and I'm proud to be liked by her."

"I expect Carter'll come around. He's a fool for good-looking women. His wife was a beauty. Beautiful voice, too. Died real young. Josh was her only child."

"Josh says he still misses her."

"I don't wonder. He told me today you have added so much to his life. And, Lord, he's excited about the baby. Says he's on cloud nine and climbing."

"Yes, he's very happy about the baby."

Papa Isaac narrowed his eyes. There was something amiss here. His granddaughter's eyes sparkled with joy when she talked about her baby; talking about Josh, she was subdued. What was going on?

"You know," he said, "your grandma and I got married when I was really young, and your mama followed suit. I never regretted it. Your grandma and I had a wonderful life together, but your mama was just starting to live when she and your father died in that plane crash. When you were little, she used to ask if I would take care of you if anything happened to her. It's like she knew what would happen."

His voice was gentle, grieved. "And I've done the best I could."

"You did a good, no—a great job with me," Maura said, "and I love you for it."

Maura was thoughtful as she entered her house that same afternoon. Josh would be at his office, most likely. Her conversation with Papa Isaac still lingered in her mind. He was doing well, and she could only now let herself know how scared she had been that she would lose him. Bless Josh for his help.

She entered the hall and was looking down when Josh spoke. "Hi! I brought shrimp home. Thought I'd use that crabmeat to fix us a fancy lunch."

Maura looked up and longing swept through her like wildfire. Josh's chest was bare, his muscles rippling under his tan skin. He wore jogging pants and had been working out.

She caught herself to keep from rushing into his arms, and she closed her eyes against the onslaught of emotions sweeping her toward him.

She would have sworn he felt something, too, but he smiled and chucked her under the chin.

"Does shrimp for lunch interest you?"

"You interest me," she wanted to scream. "Take me and press me against your muscular chest until I faint with desire; but no, I'm already fainting with desire. How much more of this can I take?"

Shaking, she forced herself to smile. "I'm sorry. I had lunch at Papa Isaac's. Oysters and shrimp. I think I'll lie down. I feel sort of tired."

If Maura had been looking at him, she would have seen how crushed he seemed, but she couldn't look at him. If she did, she'd burst into tears of frustration.

For a moment, Josh's mouth clamped shut. She was pulling away from him. Did she think he was putting the moves on her? He was her husband. He had tried to go easy in this department, let her come to him so she wouldn't feel used.

He was flying sky high when he thought about the baby, but the relationship he and Maura had undertaken saddened him. Was she going to choose to move on at the end of the year and a half or so? He shook his head. Damn the fear that wouldn't let him love again. But, next time, he felt he could completely go under, the way he nearly had when he had broken up with Melodye, or she with him.

Maura stood rooted to the spot. Until he responded, she couldn't turn away.

"Is there anything I can do?" he asked.

She gave him a wan smile, still avoiding his gaze. "No, I'll just rest. Thank you for taking Papa Isaac to the doctor."

"Glad to do it. I'm really fond of him."

"And he's fond of you."

She wanted to tell him that she was sorry about the lunch he'd been about to prepare, but the words stuck in her throat. She wanted him with an urgency she'd never known before. Her very soul cried out for him.

For him, she thought, it was a marriage of convenience. He needed a child and she was bearing one for him. Physically, it was going like clockwork. She had never felt better. But her gut was being ripped apart with love and longing for Josh. Her heartache was the worst she'd ever known.

In his room, Josh sat on the side of his bed, his legs apart and his hands hanging down between them. Out there, a moment ago, he'd wanted to pull Maura to him so badly, feel her soft warmth and hear her heart thud the way it did sometimes. He felt she liked him a lot and he often thanked heaven she'd agreed to bear his child, but she wanted a baby, too. How did she really feel about him?

Sliding up on the bed, he moved to the night table and reached for the pair of plane tickets to San Francisco that were lying there. He needed to tell her, no, ask her, tonight about the trip. Taking a deep breath, he got up and pulled on a white T-shirt.

He found her sitting on a couch in the living room, listening to a Nancy Wilson love song.

Smiling, he dropped down beside her and showed her the tickets.

"I have to go out to consult with someone. I got you a ticket in case you want to go."

She looked at him, her breath catching in her throat.

"I'd love to go," she said. "I need a break, and my work has slacked off."

She pulled the ticket from its jacket and looked at the date. Two weeks from that day.

"I thought we'd stay three or four days."

"It sounds wonderful. I love San Francisco."

"So do I. I've often thought of settling there."

"It's not too late."

"Let's talk about it. We'll look around. I'm set up here, but what the hell, we only live once and we ought to do it up right."

"You've got a wild side," she murmured

"You don't know the half of it."

In her home office, Maura was doodling a bit when Josh stuck his head in the door.

"Do you really want to make this trip?" he asked.

"I'm excited about it, yes. It will be good to get away."

He stood at the end of her drafting table. His look at her was oblique and she wondered what he was thinking.

As she worked with the drawing of the Midland Heights dwelling, he bent down to examine it.

"You're really good at this," he said.

"Thank you."

"What if I come in on it? I could help a lot."

"Well, you're an architect and a builder, so of course you could. I'm sure my board would love having you. But you're so busy."

"I'd make the time. I believe in what you're doing. I get asked questions about Midland Heights by my fellow architects."

"Oh?"

"Yes. You're becoming well-known for trying to make the world a better place. Or at least this little neck of the world."

"I'm glad."

Suddenly, as Maura straightened, she felt a movement in her belly. Her eyes widened.

"What is it?"

She looked at him a moment, silent. Then she felt the movement again.

"The baby moved."

His face lit up as he went to his knees and felt her belly.

"Yes, I feel him. He's kicking late."

Maura laughed. "How would you know?"

Josh looked at her levelly. "I've been studying everything I can get my hands on."

"Between you and Dr. Smith, everything has to go well."

He hugged her waist and pressed the side of his face to her body. "Lord, you've made me so happy. Are you as happy as I am?"

Maura pondered this a moment. "Yes, I'm sure I am. Sometimes I feel I'm in another world."

He came away from her reluctantly. Even without love, this was a precious time. And they cared so deeply for each other. That was what mattered, he thought.

Just as Josh was leaving the room, the phone rang. It was Odessa. Bubbling, Maura told her about the baby's movements.

"Typical male," Odessa quipped. "Can't wait to get started."

"Others are earlier."

"Nothing's going to get ahead of this one. You wait."

"Odessa, I feel so wonderful."

Odessa sighed. "You make me want to get my show on the road before I'm ready. But soon. Congratulations on really beginning to feel motherhood."

"Thank you."

She wanted to tell Odessa how touched she was by Josh's tenderness a few moments back, but she hugged the memory to herself.

"We're taking a trip to San Francisco in about two weeks."

"Lucky devils. You'll be marking your child to be passionate and artistic. Oh, Maura, you must get in touch with my cousin. You know the one I talk about so much, the artist?"

"Dale Borders?"

An important message from the ARABESQUE Editor

Dear Arabesque Reader,

Because you've chosen to read one of our Arabesque romance novels, we'd like to say "thank you"! And, as a special way to thank you, we've selected four more of the books you love so well to send you for FREE!

Please enjoy them with our compliments, and thank you for continuing to enjoy Arabesque...the soul of romance.

Karen Thomas
Senior Editor,
Arabesque Romance Novels

Check out our website at
www.arabesquebooks.com

ARABESQUE
®
A PRODUCT OF
BET BOOKS™

3 QUICK STEPS
TO RECEIVE YOUR "THANK YOU" GIFT
FROM THE EDITOR

Send this card back and you'll receive 4 FREE Arabesque
novels! The introductory shipment of 4 Arabesque novels – a
$23.96 value – is yours absolutely FREE!

There's no catch. You're under no obligation to buy anything.
You'll receive your introductory shipment of 4 Arabesque
novels absolutely FREE (plus $1.50 to offset the costs of
shipping & handling). And you don't have to make any
minimum number of purchases — not even one!

We hope that after receiving your books you'll want to
remain an Arabesque subscriber. But the choice is yours to
continue or cancel, anytime at all! So why not take us up on
our invitation to receive 4 Arabesque Romance Novels, with
no risk of any kind. You'll be glad you did!

Call us
TOLL-FREE
at 1-888-345-BOOK

THE EDITOR'S "THANK YOU" GIFT INCLUDES:

- 4 books absolutely FREE (plus $1.50 for shipping and handling)
- A FREE newsletter, *Arabesque Romance News*, filled with author interviews, book previews, special offers, and more!
- No risks or obligations. You're free to cancel whenever you wish... with no questions asked.

BOOK CERTIFICATE

Yes! Please send me 4 FREE Arabesque novels (plus $1.50 for shipping & handling). I understand I am under no obligation to purchase any books, as explained on the back of this card.

Name _____

Address _____ Apt. _____

City _____ State _____ Zip _____

Telephone ( ) _____

Signature _____

Offer limited to one per household and not valid to current subscribers. All orders subject to approval. Terms, offer, & price subject to change. Offer valid only in the US.

Thank you!

AN110A

Accepting the four introductory books for FREE (plus $1.50 to offset the cost of shipping & handling) places you under no obligation to buy anything. You may keep the books and return the shipping statement marked "cancelled". If you do not cancel, about a month later we will send 4 additional Arabesque novels, and you will be billed the preferred subscriber's price of just $4.00 per title. That's $16.00 for all 4 books for a savings of 33% off the cover price. You may cancel at any time, but if you choose to continue, every month we'll send you 4 more books, which you may either purchase at the preferred discount price. . . or return to us and cancel your subscription.

THE ARABESQUE ROMANCE CLUB: HERE'S HOW IT WORKS

PLACE
STAMP
HERE

ARABESQUE ROMANCE BOOK CLUB
P.O. Box 5214
Clifton NJ 07015-5214

"That's the one. We grew up practically as brother and sister. Wait. I'll give you his number. Don't you dare forget to call him."

"I'd be afraid to forget, you're so anxious. He comes across in his photo as a really nice man."

"You don't know the half of it. He's a really good artist, too."

"Has he ever been here?"

Odessa laughed. "No, the wretch says he can't bear to be away from Frisco for even a short time. He's in love with it. Here's the number. I had it in my book in the drawer beside me."

Getting a pen, Maura took the number.

"As you know, I've been out on several visits and he always shows Mike and me a wonderful time. I just wish I could get him to come here."

"I'll extend him an extra invitation."

"Please do. How're the drawings and plans for Midland Heights coming along?"

"Splendidly. I've got one house that I've finished the drawings for. I think you're going to fall in love with it. You've seen some of the older, small-scale models."

"I've seen them and I like them all."

"This one is special. I think I drew it with you in mind. And, oh, yes, I've got a great idea if we move to another home."

"What is it?"

"Remember my telling you about Val Thomas's doctor's office in Alaska, the one with a room the shape of an egg?"

"I do. Wow! That's going to be something. I like the idea."

"That's going to be the shape of my nursery, which reminds me, I've got to get busy fixing a nursery for this little tyke."

"Joshua Isaac Carter?"

"You remember well. Should we name him so soon?"

"Why not? Josh is so eager. Is he going to make it through to the birth?"

"He'll make it. He's being extremely good about this."

"Well, he loves you and you love him."

"Um-m-m." Maura thought it best not to try to answer that. It seemed that every day the baby grew inside her, the deeper her feelings got for Josh. And what did he feel? He cared, she thought she knew that. And he loved his unborn son. That was all he was able to give. With a heavy sigh, she got up from the drawing table and went to the window. The leaves were turning a deeper red and gold. Beautiful.

Fifteen

Maura never went to San Francisco without being fascinated all over again. The morning after they arrived, Maura and Josh set out to enjoy the sights of the city. Josh was especially fond of the tallest building there, the Transamerica Pyramid.

"It's a city of magic," Maura declared, and Josh agreed.

Dressed in a navy and white pantsuit, Maura felt exhilarated. Josh was garbed in tan trousers and a navy jacket. They had eaten no breakfast, because they planned a picnic in San Francisco's huge Golden Gate Park.

With sourdough bread and fresh cooked Dungeness crabs, they were on their way from Fisherman's Wharf to the park when they spied Dale Borders, Odessa's cousin, just setting up his artwork.

He came to them excitedly, leaving his easel.

"When you called last night, I know I said I would not be out this morning, so you expected me this afternoon, but I had a change of plans."

A replica of his photo, the medium height, maplewood-colored man with his bristly black hair and Jack Frost eyebrows shook hands with them. He wore, as he'd said he would, dark-blue trousers, a blue artist's smock, and a red scarf tied at the throat.

"How wonderful to meet you both."

A certain joy seemed to surround him. As they came to his easel, they saw he was painting a portrait of a small boy.

"You're very good," Maura complimented him.

"It comes from my heart."

Josh eyed Maura speculatively, and Dale interpreted the look. "You would like me to paint your wife."

Josh nodded. "That I would. We're only here for three days. Will that be enough time?"

"I could do a quick painting. The one I would like to do would of course take much longer."

"I think I'll take you up on the quick one for now."

Josh turned to Maura. "I want you with me for most of my visit here, but I want a portrait of you. None of the appointments I've made are particularly interesting They're almost entirely about the new modular construction, and you're way ahead of me on that. What do you say?"

Maura felt excited. "Yes, I would like Dale to paint me. Just be sure you take plenty of notes at your meetings."

"I'll do that. Dale, will you be here this afternoon?"

"All day. Yes."

"Then we'll see you in the early afternoon, around two."

"I'll look forward to that, and please call if your plans change." He scribbled his cell-phone number on his card.

Fisherman's Wharf was alive with mimes, artists painting and hawking their wares, musicians, clowns, and cartoonists. Many crafts were displayed there.

A pretty young girl passed before them with a wooden tray of free oatmeal cookies.

"You must try one," she said, standing in front of Josh, Maura, and Dale. She laughed and said to Dale, "You I know, but have another. You're one of my best customers."

Josh looked at Maura and smiled. "Let's see how your cookies measure up."

"Be careful. No comparisons," Maura said. "Mine are made with a special ingredient." She flinched. She had been going to say that her cookies were made with love. Josh's eyes shifted away from hers, as if he knew what she was going to say and didn't want her to.

"An extra measure of butter," she said lamely, which was true, but not the whole truth. Biting into the chewy cookie, Maura exclaimed, "These are really good."

Josh grinned. "Almost as good as yours."

Smiling, the young girl thanked them and passed on, and a man came up to them, dressed in a white clownsuit with black coin-sized dots and a bright red nose. A red fright wig bushed around his head under the tall, pointed cap.

"San Francisco," he said to them, "city of dreams."

"You're right about that," Josh responded.

"People fall in love with San Francisco," the clown pressed on, his white painted face alive with happiness.

Love, Maura thought. That word was coming up often here. Well, it was a city of artists, and artists operated from the heart. She glanced wistfully at Josh, who took her hand.

The clown waltzed away, blowing them kisses.

A dancer tapped over and did a few minutes of intricate tapping in front of them. Maura tipped him, and he moved away. She was glad they had brought plenty of small bills to tip the clown and the dancer and any others who came up.

For the second time, Maura thought it was a magical place.

"I'm starved," she said, "yet I don't want to leave."

"We don't have to leave. We can put this food aside and eat at one of the restaurants here."

"No. I'm anxious to see the park. It's as if I want to experience all of San Francisco at once."

Maura thought Josh probably had no inkling of how dear he had become to her as the father of her growing child. And looking at her, he felt sad. She deserved more than he could ever give her. She deserved more than the loveless marriage he could offer. She deserved the world.

They found a spot on a high hill in Golden Gate Park and sat down. There was a magnificent view of the Golden Gate Bridge. The basket packed for them included plastic utensils, strong paper plates, and sealed drinking cups filled with ginger ale. Spreading the paper tablecloth, they sat down.

Pulling the meat from one of the already-cracked crabs, Maura held the morsel out to Josh and he took it into his mouth, playfully biting her fingers lightly.

"Greedy." She laughed.

Looking at her, he thought she just didn't know how greedy he was for her. A shudder ran the length of his body as he again remembered the pain he had endured after the breakup with Melodye. Would it never leave him?

To break the sad spell, he began to tell Maura tidbits about San Francisco.

"Did you know Chinese fortune cookies got their start right here in San Francisco, and not from the Chinese? They were introduced by a Japanese restaurateur, and they caught on like wildfire."

"That's a nice information nugget."

"San Francisco," he murmured, "the gateway to the Pacific."

"I love it, but I think we're too rooted where we are ever to move here. We could just come out far more often."

"Good deal. Maura, did the baby kick again?"

"How did you know?"

"I saw a look of pure joy cross your face."

"Yes. He kicks often now. Odessa says he's a typical male, raring to go."

A sense of happiness flooded Josh. That made two of them anxious for him to be born.

The sourdough rolls were delectable and complemented the fresh crabmeat. Far below them spread the park and its wonders. Among them were the Morrison Planetarium and the Steinhart Aquarium. Small groups of people sat on the hillside, and a blue-bowled sky held them in its dome.

"Another nugget," Josh said. "The Conservatory of Flowers is the oldest building in the park, here since 1879."

"You know a lot about San Francisco.

"I know. I love it."

Maura glanced at him, her lips slightly open. So, he could speak of love casually, but not of love between him and a woman. Not of love between him and her.

"I'd like to walk you all over San Francisco," he said, "and enjoy it with you. But tomorrow I've got to get cracking on more meetings, and I don't want you getting tired."

"I feel strong."

"Promise me you won't overdo it."

"I won't. You have nothing to worry about."

"You're carrying precious cargo." He reflected a moment. "You are precious cargo."

She reached for his hand. "It's sweet of you to say that. Thank you."

"You deserve it all. You know that, don't you?" His voice went husky.

"I guess I haven't thought about it very much." She sat thinking that that was a lie, because she did think of it, not often, but enough. Amazing the way he could say things that pleased her so, yet what she wanted him to say most was missing.

No, that wasn't true anymore. She had the baby to think of now, and that wasn't missing. He was inside her, flourishing, and the thought of it made her happier than she had dreamed she could be.

When they had finished eating, they laid back on the grass and gazed up at the cerulean sky and the white cumulus clouds drifting lazily by. At that moment, Josh thought he had nearly everything he wanted in this world. He felt close to this woman and to his unborn child. But, yes, there was something missing—would he ever be able to do anything about it?

Getting up, he pulled Maura to her feet. They gathered the refuse from the picnic and found a trash can.

"Now for the cable cars," Josh said.

* * *

Maura and Josh found the cable cars another delightful San Francisco treat. They rode up and down the hilly terrain, thrilled and laughing, weaving in and out of the curved streets.

An older woman sat in the seat next to theirs and smiled at them. "Visitors?" she asked.

"Yes. You have a beautiful city."

"Thank you. We love it. Welcome. I happen to work for the Chamber of Commerce. I could tell you were visiting, because of the sheer delight on your faces. Some of us have become rather blasé about our fair city."

"It would take a long time for me to get blasé about all this beauty," Josh assured her.

The woman got off at the next stop. "Enjoy your stay," she said.

They rode for an hour or two, then, going back to Fisherman's Wharf, they found Dale sketching a family.

Assuring them that he'd be through in a half hour or so, he suggested that they watch the beautifully painted boats along the wharf. Sitting on one of the benches, they watched a boat called *Neptune's Dream* for a long while. Painted in gold, blues, and greens, the scene depicted the god of the sea surrounded by other gods and goddesses.

A juggler paused before them juggling large oranges. He turned to face them, then away, all the time keeping the oranges in the air. Josh and Maura watched in amazement.

"You put on a great show," Josh complimented the man, when he had finished.

"Thank you."

Josh tipped him and the man bowed. "Thank you again."

Their attention reverted to the many boats at the wharf.

"There must be every color here under the sun," Josh said. He glanced at his watch, as Dale came up to tell them he was ready to begin.

* * *

Maura and Josh got back to their hotel late that afternoon. Named the Rubaiyat, the hotel was one of a kind. Built of white stucco with a dark-red tiled roof, the front walls had floor-to-ceiling windows, giving a magnificent view of the Pacific Ocean. Their balcony was deep, fitted with padded sea-green lawn furniture. Maura kicked off her shoes and shed her jacket.

She stretched out on the bed, then rose on her elbow to watch the wonderful view of the tide sweeping against the shore, and to enjoy the brisk winds that danced in. She picked up the quick sketch Dale had done of her and studied it. He was really good, she thought.

Hearing the water running in the shared bathroom, she found herself picturing Josh in the shower, his powerful body glistening with soap. She blushed.

He tapped and came in. "I wondered if you want to shower first."

"No. You go ahead. I'm just enjoying more of the view."

He sat on the bed and took the sketch. "Dale's really talented."

"Yes. I'd like him to do you, too."

Josh shrugged. "We could always come back."

"Oh, after this trip, I'm going to insist on it," she said. "Where are we having dinner?"

"Well, I thought about Chinatown, or back to Fisherman's Wharf, but I'm told there's a wonderful place not far from here."

"I trust your judgment. You've got excellent taste."

A white T-shirt covered his smooth, tanned, heavily muscled chest. He looked good, she thought, better than in the fantasy. She closed her eyes.

"Sleepy?"

"No, not really."

He seemed to be about to say something but thought better of it.

"I'll go shower."

"Okay." As he got up and left the room, Maura wanted to

call him and blow him a kiss, but she restrained herself. They didn't have that kind of free and easy relationship.

She got up and went out on the balcony, sat in the sea-green, cushioned, iron chair, and tucked her feet under her. The breeze caressed her face, and she wished it were Josh's hands caressing her.

At moments like this, the world seemed unreal to her, until she touched her belly. Wonderful, but unreal. Time was passing swiftly. They had given themselves a year and a half. Would they last past that time? She had begun to be very sympathetic to Josh and his pain. Sometimes the look of a hurt child came into his eyes, and she wanted to kiss away his pain. Damn Melodye. But, if Melodye hadn't left him, he wouldn't be hers now. And with mild bitterness, she reminded herself that he wasn't hers, romantically or with love. He was her baby's father. And he was a decent man who was very, very kind to her.

She briefly fell asleep in the chair and woke to the trilling of a robin on the branch of an oak tree.

Stretching, she smiled. What would she wear? She wanted to look especially nice tonight. Getting up, she called to Josh, who had finished showering and was shaving. He had changed into a white undershirt and bikini briefs. He reached for a robe hanging behind the bathroom door.

A devil of mischief took her. "Don't," she said. "I'm your wife. I have a right to see you in the altogether and you're not quite there."

Josh drew in a swift breath, his eyes crinkling with laughter. "You have a right to anything I can give you," he said.

They seemed on the verge of something deeper than they had had, but he turned away after her statement.

After a moment, she asked, "What kind of restaurant is it where we're having dinner?"

"Dressy. Truly beautiful, like this hotel. Unusual. Would you like something less formal?"

"No. I feel like dressing up."

"Good. I hear they have a marvelous dance floor and a damned good orchestra."

Again, she felt very drawn to him as he sat on the edge of his bed. She wanted to kiss the top of his head the way he sometimes kissed the top of hers. Affectionate. Nothing more. Going into the kitchenette, she selected juice oranges and went to the doorway.

"Would you like fresh-squeezed orange juice?"

"Sure. Why not?"

He got up and came toward her. "I was going to ask if you wanted me to squeeze them. Do I pamper you too much, Maura? I told you I want to take the best care of you I'm capable of."

"You do, you know, but I don't need to be overly pampered. I'm pretty strong and healthy."

"I can't help it. Something about you makes me want to take care of you. I'm sorrier than you could ever know about the hell I live in, but we can be friends, can't we? Warm, caring friends. I want that so much."

She looked at him steadily and placed her hand against the doorjamb as he moved closer.

"We *are* friends, Josh," she said. "I feel you care about me, and God knows I care about you. We've having a child together. I hope everything goes right."

Something leaped in him then, a kind of unbounded joy. His baby was in her beautiful body. He kissed her cheek, not trusting himself to kiss her on the mouth.

Pacifica was the restaurant they went to that night. Near the Pacific Ocean and the Golden Gate Bridge, it was formal with its snowy-white tablecloths and potted palm trees. An orchestra played soft pop music and golden oldies.

Dressed in sheer navy lace and navy satin sandals with a navy satin band holding back her lustrous hair, Maura felt she looked her best. Small diamond teardrop earrings swayed gently in her ears and a thin circlet of diamonds was fastened around her throat.

She thought Josh looked very handsome in his white dinner jacket and black pants, a red carnation in his buttonhole.

"Mrs. America," he called her, as the maître d' led them to their table.

"Oh, Lord, but you're handsome," she told him.

"You're very kind."

"No. You never seem aware of the impression you make."

"I'm only aware of the impression you're making on me. I want to spirit you away and never come back."

"Selfish."

"Yeah. Selfish where you're concerned. Maura, we ought to talk more. Clear the air."

Yes, he thought, *we ought to talk about love and if we can get over pain so deep it shatters us.*

"I'm willing," she said, as the maître d' seated them.

They ordered Beef Wellington and potatoes au gratin, Brussels sprouts, and big green salads. When the food came, the greens of the salad and the ripe, red, juicy tomatoes together with the other food made a colorful palette that made Maura think of Dale and his painting.

They ate slowly, savoring the food and the delicious buttered sourdough rolls. Josh reached across the table and took her hand, stroking her engagement and wedding rings. He wanted to kiss her hand, but held back, thinking that he never wanted to lie to her. He could give what he could give and he prayed it was enough. He also prayed that he would be able to give her more.

They sat there, playing games with their eyes—beautiful games, meaningful games. She gazed at him shyly, then grew bolder.

"Don't make it too hard for us to break up if it comes to that," he said, and could have kicked himself for saying it.

"Sorry," she said, softly. "I'll try not to make that mistake again."

"Honey," he said suddenly, "I never meant to hurt you. I keep saying I want you to understand, and how in the hell can you when I don't understand myself? Maura, you've given me more than any woman has ever given a man, and believe me, I'm grateful. Truly grateful. Will you accept my apology?"

Maura was silent a long moment. "You're running scared," she said, "and I can understand. I've never had the kind of pain you've had, but I can empathize. I see it on your face sometimes, and I ache with wanting to take it away.

"I want this baby, Josh." She added silently, *as I want you.*

They danced to the old forties tune of "Besamé Mucho" and, as the music eddied around them, Maura felt his lithe body hard against her and thrilled at his closeness. His cheek brushed hers, and when she turned her head, his mouth caught a corner of her lips.

After a moment, he said, "This is incendiary. Let's sit down and come back out in a little while."

Maura laughed shakily. So, the night was getting to him, too.

Their dessert was a simple vanilla-bean ice cream laced with crème de cocoa and huge, ripe strawberries, the stems intact.

She lifted one of the strawberries from her crystal dish, shook the liquid from it, and fed it to him. As he finished it, he took the stem and put it on his dish.

"I'm getting in the habit of feeding someone else," she said softly.

"Thank you." He should, he thought, be telling her about now how he loved her. Now, he felt too restrained to even tell her how much he cared.

Dancing again to a less romantic tune, Maura remembered that the words of "Besamé Mucho," the song they had danced to, promised to be in love forever and make all their dreams come true. In the circle of his arms, she felt magic in the air. San Francisco magic. Gateway to the Pacific. Oh, Lord, why couldn't it be the gateway to love?

Sixteen

When Maura and Josh reached their hotel after dinner, Josh turned to her.

"I have a surprise for you. We'll need to let our food digest first, though."

"You're full of wonderful surprises."

"Because you enjoy them so."

They walked around the beautiful grounds of the hotel, sat down a while, then stood on the edge watching the stunning, restful, deep-blue Pacific.

"You're such a marvelous person to be with," she said.

"You're even more so."

Time seemed to move swiftly. When an hour had passed, he led her to the concierge.

"I believe I've found the perfect spot for you," the small blond concierge said, smiling as she led them to a large, pagoda-shaped building and inside.

There were twenty or so small rooms, each with a hot tub; a table stacked with big, thirsty towels; chairs; plants; and a small refrigerator. Their room was coral and pale green with lavender orchid plants. Padded hangers for their clothes were in the narrow closet. The concierge spoke into her cell phone and, in a few minutes, a bellhop appeared with two bottles in a bucket of ice.

Smiling, the concierge told them, "Enjoy your stay. If there is anything you need, simply call me." She gave Josh her card.

There were matching navy swimsuits laid out for them on a long, slender table.

Beginning to remove her clothes, Maura felt shy and went behind a screen. Josh had seldom seen her naked. They had been together only enough to bring about the desired consequences.

When she came from behind the screen, she asked him, "How did they get my right size?"

"I guessed," he said. "The concierge guessed, and in the end we called Odessa. I wanted this to be special."

Glancing around her, listening to the soft strains of a sensual Teddy Pendergrass tune, Maura nodded. "And it *is* special. Josh, thank you."

"You're very welcome. Nothing I will ever own is good enough for you."

He opened the two bottles. One was champagne for him; the other was nonalcoholic sparkling champagne for her.

"We're going to bring a grand baby into this world," he said. "Dr. Smith . . ." he began.

"Doesn't think I should have alcoholic beverages," she finished for him. "One little sip."

He tilted his glass toward her, and she swallowed a small amount, which tickled going down.

"I'll be glad to be back on track."

"You're just getting started."

The warm water in the hot tub churned, immersing them in its eddies and swirls. Josh stroked her back, then she stroked his. There were two dahlias lying on a low table beside the tub. Josh leaned over, selected one, and broke off most at the stem. He tucked the flower behind her ear and lightly kissed her face.

"Did you know," he said, "that dahlias are San Francisco's official flower?"

"It figures. They're one of the most beautiful flowering plants. I like everything about San Francisco."

The water felt so good against their bodies, Maura thought.

It all seemed like a dream world. Other units were occupied, but it was quiet, serene, noise controlled.

"Josh?"

"Yes, baby."

"We will come back soon. I want Dale to paint you."

"It's only important that he get you."

"No, I want a portrait of you for myself."

"Okay. We'll come back and spend a couple of weeks. We've got a vacation coming."

"Good. I'll be going back to Dale tomorrow while you're stuck in some stuffy office in meetings."

"Don't gloat. You'll be joining me in those meetings the next day."

Maura grew quiet. They worked well as a pair.

After a couple of hours of utter contentment, Josh said, "We'd better be going in. You have to get your rest."

"You say that to me so much. I'm not a fragile woman."

"But, you're a *pregnant* woman."

"I could never deny it."

Undressed and ready for bed, Maura got a CD of the music that had been playing in the hot-tub room that they'd requested. The music was so affecting, she thought. Was the artist a happy man? Had he loved more or less than most?

She was dressed in a soft, lacy, ivory nightgown and robe, trousseau items, when Josh knocked and came in at her invitation.

He closed the door and stood gazing at her, his voice caught in his throat.

"Why are you looking at me like that?" she asked softly, to stem the tide of her rushing emotions.

"Can't you guess?"

A pulse beat in her throat. He was so handsome in his blue pajamas. Swiftly, he crossed the room to where she stood and, without any preliminaries, took her into his arms.

"Maura," he murmured. "Sweetheart, please don't turn me down."

Pressed to him, her heart leaped like a wild thing going toward him.

"I won't," she whispered, and to herself murmured, "No, my darling, I won't."

He slipped the low-cut robe from her body, then the gown, and stood admiring her brown flesh.

"You're so beautiful."

"So are you."

Maura stood with his big hands stroking her and thought that if she were to live forever, it was moments like these she'd treasure most. And, holding her, Josh thought that with her in his arms the world itself belonged to him.

Gently, he led her to the bed, turned the deep rose covers down, and pressed her back onto the pillows. She was so overcome, she could hardly catch her breath. The shaft of his maleness rose mightily against her hips as they lay there.

He planted soft kisses over her body and, with his tongue, took the honey from her silken skin.

"Oh," she breathed. This was the first time they had been together with this depth. Not since the baby had been conceived had he come to her. She thought she knew that he didn't want her to think he was using her body for his own pleasure. And this was what he in fact felt, but tonight was different. There was the magic of the city in the air and in them. The world was artistic in San Francisco.

She ached for him inside her as he moaned, holding back so he could last. Her soft breasts filled his mouth as he sucked them gently. Glory days! Tantalizingly, he went the length of her body with his soft kisses. Now and then his tongue teased her body, and he stopped midway and lingered there.

"Oh, Lord," she moaned. "Now, Josh. Please. Now!"

He did as she asked, and his engorged shaft slipped into the nectared sheath of her body and clung there, bringing riotous joy and pleasure to them both.

They were the earth itself. The moon and the stars. The firmament. They were waves and rippling water. Earthquakes. All the magnificent passions of the world.

Tears filled Maura's eyes as she stroked Josh's muscular back, then his hips and flanks. He arched above her, his body burning with desire.

"We belong together," he whispered. "Trust me, Maura. One day we'll have it all."

Was he promising her love? She didn't know. He didn't know. He was a bitterly hurt man and there was no way he could know if that hurt would ever heal.

In the shadowy room, with the light from the streetlamps outside creeping in and the sounds of the pounding Pacific Ocean as the tide crashed ashore drifting into their room, they held each other.

"This is so good," she murmured.

"So good," he echoed.

Music filled the room and their hearts. The scent of roses Josh had bought her while they were out for dinner was in the air, and Maura marveled at how beautiful the whole earth seemed.

Gently working her, Josh went into a deeper place and shuddered. How could he last? He had been so long without her. She wrapped her legs across his back and drew him closer as he exploded into a world of starbursts.

Lying beneath him, Maura's breath came faster. Everything in her seemed welded to the man arched above her. Her body felt weightless; she felt full of wonder as a sharp surge of pleasure took her, and with him momentarily locked into her body, she felt the surges of passion that took her over the edge onto an island of perfect bliss.

They slept then, and Maura dreamed of a wide, rippling, clear river. On the banks of this river, Josh came to her, kissed her, and a boy-child blossomed alongside them.

"We are a family," she said to the child, who seemed to be about three years old.

"Family," the child echoed.

Josh picked up the boy and kissed him. "Yes, family," he said.

They were all so happy.

"I love you," the boy said to them.

Maura's throat closed in pain and Josh looked at his son, saying nothing.

Time was so short for them. Their agreement was for a year and a half of marriage. By the time their son was three, they would have been separated for more than a year and a half. And what of the boy? Maura felt her heart grow heavy with sadness.

She came awake to Josh gently shaking her.

"What's wrong?" he asked.

"I had a bad dream."

"Tell me about it."

Maura shook her head.

"No. I'll be all right. Thank you."

His face above hers was so clear.

"Maura?"

"Yes."

"Was the bad dream about us?"

Maura drew in a quick breath. "That dream was about us. You were leaving me. Josh, please, I don't want to talk about it."

He took her in his arms and held her until she said, "I'm fine now. I want you to kiss me again."

His lips found hers and his mouth roved over her face before he said, "I don't ever want to hurt you. Are you sorry?"

"Sorry I agreed to bear your child?"

"Yes."

"No. It was something I wanted too. It will be all right, Josh. We're not the first ones to do this. We'll both love the boy. You care about me and I—"

"And you?"

"I care about you." And she silently amended, *more than you'll ever know.*

"I love you," he said, so softly she wasn't sure she heard him.

With her voice trembling, she asked, "What did you say?"

"I love you. I should have said it long ago."

"And I love you," she told him in wonder. Did he mean it? Was it the passion of this time, this place? It didn't matter, her heart told her.

He pressed his face into her throat for long moments, then looked at her.

"God help me if things don't work out between us," he said, "but I'll love you and want you for the rest of my life."

With his kisses, her body grew warmer. Passion seemed to come into every cell again. She alternately tapped him lightly and stroked him. His fingers traced the lines of her face, then her body.

"We are so good together," he told her.

She was so full she couldn't speak, so she drew his mouth down to hers and kissed him, their open mouths both savoring and giving honey.

Her lightly swollen body thrilled at his touch. He turned her over to arch above him and caught her hair, lifting her lovely face above him before he brought her lips down hard on his.

"What is it you do to me?" he asked her. "I have never felt the way I feel with you."

"I'm glad," she whispered. "I feel the same way."

Shards of fear struck through him. He had once felt so much for someone else, and the betrayal and loss had emotionally gutted him. Lying there, he wanted to give this woman everything he had, but he sought to hold back. Suddenly she lavished kisses on him, and he knew that in many ways he already belonged to her, but he doubted if he would ever know the freedom to love that he'd known in the past.

He had told her he loved her. He'd said it and could never go back.

Turning her onto her back, he went deep into her and heard her soft cries beneath him. He added his own passionate sounds until they were breathless, spent, and wondrously enmeshed in each other's arms.

The next morning, Maura went to Fisherman's Wharf. Josh went to the first of two meetings with fellow builders.

Dale made her comfortable. He had gotten her a padded chair for her sitting. It was fairly crowded around them.

"I want you against the Fisherman's Wharf backdrop," he said, his eyes following her every move.

It was warm that day. She wore a natural fishnet dress over a blue linen sheath. Her blue strap-and-rope sandals were comfortable and showed off her slender feet to good advantage.

At Dale's request, she lay back in the chair and let the sharp breeze fan her. She smiled as he studied her.

"Madonna," he said softly.

"You flatter me."

"You're a great model, or at least I think you're going to be. I can usually tell early on. I wish you were here longer. Are you free tomorrow?"

"I'm supposed to go with Josh to a couple of meetings tomorrow morning. Why do you ask? You're doing a quick painting and you'll finish today, right?"

He chuckled. "I keep getting sidetracked and we've hardly begun. I see so much in you that I want to bring out. I could take a year and never show all the things I want to show."

Maura glanced at him in surprise. She didn't really have to go with Josh tomorrow. She was well-read on modular construction, which was what the meetings were about.

"I suppose I could come back tomorrow," she said. "I'll talk with Josh. Will one more day really make a difference?"

"Not the difference I want it to make, but it would help."

She shrugged. "I think he wants a good painting of me. He'll be willing to go alone."

"That would be wonderful. Now tell me if you get tired and we'll stop and go into one of the restaurants."

"Thank you. I don't tire easily."

By noon, he had a good likeness of her face and upper body. He worked rapidly and well.

"There is not enough time for the oil I want to do of you," he said, "so I'll settle for acrylic, not my best medium."

"Have you been painting a long time?"

"All my life."

"That's not a very long time."

"My mother is an artist. I'm thirty."

"A tender age. I'm thirty-two."

He studied her for a long moment. "You're so lovely," he said. "I'd like to do many portraits of you. I'd love to paint you as your pregnancy progresses. You're going to be even more beautiful."

Maura gave a little gasp of surprise. "Thank you," she said softly.

By midafternoon, he was more than halfway through the painting.

"I'm thinking of your comfort," he said, "and I'm hurrying, which doesn't let me do my very best. But I think you will like it."

"May I see the painting?"

He shook his head. "No. I want you to be pleasantly surprised."

They ate a light lunch of stuffed flounder. The little restaurant was dim and cool. He told her a lot about his life and asked about hers, and she smiled inwardly, wondering what he would think of the bargain she and Josh had struck that was starting to turn out very well.

Going home, in the air over San Francisco, Maura felt as if she were leaving a friend.

"We have to come back," she said, as Josh took her hand. It was night and they were high up in the firmament. Maura had a window seat and found the star-laden sky beautiful.

"The painting of you is lovely," Josh said. "I can't wait to get him to do an oil version."

"You're next."

"Why can't we have him do one of us together?"

"Good idea." He leaned back, a beatific expression on his face. "As much as I missed having you with me at the meetings, I got everything accomplished I wanted to. This has been a great trip."

"I couldn't agree more." Maura found herself thinking of the night they had spent in each other's arms. He hadn't gone back to his room that night and she blushed, thinking of the splendor of what they had known together. His eyes rested on her, and he smiled roguishly. He, too, was remembering that night.

"I want to come back here on our delayed honeymoon," he told her. "We'd spend at least two weeks."

"Oh, yes," she responded, her heart singing with joy.

Seventeen

Two mornings later, Maura sat in her home office leafing through some drawings of the Midland Heights project. She nibbled on a ham and cheese croissant. If she had her way, Midland Heights was going to be a marvelous feather in her cap.

It seemed almost a dream that Josh had said he loved her, but he had. She hugged his words of love to her heart and was happier than she had ever been.

She picked up her cell phone on the first ring. Dr. Smith had told her to get in the habit of picking it up on the second ring; he wanted her under as little stress as possible.

Odessa's rich contralto voice came through. "How was Frisco? I've been in South Carolina. Mike said you two were back."

"Superb. And, as you know, they brag that only out-of-towners call it 'Frisco.' Natives like 'San Francisco.' "

Odessa chuckled. "Whatever. Sounds like you're going over to their side. My cousin called me in South Carolina to sing your praises. He thinks you're an artist's dream."

"Pregnant and all."

"Somehow it adds to your allure for him. He painted you?"

"Yes, and it's a really lovely painting, but he swears he can do one that will eclipse this one by many miles. We're going back soon, Dessa. We've got to. Maybe the four of us can go."

"Don't tempt me. I've had a wonderful time every time

I've gone to San Francisco. They're some pleasantly far out people."

"And some very nice ones. You're picking me up around one for that ball planning meeting?" Maura asked.

"Yes, ma'am. We'll traipse over to Carter's mansion and meet with the false Queen Bee, Melodye, and with the *real* Queen Bee, Grandmother Addie. I have all kinds of ideas to bring to the table."

"So have I. It's going to be hard spending two hours or more in the room with, as you say, the false Queen Bee."

"Never mind her. Dale really complimented you."

"He's kind."

"He sounds smitten, to me. But that's too bad because you and Josh have it all together. Love bugs."

Maura sat down. "I'm glad you think so. We've got a lot going for us, I'd say."

"Not to mention a little bambino on the way. Dale calls you his madonna. He says you were a real inspiration. And he's not a flighty guy. He says himself you were like a bolt out of the blue, that he's never had an attraction quite like this before. He laughed, you know, and said he realizes you're all taken and he isn't about to get out of line. But he's crazy about the painting he did of you."

"That makes three of us. Josh loves it."

"Have you hung it yet?"

"Josh insisted we get it hung right away. Dale wants to paint Josh, or rather I want him to paint Josh."

"My cousin, the artist. Listen, honey, I've got to run. I'll pick you up at one."

Trina Ware, Maura's newly hired part-time assistant, came into the room.

"Should I get the package together to send to have the large-scale model made up for Midland Heights?"

"Yes. And it's too early to ask, but how do you like working here so far?"

"Two weeks," Trina said, "and I love it. It's the best first job I could have. You know, I want to be an architect."

"You've changed your mind about being an English professor?"

"Yes. Just since I've been here. I thought about it a lot in high school, but every minute I'm getting closer to deciding on architecture."

Maura looked at the small, very dark-skinned, and very beautiful young woman. Eighteen, a recent high-school graduate, and a darned good assistant, she got more done in her part-time role than most assistants did full time.

Maura finished her croissant and blue cohosh herbal tea and went out into the living room. She stood before the painting, admiring it. Dale had said he wanted to paint her in a fabulous ballgown, adding, "Not that you need the trappings of beauty. I could paint you in sackcloth and ashes and you'd be lovely."

She thought about his merry face and smiled. She drew in a sharply passionate breath when she thought about Josh and that special night in San Francisco. She still felt a glow from that night of love.

She answered her door chimes to find Papa Isaac standing there. Throwing her arms around him, she kissed him on the cheek.

"Ah, I'm glad to see you, and I've got something for you."

Papa Isaac kissed her cheek. "You wouldn't be you if you didn't have a gift for me."

"Would you like to come back to my office?"

"Sure. What have we got here?"

He paused before the painting. "It's a good one."

Papa Isaac studied the painting with its acrylic sheen and its pastel colors. Maura's lovely face looked slightly wistful and happy.

"This man can paint!" Papa Isaac said.

"He's a nice man, too. He's Odessa's cousin."

"You don't say. It's a small world."

"And getting smaller. Oh, Papa Isaac, you've got to go to

San Francisco with us at least once. You look so happy, I haven't asked how you're feeling."

"Better every day. I'm on my way out to the farm to check on that winter squash. I've got a lot of orders from DC restaurants. Carl's doing a good job. He's kept things going."

"How's Lona?"

She could have sworn he blushed. "She's fine. As up to snuff as usual. She's a good woman. She's been good for me, I know. I think I've gotten better faster because of her."

"Be sure you tell her so."

"I already have."

Maura's present to Papa Isaac was in a desk drawer. He opened the package and a big smile spread across his face.

It was an antique gold pocket watch.

"It's the cat's whiskers!" he exclaimed.

Trina came in. "Hello, Mr. Allen. Can I get you coffee or anything?"

"Well, now, I could surely use some of that Colombian coffee you served me when I was over last time. Maura got me a big pack, and it's about gone. And I'll take a doughnut if you've got one handy."

"I think we're out of doughnuts," Maura said. "But we've got some great apple crisps."

"That's even better. D'you see the wonderful present my granddaughter brought me?"

He held the watch up for Trina to see.

"It's beautiful," Trina said.

Trina went to the kitchen and Papa Isaac walked around the room. Looking at the photograph of Fallingwater, he put his hands behind his back.

"So many people," he said, "making the world a better place to live."

"And you're one of them," Maura said.

"So're you."

Trina brought in the coffee and apple crisp on a tray and set it on a table near the window. Papa Isaac sat down, took a bit of apple crisp, and sipped his coffee.

"Must be hard on you giving up coffee."

"It certainly is, but we want the healthiest baby possible."

"How's he coming? Kicking like everything?"

"You'd better believe it. This kid."

"He knows what a good life is planned for him."

Maura touched his cheek.

"With you as a great-grandfather."

"And Josh and you as parents. Lucky youngun. I think you and Josh make a great pair. He's a fine man, Maura. Never lose sight of that."

Somberly, Maura said, "No, I won't." She veered abruptly with the conversation. "You know, next spring or summer I'll be selling my land to the Midland Heights project. That will make a substantial payment on what we borrowed from Josh. Oh, I know he told you he doesn't want it paid back, but I want to. You took care of me. I want to take care of you."

He looked at her cell phone on the desk.

"I've been hearing on TV and reading as how these cell phones may cause cancer, so you be careful."

Maura looked up and nodded. "I've been hearing and reading about that, too. I'm using mine less."

He smiled. "You and me. We always were on the same line."

At the ball-planning meeting in the conference room at Carter's magnificent house, Grandmother Addie greeted Odessa and Maura.

"You're the first guests here," she said. "You both look lovely."

"We don't hold a candle to you," Maura said, and Odessa concurred.

Grandmother Addie smiled. "You wouldn't say that if you hadn't come over yesterday and fixed my hair," she said to Odessa. "Thank you again."

She patted her expertly coiffed snow-white hair and fingered the small diamond ear-clips, looking down approvingly at her bright blue damask dress.

Melodye came in and looked around. "Well, I'm glad you ladies could make it. Three more people and we begin. I saw Rhea Fillmore pulling in. That only leaves Mavis and Carole and we can get our show on the road. I've got a scrumptious luncheon coming up."

"It was ordered yesterday," Grandmother Addie said dryly. "I took the time to find out all you ladies' favorite dishes."

Frustrated, Melodye looked sharply at Grandmother Addie. The old lady, she thought, never gave her a break. What did they care who ordered the luncheon? Couldn't Grandmother Addie ever move aside for her?

A maid shepherded in Rhea Fillmore. Melodye kissed her cheek.

"How gorgeous you look, as always," Rhea told Melodye. For a moment, Rhea said nothing to the other three, then she smiled widely and disarmingly.

"Of course, you all look lovely, but Melodye somehow just always seems to steal everybody else's thunder. You're looking well, Mrs. Pyne," she said to Grandmother Addie.

Melodye did indeed look lovely in her black cashmere suit and gold jewelry, but Maura, in her pale fuchsia maternity outfit, and Odessa, in her off-white boxy suit, looked equally lovely.

Melodye smirked. "You say 'Mrs. Pyne.' You know there are *three* Mrs. Pynes in the room, Rhea," she said, exchanging a conspiratorial smirk with the woman.

Grandmother Addie pulled her glasses onto her nose and said airily, "Only one has the man to go with the name."

For a moment, Melodye's mouth twisted with anger, then she carefully arranged her features into a smile.

Carole Jones was ushered in, then Mavis Bradford, and the group was complete. Grandmother Addie was chairman of the committee to oversee the Crystal Lake Winter Ball to be held in January.

Each woman kissed Grandmother Addie's cheek, told her how lovely she looked, and complimented the other women.

Before they sat down, Rhea said, "I was almost late. I ran into Rafe Sampson, and he began to go on about the Theena legend and how he hadn't heard her crying in more than a year. I couldn't help asking him if he really believed that foolishness."

"Well, strange things do happen in this world," Grandmother Addie broke in. "I've seen what looked like a ghost to me. I wouldn't say it couldn't happen."

Rhea's tan skin flushed. "He's just so tiresome, always talking about Theena. Has anybody else heard her?"

Carole said slowly, "He's talked to me about Theena. . . ."

"He talks to everybody about her," Rhea said. "I wish he'd stop it."

"I don't mind," Carole said. "He told me it's been more than a year since he's heard her. That was just after . . ."

Carole broke off, flushing. She had been about to say it was just after the Iverson girl jumped, but she thought about the fact that Rhea's son was said to have gotten the girl pregnant and dumped her.

"Well, ladies," Grandmother Addie said, wheeling her chair up to the long, polished mahogany table with pads, pencils, ballpoint pens, and other useful paraphernalia at each woman's place setting. A smaller table was set for lunch. "Shall we begin lunch first?" Grandmother Addie asked.

The ladies sat down to a light snack as a maid pushed in a cart with coffee, tea, hot chocolate, doughnuts, and blueberry muffins.

"What shall I get for you, Mrs. Pyne?" the maid asked.

"Some of that strong, strong coffee. I suppose you've gone off coffee, my dear," Grandmother Addie said, nodding at Maura.

"Dr. Smith has forbidden me," Maura said, "and, frankly, coffee no longer tastes good to me."

After the maid had served Grandmother Addie her coffee, the other women served themselves.

"I don't know how I'd ever give up coffee," Melodye said. "Talk about sacrifices. And the first thing to go is the figure." She glanced maliciously at Maura.

"The figure doesn't matter," Grandmother Addie said, "in the face of something as glorious as having a child. My husband always said he loved me more than anything when I was pregnant."

"But you only had the one son," Melodye said, "Josh's father."

Grandmother Addie looked down and hesitated. "Oh, I had twins before Carter. They died when they were three days old. I don't talk about them, except to special people."

Their lunch was small bowls of New England clam chowder, rich with cream and loaded with succulent clams, then wonderfully juicy roast beef, baby lima beans, corn and a big green salad. Dessert was cherry tarts with whipped cream.

Maura made a mental note to go back to the kitchen and congratulate the Pynes' cook. She ate well, but the doctor had warned her against gaining too much weight.

With their lunch finished, the women turned to the business at hand. There were colorful brochures outlining the ball, but before they began, Grandmother Addie asked for a moment of silence to pray.

"Oh, Lord," she began, "help us to realize and be thankful for what you have bestowed upon us, and help us to share with those who are less fortunate. Amen."

Finishing, she held up a brochure. "This is a great job, Maura, as always. If everything turns out well, we'll have another beautiful ball this year. Mavis, how are things going with your group?"

A homemaker whose husband was a school custodian, Mavis looked up. "Very well. Mrs. Pyne, we're awfully grateful that you always include the less influential members of the community in on this ball . . ."

Grandmother Addie held up her hand, her diamonds flashing fire.

"No more of that, Mavis. God made us all, and some of us just got lucky. I would be the first to tell you that sometimes money counts for very little. It's love and respect we need so badly. This is the third year I've worked with you on this project, and every time you've come through like a trouper. And do call me Grandmother Addie."

"Thank you." The small, brown woman smiled. "I'll always do my best, and my workers are with me one hundred percent. We'll have food this year that will outdo anything we've seen before."

"Splendid. Now, Maura, you're handling the entertainment. What great things are you dreaming up?"

Maura thought a moment and looked at her notes. "We've got two bands," she said, "since a lot of our young people have expressed an interest this year. Our own Rich Curry's group, Love'n Us, will play, and I've engaged a dance band from DC, Masters of Music. We have old-fashioned games for the more mature and a separate dance floor for the teens and younger adults. I'm going to make a complete list after I've gotten all your input."

"Sounds delightful," Grandmother Addie said, "but, then, I expect the best from all of you and I'm sure I'll get it."

"Odessa, you're so quiet," Grandmother Addie said. "Is there anything wrong?"

Odessa shook her head, smiling. "No, I feel quite well. I'm just in awe of this beautiful house, and"—she grinned inpishly—"your magnificent presence."

Grandmother Addie blushed. "Come around more often, my dear. You and the house complement each other."

Carole was in charge of the building and coatroom, and reported that she had engaged three hatcheck girls.

The ball was to be black tie, and spirits were high as the women discussed the event.

"Have you forgotten about me?" Melodye asked, petulantly. "Or have you just saved the best for last?"

"You're hardly forgettable, my dear," Grandmother Addie said, evenly. "How're the invitations going?"

"Splendidly." She held up an engraved invitation. "I'm spending more than I should, but I believe in quality, and so many of the people I have invited are top quality."

Grandmother Addie fixed her with a stare. "*Every* guest is top quality, Melodye. Every single one. Don't you know that by now?"

Melodye drew in a quick breath and looked down, frowning, then laughed shortly. "Oh, you know the old quote about some being more equal than others."

"Not in God's world that I inhabit," Grandmother Addie said, sharply. Then, "Do you have notes to share with us?"

"I'm afraid not. I'll run them by you later."

"We're working together on this," Grandmother Addie said. "I want all the ladies to know what you're planning. And they can give you good advice, I'm sure."

"Of course," Melodye murmured. "I'll see that you ladies get all my notes."

"This is a ball on the theme of bringing us together—all of us—who live in Crystal Lake," Grandmother Addie declared. "As more and more people move in, we're separating into widely divided cliques. We've had much less of this before. I think Crystal Lake is a great city to live in because we've tried to be inclusive rather than exclusive. What do you ladies think?"

Each woman murmured assent and Grandmother Addie went on, "Crystal Lake could be one of the best cities on earth. Just as this ball helps to pull us together, there are so many other things we can do."

She looked at Melodye. "Let our hearts overflow with love. And in the Christmas season that precedes this event, let us resolve to have a splendidly humanistic season that spills over into the ball. Are we game, ladies?"

Each woman gave assent and only Melodye looked a little bored by it all.

Grandmother Addie cleared her throat. "I've made arrangements with a consignment shop in the district. If there is any woman who feels she can't afford a simple ballgown, I've made arrangements for her to get one there. Maura, I wish you'd look after this for me. You'll be good at this kind of thing. Just see that anyone who wants to come gets there. Will you?"

"I certainly will." Maura nodded. Delight in planning this ball was seeping into her every cell. But, then, there was delight in all the world. Josh loved her.

Eighteen

That same night, Maura mulled over the winter ball meeting. Grandmother Addie certainly had paid her a lot of attention. The old woman was so sweet.

Maura had come home after the meeting and gone to work on plans for Midland Heights. What an addition this was going to be for Crystal Lake.

Josh called to say he'd be late coming home. He had a meeting with Carter and the two men from Mexico who wanted to buy the old Halaby plantation plots. Maura reflected that she wouldn't be selling them her acres, nor would Ellen sell hers. Both were promised to Midland Heights acquisition. Josh had tentatively said he'd side with Maura. That left Carter. Not nearly as much land as the men wanted.

Maura got up and went to the window. The autumn leaves were gorgeous—red, green, and gold—in their well-tended yard. She walked about her office, picked up a set of plans, and began to unroll it, when a small pain sliced through her stomach. She sat down at her drawing table and waited to see if the pain recurred. After fifteen minutes, when it didn't come again, she began to move about more freely.

It had been a tiring day, she thought, and at about eight-thirty she undressed for bed. She held up the blush-pink cotton, fleece-lined gown with sheer lace inserts. It was a maternity gown Josh had bought for her. It was empire style and would be useful when she was no longer pregnant, as well.

Sitting down at her dressing table, she creamed her face, then spread a special night cream over it. Thirty-two. Bearing her first child. Looking in the mirror, she thought she looked well, and heaven knows she had never felt better. What had that twinge of pain been about?

Gingerly, she felt her stomach as the baby kicked again. "In a hurry, little one?" she asked, smiling.

She switched off the bedside table light and was dozing off when the phone rang, and Odessa's throaty voice came on the line.

"Girlfriend," Odessa said, "you did yourself proud today. My congratulations to you."

"You're talking about the meeting?"

"What else?"

"Well, you didn't do yourself any harm. I thought you came across very well."

"Thank you. Grandmother Addie is crazy about you. She doesn't seem too fond of Miss High and Mighty."

"Mrs. High and Mighty. We were reminded that there were three women in that room who bore the same surname."

"Oh, yes. But you're the one who has the good lady's heart."

"Grandmother Addie loves most people. Who else at the age of eighty-four would be fretting over a ball?"

"Right. But that's probably why she looks a lot younger. She's a people lover, all right. Most people."

"Well, let's not forget that Melodye has Carter's heart."

"Maybe they'll elope. I wouldn't put it past her."

"It's their right if they want to."

"Do you think Josh would go off if they did?"

"Why would he?"

"Oh, don't get me wrong, not from her standpoint, but I think he loves his father."

Maura shifted in bed and stroked the satiny gown. "In this world, we never know what comes next."

"Well, one thing's for certain, we're going to have a really grand ball this time around. You sound sleepy."

"Yes, I had turned in. Josh is out late." She started to mention the flash of pain a little while back, but decided against it. Odessa worried about her.

"Well, I'll say good night. I'm clipping hairstyles for mounting from Italian magazines. You'll like one of them very much, I predict."

"Next time, I want the big corkscrew curls."

"You'll look great in them. I also predict you'll turn Josh's head until he loves you even more."

"Good night, you flattering woman."

Pressing the phone gently into its cradle, Maura still felt sleepy. Her head began to hurt a little as she drifted off to sleep.

The dream came early. Josh, Melodye, and Maura were in a many-acred meadow of red clover blossoms. Melodye was dressed in a beautiful filmy lace dress, which could have served as a wedding gown. Gloating, Melodye went to Josh and took his hand. "It is Josh I want, as I wanted him in the past. It is Josh I must have again."

For long moments, Maura felt she hadn't known there was so much hurt inside her. Her heart seemed to squeeze dry as she looked at Josh. Suddenly she cried, "No! No, please don't leave me!"

Josh went toward Melodye as if he were in love with her again. Maura woke up gasping, tears coursing down her face.

"No, Josh," she said, softly. "Don't."

She sat up, reached over and switched on the light next to her bed. Glancing at the clock, she saw that it was ten-thirty.

Getting up, she felt a twinge of panic. The room spun around her, and she relaxed to go down gently, protecting her child. There was velvet darkness and she heard herself say again and again, "Josh, no!"

She came awake with Josh bending over her, calling her name.

"What time is it?" she asked.

"Thank God, you're coming to," he said, sitting on the edge of the bed. "I called Dr. Smith. He wants me to bring you to his home office. He has equipment there he needs. What time did you pass out? Do you know?"

She thought a moment. "It was just after ten-thirty."

"I got here at eleven-fifteen. Lord, Maura, I was so worried."

He smiled grimly. "I'm going to get some socks and shoes onto you and bundle you in a lap rug. Dr. Smith is waiting for us."

Dr. Smith's face bore a worried look as he ushered them into his home office. Leaving Josh in his small, cheerful anteroom, he shepherded Maura into his office and onto the examining table.

After probing for a few minutes, he asked her to sit up.

Frowning, he said, "I don't find anything wrong on the surface. I'll want you to come into my office downtown first thing in the morning. There are other tests I need to run. This is the second time you've passed out, and I want to know why."

Suddenly, his countenance brightened. "You might have the beginning of a virus. Or flu. Maura, did you by any chance turn around hurriedly?"

She thought a moment. Yes, she had gotten up suddenly and turned toward the door, just as she had the first time she'd fainted.

Dr. Smith expelled a long breath. "I think you might be developing inner-ear trouble. How do you feel now?"

"Much, much better. I fell as gently as I could to protect my baby."

"Wise move. Are you nauseous?"

"No. I kind of felt myself sliding along the edge of the bed. It broke my fall."

"Has this happened before the last time and now? Even a long time ago?"

Maura thought a long moment. "Once when I was in my late twenties. Thinking about it now, I did turn suddenly then and passed out. I hit my head on the wall and fell over a telephone. That's the only time I can remember. The doctor found nothing wrong."

Dr. Smith patted her back. He didn't think her fainting a while back had any connection to this.

"I'm not going to give you any medication. Just drink a cup of valerian tea if you can't sleep. That should do it. How're you coming with the herbal blue cohosh tea?"

"Fine. I drink a couple of cups daily and I feel really good. I was shocked to find myself fainting."

He nodded, "I'll test you for inner-ear trouble."

He looked at her quizzically. "I'd like to talk a bit with you and Josh, if you feel up to it."

In his small office, Dr. Smith sat opposite Maura and Josh.

"Is everything going well with you two? I don't mean to pry, but first babies can bring on a raft of problems. Would you say you have a comfortable relationship?"

Both held their breath, blushing, then Maura spoke, "Splendidly."

She and Josh smiled at each other, their glances locking.

The doctor grinned. Nothing wrong here. "Well," he finally said, after a few more questions, "you've got the list of herbs I want you to take, and continue to drink fresh-squeezed orange juice and V-8 juice daily. Eat well. You're a professional woman. I don't have to tell you how that can affect your energy level. Get plenty of rest and sleep."

His voice went lower, warm in its intensity. "I don't have to tell you either that these are some of the most precious moments in your life. You're shepherding in a new creation here. Enjoy this time of your life. Glory in it."

Josh nodded. "Believe me, we are," he said.

Two days later Maura saw the ear, eyes, nose and throat specialist who examined her carefully.

"Let's hope you don't have Meniere's disease," he said thoughtfully. "It's serious and passing out is one of the manifestations of it."

Probing carefully, he frowned. "Did you know that one of your eardrums is underdeveloped?"

"No, I didn't."

"It isn't likely to give you trouble, but you should be aware of it. It can be enlarged. Ah yes, I think I see the trouble here. There's an infection."

He beamed then, loading the swinging arm small table attached to the examination chair.

"We can nip this in the bud," he said, putting a powder atomizer nozzle into her ear.

When he was done, he said gently, "Please come back and let me check this again in a week or so. If this doesn't work— and I think it will—I have other nostrums."

Nineteen

The mid-January Crystal Lake Winter Ball came all too soon for Maura. There had been no further trouble with dizziness, and she was careful not to turn suddenly.

The Crystal Lake College gym was beautifully decorated in a winter wonderland theme of crystal icicles, poinsettias, and bunches of mistletoe. Faux snow was sprinkled everywhere.

As the Masters of Music played a fifties tune, a few couples were on the dance floor.

"You look gorgeous," Josh told Maura, as he had done before they left the house.

"And you are a walking advertisement for tuxedos."

"Thank you, ma'am. Pale yellow is one of your best colors, but you look good in anything."

"Thank you." Maura looked down self-consciously at her pale-yellow silk, empire-style dress that covered her ever-growing pregnancy well.

"Remember these?" she asked, touching the twenty-two-carat gold and yellow-diamond necklace and dangling earrings.

"They're my first ever Christmas gift to you, and you flatter them."

"You spoil me."

"And I intend to do more."

Maura thought she looked well, but she felt top-heavy and awkward.

Carter came in the far door, wheeling Grandmother Addie. They came straight to Josh and Maura.

"Oh, my dear, you look lovely." Grandmother Addie beamed her approval. Dressed in dark-blue velvet that set off her white hair, she twinkled in her diamond tiara, necklace, and rings.

Maura went to kiss Grandmother Addie, who then kissed Maura's cheek.

"You're going to be the most beautiful woman here tonight, except for my wife, Grandmother," Josh said.

Grandmother Addie laughed, saying to Maura, "I raised him to say all the right things, didn't I?"

"You did, you know," Maura replied.

For a moment, Grandmother Addie looked wistful. "Listen to that music. They're masters, all right. The one thing I've missed in the past few years is dancing." Her eyes lit up. "But I still dance in my imagination. Oh, how I dance!"

Looking at the woman, Maura had a sudden vision of her as a girl, a young woman, and in all the stages of her life. If Maura were to bear a girl in the future, she would want to name her for Grandmother Addie.

"My dear, you're lost in a wondrous daze. As they say these days, Hello!"

"I was just thinking, I guess, about you."

"About me? Tonight is for enjoyment. Entertainment. No deep thinking permitted. Well, I see our fellow board members drifting toward us. Are we ready for them?"

Maura followed Grandmother Addie's gaze to where Rhea came up with Carole and Mavis, two the other ball directors.

"Are we ready to strut our stuff, ladies? Show them how to give a ball?" Grandmother Addie inquired.

"We've set it up," Rhea answered. "Aren't the decorations beautiful?"

"Yes," Grandmother Addie said. "And that band sounds wonderful."

Odessa approached, touched Grandmother Addie's cheek, and hugged Maura.

"You do look splendid, girlfriend," she told Maura.

"What I feel is six months pregnant."

"Oh, that," Odessa said, laughing. "Three more little months will take care of that."

"But the ball is tonight."

"Count your blessings, girl. You're glowing and you've got that soft, soft look that goes with a happy pregnancy."

Carter had stayed close to his mother's side, saying little before he said to Josh, "I wonder what's holding up Melodye."

"I haven't a clue," Josh said dryly. "I'm sure she'll be on soon enough."

As if by magic, Melodye swept in, leaving a trail of muted wolf whistles. Dressed in a black panne satin gown and emeralds that set off her pale skin and dark-auburn hair, she was supremely sure of herself.

"Well, of course I had to be late," Melodye said, laughing gaily. "You all look so elegant. Maura, I'd never have thought you could find a gown to hide your pregnancy so well."

"I could never hide it, even if I wished to, which I don't," Maura said, mildly.

Grandmother Addie gave Maura the A-OK sign.

"Pregnancy is one of a woman's best times." Josh put his arms around Maura. "They don't come any more beautiful than this."

"If you say so," Melodye murmured. She smiled at Josh and sent him a flirtatious look. "You always did know what to say. You're a chip off the old block."

Now, she turned her wiles onto Carter, who demurred. "Honey-tongue was never my strong suit," Carter said. "I've always been too busy with other things."

"Which explains your outrageous success," Melodye complimented him.

Carter held out his hand. "*You* always know what to say. Would you like to dance?"

He led her away and Grandmother Addie scoffed. "Trust her to waltz off when the group of us is gathered and we need to put the finishing touches on our ball. By the way, Mavis, Rhea, Odessa, and Carole, you all look so lovely in your gowns. Mavis, velvet is one of my favorite fabrics."

"Thank you. My daughter helped me make this dress."

Grandmother Addie raised her eyebrows. "She did you proud, but that dress must have taken up a lot of your time. You could have gotten a dress on me." She held up her hand. "Never mind. They could sell you nothing finer than you have there. Give your daughter my compliments."

Mavis left them to supervise the elaborate catering setup. She smiled. Trust Mrs. Pyne to pay the heartfelt compliment. She wished her daughter could have come with her, but she had to work.

The city was well represented at the ball. For the past ten years, under the stewardship of Grandmother Addie and her fellow directors, the Crystal Lake Winter Ball had become one of the most enjoyable affairs of the year. When Grandmother Addie had taken over, the event had been much smaller and only for those considering themselves the town's elite and a few middle-income inhabitants.

Grandmother Addie had changed all that. She made it known that all were invited if they were willing to abide by the rules and regulations. Oddly enough, it grew to be a lovelier ball, with none of the hard drinking and occasional highbrow scuffles that had gone on in the past.

After Mavis returned and Melodye came back from dancing with Carter, the directors of the ball huddled and exchanged notes.

Now, the gym was beginning to fill with revelers. Crystal Lake College was well represented. And more young people were in attendance than the party planners had thought would be there.

Maura walked over to the bandstand where Masters of Music rested between sets.

"How have you liked our music?" the young bandleader asked.

"I've heard you before," she said. "I've always thought you top-notch, Mr. Masters. Congratulations on your new CD release."

"Thank you. Call me Lenny, please."

"And will you call me Maura? Mrs. Pyne is very pleased with your music."

"Ah, yes, the stately queen," he said.

"That's Grandmother Addie. Please go by and say hello to her, will you?"

"I'd be delighted."

Going back to Grandmother Addie, Maura stopped to talk with Fairen and Lance Carrington.

Fairen smiled. "You remind me of myself when I carried my own little love a year ago," she said.

"Enjoy this time," Lance counseled Maura. "I think you'll look back on it as one of the most precious times of your life."

The band started again with the old favorite, popularized by Nat King Cole, "Nature Boy." A number of older couples went out on the dance floor, dancing closely, enjoying the music of yesteryear.

Josh came up and greeted the Carringtons.

"How's Dave?" Josh asked, inquiring about Lance's father.

"He's doing really well," Lance answered.

"You don't know how glad I am that you decided to stay here," Josh said. "For my money, you all add a whole lot to this burg."

"Thanks. Those are my thoughts where you're concerned."

"Are you enjoying your professorship at Crystal Lake College?"

"Wherever I can study stars. I might as well be content, because my father will never be happy anywhere else."

"Could we get together for dinner sometime?" Maura asked.

"Just call me, or I'll call you and we'll set a date," Fairen replied.

Fairen and Lance danced away and Maura went into Josh's arms.

"The greatest thing," Maura began, following the music, "really is just to love and be loved in return."

Josh smiled and they danced in silence, with her cheek nestled against his.

"Believe me, I know you deserve more than I can give you," Josh said softly, holding her closer. "Watching you grow heavier with my child, listening to you as you support me in everything I want to do . . ."

"You support me beautifully and I'm grateful."

"It's not a drop in the bucket when I compare what I do for you with what you do for me. Maura, I think I've managed to show you how much I care, haven't I?"

"Yes. I believe you care about me. You're a very kind man."

Josh shook his head. "That isn't enough. I feel so much more for you."

His voice drifted off and she leaned back and looked at him. His face was set, almost harsh. He loved her but he was still afraid.

"Perhaps with time," she began.

"What are you saying?"

"Nothing. Josh, let's enjoy the ball. We love each other. We'll see it through. I'm not unhappy. Are you?"

He drew her close and kissed her eyes. "But you're not happy either. I see the sadness on your face sometimes. I'm happier than I've been in many moons. You don't know how much I wish it could all be different for us."

Maura placed her finger against Josh's lips. "Hush! I am happier than you know." She broke off, exclaiming, "Whoa!"

"I guess we both know what that is. I felt it."

"He's dancing with us," Maura said, laughing. "This is going to be some kid."

Being in Josh's arms felt good to Maura as she snuggled against him, the night in San Francisco filling her mind.

The set ended, and they went back to Grandmother Addie, who sat with Carter and Ward and Rhea Fillmore.

The mayor was psychically onstage as usual. "I'd say you

ladies put together a magnificent ball. I know my wife has worked extremely hard."

Rhea beamed. "I'm always happy to do anything to make Crystal Lake the place we all want it to be."

Their son, Lonnie, came up. Maura gave him a cool glance.

"Dad, I'd like a word with you."

The mayor nodded and stepped aside.

"I'm going to leave for a while," the youth said.

"That's hardly the outfit in which to be riding a motorcycle," his father told him, glancing at his tuxedo.

Lonnie shrugged. "I get restless, Dad. You know that. I'll be back in a short while."

"Why would you need to leave?"

"I've got a few matters to take care of."

"Mind telling me what?"

"Dad, I'm nineteen, not seventeen."

Mayor Fillmore's eyes on his son were anxious, frustrated. "You needed me when you were seventeen. Remember? You need me and your mother at nineteen."

Lonnie shook his head stubbornly. "I've got to make my own way someday. Might as well start now."

Mayor Fillmore rubbed the side of his face and saw his wife's anxious glances at him and their son.

"I've asked you this before," the mayor said, his voice catching in his throat, "Are you on drugs?"

Lonnie shook with laughter deep in his throat. *Define 'on drugs,'* he thought. Marijuana was a substance he didn't count as a drug. One day he might do a graduate course in the hard drugs, but for right now—

"No way, Dad," the boy said evenly. "Trust me, okay? I won't go out except for a bit of fresh air. I'm restless, planning my future. I'm going to make you and Mom proud of me."

Mayor Fillmore patted his son's back. "Get some fresh air, son, and take care of whatever business you need to." He winked broadly at his son. "No more knocking up some silly goose of a girl though, *if* you did that to the Iverson girl."

"Ah, Dad, I wasn't the only one."

The mayor's eyes narrowed. He wanted to believe in his son, he *would* believe in his son. The boy was all he and Rhea had, and if they spoiled him, well . . .

As the mayor walked back to the group he had stepped away from, Rich Curry joined them. He complimented the women in the group and slapped Josh's back.

"Where's Ellen?" Maura asked.

"She's in one of the dressing rooms rehearsing a new song we wrote. Odessa's with her."

"My friend has got her hands full tonight," Maura murmured.

"I think we'll give you a good show. The other dance floor is going to be packed with young ones."

"You speak for yourself," Grandmother Addie quipped. "Time was when I would have been out there with your music. Love'n Us. I've heard some of your recordings and your group is good."

Onstage, Carter took the microphone, one arm around Melodye's shoulders.

"May I have your attention?" he asked. "I have an announcement to make."

The crowd grew silent.

"Please congratulate me on taking as my wife the most beautiful woman in the world." His voice rose to an impassioned embrace. Then he pulled Melodye into his arms and kissed her.

When he let her go, she took the microphone and cooed to the audience. "I'm the one who should be congratulated. I've got as my husband the most wonderful man in the world."

They kissed again.

"Oh, good Lord!" Grandmother Addie scoffed, her hand over her heart.

"We were married in Aruba, and soon I'll be throwing a celebration that will rival this one to celebrate our union."

Josh looked stunned, then laughed. "He's got to be out of his mind."

Maura squeezed his hand. "Does it matter to you?"

"No. Not really. It just comes as a shock."

But Maura thought he looked somber. He had said he loved Maura and she believed him.

People thronged to congratulate the newlyweds and Carter felt that he was on top of the world.

Finished rehearsing, Ellen looked over at Maura's group and hesitated. She wanted to speak to Grandmother Addie, but she didn't want to be in the group with the mayor and his wife. They had savaged her once to save their son; she wasn't going to give them a chance to do it again. As she focused on the people in front of her, but a distance away, Lonnie walked up and put his arms akimbo.

"Well, don't you look a sight," he said.

Ellen looked down at her black cashmere turtleneck sweater and tight black leather pants. She tossed back her hair and set the gold hoop earrings swinging. She said nothing.

"I guess your group is going on after the buffet," he said.

Still Ellen said nothing.

Lonnie grinned. He enjoyed taunting her. "Cat got your tongue?"

"I have nothing to say to you," Ellen said evenly. "And that's what I'm saying."

"Like the bitch you are."

Ellen's face turned blazing hot, and Lonnie nearly closed his eyes, laughing.

"I'm leaving for now," he said, "but I *will* be back. I'm even going to dance to your music. I'm especially going to dance to your music."

He turned on his heels and walked away, leaving Ellen so angry she gasped for breath.

Frowning, Rich saw the conversation from where he stood. Lonnie was quickly gone, so it couldn't be too bad. He hoped the young fool didn't make a scene before the night was over. If he did hassle Ellen, Rich meant to deal with him.

As the ballgoers prepared to break for the buffet, Melodye came up and extended her arms to Carter.

"Dance with me, husband?"

"Hey, I'm an old guy and I'm winded." Looking proud, he commanded Josh, "Dance with her, Josh. Do me a favor."

More people had come up when Melodye extended her arms to Josh.

"Dance with me at least once?"

Josh felt a flash of anger at his father for putting him in this position. He didn't want to humiliate his father and Melodye, and he surely didn't mean to humiliate his wife. He turned to Maura. "Do you mind, sweetheart?"

Maura shook her head. "No," she said. "Not at all."

"As a matter of fact," the mayor said, "I've wanted all evening to ask young Mrs. Pyne to dance." He laughed. "All these Mrs. Pynes . . ."

Josh smoothly danced Melodye onto the dance floor, with Melodye pressing her body close to his. They made quite a couple. Maura told herself she wouldn't stare at them. The mayor bowed in front of her, and she let him lead her onto the dance floor.

"What did you have in mind?" Josh asked Melodye. "We haven't danced in a very long time, and I'd just as soon we never did again. Oh, yes, congratulations."

"Oh, Josh," Melodye said, pouting. "Must we be enemies forever? I'm going to make Carter happy. He loves me."

"But do you love him?"

Melodye shrugged and didn't answer.

Hard words came in a rush to Josh's lips. "Melodye, I'm not going to ruin my life with never forgiving you, but I'd be lying if I said I thought I could ever forget."

What he said didn't seem to affect her. "You can't forget me. We were in love, darling. Surely you haven't forgotten that?"

"Just dance, Melodye, and shut up."

They were near the admittance door. "I'm sorry, Josh," Melodye said contritely. "I shouldn't play games with you. Life hasn't been exactly kind to me since we broke up."

"I'm sorry. Maybe you're not being kind to life."

Suddenly, Melodye's face paled. "I feel faint," she said. "Come outside with me for a breath of fresh air."

"Melodye, I don't know about that."

"Please, Josh. I feel like I'm going to pass out. I've had too much champagne."

Damn it, Josh grumbled to himself, as he took Melodye outside past the security guard into the biting January air.

"You need your coat," he said, taking his off to wrap around her.

Once outside in the bracing air, she revived quickly. "I was afraid I was both going to pass out and throw up," she said.

"Well, thank God, you've done neither. Feel better now?"

She leaned against him. "Josh, would you kiss me, just once for old times' sake?"

Josh expelled a harsh breath. "Don't talk like an idiot. Were you really feeling light-headed and ill, or was this just a ploy to get me out and hurt Maura's feelings?"

"No, I swear I was on the level."

Josh doubted it. "Okay, if it was a game, it's over," he said. "We're going back inside." The security guard let them back in and Josh removed his coat from Melodye's shoulders and put it back on.

Mayor Fillmore had maneuvered Maura near the entrance where Melodye and Josh came in.

"I trust you're okay now," Josh said tautly to Melodye. "You're on your own." And he cut in on Mayor Fillmore.

"Welcome back," Maura told him, as he took her in his arms. "You're cold. I saw you put your coat back on."

"Yes, I'm cold, but I'm mad as hell, too. Melodye swore she was about to faint and felt like she might throw up."

"Oh? You don't think she was going to?"

"It wouldn't be the first time she's lied. I'm sorry. I don't want you embarrassed."

"I'm not embarrassed," she said. "I'm not a great one for worrying about what others think."

"You have so many characteristics I'm grateful for. What do you think others will think if I kissed my wife long, deep, and hard on a public dance floor?"

Maura threw her head back, her laughter pealing through the music. "You're a madman, Joshua Pyne," she said. "I want your precious kisses behind closed doors."

"A little one?"

Maura's lips were smooth and soft beneath his. It would be a perfect time, he thought, to say he loved her, and looking deep into her eyes he told her, "I'll love you forever."

Twenty

The caterers had put together a magnificent array of foods and beverages for the Winter Ball.

"My dear, you have outdone yourself with this," Grandmother Addie told Mavis. Grandmother Addie was pleased that under her tutelage the shy woman who had enjoyed few material things had blossomed into a far more effective and happy person.

Standing nearby, Rhea Fillmore flashed Mavis a cool smile. Rhea had wanted to be committee chairman for foods. Instead, she and Melodye were joint chairmen of the decorations committee. She shrugged. She enjoyed working with Melodye, who had so much class. Quality counted, she felt, no matter who said it didn't.

Walking hand in hand, Josh and Maura traversed the dance floor.

"I think it's time you sat down," Josh said. "I don't want you getting tired."

"I feel more energetic than usual. I'm having a good time."

"I won't have you overdoing it. I'll get you a plate."

"Not on your life. Only I can decide on what I want."

The bank of white damask-covered tables were festive with poinsettias; silver urns; silver pots of coffee, tea, and hot chocolate; and crystal pots of herbal teas. Big silver-covered dishes held roast chicken with sliced kiwi, ham, roast pork, roast beef, and roast lamb. Platters of raw vegetables added delightful color. Jams and jellies—mostly homemade—added a special flavor.

Maura's eyes went the length of the table. Josh took her arm. He had picked up a bunch of mistletoe and now held it over her head.

Without a word, he kissed her thoroughly as people around them clapped. She felt so precious in his arms.

"Way to go, Josh!" Mayor Fillmore said.

The mayor's wife gave them a thin smile. She didn't hold with public displays of affection.

"Walk me to the dessert tables," Maura said.

Those tables held both elegant and plain desserts that made Maura's mouth water: moist coconut and chocolate cakes; fruit-cakes; blueberry and strawberry tarts; lemon, chocolate, fruit and coconut and custard pies; and ice cream, some of it served from an old-fashioned ice cream freezer. She reminded herself not to overindulge.

"Where on earth did you finally find the freezers?" Maura asked Mavis.

"It wasn't easy, believe me. I found three freezers just the other day deep in the Appalachian region. Grandmother Addie suggested it. It's cold for this, but the ice cream made in them is out of this world. Be sure to try the vanilla bean."

"How about trying it now?"

The young man helping with the buffet dessert tables brought out a small dish and a spoon. "You're eating it before your other food?" he asked, glancing at her belly.

Maura laughed. "Pregnancy brings on strange cravings. Yes, I'll sample it now."

Josh twisted his mouth comically. "I'm not sure I approve. You need more solid food first."

The young server hesitated.

"Dip the ice cream, man," Maura said to him mockingly. "What have we here? It's only a *husband* talking." She pecked Josh on the cheek.

With a mock frown, Josh told the man, "I guess I'll let her get by with it this time since it's a special occasion."

"I like what happens between you two," Mavis said. "You have fun together. My husband and I have a lot of fun."

"She's a handful to keep on track sometimes," Josh said. "Hardheaded." And he added, "But I wouldn't take the world for her."

"You're sweet," Maura told him, lightly skimming layers of the vanilla-bean ice cream into her mouth.

"Why isn't Bert here?" Maura asked Mavis.

"Lodge meeting. They're having their annual initiation. I was so disappointed. He would have enjoyed this."

There were plates and small platters for the food. Maura selected a bit of many foods and two of the delectable Cornell homemade rolls, which included five kinds of cheeses and white potatoes. They sat down with Grandmother Addie.

Again, Mavis came to Maura and Josh and sat down. "Do you like the rolls?" she asked.

Maura took a bite. "Um-m-m. Out of this world."

"I made them."

"Did you, really? They're the best I've ever tasted."

Both Josh and Grandmother Addie said they felt the same.

"It's an old health-food recipe. My family is crazy about them. I wish I could have made enough for everyone to sample."

"I'll be selfish and say I got mine and I'm glad," Grandmother Addie said.

From the corner of her eye, Maura saw Carter and Melodye in another group, eating, and she breathed a sigh of relief. Carter looked like the cat that swallowed the canary. Holding her tray of food, Maura thought it the most delectable she had tasted lately and added to herself, it was on the level with that in San Francisco.

"You must try the vanilla-bean ice cream," Maura told Grandmother Addie.

Josh got up, setting his plate on a nearby table. "I'll get us some. Would anybody else care for ice cream now?"

The others demurred and Mavis said, "Please let me get it for her." She set her plate aside.

As Josh sat back down and Mavis walked away, Grandmother Addie said, "She's coming to be one of my favorite people. By the way, where is Odessa?"

"She's rehearsing backstage with Rich and Ellen. Here comes Mike, though."

Mike Martin came up and gave Maura a big hug. "You're looking great, girl. Love those yellow diamonds."

Josh put his thumbs in imaginary suspenders. "Compliments of me, my good man."

"Beautiful choice. I'm late because I knew my wife would be involved in other things, and I intend to stay until the very end."

"You're doing that tuxedo proud, yourself," Maura said. "This is one of their first good-size gigs. Odessa is on top of the world about now."

"When do they play?"

"For a couple of hours, just a little later. Mike, do hurry and get some of that delicious food. And whatever you do, don't pass up the vanilla-bean ice cream."

Josh pursed his lips. "If I had a product, I'd want you to plug for it. And my compliments to you for the entertainment. It's splendid. Mavis, you make a great food chairperson."

Papa Isaac and Lona came a little late. Papa Isaac was resplendent in his tux, and Lona wore a beaded lavender gown. Grandmother Addie claimed them immediately.

There were compliments all around and Grandmother Addie said wistfully, "Remember how we used to dance, Isaac? You were a young man when I began dancing with you."

Papa Isaac looked at her with affection. "I could never forget," he said.

"Now, you dance with Lona. Whirl her the way you used to whirl me. I'll watch the two of you and dream."

"We'll be back," Papa Isaac said, leading Lona onto the dance floor.

They danced over to Josh and Maura, as Josh led Maura in a lively waltz.

"My girl, you look fabulous," Papa Isaac told Maura. "You couldn't be more beautiful."

Maura blushed. "You two make a stunning couple. Lona, that gown is lovely."

"Yours is the one," Lona responded. "Those diamonds—" She shook her head.

"Josh's Christmas gift to me."

"You've got taste, man," Papa Isaac complimented him.

As Papa Isaac and Lona danced away, Josh brought Maura closer, her cheek nestled against his.

"You've made me a happy man," he told her. And, on impulse, he added, "Maura, I think one day things may change even more for us. I'm trying to get over my hurt and make it happen."

Maura leaned back in his arms. "I know you are," she said, feeling shy. There was so much she wanted from this man. And there was so much she had with him.

Josh took the podium to speak. Maura felt so proud of him.

"Ladies and gentlemen, tonight we are gathered together on what has become a special occasion, the Crystal Lake Winter Ball. We have a good town and we are going to make it a *great* town.

"We have problems that we are going to solve, needs that we are going to meet, and obstacles that we are going to overcome.

"We are striving to become a city of equals in spirit and in love and in humaneness."

Clad in a black cashmere turtleneck sweater and tight black leather pants—Love'n Us's trademark winter garb—Rafe Sampson came up, smiling.

"Mr. Sampson," Grandmother Addie exclaimed, "how sharp you look. I'm looking forward to hearing you play. I understand we're in for a treat."

"Thank you ma'am," Rafe Sampson said, shaking her proffered hand. "You're real kind. I'll do my best."

Onstage, Josh swept on. "We need the talents of everyone as we pull together and work toward the town we all deserve."

He had caught the crowd's attention and they were quiet, listening.

He kept his speech short and introduced Mayor Fillmore. The young people in the crowd got a bit restive. The mayor was noted for his long speeches. Josh whispered to him, "Keep it short, Ward."

Ward Fillmore nodded. He loved to talk, especially to a captive audience, but for the life of him there was little for him to say. Josh had covered everything of importance. Was Josh aiming to be Crystal Lake's mayor?

"Let's get back to this delicious food," the mayor ended after a brief speech, "and this splendid music."

People were deep into their food when Love'n Us came onstage in black leather and cashmere outfits, gold jewelry sparkling.

Mike sat with Maura, Mavis, Grandmother Addie, Papa Isaac, and Lona.

Rich introduced his group to the audience, and the college students and other young people whooped.

"They've got a loving audience," Mavis said.

"Looks like it," Mike agreed. He swiftly finished the last of his food and excused himself to walk over closer to the bandstand.

With his guitar strapped across him, Rich's velvet-smooth tenor flashed:

I don't need you anymore!
Don't need the lies,
Don't need the heartache.
Go on, walk right out my door.
Every vow you've made's a real fake.
Don't come back, or write, or phone.
I can make it on my own, and
I don't need you anymore!

The young members of the audience thronged onto the dance floor, fervently stomping their feet and enjoying the music.

Odessa's contralto and Ellen's sweet soprano blended perfectly with Rich's voice. Their guitars supported his and the bass guitar player and bass drummer strutted their stuff.

In an early solo spot, Mr. Sampson closed his eyes and became one with his harmonica. Wonderful ripples of melody set fire to the tune he played, and he was a man dismissing a hurtful lover in his song. The crowd went wild. A shudder of delight went through Maura as she listened.

Ellen was having the time of her life. She was with Rich and that was what mattered. She was happy for the first time in her recent past. She and Rich looked at each other often.

The group swung into a love song popularized by another current rhythm-and-blues group, and their audience loved it. It was plain that Rich and Ellen sang to each other. Odessa threw Mike a kiss from the bandstand. He went closer, proud as a peacock of his wife.

"I hope there's no trouble with all the young people," Rhea Fillmore said, as she sat with Maura, Josh, Grandmother Addie, and others, their food finished.

Grandmother Addie leaned back in her wheelchair, all but ignoring Rhea. "Mavis, my dear. That was the best repast I've enjoyed in ages. I see you know the importance of food in the human social system."

"It was wonderful of you to ask me to chair the committee." Mavis's eyes were damp.

Grandmother Addie patted her hand. "You handled this ball splendidly."

Rhea restated her earlier thoughts about young people and trouble. Now, Grandmother Addie's voice came through a trifle sharp. "Please give young people the benefit of the doubt. They deserve it."

Rhea looked down. Trouble was always just around the corner for her.

Lonnie came back into the gym. What he had under his belt

soothed him, made him feel like that much more of a man. So the hussy, Ellen, and her boyfriend and the rest of the band were performing. He had to admit they were pretty good.

Mayor Fillmore came up to his son. "You were gone a long time."

Lonnie shrugged. "You know how it is, Dad. Time just gets away."

"Get your food. It's good."

"I'm not hungry." He was full of everything that mattered, he thought to himself. *Cannabis, you're the greatest!*

Ward Fillmore walked away, sighing. Had the boy been drinking? He smelled nothing on his breath. When he reached Rhea, she looked worried.

"I'm glad Lonnie came back," she said. "Perhaps we made a mistake saying he could stay out of college a year."

"It's okay," Mayor Fillmore said. "The boy is going to be fine. I was a bit of a wild one when I was that age."

Rhea's mouth set in a hard line. "My daddy didn't want me to marry you, but we've come along just fine."

Ward Fillmore smiled and patted her hand. He started to kiss her cheek, but remembered that she didn't like public displays of affection. Hell, he grumbled, she hardly liked affection at all.

Lonnie hunkered down near the bandstand, grooving to the music. Once or twice, a student he knew from Crystal Lake College came up and spoke, but Lonnie didn't feel socially together tonight. He just felt like listening to the music, listening to the little chick jive. Had you asked him, Lonnie could not have told you why he continued to needle Ellen. He was still angry with her for going to his father about what she called "the rape." He called it "taking advantage of a lively situation." She had come on to him. He was sure of that inside himself.

Several times, Rich cut his eyes at Lonnie and Lonnie grinned. He guessed they were getting it on these days. They sure spent enough time together.

Ellen was jittery. Lonnie made her nervous. She sang in her

clear, sweet soprano with a hint of gutbucket blues. She and Rich and Odessa and the bass guitarist and bass drummer were a lively combination.

What was Lonnie up to now? Both Ellen and Rich wondered. Across the room, Maura and Josh wondered the same thing.

"He's such a jerk," Maura told Josh, not needing to identify Lonnie.

"He's probably had too much to drink."

"We decided not to serve liquor, except in the eggnog, just to avoid trouble," Maura said.

"Speaking of eggnog, I think I'll have some. Would you like me to bring you something?"

"I'll go with you. You're so handsome tonight, I have to keep my eye on you."

"You're stuck with me."

"Well, you two certainly have stuck pretty much to yourselves tonight," Melodye said, coming up with Carter.

"We prefer each other's company," Josh shot back.

Carter laughed. "Now, now. People who quarrel care for each other."

Josh didn't answer that one. Melodye smiled widely. "I don't suppose you'd like to change partners and dance again."

Josh shook his head. "No, I wouldn't, thank you."

Melodye turned to Carter, half closing her eyes. "That number they're playing, 'Losing at the Loving Game,' seems to be my signature song tonight."

"Don't get maudlin on me," Carter caught her arm. "Take it from me, you're losing at nothing. As my wife, you're a winner all the way."

But Melodye couldn't seem to tear her eyes away from Josh. They had had so much, she stood thinking, and she had thrown it all away. She liked Carter, but she still loved Josh, and she wasn't a woman accustomed to losing for good.

The eggnog was the fabulous recipe that Grandmother Addie had once clipped from a women's magazine: White House Eggnog. It was smooth and rich with vanilla-bean ice cream and heavy and light cream, several spices, and varied liquors.

"Grandmother Addie," Mavis said, "I've got to have this recipe." Grandmother Addie smiled, always delighted to bring more joy into the world.

Rich sang, "Folks say that I'm an all-time winner, but I'm losing at the loving game."

In spite of her nervousness over Lonnie, Ellen was having a ball. She murmured, "You're winning all around, my guy."

Rich smiled and, in a few minutes, when the lyrics were concluded with, "Gonna win, win, win the loving game," he kissed Ellen's cheek.

Lonnie stared at them as they played a riff on the tune. Odessa looked as if she were flying with happiness, and Mike was happy for his wife and enjoying the performance.

Something about what lay between Ellen and Rich got to Lonnie. Before Rich, she had been so sad and depressed, and Lonnie felt she was properly punished for running to his dad, tattling. Now she had moved on and he didn't like it one damned bit.

All the venom came up at once, enveloping him as he went toward the bandstand and leaned forward.

"You're a happy little bitch tonight, aren't you?" he snarled at Ellen.

She tried to ignore him. Lonnie got onstage. "Trouble with you is you've never known your place."

Ellen moved farther back onstage as Rich grated, "Knock it off, Fillmore."

"No, I won't knock it off. Who the hell does she think she is? You balling her, that makes her somebody?" He turned aside and spat.

All the times Ellen had cried in his arms about what Lonnie Fillmore had done to her crowded Rich's brain, and he lashed out, his fist connecting with Lonnie's jaw in a sharp crack.

Somebody yelled "fight," and Mayor Fillmore rushed toward

the stage as two security guards came up and helped Lonnie to his feet.

"Arrest the bastard! He hit me!" Lonnie squalled.

"You do no such thing," Mayor Fillmore said. "Don't even call the police. I'll get to the bottom of this."

"Are you all right, sir?" one of the guards asked Rich, who nodded.

By this time, Maura and Josh had come to the bandstand. Josh stepped onto it; Maura hesitated and went onstage too. She took Ellen into her arms.

"Honey, what happened?"

As Ellen began to tell her and as Josh talked to Rich, Mayor Fillmore grimly led his son away. As a member of the ball committee, Rhea needed to stay until the ball's end.

As they went toward his car, passing Lonnie's chained motorcycle, Mayor Fillmore felt choked.

"What in the hell got into you?" he raged. "Brawling that way. Can't you let that little hussy alone? Sometimes I wonder if she wasn't telling the truth."

Lonnie was silent, his jaw achy, then he muttered, "She was trying to get my dander up, kissing that bastard . . ."

"Did you, boy? Did you do what she said you did to her two years ago?" He couldn't bring himself to name the act.

"No. She came on to me. I swear, Dad."

The air was cold, bracing, but Mayor Fillmore felt a vicious headache coming on. He stopped by his car.

"I'm taking you home, and I want you to stay there. I'll come back and get someone to bring your motorcycle. Listen, boy, I run for mayor next year and I don't want you screwing up things for me. I've always been a winner, the way I want you to be. Seems to me like you're mostly losing these days."

His words—so like the song Rich and Ellen had been singing—cut Lonnie to his heart, but he was silent. He wanted to say he was sorry, but he wasn't. He wanted to fall on his father's shoulders and have him hug him the way he had almost never done. His parents were not affectionate people. Hell, he didn't need affection. He patted his side pocket. He had just what he needed in his pocket. Cannabis the great!

Lonnie had the presence of mind to say, "I'm really sorry, Dad. I don't know what got into me." There, he thought, he could apologize, make any amends necessary, with his mind full of dreams of being alone with the stuff in his pocket.

"I promise you," he said, with a contriteness he didn't feel, "it won't happen again."

They got in the car with Lonnie aching to be held, and they drove out of the parking lot. Scalding tears lay in Lonnie's eyes. He was glad his father didn't talk further because he couldn't have answered him.

Inside the gym, students crowded around the bandstand with support for Rich. They loved a fight, especially a romantic one. Rhea Fillmore had gone as close as she dared. Sick with shame over her son, she held her head unnaturally high and smiled stiffly.

The tiny Ellen took over the situation first.

"Let's get back to singing in a hurry, Rich," she said. She held out her hands as if leading the band.

Odessa hugged Maura. "You okay, little mother?"

"I am. This could have gotten really nasty."

"I wish I hadn't needed to hit him," Rich said ruefully, "but I couldn't let him treat Ellen that way. After what happened some time ago, I guess I wanted to kill him."

"It's all right, Rich," Josh said, somberly. "We all have our breaking points."

At the mike, Rich hailed the crowd. "We've got a new song we want to introduce to you, 'I'll Be in Love With You Forever.' "

Odessa grinned and told Maura, "I had a heavy hand in this one. You'll like it."

As Maura and Josh left the stage, Josh squeezed her hand.

"Cupcake," he said softly, "you didn't get too upset, did you?"

Maura shook her head. "No, but my heart does go out to

Ellen. What is Lonnie's problem? Why doesn't he let her alone?"

"I think Lonnie Fillmore is one sick kid," he said, slowly. "And if someone doesn't do something, he's going to make a whole lot of trouble for himself. Too bad that someone else will probably be involved as well."

After the ball was over, Josh drove to a place along the Chesapeake Bay that had guards at night. The water was calm, with shorelights sparkling on it. A clear night, there were millions of stars spangled across the sky as Josh and Maura watched a new moon.

In the distance, they could see a guard coming toward them. Other cars were parked, watching the magnificent scene.

"You looked so beautiful tonight," Josh said.

"You keep telling me. Do keep telling me."

Josh drew in a deep breath. More and more now, he thought, it seemed a great time to say what he once couldn't say—that he loved her. She placed a finger alongside his mouth, and he took her satiny hand in his. He was in a hell of a bind, not wanting to be hurt again and wanting her so badly, caring so much. His heart hurt with remembered pain.

He said very softly, "I'm going to try to give you everything you deserve."

Maura lifted his hand to her mouth and kissed it. Then she placed his hand on her belly.

"You've always done the best you could," she said, gently.

"Are you sorry?"

He had asked her that question so many times.

"No. I'm not sorry. I love you and you love me. I'm carrying your child. And something good has to come from this."

As his nearness made her dizzy with desire, she thought of the song the group had played, "I'll Be In Love With You Forever." She would settle for much less than that.

Twenty-one

Rich came by the next morning as Maura and Josh sat with cups of steaming herbal tea and New England clam chowder.

"Pull up a chair and I'll get you a bowl," Maura said. "That is, if you can stand something this heavy before lunch."

"It's one of my favorites," Rich said, grinning. "I could eat it anytime."

"You look worried." Josh probed his best friend's face and body language.

"Yeah, I am."

"Lonnie's father isn't going to let him press charges. Not with an election coming up and your being so active with young people in this town."

"That's not what bothers me."

When Rich remained silent for so long. Josh said, "Shoot!"

Rich took a deep breath.

"It's Ellen I'm worried about. She's been through so much and she's done it alone."

"Now, she's got you," Maura said, softly.

"You bet she's got me, and she's got you. I don't want to have to hurt Fillmore to make him leave her alone."

Rich fell silent again, then after a moment, he spoke.

"I watched Lonnie Fillmore from the time he came in. His face was malevolent from the beginning. The kid's got some mental problems, and he's out of control."

A DEEPENING
OF LOVE

Twenty-two

Maura lay propped up on the white hospital bed, her breath coming faster. It was time. Surrounded by hospital staff in masks, with Josh also in a mask, the miracle of birth was set to begin.

"Bear down," Dr. Smith told her, as Josh held her hand. "Bear down!"

Maura bore down as hard as she could. Pain shot through her with a vengeance, and she gasped and bit her bottom lip. Josh's eyes were hot with sympathy and a longing to bear some of the pain for her.

"You're doing fine. That push was great. Try to relax between pushes."

A second push and Dr. Smith exulted, "There's the head. Good going. Now, push harder."

With all her might, Maura bore down and felt shockwaves go through her, but, Lord, she felt strong and powerful. The herbs, blue cohosh, and the angelica, the daily freshly squeezed orange juice, and the V-8 juice, and her special diet, wonderful doctor, and Josh's tender care were all paying off.

For several minutes, she moved in a shadowy world, semi-blacking out from the pains of birth. Yet, she was remembering the times she had slept with Josh and the glory of it. So this was the culmination. San Francisco. The first time he had taken her in her bedroom. His passion for her, even when he could not love her, even if he could love no woman ever again. She wept for Josh as she wept for herself.

The smell of antiseptics permeated the room. In the cool darkness of her mind, she began to rally and came more fully awake again, groaning.

"Bear down harder!"

"Come on, sweetheart. You can do it!" Josh's warm voice cut through all the others, and her nails bit into his palms as he grasped her hand tighter.

They didn't know, she thought; they couldn't know the agony that mingled with the joy of childbirth. Her flesh felt blessed with love and wanting even as it hurt. How much longer would it hurt so badly?

"I'm—I'm trying," she said, and bit her lip again.

"I know you are, my darling," Josh said.

She came fully to herself and felt the savage rendering of her body. Her breasts felt full and ripe to bursting. This was a mission she would never forget; no, not if she repeated it a dozen times.

"Don't pass out on me now," Dr. Smith said. "I know it's hard, but we don't have too much further to go. Push!"

Maura pushed with everything she had in her, but it didn't seem enough. The baby's shoulders weren't coming through. Dr. Smith frowned. *Damn it,* he thought, why were these first births so often so difficult? He hated to see suffering; it was his job to alleviate it. If she could just hold out a little longer, and not pass out as new mothers sometimes did.

Maura fought to stay out of her daze, to focus. Yes, focus! So much depended on her. Josh wanted a child by her, and she was going to give him one. Focus! Bear down! Push!

With every bit of strength she possessed, she tried and kept trying. Cruel anguish cut through her body, and she cried out.

"Go ahead. Cry. Scream. It's all right. It will help."

She felt like such a coward as she screamed, "Josh! Help me!"

"I'm trying baby," he told her, tears coming into his eyes. "You don't know how I'm trying."

Her body was pierced by a dozen knives of pain now. She was being ripped apart.

Again the doctor told her what he wanted from her. Deliver this precious cargo, and now.

All their faces were wet with sweat. Sweat streamed down her body in rivulets. Oh, God, how long? She could no longer see Josh or the doctor, she was so focused on what she did. The nurse watched her carefully, but she was not aware of the nurse, was no longer aware of any of them.

"Give it all you've got," the doctor demanded. "Give it everything. Push!" he bellowed.

And this time, she went beyond what she could do, what they could help her do, and put her faith in God. "Help me bring my child into this world. Please help me, God!"

And like a small miracle, the shoulders slipped from her body and the birth canal, and the rest of the tiny body followed.

With a whoop of joy, the doctor held the infant by his heels and slapped his buttocks lightly.

"Hooray!" the doctor cried. "We've got us a fine boy!"

Both Maura and Josh wept with joy. She had done it! There were only the mopping-up operations to take care of.

A little while later, as the infant lay facedown on her body, she looked at Josh and wanted to kiss him.

"We've done it!" the doctor exulted again. "He's bigger than average. That was the problem. I'd advise you to leave for a bit, Josh. You're wrung out. I'm proud of you both."

"I can't leave now," Josh said, humbly. "I wouldn't miss a minute of this wonder."

The doctor laughed. "I never get used to it. But you might as well leave soon. I'm sedating your wife. After that long bout, she needs rest and sleep. I'm not just being an ogre. I know you want to stay, but think about her."

"She's *all* I'm thinking about."

The doctor patted Josh on the shoulder. "Get some rest and think about names."

"We've had names almost from the time we knew she was pregnant."

"You two were really looking forward to this."

"You can't imagine how much."

Maura slept hard and blissfully for a few hours. When she was small, her mother had given her an old children's book that had belonged to her grandmother, "The Bluebird of Happiness," by Maurice Materlinck, a Swiss author. It told the story of how a child had searched the world over for such a bird and had found it in his own backyard. Now Maura had her own bluebird of happiness.

"You're waking up. Good," the nurse said. "I'm going to bring you a present."

She returned a few minutes later with the baby in a cap and a blanket and put him to Maura's breast.

Maura gasped with joy as the baby blindly sought her with groping little fingers. She guided her breast into his mouth and felt him begin to nurse with fervor. She smiled.

"You will always be passionate," she told him. "You're like your father. And like me. Like Papa Isaac. And Grandmother Addie." Carter? Well, Carter was a different story.

As she bent to nuzzle her child, the door swung open and Josh came in, his arms filled with red roses, maidenhair fern, and white baby's breath.

A wide grin split Josh's face as he looked at his wife and baby. "Hello-o-o-o," he called. "Hello, life!"

"Oh, Josh, you're so extravagant," Maura said, looking at the roses.

"No. I should have gotten a couple of dozen more. I'm starting this kid off as a Romeo, in the best sense of the word."

A nurse came in. "I'll take those, Mr. Pyne, and find a vase or maybe two for them. They're beautiful."

"Yes, they are," Maura said. "It's not that I didn't mean to thank you and tell you they're beautiful. I guess I'm a bit over-whelmed."

Josh sat by the bed and lightly touched his son. "Over-whelmed," he repeated. "That makes two of us." But his face was grave. He felt a world of fear now. Yet, he had never felt so powerful. He had to help this baby grow and thrive. He and Maura.

"You look beautiful," he told her.

"Thank you."

Looking at her silken brown face and her lovely, long-lashed eyes, there was nothing he wouldn't do for her, nothing he wouldn't try to give her that she wanted.

"While I was out, I picked up a couple of things for you at your favorite boutique."

"When did you rest?"

"I'm moving on happiness. A man with a newborn son doesn't need rest. He needs something to do to use all that energy."

"What have we here?"

A happy Odessa and Mike swept into the room.

"Oh, that baby!" Odessa exclaimed. "You're giving my hus-band ideas."

"Ideas I've had all along," Mike said. "Get ready for me to be urging you."

"I think I'm ready," Odessa said, laughing.

"He's a real beauty." Odessa bent over the baby, her index finger tracing his cheekbone.

Mike took his wife's coat and his and hung them on the coat tree.

Dr. Smith came in and Josh introduced him to Mike and Odessa. "I'm really proud of myself for the job I've done to-day," Dr. Smith said. "I have to ask you not to stay too long, because this lady has really worked hard and needs rest."

"We hear you," Mike said. "And we couldn't agree more."

* * *

At home, everything was ready for Maura. The renovated room converted to a nursery was egg-shaped, pale blue with ivory trim. There were pastel cutouts of stars, and across the ceiling, cutouts of animals romped around the walls. There was a rocker crib sent to them by Del and Val Craig whom Maura had met on vacation in Nome, Alaska a few years earlier. The crib was covered with reindeer hide and had hand-carved, brightly colored beads strung around the top.

Now that Papa Isaac was in remission, Lona would help Maura. At the door, she took the baby and cuddled him.

"Joshua Isaac Carter," she sang softly. "Best of the babies. He is a love."

"He's surely *my* love," Josh said, and could not help glancing at Maura.

Maura touched his hand. Did she understand how much he loved her? he wondered.

After hanging their coats up, they settled down. Lona put Baby Josh in his white flannel-lined bed and lightly stroked him. Josh had sat down to watch the baby when he remembered the present he had for Maura. He went out and came back with a package that bore the wrapping of a prestigious DC boutique.

Smiling as she took the big package, she undid the multi-colored ribbons and gasped with delight as she held up several garments. One ivory and one coral bedjacket, both with dyed-to-match lace inserts and a soft-as-silk midnight-blue nylon tricot nightgown with a sheer lace top.

"Oh, Josh, thank you. They're beautiful."

"I should have bought out the store."

Maura smiled. "It isn't every day that a man becomes a father," then added, "or a woman a mother."

"Congratulations to you both." Lona's face was wreathed in smiles.

Maura found herself wanting to say to Josh, *Congratulations, my love, on getting what you've wanted so badly for so long*.

Catching a look from her he couldn't fathom, he ran the back of his hand down her cheek.

"Lovely Maura," he said softly. "My wife."

She looked up at him. He was so tender, and she ached for him. He had to deal with so much—first, his mother's death when he was so young, then Carter's inability to tear himself away from his business long enough to be a real father, then Melodye and her betrayal. It would have broken a lesser man.

Fortunately for him, he had had Grandmother Addie's love.

The baby slept, his little face serene, the tiny fists balled up and pushed into his cheeks.

"Lord, but he's precious," Josh said. "I'm going to have to go in to work, but I hate leaving you both."

Maura didn't want him to leave. Ever since San Francisco, she had felt unbelievably close to him.

Maura's office assistant, Trina, let herself in through the side door and came into the room.

"What have we here? Is this a darling baby?"

Her face lit up with longing. There were so many years to go before she could get pregnant. She had to be an architect, following her dream.

Maura looked at the young woman, whom she had so quickly grown fond of and who had proved to be so helpful. She came over to Maura and hugged her.

"I want you to know," she said, "that I'll help Lona in any way I can with the baby. I'm crazy about babies. I intend to have a passel."

At the moment, Josh felt that he, too, would like a passel of children, but he was silent.

Lona answered the door chimes and found Odessa on the porch, loaded down with packages.

As Lona helped, Odessa said, "Go straight through to the kitchen. This is lunch for everybody." She then made a beeline for the nursery.

Giving Maura a bear hug, she extended her hand to Josh, who took it.

"Congratulations again. You two have outdone yourselves."

"I'd never deny it," Josh said.

"Now you've got two loves," Odessa chirped. "You lucky man. My husband's crowding me on the subject, and I'm coming around."

"You'll make a good mother," Maura told her.

"So will you. And I'd better, if I don't want Mike on my case. I sneaked out from the shop and made lunch for you all. Shrimp-stuffed flounder, your favorite, Maura, and oyster bread, a great salad, and chocolate chip cookies from your recipe. Am I a friend, or what?"

"You're the best." Maura got up and hugged her.

"You go ahead and eat," Trina said, "and I'll be happy to watch this doll. But don't blame me if I run away with him."

The door chimes sounded again, and Maura answered them to find Carter standing there.

"Carter, what a pleasant surprise. Come in."

She took his coat and hung it in the hall closet.

"I came to get another look at little Carter."

"Joshua *Isaac* Carter." She was going to set him on the right track from the beginning. He grinned.

"Okay, so Isaac gets first dibs. I can live with that, I guess. You could call him Isaac for the first six months of the year and Carter the second six months."

"Oh, Carter, you're hopeless. As if the world isn't mixed up enough."

"You've made me a proud grandpa, Maura, and my son is beyond happy. There just aren't enough words for what he's feeling, I wager."

"We're having lunch. Would you care to join us?"

Carter thought a moment and nodded. "Yes, come to think of it I am hungry. I missed breakfast."

"Since I know you're anxious, I'll show you the baby first."

She led him into the nursery, where Trina sat gently rocking Baby Josh Isaac. Carter spoke to the girl and bent over his grandson.

"I won't touch him," he said. "I want to keep every germ possible from him. He's so precious."

The baby slept on, squirming a little. Carter looked around. "This is a great room," he said. "Whose idea was it?"

"Well, actually a friend had one like this for her baby. She got the idea from her doctor's office. The decorations are my idea."

"They're both great ideas."

"Thank you."

"Melodye wanted to come by to see your baby. *Our* baby. That is, the Pyne clan's baby. You're going to have to get used to that."

"I can live with it," Maura said evenly, "but he's mine first. Mine and Josh's. I'm sure you know it has to be that way. I don't want my child spoiled, mixed up."

Carter looked at her with admiration and chuckled. "Agreed."

After lunch, Josh and Carter left. Lingering for a few more minutes over the food, Maura chatted with Odessa and Lona.

"We'll help you stack the dishes," Maura said.

"No. I'll have them in the dishwasher in a jiffy. You two go ahead and indulge yourselves in girl talk. Odessa, this was a really tasty lunch you prepared." She patted her stomach. "My stomach thanks you."

"Anytime."

Seated in her office with Odessa, Maura told her all about the relationship behind her and Josh and how they'd fallen in love.

Odessa began smiling. She got up and hugged her friend.

"What a glorious story," she said. "What I think is you two are forever."

Maura got up, went to the small-screen TV, and switched it on to get the weather forecast. She was greeted by a picture of a tornado in progress about a hundred miles from them, below Richmond.

"Oh, my God," Odessa wailed. "Those poor people." The announcer's voice went on telling about the devastation left in the storm's wake.

"This isn't the season for storms," Maura said. "This is a surprise."

"They come at any time, it seems. I remember someone saying that they once struck here far more often. A few people have storm cellars in the outlying areas."

Maura sighed. "We'll have to do what we can to help."

"Yes," Odessa responded.

The announcer segued to another story and the women spent a moment in silence, then moved on to other subjects.

Twenty-three

When Baby Josh was three weeks old, Maura took him to see Grandmother Addie. In her suite of rooms, the dowager queen held sway. She had had her maid get an old bassinet to put the baby in. Hugging Maura, she said, "You'll stay for lunch."

Maura shook her head. "I'm afraid I can't. I have several projects I'm working on, and we're working with the lawyers for land acquisition for Midland Heights."

Grandmother Addie sighed. "Just my luck to find a young woman I care so deeply for and she's busy as a bee."

"That doesn't mean I don't think of you often and love you."

"Yes, I think you do. Give an old lady a kiss."

Holding the baby, Maura bent and kissed her cheek. Then, taking the outer wrappings from the baby, she placed him in the lace-decorated, white bassinet the maid had brought in. She exclaimed over the baby, "Look at those round cheeks, will you?"

"That's his wise old owl look. Already he has Carter's commanding mien, but then he reminds me of Isaac. Has Isaac ever told you how we used to dance at parties?" Grandmother Addie asked.

"Yes."

"He was my favorite partner." Her eyes misted. "Your falling in love with my grandson and marrying him is the icing on the cake for my very long and mostly happy life."

"I think you've had a wonderful life."

"So do I." She rang for the maid, who had left the room. When the young woman came back, Grandmother Addie smiled and told her, "Please fetch the things you've gotten together for Maura."

The maid went in and out several times, bearing articles of clothing and stuffed animals and other toys.

"Oh, Grandmother Addie, you shouldn't have gone to so much trouble."

"Oh, yes, I should have. No child is going to be more loved than this little boy. We won't spoil him, but we'll always let him know he's the apple of our eyes."

"You're so sweet."

"No. *You're* so sweet. Anytime you need someone to baby-sit, I know Trina is willing, but Thelma is too."

"Believe me, you'll all get your chance. I'm working now on the Teen Center Dance. As soon as I get back into some kind of shape, I'll be working harder. This is one of the last affairs we'll sponsor to raise money for the Midland Heights development."

"This means a lot to you, doesn't it?"

"You bet it does. I plan to make this one of the finest moderately priced developments in the country."

"You're quite a woman, my dear. I always tell your husband how lucky he is."

Maura swallowed. "I'm the lucky one."

"Well, you two fit like a hand in a glove."

"You're always so kind. I think that's where Josh gets his kindness from."

"It never hurts to be kind."

"Well, examine what I've put together for you."

Maura got up and looked at the assembled items, oohing and aahing over each piece.

"You've got exquisite taste."

"Oh, the store sent a young woman out to talk with me and

she selected the articles. I ordered a lot of educational toys, although I know you've got or are getting plenty."

"Yes, we are, but he can't have too many."

Maura held up a musical foot roller, a long object that fit across the bed at the baby's feet that he could push and make music. Maura smiled at the picture on the box of a baby using the toy.

"I've set up a fifty-thousand-dollar trust fund for him," Grandmother Addie said. "You should be getting the papers soon. I've written him into my will. Josh never really needed my help; he's self-sufficient. Baby Josh may be different."

"I want him to be self-sufficient."

"I know you do. Well, it's always better to have more than you want rather than not enough."

There was a knock on the door and Carter entered with Melodye at his side. *Déjà vu*, Maura thought. The first time she had visited Grandmother Addie, Melodye and Carter had come in.

Carter and Melodye spoke to Maura, then Carter bent over the bassinet and lightly chucked Baby Josh under the chin.

"Well, grandson, how's it going today?"

The baby squirmed and drooled, doubling his tiny fists.

Carter wrapped a big hand around the fist, as Melodye went to his side and looked at the baby, but didn't touch him.

"I think people move little babies too much," she said. "All those germs."

"If they're not touched," Maura said gently, "then they're really in trouble."

"I would have come to the hospital with Carter, but I don't like being reminded that there's such a thing as childbirth." She shuddered. "I'm glad you came through okay."

"Yes, so am I."

Dressed in a black cashmere pantsuit with a lot of gold jewelry, her hair flowing around her shoulders, Melodye looked well and knew it. Her figure was never going to be ruined by childbearing.

"Maybe you'd be better off if you'd try to bear a child," Grandmother Addie said.

"Mother!" Carter scolded.

Melodye gave him one of her loveliest smiles. "It's all right, Carter. To each his own." She looked somber then as she took in Maura in her simple buttonfront coral blouse and skirt. No jewelry for Baby Josh to pull.

Getting up, Maura said, "I have to nurse him now." As Carter got up, she said quickly, "No, you don't have to go. I have a cover for me, and I can sit over there."

"Well, if you're sure," Carter said and settled in.

Maura got up and got Baby Josh from his bassinet. He was very quiet. She got a diaper from her tote bag, sat down, and unbuttoned her blouse, covering her breast with the diaper. Hungrily, the baby's mouth went to her body with a homing pigeon's instinct, but he fussily came away before he began to pull harder on her breasts.

"Ah, you," Maura said softly, her body thrilling to the joy of nursing her infant.

She could see the spacious grounds of Carter's estate from the window. His house was the showplace of Crystal Lake. It seemed odd to her that he would settle here. DC would have been a more likely place, but Carter liked to stand out. In DC, he would have been one of many.

Cooing to her son, she murmured, "It's your grandpapa I'm thinking about, love."

She was suddenly aware that the baby squirmed and fussed a bit more than usual. Placing her hand on his brow, she found him feverish, reached into her tote, took out and unsheathed a baby thermometer. Soon it registered one hundred five degrees.

Her pediatrician, Dr. Patricia Wineglass, had told her that a baby was apt to run temperatures that in an adult would be dangerous, so she held her cool, but felt she should take him in to the doctor.

Calling Dr. Wineglass on her cell phone, Maura left a message. The three people in the room looked at her.

"What is it?" Carter asked.

"He has a high temperature."

Grandmother Addie wheeled over and felt the baby's forehead.

"Yes. You were calling the doctor?"

"I left a message. She's very good about calling back."

"I guess it runs in the family," Grandmother Addie said. "Carter ran temperatures so many times, and Josh had quite a few."

Maura breathed uneasily. Dr. Wineglass had prepared her to be aware of many illnesses. Which one was this? Fifteen minutes or so later when the cell phone rang, she nearly dropped it.

Dr. Wineglass identified herself and asked what was wrong.

"First, thank you for getting back to me so fast. He's got a temperature of a hundred five."

"Diarrhea? Vomiting?"

"A little of both earlier this morning, but it was short-lived so I didn't think much of it, and he had no fever then."

"I think we'd better nip this in the bud. I have some idea what this is, but I want to see him. Can you bring him in as soon as possible? I'm at the hospital."

"I'll be there immediately."

"I'll drive you," Carter offered.

"You'll do no such thing," Melodye told him. "Your hands are shaking. I'll drive you both in your car. Joseph can take Maura's car home." She shrugged her shoulders. "Or Carter can drive you if you'd rather I not do so."

"It's fine with me if you'd like to drive. I just want to get him there as quickly as possible."

"Poor little lamb." Grandmother Addie sighed and said to Maura, "I know you're frightened, and may God go with you."

"Thank you," Maura said. "That always helps."

Dr. Wineglass saw them immediately, her dark-brown face deeply concerned. She took the baby from Maura and put him on the examining table, where he promptly threw up.

"Oh, dear," the doctor said. She took the baby's temperature. "It's gone a bit beyond one hundred five. I may have to keep him overnight."

"It's that serious?"

"I just don't know. There are several possibilities here. Let me clean him up and examine him."

"If he has to spend the night . . ." Maura began.

"Oh, you'll stay with him—definitely."

The doctor cleaned up the baby and set about examining him again. Fever. Diarrhea. Vomiting. She had seen far worse. She was pretty sure it was nothing more than gastroenteritis and told Maura so.

The doctor added, "This is only the second case that I've seen of a baby on its mother's milk getting gastroenteritis, and so early, but I really don't think it's that bad."

Maura breathed a sigh of relief.

"We now have excellent medications for this." She lightly pinched the baby's fat cheek. A forty-year-old who looked younger, she had six children of her own and never tired of being around children.

She buzzed the pharmacy and, in a little while, the aide came in with the medicine for the baby. Uncapping the cup and carefully spooning the pink liquid into his mouth, she smiled. "Well, he's taking it down like a trouper."

"He's a good kid. I'm having so much fun with him."

"I have an idea you're both good parents."

"We try to be."

The doctor finished her exam, and in a little while, the baby was sleeping. The doctor asked for a detailed rundown on what the baby had weathered for the past two days, and Maura told her. They talked easily of children, as mothers will, until Maura's cell phone rang.

"Dad called to say Baby Josh is sick and you're at the hospital. Why didn't you call me?"

"I didn't want to worry you if it turned out to be nothing much. I'm sorry, Josh. I was beside myself."

"I'm coming right over."

"Yes. Please do that."

Turning to the doctor, Maura said, "My husband is on his way. I wasn't sure what to tell him."

Dr. Wineglass smiled. "Daddies. They really go to pieces at the slightest provocation, big and strong as they are."

"Josh is usually so laid back, but where his son is concerned, he can really get rattled."

"Can't they all? Sometimes you'd think I wasn't a pediatrician who knows a bit about babies when my kids get sick. My husband is frantic when that happens."

After thirty minutes or so, the doctor took the baby's temperature again. It had gone down to one hundred three. She pursed her lips. "We're getting there."

Josh came into the room, breathless, demanding of the doctor, "How is he? Do you know what's wrong yet?"

"Hello, Josh," the doctor greeted him. "Don't be alarmed. I think—I'm pretty sure—it's gastroenteritis, and his temperature is already going down. I thought at first I'd need to keep him overnight, but if the fever continues to go down, I'll release him."

"Thank God it's not worse," Josh said.

Maura went outside to talk a minute with Carter and Melodye, who stood just beyond the door to Dr. Wineglass's office. Carter smiled broadly when she gave them the news.

"He's a Pyne," Carter said proudly, "certain to pull through anything. He looked so sad on the way over."

"He's sleeping now. That lets you know what a toughie he is."

Melodye touched Maura's hand. "I'm glad," she said simply. Maura reflected that she would not have thought Melodye capable of the friendly gesture of compassion toward her. She thanked her.

Going back into the doctor's office, she sat in a comfortable chair, beside Josh and opposite the doctor.

"I was telling your husband I want to check your diet more

closely. I think perhaps I'd advise against you eating too many fatty foods and too many sugars. Your milk is made up of what you eat, and your baby might be getting something that isn't good for him."

"Dr. Smith had me on a special food regimen during my pregnancy."

Dr. Wineglass nodded. "And up to now, the baby's been as healthy as can be. Are you fond of sweets? Fatty foods?"

"Yes, but I largely steered clear of them when I was carrying him. Lately, I have to admit I've had a larger share of sweets and fats."

"Alcoholic beverages?"

"Only a small amount of red wine."

"That shouldn't hurt, but if this continues, I'm going to ask you to go on a stricter diet."

Taking Baby Josh's temperature again, she smiled. "It's now one hundred two." She paused, then went on. "I'd like to observe him for the rest of the afternoon. Maura, I'd like you to stay with him. Then I think I can safely say he can go home late this afternoon or tonight."

"You have no idea how good that makes me feel," Maura told her. "Josh, I know you were tied up in an important meeting. Why don't you go back? If he can leave, I'll call you when we're ready."

"Meeting or no meeting, I'll stay if you need me."

"It's all right, Josh," the doctor said. "I think this is going to be one of my happier cases."

Josh got up, thanked the doctor, then said to Maura, "Come outside with me for a minute."

Maura got up and they walked to the door. Before they went outside, he caught her hand and said huskily, "Please call me if there's any change, or if anything else happens. Keep me posted."

"I will, and I'm sorry I didn't call you. I was just beside myself and I wasn't thinking. He looked so ill."

Outside in the hallway, they walked over to where Carter and Melodye still stood.

"How is he doing?" Carter asked.

"Much better," Maura told him.

"Are you going back to your office, son?"

"Yeah, Dad. Baby Josh seems so much better, and I was hammering out an agreement with the Isom brothers."

"I know how much that means to you. Listen, Melodye and I are going to stick around a while longer. . . ."

Josh looked hesitant. "Maybe I had better do that also."

"No," Maura said quietly. "Listen, Josh, I, too, know what the Isom deal means to you. You go ahead. I'll keep in touch every hour, or less if anything happens. Carter, Melodye, you really don't need to stay. I'll be all right. Dr. Wineglass is a rock; she's all the backup I need."

"Well, okay," Carter responded. "But you call me too if anything untoward happens. This is my grandson, and I want to be in on everything about him."

Maura raised her eyebrows. Carter Pyne could in time become a difficult, overly doting grandfather.

When Maura returned to the doctor's office, the doctor had placed Baby Josh in a bassinet in a smaller room just off her office. Pointing to a tubular, padded chair, she said, "You can watch him and get a bit of rest here. I have another exam to do. If you want coffee . . ." She stopped, frowning. "You know, that's another thing. Coffee. Do you drink much?"

"I used to, but when I was pregnant, I couldn't stand the taste of it. Now I'm drinking it again, about two cups a day."

"Don't. That could be one of the causes of the upset in the baby's system: sensitivity to caffeine. Now, that's not in the medical books, but I've found it can happen. You're going to have to watch out for soft drinks, too."

"That will be easy."

"I think I'd advise that you cut out sweets entirely for right now. Eat plenty of fruit. We'll see if that doesn't take care of it. This is your first child. I was a basket case when my fourth child took ill with something that wasn't diagnosed for quite a while."

"You're so helpful."

"It's my job."

"I think you know you go beyond your job."

Dr. Wineglass smiled. "I try," she said.

Maura kept in touch with Josh throughout the afternoon, and he picked Baby Josh and her up around six. Baby Josh's temperature was normal and he was his usual gurgly, cuddly self.

Walking into their house that night, Josh was aware of something new inside him. As Maura placed the baby in his bassinet and stood up, their eyes locked, and neither could look away. This was bonding, he thought, the deepest kind of bonding.

And with her gaze locked into his, Maura felt the pull of the earth itself. Right now, this was her man and this was her child. They had love between them, between Josh and her, and she would need nothing else, ever.

THREATENED BLIGHT, THEN SAVING GRACE

Twenty-four

Baby Josh rapidly got over his ailment and was in tip-top health when Maura decided to take him out to visit Ellen. Parking in the driveway by Ellen's house, she got out, admiring the carefully tended azaleas and impatiens in the yard. She rang the doorbell and waited. No answer. Going back to the car, she blew her horn several times.

After a few minutes, Ellen came around from the back of the house.

"Maura! How nice to see you."

The two women hugged, and Ellen came around to the side of the car where the baby's seat was fastened.

"Oh, little one." Ellen gazed at the baby fondly, then stood aside as Maura unbuckled him. Dressed in a blue cotton-knit one-piece outfit with a matching cap, Baby Josh looked like a model for a baby magazine cover.

"Let me hold him while you get your things," Ellen said.

"Gladly."

A Chevrolet pickup truck came into the driveway, and Rich waved to them, parked, and got out.

Walking over, he kissed Ellen on the cheek, spoke to Maura and patted the baby's head.

"How long can you stay?" Ellen asked him.

"Not too long. I'm on my way to look over a site, and I've got to pick up two of my men and take them somewhere."

"A half hour?" Ellen queried.

"Sure. Why?"

"I was in the storm cellar when Maura drove up. I'd like for her to see it and Grandma Theena's crypt. I can show her some other time, but I seem to be in the mood for it today. Someone needs to hold Baby Josh. Are you afraid?"

"Do I look like a coward?"

"Do I need to answer that?" The look that passed between them was warmly loving.

Settling Rich in the living room, with the baby in his portable basket, Maura and Ellen started to the backyard. Maura couldn't help glancing back over her shoulder at the uneasy Rich Curry. She made up her mind to hurry back.

"I open the storm cellar so seldom that I thought since you're out here you could take a peek. And I want to show you something about Theena's crypt."

Ellen had left the storm-cellar pullup door open. A ladder led them a short distance down and into a concrete room approximately eight by eight feet. There were jugs of water and two wine casks to hold the wine Ellen made each year.

"How did you like the last bottle I gave you?" Ellen asked.

"Really good. I don't know that I'd have the patience, but I'd like you to show me how it's done. I'm curious."

"Sure. Anytime. I'll be able to supply you with grapes from my arbor in a couple of months."

"What's in the painted tins?"

"Crackers, a few snacks. People usually stay in storm cellars a little while to give things a chance to clear up."

"We had one tornado when I was a child and never since."

"But they happen around us, farther south. Just thought I'd show you. You've asked what this spot is a couple of times."

Climbing the ladder behind Ellen, Maura felt a bit anxious to get back to Baby Josh.

Once outside, they went through a gate and deep into the woods where Theena's crypt stood. An angel spread her wings over the marble structure.

"Someone's been trying to deface it," Ellen said.

And looking at the doorway, Maura saw where deep gouges had eaten into the angel's robes.

"It has weathered all the years since my grandmother had it put up here for the second time," Ellen said quietly.

Maura looked at the inscription:

THEENA MARIE HALABY
BELOVED WIFE OF LIONEL HALABY
REST IN PEACE!
(1865-1895)

This in a time when interracial marriages were illegal. When Lionel Halaby had had the crypt erected on his land, nightriders had blown it up. Now there were only shards of dust that had once been Theena's lissome frame. Theena had long lain on the air.

"Where was Lionel Halaby buried?"

"He originally came from Louisiana. His daughter took him and buried him in his family plot there. Lafayette, Louisiana. It angers me that someone would do this to Theena's memory."

"It angers me, too."

Maura placed her hand on Ellen's shoulder. "I'm so sorry. When did this begin?"

"I didn't notice it at first, not until about four months ago. I know we've still got whites who hate the thought of interracial marriages, just as they did then. But all these years since it was rebuilt, and we've had no trouble. I wish I knew who did it."

"Probably a group of hateful men."

Ellen shuddered at the thought of marauders in the woods behind her house as she lay sleeping. Her heart beat heavily. Rich had been beside himself with fury. He was such an even-tempered guy. She hated to be the cause of pain for him.

They came back to find a baby-bedazzled Rich sitting on a swing on the front porch, dangling Baby Josh on his knee. Gripping the baby's wrists, he played with him, pushing him lightly back and forth. "Handcar! Handcar! Handcar, baby, handcar!"

Both women said they remembered their mothers reciting those words to them.

"So did my mom," Rich said, "so I haven't lost my touch."

"Rich, I showed her Theena's crypt."

Rich nodded. "What kind of bastards would do this?"

"Do you think it's racial? Memories are long sometimes."

Rich shrugged. "It doesn't have to be, but it's possible. We seem to be getting more evil people about nowadays."

"No, love," Ellen protested. "Back then, the crypt was completely demolished. This time there's only damage."

"But if it keeps on," he pointed out, "there's going to be a lot of damage."

"A little more of this and I'm going to start baby-sitting that crypt at night to see what goes on."

"You've got your work," Ellen told him. "You can't take that kind of time off. You need rest and sleep."

"We'll figure something out," he said. "I'm not going to have you continually upset like this."

He went into the house and got himself a glass of water, kissed Ellen briefly, and left.

Seeing that Ellen was still somewhat down, Maura proposed that they drive into town, where she would treat her to an ice-cream sundae.

Ellen squeezed her hand.

"What a wonderful friend you are," she said.

With his binoculars, Lonnie saw Maura and Ellen as they drove away. He sat on a deserted, heavily forested plot of land across from Ellen's house. He had seen old man Sampson in town earlier and knew it would take him a while to get back home. It was extra time he had not counted on.

Sometimes he picked the back lock on the gate to the woods behind Ellen's, but this time he simply left his motorcycle chained to a broken tree hidden by bushes, crossed the road, and climbed between sagging barbed wire and the square-blocked steel fencing.

Jauntily, he walked to the crypt that stood in cool shadows. Taking a sharp tool and a hammer from his leg-length pocket, he made dents and gouges in the folds of the guardian angel's robe.

"Bitch!" he hissed, seeing the angel as Ellen. In striking at her ancestor's grave, he struck at her. Morbidly frustrated, he was growing sicker and sicker with anger.

He had had her where he wanted her, down and helpless, until this new dude had come along. He spat, then spat again.

"Damn you, Ellen," he grated.

He stood, breathing heavily, putting his ducks in a row. Rich, and now Maura, had signed on for damage and maybe death when they got too close to Ellen, and she had been targeted from the beginning. Old man Sampson was lucky he was too old to bother hurting.

At home that night, Maura picked up her phone to hear a strange voice.

"May I speak to Mrs. Pyne?"

"This is Mrs. Pyne."

"Ma'am," the soft, feminine voice said, "I wanted to call you earlier, but I've just been so busy. I want to thank you for the things you sent to help out in the tornado. We got one of your packages and they sure came in handy."

"You're so welcome, and I'm sorry about what happened."

"Yes. I guess it's just God's will, but we were lucky. Two people were killed; they couldn't get to shelter in time."

"I'm so sorry."

"I know you are. Our minister's wife said you'd called to find out how you could help. She told me about all the things you'd collected and I wanted you to know how much you helped. God bless you. If you're ever down this way, stop in and see us."

"I will, and will you do the same?"

The two women exchanged addresses and bade each other a lingering good-bye.

Odessa called early several weeks later. "I've got company that knows you very well and likes you very much."

"Dale?"

"How did you guess?"

Maura shrugged. "I'm not sure. Tell him hello for me."

"Why don't you tell him yourself?"

Dale came on the line. "Maura?"

"Yes. How are you, Dale?"

"Never felt better. Congratulations on your bambino. That gives me something else to paint."

"Oh, Dale, I thought you were going to wait for us to come back to San Francisco."

"I just got terribly itchy feet. You looked like a madonna when you visited. I can just imagine how you look now holding your infant."

"You flatter me."

"That wouldn't be possible. When can I see you?"

Maura thought a moment. She was busy with Midland Heights and other projects, but she wanted to see him.

"How about this afternoon? I'm sorry, but I don't have a lot of time."

"Let me tell you what I want to do: paint you and Josh and the baby together and paint you separately."

"That's going to take a lot of time."

"I'm a swift painter, but I want to paint a real in-depth portrait of you. I think you have something that not even you see in yourself. You're ethereal."

"Hmmm, if you say so."

"I say so. I'll see you this afternoon."

Maura hung up, smiling. What had happened to his love for San Francisco that wouldn't let him leave it even for a visit?

Trina had the day off, and Josh was working at home to help her with Baby Josh. As she sat at the kitchen table, Josh came in. She told him about Dale.

Lifting his eyebrows, he looked at her over his reading glasses.

"I think that guy's got a crush on you."

"Nonsense."

"Yeah."

"He wants to paint all three of us together and separately."

"I have to admit he's good. What did you tell him? We're both pretty busy."

"In San Francisco, he told me he worked from the live model, but also photographs. That's what he'll have to do here."

"Well, I sure love the one he's already done of you. Why another?"

Maura blushed and told Josh what Dale had said about her looking "ethereal."

Josh got up and came around to where she sat. He put his arms around her shoulders.

"He's right. You are ethereal. You're my own private angel. If I forget to tell you, you remind me."

He pulled her to her feet and kissed her, his tongue flicking quickly at the corner of her mouth. She relaxed against him, then explored his mouth with her tongue.

"Lord," he said, "the heaven we know on earth."

"If we're in the company of the right people."

"Which for me is you."

"And for me, you."

He rocked her gently, then pressed her closer.

"You're starting something we can't finish. Dale is coming over this afternoon, and I've got to get a section of those plans for Midland Heights finished before he gets here."

"Damn you, Dale, for choosing this time to visit," Josh said.

"He didn't choose this time. I did."

"Anxious to see him?"

"Jealous?"

"Hell, yes. You'd better not give him even one smile that belongs to me."

"You're more mature than that."

"You speak for yourself."

Dale came loaded down with a couple of good cameras and his painting paraphernalia.

He admired the baby and took photos of the three of them.

"How about a brief sitting of you, Josh?" Dale asked.

Josh shrugged. "You're probably going to have to do almost all of your work from photos for me."

"You cooperate," Maura commanded. "I'm dying to have a really good portrait of you."

"Bear with me," Dale bolstered her command. "Your wife deserves the best."

"And I intend to give her the best."

"That should include a portrait she can be proud of," Dale said.

Josh looked at him with a grimace. "Let's get the show on the road, man," he said.

By the time a couple of hours had passed, the photos had been taken, sketches were in order, and Dale had explained to them what he wanted to do.

"I know you're busy people," he said, "but I need to be a fly on the wall, get the basic feel of how you operate. If you could bear that for a couple of days, I would be grateful."

"I don't see any reason why not," Maura told him. "What do you think, Josh?"

Josh rolled his eyes. "In the service of a great portrait of Maura, I'll bear it."

"And in the service of a great portrait of Josh, I'll welcome it."

Maura went out, got Baby Josh and brought him back.

"Something comes into your face when you look at him," Dale said. "A certain expression. If all mothers bore that look, had that dedication, we wouldn't have juvenile delinquents or cruelly unhappy people."

Josh drew a deep breath. "You're a visionary, my friend. If the world had one quarter of what Maura is offering our son and me, the world would be a great place to live in."

Maura picked up the phone on the second ring.

"Have I lost a cousin to you two? Or you three?"

"If you're speaking of Dale, you probably have. He's going to be around us a lot for a couple of days. He says he'll get far better portraits that way."

Odessa laughed. "A likely excuse to hang around you."

"Josh is here."

"Artists are famous for not caring about husbands of women they covet. And he does covet you."

"You're way off base."

"And if you think that, you're in trouble."

"Listen, since Josh and I have pretty much knocked off for the day, why don't you grab a bucket of fried chicken from whatever fast-food shop you come by and bring it over. With you and Mike here, I can be even more ethereal."

"Ethereal, huh? You're more the Dorothy Dandridge-in-her-heyday type. You're a good-looking woman, but I wouldn't say you're ethereal."

"I thought it was a nice touch."

"You be careful. Josh is a sweety pie, but he's got a temper."

"I know. I've got a temper, too."

After they had finished talking, Maura looked at Dale and reflected on how much the bone structure of his face was like Odessa's.

In the kitchen, the three of them set about making a massive salad of romaine lettuce, tomatoes, celery, radishes, croutons, grated parmesan cheese, and the wonderful dressing that was Josh's specialty.

The baby lay in his bassinet in the room with them, gurgling and cooing.

Dale went over and squatted by Baby Josh.

"This is a great beginning, kid," he said. Don't you ever forget it."

Maura's heart went out to him at the wistfulness in his voice. He deserved someone wonderful.

She heated frozen rolls she had made from scratch and buttered them.

When Odessa and Mike came, there was general merriment. Odessa squatted by the baby, then picked him up.

"Listen, I've got an idea," Dale said. "Let's go back to some point in our childhood. Let's sit on the floor and picnic."

"I've got a better idea," Josh said. "Let's go out on the terrace. We'll have a ball there."

Dale was amenable and they trouped out to the terrace, bringing blankets and rugs to sit on.

Maura thought at length about the wistfulness that had lain in Dale's eyes. How much was hurt, and how much was longing?

"Hey, Mama," Josh teased her. "Don't abandon us. We love having you around."

When Maura had driven to the supermarket that morning, she had parked at the curb, thinking she might go back out. That same night, she told Josh she would put her car in the garage.

"I'll do it for you."

"No. You're busy. I'll only be a minute."

Drawing on her coat, she went out to the curb and looked at her Lexus. She loved the lines of the car. Almost at the car, she stood in sudden shock. The flat tires said someone had slashed them. Going slowly around to the other side, she saw the same thing there.

"Oh, good Lord," she said. "Don't tell me we're going to have a wave of vandalism."

Going back into the house, she told Josh, who immediately

took her keys and went to examine the car; then she called AAA.

Coming back in, Josh looked puzzled.

"That was savage slashing," he said. "It didn't take those deep cuts to deflate the tires. Did you notice that the driver's side has a deep gouge?"

"No. I guess I was too upset."

"I got a flashlight from your glove compartment and went over the car. It looks like someone was very angry."

She reported the incident to the police, who said someone would be out in the morning.

"I've lived in this neighborhood eight years and never had anything remotely like this happen," Josh said. "This kind of thing frequently comes from someone holding a grudge."

"Or it could be some kids mad with the world—and their parents."

Baby Josh slept peacefully. Maura looked at his angelic face and said a prayer that he would always feel secure enough to live in harmony with his world.

Twenty-five

The Crystal Lake Town Center bustled in late September. A dance was being held to raise money for the Midland Heights development. With land sold at a lower than usual price by Maura, Josh, and Ellen, the holding company was set to begin land acquisition. The land of several nearby landowners would be desirable. One more year should do it. Especially since Josh was now an integral part of the project.

Gaily decorated with light blue, dark blue, red, and white streamers of crepe paper, the hall bore a rakish air of merriment. White-clothed tables lined the entire wall of one side and would hold the informally served food, to be brought in later.

The lights were bright as Rich, Odessa, Ellen, and Mr. Sampson rehearsed.

Lona was baby-sitting with Baby Josh so Maura and Josh could attend. The only ones on the floor, they danced to a slow tune that Love'n Us played. Going to the bandstand, Josh stopped dancing and teased the group.

"Some record producer's going to snatch you away from us in a hurry."

Rich grinned. "We've got a way to go yet."

"Not from what my ears tell me," Josh assured him.

Others soon joined Josh and Maura on the dance floor. Maura smiled thinking that this was a far cry from the winter ball, so grand and stately. She had been very pregnant then; now Baby Josh was here.

Leaning back in Josh's arms, she told him, "I keep wanting to call Lona to check on the baby."

"Give it a rest," he said. "We haven't been gone an hour."

Maura laughed. "I know, but this is the first time we've left him with someone else. Don't you worry?"

"A little, but he's in good hands."

"Remember the last big party we attended, the winter ball, with me as big as a barrel?"

"A pretty barrel. And look what came from that. You're looking great, honey. You looked great to me then."

"Thank you. You're not so bad yourself."

And he did look handsome in a natural-colored gabardine shirt, brown slacks, and a tattersall checked jacket.

She smiled and nestled the side of her face in the hollow of his leathery cheek.

Maura wore a very dark red, closely fitted dress that made her skin glow, with gold and pearl jewelry and black suede pumps. Her hair was bound into a french twist with tendrils around her face. She snuggled closer to Josh, feeling the heavy beat of the music.

"Whoa!" he said. "The evening's young and I'm building up to a fever pitch fast. Hold it!"

"Did anybody ever tell you you're sexy?"

"I'm a realist. Where you're concerned, my fire gets lit in a hurry."

"Do you imagine I don't feel the same way about you?"

"All I know is you please me, one hundred percent."

The music stopped as Rich looked over at them and grinned, then gave them the A-OK sign.

Withdrawing a little of her attention from Josh, Maura noticed that Ellen looked a bit drawn. As the band put their instruments aside, she excused herself and went to the bandstand.

"How're we doing?" Odessa asked.

"Splendidly. Keep it up. I like your newest, 'I'm the Mama, You're the Papa.' It's got great rhythm."

"I was in on that one," Odessa said. "I'm having the time of my life."

"Where's Mike?"

"He's going to be a little late."

"Ellen," Maura said, "may I talk with you a moment?"

"Sure." Ellen gave her a sweet smile and stepped down off the bandstand. They stood near the beginning line of tables.

"Are you okay?" Maura asked.

Ellen sighed. "I wish I could say yes, but Maura, Lonnie is driving me crazy. He's roaring by at least once every night, and he whistles some unearthly, shrieky whistles, like sounds from hell. . . ."

"Has any more damage been done to the crypt?"

"Yes, not a whole lot more, but some."

"Could Rich stay with you?"

"It looks like he's going to have to. I'm getting to be a bundle of nerves."

Maura stroked her arm. She looked pretty in the band's trademark black cashmere turtleneck sweater and buttery-smooth, tight black leather pants.

"You hang in there," Maura told her, anxious to give words of comfort, but seeing little that she or anyone except Lonnie's parents could do. And it was too late for even them to help her.

"Walk with me to your dressing room," Maura said.

"Okay."

Once there, Maura got a key from her small purse, unlocked a drawer in a cabinet, and got her tote bag. She pulled a pair of black flats out, took off her pumps, and slid on the flats.

Turning her attention back to Ellen, she told her, "I don't mind saying that I'm worried about you. I don't know how much more of this you can take."

Ellen's laugh was bitter. "I've stood it now for more than two years. The vicious gossip, the catcalls. I'm so lucky Rich came along. I feel I can take anything now."

"You shouldn't have to."

"Any more trouble with someone vandalizing your car?"

"No. Thank God for small favors. Listen, call me anytime you need me. I'm always available to you."

Ellen hugged her. "Thank you, Maura. I guess I know now the hell Theena went through. Evil thrives in every century."

"You just be careful. And good luck with your performance tonight."

"Thank you. You're a wonderful person. Josh is one of the luckiest men alive to have you."

"That goes double for my having him."

They walked back out. Ellen got onto the bandstand and Maura rejoined Josh.

"I was about to abandon you," he said. "See the little fireball over there in the scarlet dress, brown skin gleaming, rivaling a Coca-Cola bottle for shape?"

"I see her. Was she hitting on you, you poor baby?"

Josh laughed and hugged her. "Everybody knows I'm off limits by now. I just looked at her out of the corner of my eye. I've got my cola-bottle baby in my arms. I need nothing and nobody else to keep me satisfied."

"Are you bragging or complaining? If you ask Miss Coca-Cola bottle to dance, I don't mind."

"Please. She's all of eighteen. I'm nearly twice her age."

The girl walked slowly by them, moving slinkily, looking at Josh out of the corner of her eye. Maura grinned and narrowed her eyes.

"Romeo," she said, laughing. "Now, do you believe me when I say you're a handsome man? But that chickadee is asking for trouble. I believe in fighting for what's mine."

"I come to you without you fighting for me. We just happened to find out we belong together."

The band was getting a lot of requests for the 'Mama-Papa' tune. At one point, the other instruments were lulled and Mr. Sampson went into a really epic hot riff on his harmonica. The dancers went wild. They stomped and cheered him and he played harder.

Finally, winded, he stopped as they cheered him, and got a

glass of water from the refreshment table onstage. His face bore all the joy of a pleased Santa Claus.

The floor was beginning to get crowded. Maura reflected that there were a whole lot of people there. Out of the corner of her eye, she saw Dale and Mike come in and waved to them. They waved back, and Dale started over. Mike went to the bandstand.

Josh ran his tongue over his bottom lip. He'd be damned glad when Dale finished his painting and went back to San Francisco.

Dale reached them as the music stopped. Dressed in a navy turtleneck and tan jacket and slacks, he looked good, and he seemed highly pleased about something.

"Hello, you two lovebirds," he said. "I don't mind telling you that my portraits are coming along fabulously well. Late next week, I can start on your baby."

"We're going to owe you a fortune," Maura said.

Dale shook his head. "They're a gift."

Josh frowned. "That's a great gesture, Borders, but I want another portrait of Maura for my office, she wants a portrait of me, and we both want one of the baby. So set your price where you will. We'll willingly pay."

"My fee will be one dollar for each portrait. That's the price I set. I am paid by knowing you two and your baby."

Josh was taken aback. Talk about your smooth artist types.

"We'll find some way to pay you, even if we have to go through Odessa," Josh told him.

The slow, melodious strains of another of their tunes, "You're Mine Tonight," started and Dale bowed.

"If you will permit me the pleasure of dancing with your wife and if she will dance with me, I will be repaid better than you know."

Josh shrugged. "Of course."

Maura reflected that she felt better than she had felt in a long time, here with this music, the energetic young crowd, and the food now being brought in. As she left Josh, she said out of the corner of her mouth, "Now don't drink Coca-Cola while I'm gone."

Josh lifted his eyebrows and smiled. "Hurry back," he said.

As they danced away to the slow tune, Josh stood thinking that this poor slob had it deeper than he knew. Except Dale was no slob, but a very attractive, gifted man. He watched them as they danced on the packed floor. They were graceful together.

The little cola kid walked over to him, smiling, and held out her hand. "Care to dance?"

He smiled from ear to ear. "Thank you, but not just now."

"Later?" She was persistent. "Your wife or your girlfriend is dancing with someone else. They seem to be having a good time."

She was nettling him. "She's my wife," he said smoothly. "And I guess you're right. They *do* seem to be having a good time."

"Then why won't you dance with me?"

"No good reason," he said, smiling again. "Right now, I just don't feel like dancing."

"Mind if I stay here and talk with you?"

"Not at all."

"I need a cigarette, so I'll have to go outside. Would you go with me?"

Josh shook his head. "I'd rather not. You shouldn't be smoking."

She looked sad. "So much in my life isn't the way it should be." He looked at her closely then and saw the pools of sadness in her dark-brown eyes as she left him to go outside for a cigarette.

Out on the dance floor, the song ended and Rich took the microphone to announce a dance contest.

"The Funky Chicken," he chortled. "Who can dance it best?"

The crowd clapped as the band went into "I'm the Mama, You're the Papa."

"I'm a master at the Funky Chicken," Dale said. "Are you with me?"

Maura was a master at the Funky Chicken, too. She had been on her way back to Josh, but knew he didn't like the dance.

"I'm game," she said, and they began the ultra-lively dance. As they shook and spun around, others dropped back to watch them. Maura felt on top of things, in command. The music filled her, lifted her spirits. Dale was really good at this.

In spite of himself, Josh couldn't help watching his wife from the sidelines. She was so lithe. He was a good dancer, but he preferred the older dances. He had never learned the Funky Chicken. Now, he watched her with pride mixed with his jealousy. She was better at the dance than most of the young people out there.

Mr. Sampson went into one of his prolonged hot harmonica wails as more and more couples dropped out to watch the best dancers. The judges watched from the sidelines.

When the second set ended, about twelve couples were left on the floor. The lead judge announced the number one choice—two teenagers—who gave each other high fives.

"And prize number two goes to Maura Pyne and Dale Borders!" the judge intoned.

Maura gasped. "Oh, no," she said.

"Oh, yes," Dale responded. "I told you we were good."

She was hardly conscious of the last two couples to get prizes. Their own prize was a two-pound box of Godiva chocolates. Dale took it and handed it to her. "Without you, I couldn't have done it."

"I don't need the pounds."

"Take it," Odessa said, coming up. "You can always give it to me. You two did a fantastic turn."

"There're a lot of things you don't know about me, cousin," Dale said, grinning. Maura handed Odessa the candy.

"Something wonderful has happened," Odessa said. "A scout for a major record company wants us to cut a CD."

Maura hugged her. "You and the group go, girl!"

Maura felt a tap on her back and Josh was there, smiling broadly. "Congratulations! You two were really good. Now that I know how much you like dancing the Funky Chicken, I guess you'll have to teach me."

Maura kissed his cheek. "Darling, I'd love to."

"Now, may I have this dance?"

"Please do."

The band played the oldie, "Nature Boy," and Maura slipped into Josh's arms. She placed her hand on the back of his head, bringing him closer.

"I was jealous," Josh told her as they danced, barely moving.

"Why? You know I belong to you completely."

"Borders is a personable guy."

"You're more than that. You're my man." Then she added somberly, "Forever," pulling his head even closer and kissing him.

"You've got all sorts of talent," he said huskily.

"And you imagine you don't?"

"They only come out where you're concerned."

Lonnie peered into the window of the Town Center and felt sick with envy at Ellen and Rich performing, having a good time. She wasn't going to be a star. She wasn't going anywhere, he grated to himself. And again he reflected how he'd had her where he wanted her: down and out. Then this clown had come along. She was all hugged up with the architect woman, too, and he wasn't going to have it on either count. He had staked her out. She was his. He walked back to the fence a hundred or so yards away from the building. In the weeds along the fence, he had hidden a can of gasoline and he had a pocketful of easy-strike matches, the kind you could flick your finger across and ignite.

He ground his teeth. Why did he feel sick so much of the time? His parents were constantly haranguing him now when they never had before, telling him they only fussed at him because they loved him, wanted him to be somebody. Well, he had news for them. He *was* somebody—his own man. His mother wanted him to go to church with her. That was a laugh. He'd flirted with satanism and thought he might go back to it. It could give him some ideas on what to do about Ellen. Hell, he didn't need satanism to tell him what to do about Ellen. Her number was almost up. He'd bet she'd lose that glowing, happy look if she knew about that. She had also looked peaked at times lately, along with her happy looks. As if she felt something was about to happen.

Too bad about the architect woman. He was going to have to get to her and Rich too, because they'd guess that he'd killed Ellen. Kate Sampson would guess, too, but he didn't matter. Stupid old man living back in the woods. Who'd listen to him?

A siege of nausea took him as he looked at the lighted room from his vantage point and leaned against the fence. The barbed-wire strands across the top of the fence pricked his body, but they eased the pain inside him.

There was a fever raging in him that had Ellen's name all over it. And that fever had grown worse since she'd been cavorting around with Curry. Lonnie didn't love her. What did he care? Sometimes, he thought, it had nothing to do with love. A woman was just yours and you claimed her until another one came along.

Lonnie had had only one girlfriend, Iris Iverson. She'd been sweet, but dopey, knocking herself up like that when he'd told her to use birth control. When she'd gone over that bridge rail, he hadn't really felt it, just felt an emptiness. He wasn't going to have a baby messing up his life. And her mother had talked about making him marry her. He had felt cool and superior at her death. Almost as if he had pushed her.

His head was messing up again. The music was in his loins and he wanted to dance like the people inside. Be like them. He felt drawn back to the windows and looked straight into Ellen's face. He stared malevolently at her and moved back into the shadows of a tree. From his perch a short distance away, he saw her say something to Rich, who looked in the direction she had pointed and hugged her.

Lonnie grinned evilly. "You hug her, bastard. You hug her tight tonight, because she won't be around for long."

At that moment, he thought, he had made up his mind what he wanted to do. Three people would go out by his hand. He wasn't sure just how he'd do it, only that he would. That little bitch Ellen. The architect lady, Maura. Yeah, he was glad he ruined her tires. And that bastard, Rich Curry. It was as if by the thinking, a load had been lifted off his shoulders. The way it had happened which Lis Iverson jumped off that bridge,

On the bandstand, Ellen licked her dry lips. Was this jerk going to haunt her life forever? Rich kept looking at her tenderly after she pointed out Lonnie at the window.

"Easy, baby," he said softly, between snatches of song.

Ellen shuddered. That had been a devil's face at the window. Make no mistake about it.

"I'm going to teach you the Funky Chicken right now," Maura said, as she danced with Josh.

"And show me up before Borders?"

"You're a good dancer. You just aren't too fond of some of the dances. Don't knock it if you ain't tried it."

"Tell me about it. I'm game."

They sat out until the next suitable music came on and Maura pulled him onto the dance floor. Sparkling, she showed him the moves and he responded.

After a little while, she told him, "Hey, you're catching on to this like wildfire. You're a natural. And just think, I could have won a prize with you tonight."

"Well, thank you, ma'am. You're pretty good yourself."

Dale started toward them.

"If he cuts in, I'm going to punch him."

But Dale smiled and continued to weave his way through the dancers, until he got to the Coca-Cola girl and asked her to dance. Soon they had a dance competition going that was all their own.

"She's about his speed," Josh said.

"Oh? I thought I was his speed."

"You're pushing the envelope."

"You know something, you're sweet. All the way through. One day I might gobble you up." She stopped suddenly, feeling a start of alarm. "Josh."

"Yeah, babe."

"I could have sworn I saw Lonnie Fillmore's face at the window."

Josh turned to the windows. "I don't see him."

"He was there. I'm sure of it. I wonder why he doesn't come in."

"My guess would be he feels like he is—unwanted."

"That can be a terrible feeling."

"Yeah. As a kid, I never felt my dad loved me. He didn't have time for love."

"You still don't feel too much about his marrying Melodye?"

"No. I really don't."

"And his planning to have a family? That kid will get all the love you didn't."

Laughter crinkled the skin around his eyes, and his smile was beatific.

"Listen, sweetheart. I've got you and Baby Josh now. Everything I ever missed I have in my arms."

"You're happy?"

"I'm happy."

The dance ended around one o'clock. Ellen, Odessa, and Rich spent a little while making an appointment to talk in depth with the record scout the next day.

Driving along, Rich touched Ellen's hand.

"You're awfully quiet. Penny for your thoughts."

"I guess I'm bothered about Lonnie Fillmore. He was acting so strange."

"Forget him. If he comes any closer, we can get a restraining order on him."

"He's so sly. He seems to know just how far to go these days."

"Well, he'd better not slip up. Damn it, Ellen, I hate what this is putting you through, but I'm here for you now."

"I think it's almost certain he slashed Maura's tires."

"Probably. That's his speed." Rich's mouth set in a hard line, "Where you're concerned, he had better watch his step."

That night, they slept spoon-fashioned, cuddling with each other.

Lonnie waited impatiently for everyone to leave the Town Center, then waited some more. Finally, breathing raggedly with excitement, he got his can of gasoline from its hiding place and patted his pocket, which held the matches. He had added one more task he hadn't thought about: torch the stage where Ellen and Rich had been whooping it up tonight.

Hell, he thought, *why am I burning the place down? She won't be around much longer and neither will Rich or the architect woman.* They were all in the crosshairs of his psychic dementia and they were going to get what was coming to them. Nobody messed with Lonnie Fillmore. Iris Iverson had found that out. The sweet thing was she had done his dirt for him by killing herself.

The can of gasoline was heavy in his hands. Climbing carefully through the barbed wire and steel-block fencing, he stood and breathed deeply in the night air, then walked over to the Town Center.

Jimmying a window with a slim-jim he'd gotten from a mail-order place, he opened it and went in, hauling the gasoline with him. Once inside, he went straight to the bandstand, spread some of the gasoline on it, and struck a match. Flames leaped up. He had to do the rest and get going before anyone saw him.

Running now with the gasoline, he poured it up and down the floor of the frame building as he climbed back out the window. He struck the matches and watched the gasoline ignite. Once outside, he picked up the can and ran.

Climbing back through the fence, he was winded. Taking a handkerchief from his pocket, he wiped the handle of the can and the can itself and threw it aside, deep in the bushes. It was a job well done, he congratulated himself.

That night, Rafe Sampson couldn't sleep. He got up, got himself a glass of elderberry wine, went out on the porch, and sat, tapping his foot. He took out his harmonica and began to play. When he finished the tune, he put the harmonica down beside him and a chill hit him. He was hearing Theena cry!

The sound, he thought, was like nobody'd ever heard before. Soft and mournful, the pain in that cry was so deep, it broke your heart. He hadn't heard it but five times in his life, and every time, *somebody* died. Not your ordinary just passing on like people did. No, it was always a horrible death. Sad beyond the telling, like Theena's own death. Nightriders who didn't like what was going on—old Halaby taking his slave to Europe and marrying her—had poisoned her and left her at his doorstep. It took a lot to make Theena cry. One of the men who killed her had told his brother, "She never shed a tear. Unnatural, that woman."

Now, throughout eternity, she cried as a warning, and when she did, others would come to cry, too.

Reluctant to go in, Mr. Sampson sat, his hands hanging down between his legs. He had put his harmonica to his mouth to begin another tune he had helped write. All the band members had pitched in on that one and the record man thought it would be a winner.

It was then that he saw red and yellow flames in the distance and black smoke in the bright moonlight. It was the Town Center! Hastily he struck out for Ellen's house through the woods. He had no phone.

Rich heard the knocking and Mr. Sampson's hoarse cries, got up, and went to the door. From their porch, he, too, could see the flames. He went back in and called 911.

Mr. Sampson was afraid that maybe someone homeless had taken shelter in the Town Center. It was an old building, easy to get into. Were they dying? Was that why Theena had begun to cry?

It didn't always happen right away. Theena cried about the heartbreaking deaths, so like her own. With the Iverson girl, he had heard Theena cry nearly a month before it happened. But with Martin Creel's suicide, shooting himself in the head when his girlfriend had run away with money his daughter had given him for safekeeping, it had been quicker. Theena had only cried twice, but it had been nearly all day that she cried.

Mr. Sampson, Rich, and Ellen went to the Town Center as the fire trucks pulled in.

"Look, honey, the stage is burning!" Ellen exclaimed.

"I see," Rich responded grimly.

The firemen moved swiftly with their hooks and ladders. In a short while, they were on top of the fire.

"I'll want to talk to you three," the lieutenant told them. There was a police car there, too, and John Williams, the police chief, got out of it.

"Before I talk with you," he said, "please get your mind together, because the lieutenant says this is almost certainly a case of arson."

Maura was sleeping soundly in Josh's arms when the phone rang. It was Ellen, who quickly told her about the fire.

"Oh, my God."

"They put it out, but there's a lot of damage. Someone set fire to the bandstand, too. It's a good thing Mr. Sampson saw it and notified us."

"Are you thinking what I'm thinking?"

Ellen sighed. "Lonnie?"

"Yes. He looked so wild-eyed when I got a glimpse of him. Ellen, be careful. I think he's cracking up."

"What I think," Ellen said bitterly, "is he cracked a long time ago."

Back at his house, Mr. Sampson sat on the porch again, his harmonica by his side, but he didn't play. He was too tired. He was a man who believed in the Bible, but he didn't go to church. People, he thought, carried their church in their hearts. His wife had gone to church every Sunday and to prayer meetings on Wednesdays. Sometimes he used to go with her. He was so proud to show her off, proud of her dainty hands and feet.

Then, after ten years of a happy marriage, she had passed on with a rare strain of influenza. It had been a calm and peaceful death. Theena hadn't cried. He had grieved during those thirty years and had slowly become a recluse.

Theena hadn't cried then. Why was she crying now?

"People saw you hanging around, but you never went in. Why, Lonnie?"

"Hell, Chief, it's a free country. I wasn't doing any harm."

Lonnie sat, squirming. He might have known somebody'd see him and rat on him.

"Who told you they saw me?"

"I'm not at liberty to say. But you were there?"

"I might have been. I might not have been."

The chief's face turned red, but he kept his cool.

"Listen, Lonnie, I've known you most of your life. I came

here as a very young man, and I joined the police force right away. I've watched you grow up. . . ."

Lonnie put a fist to his forehead. "Now you're going to tell me what a great family I've got, and how my parents are pillars of the community."

"They *are,* you know."

Lonnie grinned evilly. "Now you want to know how come I'm so bad."

"You don't have to be a loser. You can straighten out. Go back to school. You're ruining your life."

"You think I torched the building?"

"I think there's a good chance. Did you?"

Lonnie shook his head. "You're on the wrong track. I am going back to school."

"Good."

The boy smirked inside. He didn't think he'd ever go back to school. He had other plans. Travel. Hooking up with some smart dudes who knew what was going on. Crystal Lake just didn't have his kind.

"If you did it, kid, we may be able to plea-bargain. This is not a first-time offense for you, Lonnie, but on the books it will only be a second. You've been into a lot of stuff we've never charged you for. What you did to Ellen isn't pretty."

Lonnie felt his throat closing up.

"You can't prove a damned thing," he said gutturally.

The policeman was silent.

Lonnie decided to take the offensive. He glared at the other cop.

"You're mighty silent," he said. "Cat got your tongue?"

The officer looked at him steadily.

"You're the one who's being interrogated," the chief said.

"I know why you're after me," Lonnie said, after a moment. "My old man's election is coming up this year," he said, as if Mayor Fillmore's election were assured. "You want to rat me out to hurt him."

"Don't change the subject. What do you know about that fire?"

"Less than nothing."

"Have you got an alibi?"

"I don't need one. I'm a night owl. I stay out a lot at night."

"Alone?"

"Alone."

"Are you into drugs?"

"Now you're accusing me of using drugs. Man, you're crazy. Are you picking on me to hurt my old man?"

The chief looked at him steadily. "I get along fine with your dad, but I do think he's a little too easy on you."

Lonnie smirked. "Love's like that."

"I don't think you always do credit to him."

"I try."

"I don't think you do. Where were you when the fire was set?"

"At the Town Center?"

"Yes."

"I was on my bike, riding the winds. I went a long ways out."

"Anybody who can vouch for that?"

"Not a soul. I'm a loner. Can't you take my word for it?"

"I'm afraid not. Have you been drinking tonight?"

"I had a nip or two."

"And drugs?"

Lonnie snorted. "You work too hard."

"We're going to keep on until we get to the bottom of this. Arson is a big step from the petty stuff you've done before, except for the rape."

"Be careful. I could sue you for false statements."

"I don't think you will."

The chief let him go then, and Lonnie swaggered out on his way home.

When he had gone, the chief turned to the other officer, his mouth in a sad line. "Lord," he said, "I wish we knew what makes kids go bad."

* * *

At home, Lonnie found his parents waiting up for him. He blinked as he walked into the living room.

"You're late, son," Mayor Fillmore said, clearing his throat.

"Yeah, Dad."

His mother got up, came toward him, and touched his face. "You look so upset."

"I've been down to the police station. They picked me up."

Mayor Fillmore looked puzzled. "What for?"

"Well, they seem to think I set a fire at the Town Center."

"Damnation. What poppycock," the mayor roared. "Is Chief Williams out of his mind?"

"I don't know, Dad. You tell me."

The mayor and his son looked at each other a long while. Finally, the mayor spoke. "Did you have anything to do with it? I know you didn't set it."

"Thanks. I had nothing to do with it."

"Tomorrow morning," the mayor said, "we go to my lawyer's office. He'll know how to handle this. I can make some trouble for the chief, detaining my son without due cause."

"Thanks, Dad."

"I was a heller myself, and I guess you could say I turned out all right. I've talked to you about this lately, but I'll do it again. Next year is election year, and I've got opposition for the first time I can remember. Keep your nose clean. Don't mess it up for me."

"I—I won't." Lonnie's voice went down to a near whisper. "Being mayor means a lot to you, doesn't it, Dad?"

"Yes. It means everything."

Lonnie turned away, hot tears in his eyes. "Guess I'll go to bed."

Mayor Fillmore glanced at the mantel clock. "You do that, and don't leave the house in the morning. We see my lawyer first thing."

Twenty-six

A few days after the fire, Maura sat at her desk going over drawings and checking a set of plans for the Midland Heights development. It was noon. She had gotten an early start and would sit for Dale for a couple of hours here at home.

Lona stuck her head in the door. "You said you were having company, so I fixed turkey-and-ham club sandwiches and opened a fresh bottle of wine. I did a salad, too."

"You're a doll."

"The baby is a sleepyhead. A nursing, squirming sleepyhead."

"You couldn't be more right."

Picking up a sharp number two pencil, Maura drew two parallel lines and looked at them. She saw so perfectly the shape of the homes to be built in Midland Heights. They would be top-notch and beautiful. Closing her eyes, she saw a development far better than most at the price.

Each house had more than an acre and a half of land. There would be a clubhouse. Swimming pool. Tennis courts. A playground. She had been written up in an architectural journal, and it lay open with the page on which she was featured folded back.

Smiling, she picked up the magazine. Something grand for the moderate-income crowd. There were ten floor-plans and such fancy touches as crown molding. Josh wanted their house built nearby. She looked around her. If it were left to her, she would stay in this house, but he wanted to move—away from the old pain of Melodye.

Dale came at one. The final sitting would be today; he would put on the finishing touches and begin painting Josh. Maura laughed aloud thinking what a difficult subject Josh was likely to be.

"I love that dress," Dale said, "but, then, I've told you that each time I see you."

She had changed an hour or so before into the long, simple, ivory-silk crepe gown with a boat neckline and fitted sleeves. She wore the natural pearl necklace and earrings Josh had given her for her birthday.

"I like this dress," she said. "If I'm going to be memorialized, I guess this would be my choice. When may I see the painting?"

"Not until I'm done. I'm adamant about that."

"Very well. This had better be good."

They ate a quick lunch, with Dale looking at her more than usual, then they went into the room off of the living room where she had posed each time.

"You know," he said, once she was positioned, "I keep wanting to paint you outside, the way you were in San Francisco. Your grounds here are so beautiful."

"Thank you. Perhaps you'll come again."

"It isn't as if I want to leave now."

"I remember Odessa telling me you hated being away from San Francisco, you were that fond of it."

"That was before you."

Flustered, Maura could think of nothing to say. She looked down quickly as his gaze stayed on her.

"Don't worry. I won't make a fool of myself. You're a married woman—happily married. I met you too late, and I curse the fates for that."

"You're a good man, Dale. You'll find someone."

"You've become my muse. I find myself painting in a way

I didn't paint before I met you. Can you promise me I'll find someone?"

Sunlight poured through the windows and sitting there, Maura was happy. Josh loved her. Papa Isaac was doing well. Baby Josh continued to thrive. There were few clouds on her horizon.

Only Ellen was unhappy. Maura talked with Ellen almost daily. It was plain the young woman was beside herself with fear. When she and Ellen had talked to Chief Williams just after the fire, he had said there was nothing he could do until Lonnie got more daring. But he would keep an eye on him. He was sorry, and his pale-blue eyes had conveyed that sorrow.

Dale looked at her closely. "Maura?"

"I'm sorry. Did you say something?"

"I asked if Josh is ready to pose for me."

"I think so. I'll ask him tonight, or he might come home while you're still here. We have irregular hours."

"Best of both worlds. And don't forget the baby. Baby Josh."

"Why not paint him next, then Josh? That'll give Josh more time to get used to the idea."

"Good thinking. You're not aware that you're beautiful, are you? Nothing about you says, 'I know I'm beautiful.' "

"I could hardly be aware of what isn't true. I'm attractive. So many women are attractive."

He shook his head. "I'm an artist, and I know beauty when I see it. Inside yourself, you're pure gold, diamonds, and those pearls you wear. The inner you emerges into the outer you, and there are few comparable women in this world."

"You flatter me, you know."

"I don't, you know."

They fell silent as he painted. He had reached the point where being with her hurt, even as it nourished him. Holding his easel, he thought he had never done such superb work. He picked up a sable-tipped brush. These were the finishing strokes for the sitting. He would put on the final touches at

Odessa's house. No painting he had ever done pleased him more.

"Can you excuse me a moment?" she asked.

"Certainly."

She got up and went into the bedroom, where Lona and the baby were. "I was thinking about coming to get you," Lona said. "His highness is wide awake."

Maura went to the closet, slipped off her dress, and got a robe. Putting it on, she took off her jewelry to guard it from the baby's prying hands, came back, and picked him up.

Nursing the baby, she thought she had all that heaven allowed.

"Dale is a wonderful painter," she crooned to him, "but he will never be able to capture the perfection of you."

The baby gurgled and his muscles twitched into a disarming smile.

Later, back in the room with Dale, she thought about a woman she could introduce him to and came up blank.

After a half hour or so, he told her that the part of the painting that required her presence was done. "In a couple of days, I will bring the painting to you."

"I can't wait to see it."

"You'll be pleased. I can promise you that."

Josh came home early. "Would you like to go out for dinner?" he asked.

She shook her head. "No. I posed for Dale this afternoon. Remember? I don't like being away from Baby Josh too much."

"You're a good mother."

"Am I a good wife?"

They sat in their bedroom, and he bent down beside the chaise lounge she sat on and took her hand. "Sweetheart," he told her, "they don't make better wives, don't make better women, than you."

Her other hand went to her breast, then his hair. As their

eyes locked in love and a marvelous belonging, she told him, "No wonder I love you so."

They went to bed early and lay for a little while in each other's arms before drifting off to sleep.

Maura's dream came early, lifting her. Josh and she were on a jet plane making love. His big hands stroked her gently and his tongue probed her mouth relentlessly. She was ripe with love for him and woke up moaning faintly.

Josh was fast asleep. She rolled over and kissed the side of his face, squeezing his shoulder.

"What is it, honey?" he asked, groggily.

"I can't sleep."

Josh came wider awake, rolled over, and sat up. "Is something bothering you?"

"No. Far from it."

"Then why can't you sleep?"

"Heaven knows you're sleeping hard enough for the both of us." She chuckled. "Wake up and keep me company."

"You've got a rough day tomorrow, remember?"

She sighed. "Yes, I remember. Sweetheart, I want you so bad."

Josh laughed. "Why didn't you say so?"

Caressing her in broad strokes, his mouth found hers and drew the honey from it. It thrilled him that she had wanted him enough to wake him.

"I'll put on some music," he said, starting to get up.

"No. I don't want you to go away from me."

"Okay, you've got it."

His mouth found hers again, and his tongue probed the sweetness of her body, the soft, silken flesh that aroused him to fever pitch. It was so quiet. Then, as his hands stroked her, the winds rose outside, and they could hear the sharp patter of raindrops against the window.

"There's the rain we were promised," he said.

"Don't talk. Just make love to me. I'm dying for you."

Josh felt wonder at the things she said to him. He had not

known her to be this fervent, not even in San Francisco. Pushing him onto his back, she sat astride him. He positioned his hands on her hips and bore her down onto his mighty shaft. She gasped with pleasure as he took her.

She stroked his hairy chest and ran her tongue over his nipples, knowing it thrilled him. And he responded by moving more swiftly, his thrusts now going deep.

What was the matter with her? she wondered. She was going mad with desire. Too soon, she felt the tremor of his loins and he clutched her tightly. Still astride him, she whispered, "Oh, my darling," and in a short while her climax took her, left her shaking, and she relaxed.

"Satisfied?" he asked her.

"For now."

He laughed. "Well, I want more. I want all that heaven allows."

"You're so good."

"And you're not?"

"I hope I am. I know we're good together."

"I'm not sleepy anymore. I could use more of the same."

"Don't be greedy."

"I can't get enough of you."

He leaned over and switched on the lamp, and the room was flooded with the soft light as the rain and wind swept around the house.

"Making love when it's raining," she said. "Isn't it glorious?"

He grinned. "I don't need the rain. I don't need music. I just need you. Why didn't you want me to talk at first?"

She pondered his question. "I don't know. I guess I wanted to feel like a part of you. Fusion. I didn't need to talk. You were me and I was you. I felt strange, Josh. Really strange."

"Well, you felt wonderful."

"And you felt to me like an African god."

"Thank you. Repeat performance?"

"Need you ask?"

He rolled her over onto her back and kissed the length of her body, beginning with her toes. His hands stroked her as his lips touched the depths of her soul. Pausing at her waistline, his hands grasped the smallness of her waist and pressed in, and she moaned with desire. Intense thrills were flooding her body, and she was lost in wonder as he found her breasts, gently sucking first one, then the other.

Her hands were busy with his body, and with her movements she cheered him on. He kissed the sweetness of her fragrant, buttery scalp, then slipped his tongue into her mouth and kissed her as if he could never stop.

This time, they were slower, getting and giving honey, lost in the ambience of their love and found in its glory.

Rain began to pour, beating against the walls, and she held him deep inside her and moved beneath him in rhythmic strokes. He knew now why she hadn't wanted to talk. They were in the blended throes of love and they needed no conversation.

He kissed the palms of her hands and tongued them, then the corners of her mouth. He teased her nipples with his tongue and she led him on.

"Oh, glory night," she whispered to him. "Marvelous you!"

"You make it all possible," he told her. "Before you, I felt as if I had nothing."

"I'm yours."

"And I belong to you forever."

Gently, she wrapped her legs around him and pulled him in for a final thrust. Together they knew the splendor of fulfillment, the knowing glory of their lovemaking.

Twenty-seven

"Dale paints all day and most of the night. He doesn't seem to stop painting." Visiting Maura for what she termed a "pop" visit, Odessa laughed merrily. "He's a busy man."

"It's hard to believe how much he's accomplished and how well it has gone," Maura said. "Now, in a day or so, Baby Josh's portrait will be finished. Josh is really pleased, and I'm ecstatic."

"I imagine Josh will be happy to have Dale back in San Francisco. Talk about your obsessions."

"Wel-l-l," Maura responded, "it's a nice obsession, if it can be called one. He hasn't once gotten out of line. He's a sweetie-pie, really."

"He'd hug that to his heart."

"I enjoy knowing him."

"And he *loves* knowing you. I feel kind of sorry for the guy."

"He'll find someone."

"I've introduced him to a couple of my friends. He can't see them for looking at you."

"Oh, stop it."

"You know it's true. Isn't Josh jealous?"

"A little. He knows I'm faithful."

"Oh, I'm sure he knows you'd never betray him, but he can't help being miffed at a handsome guy going gaga over his wife."

"Josh is handsome."

"In spades, but you get my drift. Don't play dumb."

Maura laughed. "Okay, I won't. In a few days, Dale will be gone and that will be that."

"Care to bet?"

"Odessa, stop making trouble."

The two women went to the living room where the two portraits hung; a space awaited Baby Josh's portrait. Dale had decided to do Josh first.

"My cousin is a fabulous artist. I'll say that for him."

Maura stood reflecting that Dale had caught a certain sadness in her mien that she knew was there but thought she didn't display. He also caught in full measure her joy in living.

The door chimes sounded and, answering them, Maura found Papa Isaac standing there. She hugged him, kissed his cheek, and he and Odessa hugged.

"You're looking great," Odessa said. "Everything still okay?"

"I'm about as healthy as I've ever been," Papa Isaac said. "I'm one lucky man." He looked fondly at Maura. "Thanks to my granddaughter here."

"I only partially made it possible," she said, "Josh and I. You're the one who had the will and the drive to get well."

"You bet. I love this earth too much to leave it."

"And I was determined not to be without you," Maura said.

"What are your plans for the day?" Odessa asked Maura.

"I'm going on my daily visit to Ellen, then to see Grandmother Addie tonight with Josh."

"How's Ellen doing?" Odessa asked.

"Well, things have been quiet, but she's thoroughly spooked. She said Mr. Sampson told her he hated to have to say this, but felt he had to—he's heard Theena crying for several days. Sometimes just once, at other times nearly all day."

Odessa stroked her own arms against the chill and goose bumps she felt.

"You don't say." Papa Isaac looked concerned.

"I'm afraid I keep thinking about last summer and the Iverson girl," Maura said. "Such a pity."

"I wonder what that rat, Lonnie, is doing these days." Odessa looked grim.

"You can rest assured there's nothing good going on with him," Maura responded.

When Josh got home that same night, he looked bothered.

"What's the matter?" Maura asked.

"The baby's sleeping?"

"Uh-huh. He's waiting for us to start doing something, anything, then he'll wake up."

Josh laughed shortly. "I need to talk with you, honey."

"Shoot."

"Let's go back to your office."

Once there, seated in the comfortable chairs, Josh leaned forward, his eyes pleading.

"Castillo and Lopez have offered us a deal for the land that Carter feels we can't refuse."

He named a sum in the millions, and Maura whistled. Drawing a deep breath, studying him, she said, "But I thought this wasn't about money, but about principles, about bringing a quality of life to people who might not otherwise have it and what we want it to be."

"You're right, but I've found myself changing since Baby Josh was born. I want him to know I've always tried to give him the best. Think what this can mean."

Maura felt the start of hot tears. "I guess I'm thinking about the scores of people who could have better homes, homes they could never afford under some other aegis. My whole life is wrapped up in this."

"Sweetheart, I know it is. This is your baby, too. Oh, not in the way our son is, but enough so that it means a whole lot to you."

"You said you were with me."

"And I am," he said, stubbornly, "but I've got to think of Baby Josh and other children we'll have."

When she was silent for a long while, he said, "I hate having to ask this of you, but there's just too much involved to pass it up. I don't think we'll ever get the chance at something like this again—not soon, anyway."

Choked, she said, "And when will another Midland Heights for people who deserve it be built?"

"There're other parcels of land."

"Not so close to Crystal Lake, not for miles and miles. Midland Heights was going to help put this town on the map."

"I know. Your plans are near perfection. And together, we could build something to the glory of a whole town."

"Oh, Josh."

Josh came to her, bent over her. "I'm sorry, my love, but I've got to do it this way. I couldn't live with myself if I cheated my son out of his birthright. And what about Ellen? Doesn't she deserve the riches she'd never know otherwise?"

"Ellen doesn't care about money."

Josh sighed. "We could hire bodyguards for her if it came to that. But I want the world for Baby Josh."

That hurt, Maura thought. She didn't want her son to come up worshipping material things.

"I don't think she'd take the money."

"She would if you advised her to."

Maura buried her face in her hands. "I'll have to think about this, Josh. You of all people would want our son to know that money isn't everything."

Quite patiently, he told her, "I know money isn't everything, but it doesn't hurt to have enough."

"Is it more important than a dream?"

"No, of course it isn't. But what I'm trying to give my son is a dream, too. Okay, what if Ellen kept her land and you kept yours."

"We need the whole tract. You know that."

He nodded. "Yes. You think it over."

"You've made up your mind."

"Yes, more or less."

"When did you ever listen to Carter?"

"Only when he makes sense. Darling, please think it over carefully."

That night at Carter's, Maura and Josh found Grandmother Addie in good spirits. Still, when they walked in the door, she frowned.

"You look as if you've got something on your mind," she said to Maura. "Out with it."

"Not really," Maura said, sadly. "I'm a bit run down."

"Very well. How's that baby? A great-grandmother I am. Happy days!"

"Baby Josh is fine. He livens up the house and our lives, all right," Maura said.

They had hardly settled when Carter tapped on the door and came in. "Mother, Melodye wonders if the three of you would like to come downstairs and watch her whip me at a game of ping-pong."

He sounded downright loving of his new wife.

To their surprise, Grandmother Addie laughed and looked at them. "Carter used to beat me at ping-pong every time we played. I'd love to see Melodye give him a beating. But only if you two feel like it."

Josh and Maura said they didn't mind and set out with Grandmother Addie.

They found Melodye clad in sea-green pajamas, a large emerald pendant hanging around her neck. Maura felt good in her own lilac leggings and shadow-lace tunic top.

Melodye looked at Josh and smiled. She came to him and kissed him on the mouth and he looked uncomfortable. "I'm your stepmother," she said. "That gives me the right to kiss you."

Carter looked none too happy. "Don't play with fire," he told his wife. "Sometimes it burns you."

Melodye gasped. "Darling, it was a harmless kiss. It meant nothing."

"Let's play, shall we?" Carter told her, his mouth set in a tight line.

Maura and Josh sat on the sidelines with Grandmother Addie and watched the game progress. A netting had been drawn around the playing area to keep the ball from hitting the onlookers.

Melodye seemed nervous. She kept missing serves. Carter seemed to hit the ball with all his might, and he returned serves swiftly and effectively.

"Come on, Melodye," Grandmother Addie called out. "I know you can beat him."

But, in a short while, Melodye called time out and wiped perspiration from her brow. Smiling grimly, her glance strayed to Josh, then back to Carter.

"Darling, I guess I'm more tired than I knew I was. Let's call it a game and just visit with Josh and Maura."

Twenty-eight

Lonnie grinned sourly. It was a Saturday. Alone in the woods behind Ellen's house, he opened his knapsack and took out a sawed-off shotgun. Holding it up, he sighted the two people in Ellen's yard—Ellen and Rich—and laughed.

"Time's almost up," he growled softly. His stomach hurt with his rage at their being together. At her being happy.

Lonnie had been put under house arrest by his father for a few days after the police had questioned him about the fire. Now he was out with an admonition from his father. "You're not going to cost me this election, son, because I'm not going to let you. I like being mayor and I'm holding on to it. You understand?"

Lonnie had nodded, his throat dry and hurting. In spite of what his father had always said, how much did he mean to Mayor Fillmore? The whole damned world seemed to be closing in on him these days. But he'd set the fire on that damned stage and in the back of the building and nothing had come of it. Lonnie believed in his omnipotence. His heart hurt too much to think straight.

His shotgun sight was in perfect alignment. He could kill them both now, but he wasn't ready. Every day, at some point, the architect woman came out and stayed a short while. He had sighted her and Ellen, and often Rich, in the kitchen, laughing, and he had restrained himself, giving them more time to be on earth.

He wanted the three of them together once more. And time was running out.

At Josh and Maura's, the two of them stood with Dale and Odessa in front of the three portraits. Josh. Maura. Flanking Baby Josh.

"You've done a great job," Josh told Dale.

Maura added her compliments and Odessa hugged him and said, "Cousin, I'll admit I never knew you had it in you."

Dale smiled, pleased with himself and more pleased with his work than he had been in his life.

"You've got to let us pay you," Josh said.

Dale shook his head. "Since you insist, I'll list my favorite charities and you can contribute to them."

"Fair enough."

Maura looked at the wonderful blending of colors, the sharply etched rendering of bone structure, and the muted background.

"I'm leaving next week," Dale said.

Josh opened his mouth to say the courteous thing, that he was sorry, but bit it back. No point in lying. But Maura thought she was sorry. She would miss him.

"It has been great having you here," she said quietly, "and I've enjoyed posing for you. I can't tell you how pleased I am."

"I'm glad," Dale said, "because this is the best work I've ever done. If it's okay with you, Josh, I'd like to paint Maura from time to time as your child grows up."

"Sure," both Maura and Josh said. Odessa looked from one to the other of the three people. She was so proud of her cousin she could burst.

"I haven't run this by my wife yet, but I'll hazard offering to take you to the airport."

"I'd like that," Dale said.

Maura stood reflecting that money meant little to Dale. He would never let money stand between him and her dream of

Midland Heights. And she felt disloyal to Josh thinking that. Disloyal and angry. Hurt. Confused.

When Lonnie got home early that afternoon, he found his father pacing angrily.

"Well, welcome home, son. This *is* where you live, isn't it? Lonnie, where the hell were you last night? Maybe I shouldn't have let you have your bike again."

"Sorry, Dad," Lonnie said, humbly. "The bike broke down and I spent the night on the road. Got it fixed this morning." He was proud of how smoothly he could lie.

"Well, I hope you've eaten because we've got to go to the police station. Chief Williams wants to see you."

Lonnie's stomach plummeted. "For what?"

His father sucked in his cheeks and looked at him.

"Seems someone found some evidence linking you to the fire at the center. He wouldn't tell me what over the phone. Wash up, and we'll be on our way."

Lonnie's mother came into the room.

"Lonnie, tell me you had nothing to do with that fire," she begged him, tears in her eyes.

"I didn't, Mom. I had nothing to do with it. I swear."

"I want to believe you," his mother said. "I do believe you. I've been praying for you and whoever did this. I want to go to the police station with you."

"You'd just be in the way," Mayor Fillmore said. "I can handle this. Chief Williams and I don't always see eye to eye, but we get along."

In the interrogation room of Crystal Lake's police headquarters, Lonnie, Mayor Fillmore, his lawyer, Keith Moore, Chief Williams and a female detective sat around a battered table. A tape recorder whirred.

Chief Williams intoned an introduction for the benefit of the tape recorder and began. "What we have is a two-gallon gasoline can found in the woods behind the center."

Chief Williams was silent after that, biding his time, playing the detective game.

Finally, Mayor Fillmore said, "Well, what has that got to do with my son?"

Blowing out a stream of air, Chief Williams said, "We have a perfect thumb print of Lonnie's that compares with one we have on file from the one charge we have against him. You remember the breaking-and-entering charge at the elementary school?"

Mayor Fillmore nodded. Lonnie was numb. He thought he'd wiped off all his fingerprints.

"Have you for some reason handled a gasoline can—a two-gallon gasoline can—lately?" Chief Williams asked Lonnie.

Lonnie hung his head as his lawyer took over.

"There're lots of two-gallon gasoline cans around Crystal Lake," he said. "At some point, Lonnie might have handled the can. He's got friends. It could be that the can belonged to one of them."

"Could be," Chief Williams said, "but it's unfortunate that the other prints were smeared. Only this one was clear."

"If you ask me, that's not much evidence," the lawyer said. "You're a long way from home."

"There were the people who saw you looking in the window at the dance, and you never came inside," the female detective pointed out.

"No law against looking in a window," the lawyer said.

"Some things just looked suspicious." Chief Williams stroked his chin.

The woman looked at Lonnie levelly, her face impassive. "Did you set the fire?"

"No, I didn't," Lonnie croaked.

"You look kind of nervous," the chief said to Lonnie.

"Hell's bells," the lawyer exploded. "Wouldn't you look nervous if you had adults picking on you, harassing you the way you're harassing this boy? Give him a break. Give me a break. If you've got this wrong, Williams, you're looking at a suit against your department that'd make your eyeballs bulge."

Chief Williams nodded, seeming almost humble. "I hope, for the boy's sake, that we are wrong, but we've got to go where the evidence leads us."

"Some evidence, if you ask me. Are you through with us?"

The chief nodded. "Don't leave town, Lonnie. We'll let you know if anything else turns up."

"Oh, I'll just bet you will," the lawyer sneered. He didn't want to come on too strong with the police chief. He had to earn a living in this town, and he never knew when he'd need the chief on his side.

The group stood up. Chief Williams offered his hand to Mayor Fillmore, who shook it, then to Attorney Moore, who did the same.

"I'm sure you want to get to the bottom of this as much as we do," the female detective said. "We'll be in touch."

The lawyer laughed. "Don't call us. We'll call you."

Twenty-nine

When Maura got back home from her visit to Ellen's, she found Carter and Melodye in the living room with Josh, who was working at home. They sat on the sofa.

"We just got here," Carter explained. "We were asking to see Baby Josh."

"Yes," Melodye said, "the little tyke is growing by leaps and bounds."

Melodye and Carter exchanged glances. "Soon we'll have a kid of our own." Carter stuck out his chest.

"You're pregnant, then. Congratulations," Maura told Melodye.

Melodye laughed a bit shrilly. "That's wishful thinking on Carter's part. I'm not pregnant." She patted her flat stomach.

"Time will take care of that," Carter said gruffly.

Melodye smoothed the skirt of her dress. "Darling. We just got married. I want you all to myself for at least a little while."

"What's the hurry, Dad?" Josh asked.

"I want another chance to raise a kid. I won't make the same mistakes I made with you."

"I think Josh turned out awfully well," Maura said. Josh shot her an appreciative glance.

"Thank you."

"Oh, I'm not saying for a minute that he didn't, but it wasn't due to much effort on my part. Grandmother Addie largely raised Josh. I'll be honest. I was too busy."

Baby Josh and Lona were playing with his crib toys when Maura came to get him.

"I was afraid he might be asleep," Maura said.

"Oh, he's been Mr. Energy for the last hour or so."

Going to the crib, Maura lowered the bar and picked up Baby Josh. Feeling his soft weight in her arms, a thrill of pleasure shot through her. Her son. Josh's son. She and Lona exchanged smiles.

"He's such a good baby," Lona said.

Carter got up when Maura entered the room, came to her swiftly, and took Baby Josh.

"Come to Granddad," he said. "Tell Melodye you're going to have an uncle. You two will grow up together. I'm slowing down to be with my beautiful wife. Taking it easy. I'll have plenty of time to play with both you boys."

Melodye looked uncomfortable, Maura thought. Toying with her earring, the woman who had been a stunning beauty from birth wished she were somewhere else. She should have told Carter, she thought, that she didn't want children. She hadn't wanted them with Josh. She didn't want them with him. She shrugged briefly. Carter loved her. She would get around him somehow.

Melodye made no effort to cuddle with the boy. She played with him a bit as Carter held him.

"Fabulous baby, you two," she said, again flirting a bit with Josh. "I've always wished I had the natural talent to be a mother."

"Nonsense," Carter told her. "You're going to make the world's best mother."

Melodye shrugged again. "We'll see."

Carter gave Baby Josh to Maura and paced the room with his hands behind his back, unsmiling. He stopped in the alcove and stared at the paintings of Maura, Josh, and Baby Josh.

Turning back to Maura and Josh, he told them, "This is stunning work. I know you introduced me to the artist, but I never dreamed he did work of this quality."

"He does magnificent work," Josh said.

"You said he lives in San Francisco when you introduced him."

"Yes." Josh rubbed his day-old facial stubble.

Running his tongue over his lips, Carter was silent a little while before he said, "I'd like him to do Melodye, Mother, and me."

"I'm not sure he has plans for coming back this way," Josh said, slowly.

"I'll see that it's worth his while. You said he's Odessa's cousin?" He sat down.

"Yes."

Melodye got up, went over, and studied the paintings. She whistled lightly.

"He flatters you, Maura. This is a superb painting."

Josh chuckled. "He doesn't flatter her. My wife is a beautiful woman."

"Of course," Melodye answered him. "I wasn't implying otherwise. I'd love to have him paint me."

"Consider it done," Carter said, gallantly.

Carter and Melodye accepted drinks—a highball for him and white wine for her. Josh took cognac and Maura sipped a ginger ale. Carter cleared his throat.

"Of course I came to see my grandson, but I want to talk with you about the land, Maura. Your husband tells me he's coming around to my side. Señors Castillo and Lopez are offering a lot of money."

After a few minutes of silence, Maura said, "I'm not terribly impressed by material things. Oh, I like them well enough, but so many things are more important."

"Your son is liable to hate you when he grows up and finds you cheated him of part of his birthright." Surprisingly, this came from Melodye.

"You're right," Carter said. "I couldn't have put it better myself."

"If my son is half the man I raise him to be, he'll be grateful to me," Maura told them.

When Carter began to argue, Josh looked at him sharply. "Don't push it, Dad. I can understand where my wife is coming from."

Maura felt a rush of relief. Was he taking her side? Or simply serving as devil's advocate?

As was his wont, Carter ploughed on stubbornly. "I want you to promise me you'll think this over carefully. I've talked with Ellen. She's young, inexperienced. She'll go either way you go, Maura."

"That's not entirely true. She believes in the Midland Heights development, just as I do."

Carter was blunt. "I hear she's having trouble with my friend Fillmore's son. The boy doesn't have what his father has. He's no good. If he were my son, I'd have shipped him away to a military school long ago instead of coddling him. Now, with money, she could put this place behind her."

Maura sighed. "Ellen's family goes back for a couple of centuries here. She loves the place."

"Money would help protect her," Melodye cut in.

Carter looked lovingly at his wife, grateful for her help. She usually paid little attention to conversations he indulged in.

"We've said we'll think about it," Josh said, "or at least I've said I would. I'm not going to push Maura. It's her land. And I think Ellen is making up her own mind to a far greater extent than you know."

Baby Josh looked at the various faces, then lingered on Maura's, and he smiled widely, his fat cheeks dimpling.

"Oh, you darling rascal," Maura told him. "That's the biggest smile I've ever gotten from you."

Josh laughed happily. "He's going to be a heartbreaker."

"You see," Carter told Melodye. "You see what happiness a baby can bring?"

Melodye looked at him and said, evenly, "Happiness has a whole lot of faces, my darling husband. Just because Josh and

Maura are happy with their baby doesn't mean that we aren't just as happy without one."

Melodye got up, moved over, and sat on Carter's lap. He looked a bit embarrassed.

"I know I'm happy," she said. "And I'm always going to make you happy."

Thirty

Three days later, Maura stopped in around eleven o'clock to see Ellen and soothe her. She found Ellen looking well, but shaken.

"Even with Rich here, I'm afraid," she said. "I've never been so mixed up. Loving him has given me what I thought I'd never have, but Rich isn't God, and I'm not sure he can protect me from Lonnie."

"But he has stopped meddling with you."

"For a while, yes, but I hear things outside and it frightens me. Rustles in the night. We have a dog now, and he barks frantically sometimes."

"How long has this been going on?"

"Only for the past several nights, but I guess my dreams frighten me more than anything."

"Can you tell me about at least one of your dreams?"

Ellen thought a moment, then recounted, "That I'm alone in a field where snow is piled in banks over my head. No one else is there and wolves are howling. Circling me. I know they're coming and I'm terrified, and I wake up as soon as they come into view."

Maura pondered the dream that had become seared in Ellen's brain by way of frequent dreaming. She shuddered. She had studied creative writing in college. Snow was said to be a death symbol.

They heard Rich's key in the lock. Ellen went to him and hugged him as he barely got into the room.

"You're shaking," he said, hugging her tightly. "I came back to get some papers I left. I can stay a little while since we've delivered the drywall to Josh's site."

"I'm so glad," Ellen said. "I hate being such a coward."

"You're no coward," Rich said, staunchly. "You're a brave woman. I know what you're going through."

Rich spoke to Maura and asked about the baby.

"He's coming along at a high clip," Maura told him. "He seems to double in size every couple of months or so. I think we're going to have a football player on our hands."

Rich laughed and stroked Ellen, who leaned against him.

"It's going to be all right, baby," he said, softly. "Trust me."

The three of them went out into the backyard to see the chrysanthemums that were beginning to bloom by the fence. They would be a glorious array in a week or so.

Purple dahlias bloomed profusely in another fence-row spot. Ellen cut off several and handed them to Maura.

"They're beautiful." Dahlias were one of Maura's favorite flowers.

Cumulus clouds swept along a pale blue sky. "What a glorious day," Ellen said. Then her voice went down to a hoarse whisper. "Who would think evil could linger in a world this beautiful?"

As she spoke, rangy clouds began to overcome the sun. The sky's darkening seemed at odds with what they had just experienced.

Rafe Sampson hurried along, looking up at the sky, squinting. He had left his house very early that morning in search of bullets for his gun. He was going rabbit hunting. Miss Ellen had said she liked wild-rabbit stew cooked in wine, and he aimed to oblige her. He accelerated his pace. He could make it home in a short while.

* * *

Lonnie Fillmore found himself jumping with glee. He couldn't have asked for a more advantageous setting. The three of them close together and outside. Ellen. Rich. And the architect woman. Yeah, Maura. Maura's new baby didn't cross Lonnie's mind. He had to do what he had to do. He had to protect himself.

These three were the ones who'd ratted on him. Sure, there had been a couple of others, like Sampson, for instance, but nobody listened to Sampson. He was a nobody.

Except for the one time he'd been caught breaking and entering, Lonnie's criminal exploits had gone uncaught and therefore unpunished. He had gotten probation on the one deed that he had been arrested for. The arrest had been expunged from his record. His father had protected him all his life. The boy had a cocky faith that he always would.

He lowered the gun with trembling fingers. He needed to shoot now and get away, which might not be so easy because he'd left his bike at home and walked out. Damn! Excitement was wringing him dry. Soon he'd be rid of his burden of three good witnesses, nobody a better witness than Maura Pyne. Laughter bubbled in his throat. His father would be proud of the way he'd planned this, even if he wasn't proud of the deed. His father was a square, but he loved him.

Bile rose in his throat. Yeah, he loved him, but he knew his father's being mayor meant more to him than Lonnie's being his son. More and more, a sort of fog seemed to settle on his brain. He didn't feel loved anymore, the way he once had. His parents hassled him now; nothing he did seemed to please them. For the first time in his life, he felt they'd let him go to prison to teach him a lesson, and to win an election.

Well, the fire was history, and the evidence they had wouldn't stand up without the witnesses testifying that he had been skulking around the building. He wondered who had found the gasoline can with his thumbprint on it and turned him in.

The sawed-off shotgun was heavy on Lonnie's arm, but he

wouldn't put it down. The sky was growing darker. All of a sudden, he felt winded, as if someone were pushing him to his knees and he panicked, screaming to himself. He had to do it now! He was like Uncle Hal after all, and he liked being like him.

His mind cleared a bit. No, he wouldn't do it today. He was just too nervous. He was a good shot, but he couldn't be certain of hitting them in this condition. He would try again tomorrow, and another day if that didn't work out. He was determined.

Giggling, Lonnie reflected on how he always found out that Rafe Sampson was away before he came close to Ellen's house. And he stayed away a lot. He hunted and fished on the other side of town.

In the yard, Maura saw it first. A huge, smoky, black funnel cloud. A tornado! A twister was descending on them!

"Oh, my God!" Ellen screamed, catching first Rich's then Maura's arm. "Let's get into the storm cellar. We've only got a few minutes' time."

She lifted the hatch door that led down, and, one by one, they descended the ladder into the cellar and drew the door shut.

Maura was sick with fear. What would the twister hit as it skipped about?

Suddenly, they could hear a terrible din outside. Loud thumps and crashes. Banshee wailing of the wind. The last twister had hit forty years ago. Hell's angels were wreaking havoc outside. Here they were safe, but Maura was so worried, wondering where Josh and the baby were. She was too frozen to cry.

In the forest, not a quarter of a mile from Ellen's house, Lonnie saw the twister funnel, too, but he had no time to run before the twister uprooted several heavy oaks and one fell across his skinny body, crushing it.

* * *

Maura, Ellen, and Rich huddled in the storm cellar, waiting. After a few minutes, everything was quiet outside. They waited fifteen minutes, stunned, before they could move on wobbly legs.

Ellen put her face down to her knees and wept.

Rich put his arms around her. "Please, sweetheart," he told her, "try to calm down."

But he was shaking as badly as the two women were.

When they climbed up and lifted the storm cellar door, the chaos was terrible to behold. Uprooted trees were all around them. The mums and dahlias they had admired so fervently were beaten to the ground as if trod on by a rampaging giant. Rich saw his pickup truck in the near distance, overturned and smashed.

Gingerly, they walked to the house and went inside. "Good Lord," Ellen said. Even as she spoke, Ellen's foot went down on a jagged piece of glass and blood flowed freely onto the floor.

"Oh, my God," Rich said, "you've cut yourself."

They sat on the floor, which was strewn with debris, and he pulled the long shard of glass from her foot. Maura got cold water from the kitchen and filled a pan and put Ellen's foot in it. By some miracle, the bathroom—an inner room—had been left unscathed. Searching in the medicine cabinet, Maura found a bottle of iodine. Grimly, Rich washed the wound and took off his shirt, cut it on the glass, and tore it into strips.

Deftly, he bound Ellen's foot as Maura rummaged and found a pair of walking shoes.

"At least we can keep you from cutting the other foot."

The sky was now an angry gray and rumbles of thunder presaged rain.

Ellen's house still stood, but every window was broken, and the roof had been ripped off. Maura's tote bag was no longer on the front porch.

Maura fell to her knees and Ellen and Rich followed suit. "We have to pray," Maura said.

"Dear God," Maura began, "thank you for sparing our lives. I hope you saw fit to spare Josh and my son's and our loved ones' lives. We are grateful for all you offer us. Forever. Amen."

Still dazed, they rose. "I want to start walking into town," Rich said, "but I don't want to leave you two."

"We could both walk in with you," Maura suggested.

With a start, Maura wanted to call Josh and realized she had left her cell phone in her tote bag on the front porch.

"We have no way of knowing how deep that cut is," Rich said. "Walking into town may not be such a good idea."

Rafe Sampson stood with his mouth agape, looking at the clear line of demarcation for the twister.

"My God," he said to himself. "I'd've never believed it." Twenty feet behind him there was no sign of a storm and thirty feet ahead of him was a hell of nature's making. Trees uprooted as if they were saplings. Broken glass was all around. Cars, trucks, and buses were all around, some on their roofs, some on their sides. Bricks and stones and roofless houses were everywhere.

He had been a grown man when the last twister struck forty years ago. Young. But this twister was more devastating. Ahead of him, he could only see chaos. He fell to his knees and prayed. Had he not stopped to talk with the gun-shop owner, what would have been his fate?

Thinking about the way Theena had wept lately, he shuddered. Theena's weeping always foretold terrible death and sorrow. Who would it be this time?

Lonnie never heard the trees being snatched out of the ground, and felt for only a second the one that pinned his body down, lifeless. The smashing of the trees caused three of the bullets to go off, but Lonnie never heard the roar. The earth was a place he was no longer invested in.

* * *

"I don't want to risk your walking on that foot," Rich told Ellen. "I think our best bet now is to stay here. Someone will come. I don't know how wide a path the storm took, but someone will come."

Thirty-one

As he drove along the winding highway that led out to the old Halaby plantation, Josh found he could hardly catch his breath. He had been in his downtown office when the newsflash about the twister came in on the Internet, TV, and radio.

He had run outside, jumped in his car, and started out of town, knowing that since the twister had struck that section, trees would be down and the roads would be debris-strewn near there.

He pulled a handkerchief from his pocket and wiped his sweat-soaked face and neck. Why didn't Maura answer her cell phone? She had said she was leaving Baby Josh with Lona. He said a silent prayer for that and for Maura's safety. But if she were hurt . . . His mind veered away from that thought and he drove on, going carefully, wanting to speed, to fly to her side.

Just ahead was the storm-struck roadway he had known would be there. Trees were strewn across the road, along with twisted metal hunks of trucks and automobiles. Impossible to go through. He stopped and got out. He would walk. At least he was on the road to the Halaby plantation, on the road to Maura and his friends.

Maura, Ellen, and Rich sat huddled on the front porch. The sun had come out, overcoming earlier threats of rain; they welcomed its warmth and brightness.

Rich bent over Ellen's foot. "Is it hurting badly?"

Ellen shook her head. "Surprisingly little. Rich, don't worry. I'll be all right."

Things had happened so fast. Maura wished she could talk to Josh and know that he and Baby Josh were all right, but God only knew where the cell phone and the tote bag were lying now.

Rich's mouth was a grim line. "If help doesn't come soon, I'll carry you into town. There will be places there the storm didn't hit."

Josh felt a powerful sense of purpose as he shut off the ignition, got out of his car, locked it, and began walking. Climbing over trees uprooted and clumped together in the middle of the road, he was careful not to step on big pieces of jagged glass from car windows. Other shards of glass came from blown-out house windows and broken bottles. A car was lodged in the lower branches of a big oak tree. The countryside, placid an hour earlier, was now the portrait of devastation.

He clenched his teeth and walked on. A long distance away, he saw the three of them—at least he took it to be them—on the front porch of Ellen's still-standing stone house, and he began to trot, dodging glass and trees and debris.

It seemed an eternity, but Josh was soon bolstered by the knowledge that it was the three he sought on that porch. Through the moisture in his eyes, he saw Maura coming to meet him, climbing over debris and as careful of tree roots, fallen trees, and glass as he was.

He swept her into his arms and she hugged him for dear life.

"Are you hurt?" he asked.

"No, but Ellen cut her foot. How is Baby Josh?"

"Okay. We're all okay. The storm skipped about and struck a few houses on the edge of Crystal Lake."

"Thank God for the ones it didn't hit."

"Sweetheart, there are things I have to talk about with you. . . ."

She placed a finger against his lips. "I just want to know that you're here with me, that we're safe."

"No," he said, "I've got to tell you now." His heart raced as he talked to her. "I'm with you on the Midland Heights development. . . ."

"No. You have a right to your thoughts. Who knows, but you may be right."

"It isn't a matter of right or wrong. When I thought something had happened to you, when you didn't call, I thought I was going mad and I wanted to die without you. Sweetheart, I love you so much, no words I know will ever tell you what's in my heart.

"I want us to build together, build Midland Heights and everything else we agree on. It isn't Midland Heights that matters, it's you and me. Us."

They sat on a log behind them, its leafy branches brushing their legs. He drew her close and kissed her fervently, and she responded with her very soul going out to him.

"If only you knew how much I love you," Josh said.

"My darling, I *do* know," she told him, "because I know how much I love you."

They got up then and began to walk back to Ellen and Rich. And with his big hand covering hers, Maura and Josh knew that theirs was now a forever love.

Epilogue

In May, two years from the day of the twister, Maura and Josh had moved into their new home. Gorgeous chunks of fieldstone formed the big structure, located on five acres of beautifully landscaped grounds.

They were throwing a housewarming party, and Maura leaned against Josh as they stood in the doorway of Little Josh's bedroom, egg-shaped as the one in their former house had been.

Maura felt her heart lurch as she looked at Josh, savoring the closeness they shared.

"You look so happy," Josh said.

"I am happy. Aren't you?"

"You know I am."

Guests milled about throughout the house and on the grounds, especially where the beautiful fountain stood and near the fieldstone goldfish pond where multicolored goldfish leaped and frolicked.

Hand in hand, Papa Isaac and Lona came up to them.

"You've got a beautiful gathering here," Papa Isaac said, "beginning with my wife."

Lona threw back her head, laughing. They had been married less than a year.

Where were Rich and Ellen? Maura wondered. She asked Josh.

"He had a shipment of drywall held up, and he's checking on it. They should be here soon."

Mr. Sampson ambled up to them, his face wreathed in smiles.

"Now you're really living large," he said. "Gonna catch up to your papa one day, my man."

"I'm not sure I want to," Josh answered.

Odessa and Mike were enjoying themselves hugely. Midland Heights was becoming a reality and they would move into their new home in the fall. With a twinkle in their eyes, both frequently said they were *working* on a baby.

Maura and Josh had given up their dream of moving to San Francisco. There was too much in Crystal Lake for them.

Trina came from the house, bringing Baby Josh with her.

"He insisted on coming out," she said.

"But we were just with him." Maura patted the baby's soft cheek.

Trina shrugged. "He has a way of getting what he wants, you know?"

"Don't we know that." Josh bent and chucked his son under the chin.

Dale Borders was visiting again to paint Odessa and Melodye. He looked far happier than usual, and he had taken to coming to Crystal Lake fairly often. Maura followed his line of vision and saw the look that passed between him and Trina. Her heart lifted with happiness for them.

Maura, Josh, and Baby Josh walked over to Grandmother Addie in her wheelchair. Baby Josh climbed up on her knees and she hugged him tightly as he peered into her face.

"This is all about love," Grandmother Addie said solemnly.

And with a catch in her throat, Maura thought of the gamble Josh and she had made in fear and trembling and how well their gamble had paid off. But was it really a gamble? Hadn't they really loved each other since her high school prom?

Strolling over, with Melodye in tow, Carter reached their

side, swooped down and held Baby Josh over his head, which delighted the little boy.

"How are you, trouper?" Carter asked.

"I'm fine," Baby Josh answered clearly. He spoke well and had walked at eight months of age.

"I'll say you're fine," Carter responded, his breath catching in his throat.

Melodye touched Baby Josh's face, but didn't play with him further. Instead, she walked away to join another group.

Carter's gaze followed her sadly as he held the toddler.

"I guess I'm going to have to get used to having one son and a grandson," he said. "Melodye has declared she doesn't want children."

"But you knew that," Josh said.

"I had faith in myself. I thought I could change her mind. I was wrong."

Maura thought Carter had aged five years in the two years he had been married to Melodye.

Looking at Maura, Josh considered himself the luckiest man on earth. He had dreamed a glorious, vibrant dream and had made it come true. What if Maura hadn't accepted his proposal? He had let fear nearly destroy his life. He would never go there again.

Josh squeezed Maura's hand, lifted that hand to his mouth, and kissed the rings on her finger. Then they walked over to former Mayor and Mrs. Fillmore.

"I'm so glad you could come," Maura told the broken woman. The former mayor and his wife were practically recluses now. Had they known nothing of what Lonnie was about?

People rarely spoke of Lonnie anymore, and when they did, it was to shudder in wonder at the fact that Theena had predicted the loss of life again.

"Your house is beautiful," the Fillmores said, and Mrs. Fillmore said further, "As you know, after all this time, we're still in mourning, but I wouldn't have missed this."

An ineffable look of sadness lay on both the Fillmores's faces now. Josh wondered what they would have thought had they known the life their son really lived.

Looking up, Maura saw Rich and Ellen coming toward them and met them halfway. Rich had his arm around his wife, whose belly bulged with their unborn child. The two women hugged.

Josh walked up. "Did you get the drywall shipment straightened out?"

"It wasn't easy, but I did."

The four friends stood there with the gentle May winds eddying around them.

"This is your day for good news, so I should wait to tell you, but I can't." Ellen's eyes twinkled.

"What is it?" Maura asked.

"We're signing a contract with a really good record company, and they're releasing another CD."

"Congratulations!" Josh and Maura responded.

"Oh, congratulations to you, on all this beauty," Ellen complimented them.

As the caterers began to bring the food around, looking over at her son, as he sat again on Grandmother Addie's lap, then at her husband, Maura laughed merrily.

"We have it all, love."

And Josh nodded in agreement.

Dear Readers,

It was such a lovely experience to write about Maura and Josh Pyne, and it was fun. I hope you will know the same joy I felt in relating to these characters.

Josh and Maura made the ultimate love choice and came out ahead. In your endeavors, many of you do as well.

Your letters continue to delight me. Please keep them coming. The tidbits of information you give about yourselves are interesting and welcome. If you would like a newsletter about what I am writing and some items of interest from the world of romance, please send a stamped, self-addressed, legal-size envelope.

The best of everything for you and in your lives.

Best wishes,

Francine Craft
P.O. Box 44204
Washington, DC 20026

ACKNOWLEDGMENTS

To Charlie K., June and Bruce Bennett. Thanks for all your help and patience. You were always there for me as I hope I am for you.

ABOUT THE AUTHOR

Francine Craft is the pen name of a Washington, DC-based writer who has enjoyed writing for many years. A native Mississippian, she has also lived in New Orleans and found it fascinating.

Francine has been a research assistant for a large nonprofit organization, an elementary-school teacher, a business school instructor, and a federal government legal secretary. Her books have been highly praised by reviewers. She is a member of Romance Writers of America.

Prodigious reading, photography, and writing song lyrics are Francine's hobbies. She presently lives with a family of friends and many goldfish.

BOOK YOUR PLACE ON OUR WEBSITE AND MAKE THE ARABESQUE ROMANCE CONNECTION!

We've created a customized website just for our very special Arabesque readers, where you can get the inside scoop on everything that's going on with Arabesque romance novels.

When you come online, you'll have the exciting opportunity to:

- View covers of upcoming books

- Learn about our future publishing schedule (listed by publication month and author)

- Find out when your favorite authors will be visiting a city near you

- Search for and order backlist books

- Check out author bios and background information

- Send e-mail to your favorite authors

- Join us in weekly chats with authors, readers and other guests

- Get writing guidelines

- AND MUCH MORE!

Visit our website at
http://www.arabesquebooks.com